Pony 'n' Pals SECRETS

TWO BOOKS IN ONE!

Comet and Storm

The Pony Club Secrets series:

Also available...

PONY CLUB SECRETS

Comet and Storm

Comet and the Champion's cup

and

Storm and the Silver Bridle

STACY GREGG

HarperCollins *Children's Books*

WWW.STACYGREGG.CO.UK

Comet and the Champion's Cup first published in paperback in Great Britain by HarperCollins *Children's Books* in 2008. *Storm and the Silver Bridle* first published in paperback in Great by HarperCollins *Children's Books* in 2009. First published as a two-in-one edition as *Comet and Storm* in Great Britain by HarperCollins *Children's Books* in 2011.
HarperCollins *Children's Books* is a division of HarperCollins*Publishers* Ltd, 77–85 Fulham Palace Road, Hammersmith, London, W6 8JB.

Visit our website at: www.harpercollins.co.uk

2

Text copyright © Stacy Gregg 2008, 2009

ISBN: 978-0-00-742004-9

Stacy Gregg asserts the moral right to be identified as the author and illustrator of the work.

Printed and bound in England by Clays Ltd, St Ives plc

Comet and the Champion's cup

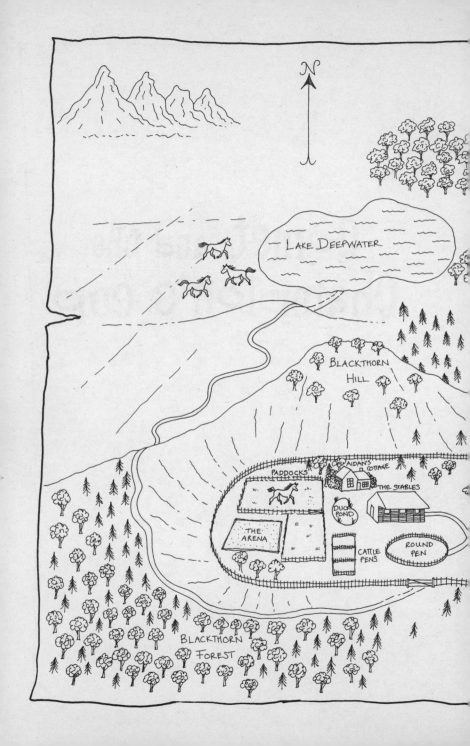

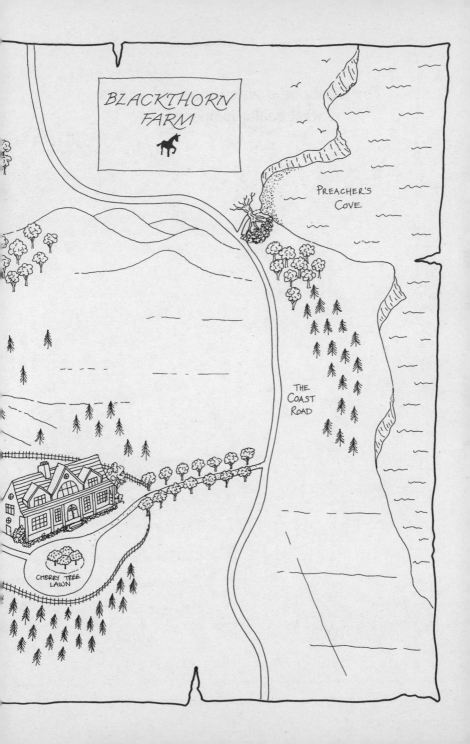

For Kirsty, who was there and knows
what really happened...

Chapter 1

The bay colt knew the girl was watching. He arched his neck proudly, delighting in her attention as he trotted by. When he passed the paddock railing where the girl was sitting, the colt came so close that he almost brushed against her knees. She giggled and reached out a hand to grab him, but the colt swerved away, putting on a sudden burst of speed, galloping away from her to the other side of the paddock.

When he reached the hedge at the end of the field his flanks were heaving and his muzzle was twitching with excitement. He wheeled about, his ears pricked forward, turning to face the girl who stared intently back at him.

The girl whistled. Her lips pursed together as she blew once, then a second time – a sharp, clear note that carried across the paddock. The colt heard her call, but at first he refused to obey, stamping at the ground and tossing his head defiantly. He held his ground briefly, his muscles quivering, before he leapt forward as if he were a racehorse, breaking from the gate. Thrilling in his own speed as his eager strides swallowed up the ground between them, the colt galloped back to her, wanting to start the whole game again.

"Good boy, Storm!" Issie giggled as the colt swept past again, once more managing to avoid her hand as she reached out to touch him.

They had played this game of tig many times, but Issie never got tired of it. She loved to watch Nightstorm move. His body still hadn't grown into those long, lanky legs – it was as if he were teetering about on stilts – and yet there was something so graceful about him.

Nightstorm was hardly recognisable as the tiny bay foal with the white blaze that had been born that stormy night in the stables here at Winterflood Farm. It was Issie who had named the colt Nightstorm as they sheltered together in the stables while the lightning flashed above their heads. Lately, though, she had taken to calling him by his nickname – Storm.

Storm was just three months old, but already Issie

could see that he was the best possible combination of both of his magnificent bloodlines. His elegant head carriage and beautiful, dished Arabian face were derived from his Anglo-Arab dam, Blaze. Physically, though, the colt was much more solid than his mother. He bore a powerful resemblance to his sire, the great grey stallion Marius. You could see it in his well-rounded haunches, classical topline and strong, solid hocks, all true signs of the Lipizzaner breed.

As the colt cantered back once more, Issie leapt down off the rails, a signal that the game was over. Storm understood this. He trotted towards her and didn't try to swerve away this time. Instead, he came to a halt right next to her so that Issie could reach out and stroke his velvety muzzle. She ran her hand down the colt's neck. Storm was already moulting, losing the soft, downy layer of fur that all foals are born with, to reveal the shiny, smooth grown-up coat underneath. Issie could see bits of deep russet bay, the colour of warm mahogany, emerging from underneath the baby-fluff.

Storm was growing fast. Sometimes Issie felt it was too quick – she wanted him to be a foal forever. At other times, she felt it still wasn't fast enough. Horses take a long time to mature – and horses with Lipizzaner blood take longer than most. It would be three years before Storm was ready to be ridden. Such a long time! Issie had bitten her lip and tried not to say anything childish when Avery told her how long she must wait to ride the colt, but inside she felt bitterly disappointed. She didn't want to wait. She wanted to ride Storm now!

It had never occurred to Issie that when her beloved mare Blaze had a foal it would mean she would be left without a horse to ride for the whole of the summer holidays. She couldn't ride Storm – and Blaze couldn't be ridden yet either, not until the colt was weaned at six months. And that was ages away!

Never mind, Issie thought. She might not be able to ride, but she loved just being with her new baby. She was amazed at how quickly Storm seemed to put his trust in her. Perhaps it was because he had watched Issie and Blaze together and he was simply following his mother's cues. His mother was the centre of his universe and if his mum loved this girl with the long dark hair, well, then Storm loved her too. Issie could have happily spent her summer goofing around with the colt, playing silly games like the one they were playing today – if it weren't for Avery getting all serious on her.

"He's just a cute baby now," Avery pointed out. "But

that foal of yours will be a sixteen-two hands high stallion one day. He's getting stronger every day, bigger too. That's why it's important to start his schooling now, while he's still small enough for you to be able to handle him. It's important to teach Nightstorm good manners and respect right from the start."

And so, under Avery's expert tuition, Issie began learning how to "imprint" her foal. She followed her instructor's advice to the letter, being firm but gentle with Storm as she taught him to accept a head collar and then a foal halter, how to walk politely beside her on a lead rein and how to stand perfectly still while she picked up his feet.

Issie would arrive at Winterflood Farm at dawn most mornings so she could spend time with the colt before school. She would bring Storm and Blaze into the stable block and spend the next hour grooming the colt while the mare ate her hard feed. The grooming sessions were a gradual process, part of the colt's training, teaching him to accept her touch as she ran the brushes over his body. The whole time she worked, Issie would talk softly to Storm, and he would occasionally nicker back to her, turning around to snuffle her softly with his velvety muzzle when she was brushing him, or closing his eyes in pleasure as she scratched him on that sweet spot on his rump.

The weekends were the best. Then she would cycle down to Winterflood Farm at dawn and wouldn't return home until dinner time. Issie couldn't really say exactly what she did at the farm all day. Sometimes she just lay in the long grass under the magnolia tree and watched Storm. She especially loved the way he would snort and quiver each time something new crossed his path. She could hardly wait until next week when the school holidays would finally be starting and she could spend all her time with the young horse.

Today, Issie had another new surprise for the colt. As she reached into her pocket and produced a carrot, she watched Storm boggle at it with wide eyes. He hadn't learnt to eat carrots yet – and he was uncertain what to do next.

"Here you go, Storm," Issie said softly, extending her hand, the carrot in her palm. Storm had watched his mother eat carrots before, but he'd never been offered one to try himself. He gave it a sniff and his ears pricked forward. It smelt good! He gave Issie's palm a snuffle, taking a tiny little bite, then he held the chunk of carrot in his mouth, unsure of what to do next. Issie giggled again at the expression on his face, those wide dark brown eyes filled with wonder.

"Here, Blaze, you show him how it's done!" Issie grinned, giving one to the colt's mother as well. The mare took the carrot eagerly, crunching it down. Issie was about to dig another carrot out of her jacket pocket and try to feed Storm again when she heard her name being called.

"Issie!" She turned around to see Tom Avery standing on the back porch of the cottage. "Your mum is on the phone. She wants to talk to you."

Issie sighed. "She probably wants me to come home and tidy my room. She's been on at me about getting it done before the holidays begin."

Avery smiled at her. "It is possible that your mother just wants to lay eyes on you for five minutes to make sure you actually exist. You've been spending all your time here with Storm."

Issie paused on the back porch to yank off her boots before padding along the hallway to pick up the phone. "Hi, Mum," she said brightly. "Listen, if it's about my room, I know I said I'd tidy it, but I couldn't find the vacuum cleaner nozzle and..."

Her mother interrupted her. "I've just had a phone

call from Aidan." Mrs Brown's voice was taut and serious. "Issie, I'm afraid it's bad news. It's about your aunty Hess…"

Hester had woken at 3 a.m. and, finding herself wide awake, resigned herself to her fate. She switched on her bedside lamp and tried to occupy herself with a crossword puzzle, but found it impossible to concentrate on the page in front of her. Her eyes kept darting nervously away from the newspaper in her hand to her laptop, which sat silently in the dark on her desk. She was waiting for an important email and, until it arrived, sleep was out of the question.

At 6 a.m., as the light came streaming in through the wide bay windows of Blackthorn Manor, she finally heard the sound that she had been longing for and dreading at the same time: the soft "ping" that signalled that an email had arrived in her inbox. She walked across the room and looked at the screen. *You've got mail!* it flashed at her urgently.

Hester held her breath as she clicked the mouse to open the email. She was so sick with nerves, she could barely bring herself to look at it. *Please let it be good news,* she thought to herself. *We need this film so badly!*

From the very first line, though, her heart sank.

```
Dear Hester, it is with great regret
that we inform you that all work has been
delayed indefinitely on our latest film
project…
```

Hester didn't bother to read any further. She knew what the rest of the email said. And she knew exactly what it meant — total disaster. She shut the laptop immediately, as if closing it would keep the bad news locked inside where it couldn't upset her any more. She felt a sudden chill and wrapped her dressing gown tightly around herself as she left her bedroom and walked downstairs.

Padding down to the kitchen in silence with the dogs following at her feet, Hester put the kettle on and began to make coffee. She looked out of the window towards the stables. The horses would be waking up in their stalls and expecting their breakfast. They had no idea about the email — or the bad news it contained.

"Well, my Daredevil Ponies," Hester said darkly, "I'd like to see what stunt you can pull to get us out of this mess."

"Hester?"

Hester turned around to find her young stable manager Aidan standing in the doorway. Aidan looked like he hadn't slept either. He ran a hand through his hair, pushing back his long dark fringe to reveal striking blue eyes that were restless with the worry and stress they had both shared over the past few weeks.

"Has there been any news? Have you heard back from the production company yet?"

Hester nodded solemnly. "It's all bad I'm afraid. They've postponed the movie – indefinitely. We're out of work again. I just don't believe it. Three film jobs falling through in a row. We've got the luck of the devil hounding us, Aidan. I just wish we had his money too. I was relying on this movie. There's no way I can keep things going now…"

"Of course you can!" Aidan said. "Hester… I've been thinking about it and you don't have to pay me. I mean, I don't need much to live on and I've got my room and board here. You can forget about my salary until you've got some money again. I was thinking maybe we could do a deal with the feed and grain merchants too. I'm sure they'd help you out. If you just told them the situation, and we promised to pay again when things get better…"

Hester smiled back at Aidan. "That's very kind, dear, but feed merchants aren't very keen on charity. And in case you haven't noticed, it's already been over a month since I last paid you. I don't expect you to keep working for me for free." Hester looked at Aidan's forlorn expression. "I appreciate your offer, I really do. But even if I wasn't paying your salary, there's still the mortgage. And the maintenance. This place is so big and so old, it needs an enormous amount of money just to keep it running. And all the horses need shoeing and there are vet's bills mounting up..." Hester sank down into a kitchen chair and put her head in her hands.

"Aidan, I've run out of money. Worse than that, for the first time in my life I've run out of ideas."

There were tears in Hester's eyes as she turned to face her stable manager. "It's over. I have no choice... I have to sell Blackthorn Farm."

Chapter 2

Sell Blackthorn Farm? Issie couldn't believe it. The farm was her favourite place in the whole world, and she knew how much her aunt loved it too.

She still remembered when Hester first bought the farm, complete with a decaying mansion, high in the hills outside Gisborne. Issie's mum had pronounced her sister "officially totally bonkers".

Mrs Brown worked for a law firm and was very practical about boring things like having a proper job. So when Hester broke the news that she was giving up her acting career, buying a rundown farm manor and becoming an animal trainer, Mrs Brown was far from impressed.

The whole farm, especially the manor, needed loads of work to restore it to its former glory. Loads of cash too.

Mrs Brown called Blackthorn Farm "Hester's Money Pit". Issie's aunt spent all of her savings restoring the buildings inside and out, including the stable block for her stunt horses.

Eventually, though, even Mrs Brown had to admit that Hester's hard work and determination had paid off. Hester's mad menagerie of movie-star animals – pigs, chickens, ducks, goats and especially horses – were considered to be the best in the business. Her Daredevil Ponies had worked on loads of films doing all sorts of stunts.

"It was all going so well!" Issie said. "I can't understand it. What happened?"

Mrs Brown sighed. "The movie business is unpredictable. Aidan told me they've been out of work ever since *The Palomino Princess*. There was a new project due to start filming this week and it fell through. Now Hester's been left with mountains of debt and no way to make any money!"

"But she can't sell the farm!" Issie said. "What about the horses?" Hester had over a dozen stunt horses in the stables at Blackthorn Farm.

There was silence on the phone. And then Mrs Brown finally spoke. "Aidan didn't say, but I guess they'll have to be sold as well."

"Mum! This is awful…" Issie felt close to tears.

"I know," Mrs Brown said gently. "Aidan is calling back soon. He says he has an idea that he wants to talk to you about, something that might help."

"I'm coming home now!" Issie hung up the phone. She turned around and saw Avery standing in the hallway behind her.

"I'm guessing she doesn't just want you to tidy your room then?" he said.

When Issie told Avery the bad news he immediately offered to give her a lift home. Issie gratefully accepted, putting her bike in the back of the Range Rover and clambering into the passenger seat. She spent the ride home in total silence, feeling sick with worry. Aunty Hess couldn't sell Blackthorn Farm. Things sounded pretty bad, but maybe there was still hope. What was this idea that Aidan wanted to talk to her about?

Issie didn't have long to wait before she found out. The phone was ringing as she ran in through the front door.

"I've got it!" she called, making a mad dash down the hallway to grab the receiver. She was still puffing and trying to catch her breath when she heard Aidan's voice at the other end of the line.

"Issie? Is that you?" She knew that they were in the

middle of a crisis here, but still Issie couldn't help smiling when she heard Aidan's voice. She hadn't seen him in ages and she had missed him. She pictured his face, the thick mop of black hair and the long fringe that hung down, almost hiding those startling blue eyes.

"Issie? Are you there?"

"Sorry, I'm still puffed from running to the phone," Issie panted.

"That's OK," Aidan said. "You don't need to talk anyway. Just listen. I have a plan to save the farm and I want you to hear it because I'm going to need your help." He paused. "Issie, I want to start a riding school."

"What?"

"My mum used to run one years ago when I was little," Aidan continued, "and I always thought Blackthorn Farm would be the perfect place to have one."

"But it's miles from anywhere!" Issie protested.

"I know," Aidan said, "but school holidays are about to start, right? We could run a school holiday camp with ponies. Kids could come and stay during the week and go home on the weekends and we could give them lessons."

"We?"

"That's where you come in," Aidan said. "I need

instructors. Hester and I have too much farmwork to do it all ourselves."

"But I'm not an instructor!" Issie squeaked.

"You've got your B certificate, haven't you? And don't Stella and Kate have theirs too? That means you can be junior instructors. Hester can run the school and you'll be her assistants."

"Does Hester think it's a good idea then?" Issie said.

"She will do once I tell her about it," Aidan said. Issie laughed, but he sounded serious. "You've got to help me do this, Issie. It's our last chance. I don't want Hester to lose the farm."

Issie took a deep breath. "When can you come and pick us up?" she said.

Issie needed to talk to Stella and Kate urgently – and she knew exactly where they would be, since today was rally day. She would find them at the pony club.

Some things never changed at Chevalier Point Pony Club. Take Natasha Tucker for instance. You would have thought, after all Issie and Natasha had been through together as stunt riders on the set of *The Palomino Princess*, that Natasha would have finally wanted to be friends. But no. From the moment the girls had arrived back at pony club this season, Natasha had become her same old super-snobby self. In fact, she was worse than ever. Issie had been really upset at first when Natasha had stopped speaking to her. Now she just tried to avoid her – which wasn't always easy.

"They must be here somewhere," Issie said, staring out of the window as her mum manoeuvred her car through the pony-club gates and into the parking area. Issie was so busy looking for her two best friends that she hardly noticed where her mum was driving until it was too late.

"No, Mum! Not here!" Issie shrieked as Mrs Brown pulled to a stop right next to the Tuckers' flashy blue and silver horse truck.

"What's wrong?"

"That's Natasha's truck!" groaned Issie.

"I thought you and Natasha were friends now?" Mrs Brown said.

"So did I," Issie sighed, "but it turns out that Natasha doesn't think so." Issie didn't know why Stuck-up Tucker was so against her, although Stella insisted that it was because Natasha was jealous.

"Jealous?" Issie didn't understand. "Jealous of what?"

"You and Dan!" Stella said. "She has got, like, a huge crush on him and you're always hanging out with him, which makes her blood boil."

It was true. Issie and Dan were pretty tight – but big deal! Stella and Kate and Ben were her friends too! Dan was most definitely not her boyfriend. Still, if Natasha wanted to be jealous of Issie's non-boyfriend then she guessed there wasn't much she could do about it – except stay out of Natasha's way.

"Mum? Do we have to park here? Can't we move?" Issie pleaded again. But it was too late because at that moment, a blonde girl with hair braided into ramrod-straight plaits emerged from behind the corner of the blue and silver horse truck. She was leading an elegant rose-grey gelding.

Issie attempted a cheery greeting. "Hi, Natasha!"

Natasha didn't smile back. "What are you doing here?" she said flatly. "It's a rally day and you don't have a horse to ride, do you?"

"Ummm… I'm looking for Stella and Kate," Issie faltered. "Have you seen them?"

"Why?" said Natasha. "What do you want them for?" Natasha's frosty stare made Issie start to babble and before she knew it she was telling Natasha all about Aidan's phone call.

As soon as she started, though, she wished she had kept her mouth shut. Natasha's face was like thunder. Even though she would never admit it, it was obvious that in some weird way Natasha was upset that Issie wasn't asking her to join them this time. Issie sighed. If she had actually asked her, Natasha would certainly have said no. Now, because she hadn't asked her, Natasha was in a total huff. You just couldn't win.

"So Aidan is looking for some pony-mad slaves to rope in to do all your aunt's donkey work yet again," Natasha harrumphed. "I hope you're not thinking of asking me this time because I've already done dung duty for her once and I'm not planning on falling for that again."

"It's not like you were her slave! Aunty Hess paid us to work on *The Palomino Princess*!" Issie said indignantly.

"What-ever!" said Natasha. "Anyway, I'd rather be riding my own horse than trying to teach some snot-nosed brats how to keep their hands steady. You probably won't even get a chance to ride. You'll be too busy mucking out the stalls and grooming all their ponies for them."

Natasha smirked at this put-down, then made a vague gesture across the club grounds to the far paddock. "Anyway, if you're looking for Stella and Kate, I think I saw them over by the main arena." And with that, she turned her back on Issie and began to busy herself with attaching Fabergé's bell boots.

Issie didn't care what Stuck-up Tucker said. Maybe the riding school would be a lot of hard work and not much actual riding. But it would still be fun just being near the horses, helping to groom them and look after them. She just hoped that Stella and Kate would both feel the same way. Aidan needed all three of them.

Issie found Stella and Kate with their horses, under the shade of the plane trees by the main arena. The girls had finished riding for the morning and were watching the other riders in the showjumping arena.

Stella was lying on the grass next to Coco, her little chocolate brown mare. She had taken off her riding helmet and her wild red curls were sticking out at funny angles with a flat patch on the top of her head where the helmet had been. Kate was standing next to her holding the reins of her rangy bay Thoroughbred, Toby. She was taller than the other two girls, even though they were all in the same form at Chevalier Point High School. Kate still had her helmet on and she wore her blonde bobbed hair tucked up neatly out of the way in a hairnet – which was actually a rule for club days although Stella clearly hadn't bothered. Stella wasn't very big on rules. Issie noticed that she wasn't even wearing her club tie underneath her navy vest.

"Issie! Ohmygod. What are you doing here?" Stella shrieked when she saw her best friend. She shrieked even louder when Issie told her about Aunt Hester's riding school.

"Us?" Stella shrieked. "Riding instructors!"

"Uh-huh," Issie said. "The kids are novices so we'll just be teaching them the basics. Plus, we'll have to help Hester to run the camp, doing all the other stuff like cooking meals and grooming the horses. She can't afford to pay us, but we get room and board. Plus you get to bring Toby and Coco with you and we can hack out across the farm after we finish schooling each day."

Stella grinned. "Cool. If I can bring Coco then I'm totally there!"

Issie knew it would be easy to convince Stella – she was mad keen on anything horsey. But sensible, practical Kate was a different story.

"Why is Hester running a riding school? I thought she trained movie horses," Kate said.

"Ummm... the movie business is having a few hiccups," Issie said. "Anyway, it's not just a riding school, it's like a camp for horsey kids like us. The riders come and stay at Blackthorn Farm for three weeks over the school holidays and learn to ride..." She saw Kate's hesitant expression. "Come on! It will be really good fun..."

"When do we go?"

"We need to spend the week before the kids arrive getting the camp ready. Aidan is coming with the horse truck to pick us up on Tuesday."

"That's only two days!" Kate boggled. "Issie, I don't know if I can. Mum will flip out if I tell her I'm going away for a whole month!"

"Please, Kate!" Issie begged. "I know it's short notice, but Aunty Hess needs us straightaway."

Issie had been desperately worried that Kate would say no. Of course she would be put off by the idea of suddenly changing her holiday plans and going all the way to Gisborne for a month. The problem was, she couldn't imagine going without Kate. Cool, calm Kate was a really good riding instructor; she was brilliant with kids and had loads of patience. All the junior riders at Chevalier Point totally adored her and Kate was always

Avery's first choice to fill in and teach the younger kids if an instructor failed to turn up for a practice session.

Kate looked thoughtful. "Issie, do you think you could get your mum to ask my mum? If your mum has OKed it, she'd have to say yes. Besides, I've stayed at Hester's before and she let me go that time, didn't she…?" Kate was smiling now. "And if I can take Toby with me, how excellent would that be?"

Issie squealed and threw her arms around Kate. "I knew you'd say yes! Oh, this is going to be so cool!"

The only thing left to organise now was Storm. Issie would miss him so much, but she was sure that Avery would take good care of the colt and Blaze while she was away. Avery had looked after Blaze when she was in foal and Issie was away working on *The Palomino Princess*. She knew that Avery would be more than happy to take care of Storm and Blaze while she was gone. She saw him over by the clubhouse and set off to ask him.

"I can't," Avery told her. Issie couldn't believe it.

"Issie, you know that normally I would do it," Avery continued. "The problem is, I was planning to go to

Gisborne myself in a week. It's the Horse of the Year Show. I'm taking Dan and Ben down to prepare their horses to compete in the showjumping. This is the first time Dan will have a chance to compete on his new horse. We've been planning it for ages."

Of course! How could Issie have forgotten? The Horse of the Year was the biggest event on the equestrian calendar.

Avery looked concerned. "I'm sorry, Issie. I can look after Storm and Blaze for the first week, but then we're trucking Madonna and Max to Gisborne to start training there and I'm afraid that leaves you stuck – unless you figure out a solution."

Issie was devastated. This completely ruined their plans. She couldn't leave Storm behind with no one to check on him and care for him each day. And she couldn't take the colt with her. There was no way he was old enough to travel all the way to Blackthorn Farm. The trip to Gisborne took most of the day in the horse truck, much too far for a three-month-old colt. There was only one solution, Issie decided. She couldn't go.

"Don't be ridiculous!" Mrs Brown said when Issie met her back at the car and broke the bad news. "Of course you're going. It's all arranged."

"But, Mum, I can't leave Storm and Blaze alone."

"I'll look after them," Mrs Brown said confidently.

"You? But, Mum, you don't even like horses…"

"Oh, for goodness sake, Isadora," Mrs Brown said. "OK, I think we're all aware that I'm not exactly Pippa Funnell, but it's not like you're asking me to ride at Badminton, is it? I've been around them for long enough now and I think it's perfectly within my capabilities to go and check on your ponies each day. I'll make sure they've got food and water and that Storm hasn't got himself tangled in the electric fence!"

"Really?"

"Absolutely," Mrs Brown smiled. "They will be just fine, I promise you."

Aunt Hester was thrilled that evening when Issie phoned her with the good news. "Aidan's quite convinced that this riding-school plan will save our bacon – and I certainly hope he's right," Hester said. "Is your mum OK about you coming here for the holidays? I haven't ruined any family plans, have I?"

"Mum's been great!" Issie said. "And she talked to Mrs Knight and convinced her to let Kate come. She's even looking after Blaze and Storm while I'm away."

"Well, well," Hester said. "It might not be too late for that sister of mine to turn horsey after all."

"I know!" Issie said. "I can't believe it's all organised and we're really coming. By this time tomorrow we'll be at Blackthorn Farm."

Chapter 3

"We're nearly there!" Issie pressed her face up against the window at the back of the truck cab and mouthed the words through the glass at Stella and Kate.

"What's she saying?" Kate was frustrated. "I can't hear her through the glass!"

"Issie!" Stella shouted back. "We can't hear you! What are you saying?"

The cab of Aunt Hester's horse truck wasn't big enough for all the girls to fit up front so it had been decided that Issie would travel in the cab with Aidan while Kate and Stella rode in the back.

The girls didn't mind riding in the back. The truck was fitted out a bit like a camper van, with a shower, kitchenette and bunk beds, and it was comfy enough travelling on the bench seats. Plus, from where they sat, Stella and Kate could keep an eye on Toby and Coco who were travelling at the very back of the truck in their stalls. The girls could see Issie and Aidan too by peering through the little window with very thick glass at the back of the truck cab.

Issie tapped on the glass and tried again. "I said… We're nearly there!"

"Oh, give up, Issie!" Aidan grinned. "They'll figure it out for themselves soon enough. We're about to reach the turn-off."

The six-hour drive to Blackthorn Farm had somehow seemed shorter this time. That might have been because she and Aidan hadn't stopped talking from the moment Issie got into the truck. There was so much for them to catch up on.

"I haven't seen Nightstorm since he was two days old," Aidan said, "so that would make him…"

"Three months old!" Issie said. "He's already almost thirteen hands. Avery reckons he'll grow to sixteen-two, and he's so beautiful. He's losing all his foal fluff and he's got the most amazing deep bay coat, with a thick black mane and tail and black points. He looks so cute with his white blaze. He's exactly like his mum in some ways, but he's kind of like Marius too. He has his own personality though – he's really smart. I taught him to wear a halter in just one day."

Aidan pushed his long, dark fringe out of his eyes and looked at Issie. "It must have been hard to leave him."

"Uh-huh," Issie said. She didn't want to tell Aidan that she had been in floods of tears when she said goodbye to the colt last night. She knew it was only a month, but it seemed like such a long time to be away from him when he was so young.

"Well, I'm really glad you came," Aidan said softly. Then he realised he sounded mushy and tried to make up for it by adding, "Ummm… cos Hester really needs your help."

Issie smiled. "Hester says you've been schooling up a few of the Blackthorn Ponies that we caught when we were here last time."

The Blackthorn Ponies were a wild herd that roamed the hills around Blackthorn Farm. On her last holiday at the farm Issie and Aidan had saved the herd from a cull. Most of the ponies had been sent to new homes, but Hester had kept a few of them with her at the farm.

"That's part of the problem," Aidan continued. "The cost of those extra ponies adds up fast. Hester has thirteen horses now – that's a lot of farrier bills and hard feed."

"So the riding school will cover the bills?"

"Uh-huh," Aidan said. "We won't make a fortune out of it, but hopefully we'll make enough to keep the farm going until the next movie job comes along."

Issie looked worried. "And what if another film job doesn't come along?"

"Something will turn up soon," Aidan said reassuringly. "I'm sure everything will be fine."

"But, Aidan, what if it's not fine?"

"Well, if things got really tight, I guess we'd have to sell some of the horses," said Aidan quietly. "Diablo and Stardust are experienced stunt horses – they're both worth quite a lot. But if that's not enough…"

"Then what?"

"Then Hester will have to sell Blackthorn Farm."

For the first time since they had set off on this trip, silence settled over the truck cab. Issie stared out of the windows at the road ahead and couldn't help wondering if this would be the last time she would be making this journey.

By the time the horse truck came through the narrow Gisborne gorge and began to travel up through the green cornfields towards the high country, Issie had pulled herself together again. In fact, she was positively filled with resolve.

"You're right. Things will be fine!" she said firmly, smiling at Aidan. The riding school would make enough money – or they'd think of something else. No matter what, there was no way her aunt was going to lose Blackthorn Farm.

Half an hour later, they reached the crest of a very steep hill. To the right, Issie could see the bright blue sea of the Gisborne coastline, and on the left was farmland and forest. Up ahead she could see a gravel road that veered to the left off the main highway.

"We're here!"

Aidan turned off down the private road, slowing down a gear as the truck struck gravel. Issie watched as the trees closed in around her and the truck became cocooned in the dense native forest that bordered the sides of the driveway that led to Blackthorn Farm. Low-hanging pohutukawa branches scraped against the roof of the truck.

"I keep telling Hester we need to prune the trees back to get the truck through," Aidan said as he heard the branches scraping the roof above him. "She just tells me to 'add it to the endless list of things that need doing'!"

A few more scrapes and bangs later and they had emerged into the bright sunlight once more. Issie's heart leapt when she saw the familiar sight of the cherry trees, their white and pink petals falling in a snowy carpet on the circular lawn in front of Blackthorn Manor.

The tumbledown mansion was just as she remembered. The enormous two-storeyed country manor must once have been very grand, but was, she noted with fresh eyes, definitely rickety and in desperate need of a new coat of white paint.

"It must have been horrible being here over the past couple of months. You know, with all those movies cancelling at the last minute."

"Actually," Aidan said, "this will sound weird, but it's been great. I mean, yeah, it's been stressful, especially for Hester. But having no film work has meant that I could spend more time riding. I've been doing loads of training sessions on Destiny."

"Like movie training?" Issie asked.

Aidan shook his head. "Showjumping. Destiny's a natural jumper. He picks his feet up really cleanly and never knocks the rails."

"How high have you been jumping?"

"He can do about a metre twenty," Aidan said. "Easily big enough to put him in the prize money."

"What prize money?" Issie was confused.

"The Horse of the Year Show," Aidan said. "I haven't asked Hester yet, but I was thinking of entering him in the novice horse class."

"Do you think he can win?"

Aidan nodded. "Yep – and it's decent prize money too. The Horse of the Year is the richest competition in the whole Southern hemisphere. There's half a million dollars in prize money. If Destiny and I win the novice class, that's worth $10,000."

"$10,000?"

"There'll be loads of competition though," Aidan continued. "There are riders from all over the country coming down for it."

"I know," Issie said. "Tom is coming down next week. He's bringing Dan and Ben. I think Dan's riding in the novice class too."

Aidan seemed to go very quiet at this news. When he finally spoke his voice sounded quite different. "That guy Dan. You go to pony club with him, right?"

"Uh-huh," said Issie.

"And he's, like, a friend of yours?" Issie nodded. Aidan went quiet again for a moment.

"Is he your boyfriend?"

Issie was stunned. She hadn't been expecting this. "No," she said, "no, he's not." Aidan looked relieved.

"Hester is probably waiting for us down at the stables," he said. "We'll drive straight through to unload the horses." He nosed the truck to the right of the circular lawn so that they swept right past the front door of the manor and headed down the limestone drive towards the stables.

"Issie?"

"Uh-huh."

"You know what I said before? About me being glad that you were here? Well, I am, Issie. I'm really glad. It seems like ages since I saw you and…" Aidan stopped paying attention to the road and stared at Issie. He was fidgeting nervously with the sleeve of his tartan shirt. "The thing is, I've been wanting to ask you something the whole way down here…"

He was suddenly interrupted by Issie who let out a loud shriek. "Stop the truck, Aidan! You're going to hit him!"

Aidan's foot instinctively went for the brake as he turned to see what had made Issie shout out. In front of them, galloping straight for their truck, was a pony.

"Aidan!" Issie yelled again.

"I see him!" said Aidan, sounding the horn at the pony.

"What's wrong with him?" Issie asked. "Why doesn't he get out of the way?" The pony was still galloping towards them. There was no way the truck could stop in time. They would hit him for sure.

"You've got to stop!" Issie shouted.

"I'm trying!" said Aidan. "It's not that simple – we have horses in the truck to think about!"

Issie realised that he was right. If Aidan slammed the brakes on too quickly then Toby and Coco would be thrown forward violently and might be badly hurt. But if Aidan didn't brake fast enough then the poor pony that was bearing down on them would be killed.

It felt as if everything was in slow motion as the pony continued to gallop at them and tyres skidded against the limestone gravel as Aidan tried to stop. The horrible squeal of truck brakes filled Issie's ears, overwhelming her in a rush of memory. She had a sickening sense of déjà vu – as if she was reliving that awful day at Chevalier Point. The day when Mystic had been killed. It was nearly two years ago now that the accident had happened. Her mind always got so confused when she tried to think about that day.

Issie remembered trying to stop the runaway horses from heading out on to the main road, her sense of horror as Mystic had reared up to face the truck. Then she was falling backwards and the tarmac was rushing up to meet her. There had been a sickening crack as her helmet hit the road, and the taste of blood in her mouth before it all went black. After that, she couldn't recall anything until she woke up hours later in the hospital with her mother calling her name. Her mother told her what had happened. She explained how Mystic had saved Issie by throwing her clear of the truck. Issie still remembered the desperate expression on her mother's face as she struggled to answer her question. "Mum? What about Mystic? Is Mystic OK?"

It was the very worst moment in Issie's life. Her first pony Mystic had been her best friend. She had loved him so completely, so deeply. Losing him was like losing her own soul.

Now, suddenly, she was living through it all over again. Only this time she was watching it all from inside the truck, powerless to do anything as she sat waiting for the awful, inevitable moment of collision with the horse in front of her.

Issie shut her eyes and held her breath. She couldn't bear to look. Instinctively she put her arms on the dashboard to brace herself for the impact. A few seconds later, when the crash didn't come, she opened her eyes again.

The truck had stopped. The horse was nowhere to be seen and Issie suddenly realised that she was crying and shaking and Aidan was holding her tight in his arms. "It's OK," he was saying, "it's all right. We didn't hit him."

"Aidan!" Issie felt like she couldn't breathe. "We were going to hit him. I was sure we were going to…"

"Shhhh, it's OK. I know. I thought we were going to hit him too. He got out of the way just in time. Are you OK?" Aidan let go of Issie and sat back in his seat.

"Uh-huh." Issie dried her eyes. "I'm fine."

"That was close, huh?"

"Where did that horse come from?" Issie wondered. "He seemed to come out of nowhere."

"He must have jumped out of his paddock again." Aidan shook his head. "That's the third time this week. He might have escaped the truck, but I'm pretty sure that this time Hester is going to kill him!"

"You mean he's done this before?"

"Yeah. Last time he jumped out, he managed to get into the garden shed and ate all of the dog biscuits. He is totally crazy, that pony. Hester is so fed up with him. She can't afford to put up deer fences to keep him in – and, knowing Comet, he'd probably jump over them anyway!"

"Comet?" Issie said.

"Uh-huh," Aidan replied. "He's one of the Blackthorn Ponies that Hester decided to keep. Although I think she's been regretting the decision ever since."

Just as he said this, Issie saw her aunt emerge from the rear of Blackthorn Manor. She had a makeshift lead rope in her hands that she had made out of the belt from her dress. She was using it to lead a cheeky-looking skewbald. The pony, for he was just a pony and couldn't have been more than fourteen-two hands, was skipping merrily at her side. He didn't seem to notice or care that Hester was looking at him with a murderous expression. The skewbald looked so pleased with himself that, despite the heart attack he had just given her, Issie couldn't help but immediately have a soft spot for him.

"So that's Comet?"

"The one and only," Aidan said darkly. "The skewbald that no paddock can hold."

As Comet came closer, Issie could see that he was actually rather pretty. The pony was a chestnut with white patches, and he had white socks and a broad, white stripe down his nose. Comet was sturdy and muscular, like all wild Gisborne hill ponies. He had solid legs with thick cannon bones, strong shoulders and powerful hindquarters made for jumping – a fact which he was clearly using to his advantage to get out of the paddock whenever he liked. The pony's conformation was powerful, but it was his eyes that had Issie totally bewitched. Those eyes! They burnt with an intensity that she hadn't seen before in any horse.

Comet seemed thrilled that everyone was paying him so much attention. As he danced along at Hester's side, Issie could have sworn he had the attitude of a champion racehorse. In his mind, this pony wasn't little at all. He was a colossus.

"Comet! Stand still, naughty pony!" Hester growled. Then she turned to Issie and Aidan. "Isadora! Lovely to see you. I take it you've already met Comet?"

"You could say that," Issie smiled.

"Well, my favourite niece, as you can see, this place hasn't changed a bit – it's still completely mad!" Hester said. "Welcome back to Blackthorn Farm."

Chapter 4

"You mean we were nearly hit by a comet?" Stella said. She and Kate had emerged from the truck and were totally confused by what had just happened.

"No," Issie giggled. "We nearly hit him. Comet is a horse!" She gestured towards the skewbald pony who was still skipping about as Aunt Hester tried to hold him with the belt off her dress.

"He escaped on to the driveway and we nearly ran him over," Aidan explained.

"Are Toby and Coco OK?" Hester asked.

"They're both fine," Stella said. "They scrambled a bit when the truck stopped suddenly, but they didn't fall over or anything."

"Let's get them unloaded," Kate suggested. "We can

check them over properly in the loose box once we take off their floating bandages."

Since the truck had been forced to stop halfway down the driveway it seemed easier to simply unload the horses there and walk them the rest of the way.

Toby and Coco came down the ramp with their ears pricked and their heads held high, as horses do whenever they arrive somewhere new. When he saw them Comet gave a whinny of greeting. His whole body reverberated as his clarion call rang out, shaking with a neigh of excitement at having new horses for company.

Hester glared at him. "Oh, do behave yourself, Comet! You really are the most troublesome pony." She turned to the girls. "I don't want you to think they're all this bad. Most of the Blackthorn Ponies we have here are very well schooled. I've got several new horses that are perfect learners' ponies, ideal for the riding school. Come on, let's put your horses away and then you can meet some of them."

The stable block at Blackthorn Farm was built from the same white-painted weatherboards as the manor. Inside it was like a giant barn, with bales of hay stacked up in one corner, a storage room for tack and two rows of loose boxes. On the door of each loose box a horse's head was carved into the honey-coloured wood above a plaque with the horse's name inscribed on it.

Issie pushed open the vast wooden sliding door and walked inside, followed by Stella and Kate leading Coco and Toby, and Aunt Hester, still with her makeshift dress-belt halter, hanging on to Comet.

"You can put your horses in the first two boxes on the left there, girls," Hester said.

"What about Comet?" asked Issie.

"I don't usually box him," Hester said. "Blackthorn Ponies don't really like it in the stable as a rule. They prefer to graze out. But I might have to make an exception in Comet's case – at least if he's in a loose box he won't be able to jump out!"

Hester popped Comet in the box next to Coco's. The stall was freshly mucked out with clean straw on the floor and water in the trough. Comet gave his new home a rather bored once-over and then craned his neck desperately over the Dutch door, whinnying to get attention. Coco stuck her head out of her stall and returned his call.

"Shhh! Coco!" Stella said, giggling. "He's a naughty pony. Don't encourage him!"

As they walked down the rows of loose boxes the girls could see familiar faces poking out of the top of each stall door. First in the row were the three palominos, Paris, Nicole and Stardust, the mares they had ridden when they were working as stunt riders on *The Palomino Princess*. Issie stopped and fed a carrot to Stardust, running a hand through her silver-white mane, admiring the rich treacle sheen of her coat. "Remember me, girl?" she asked softly.

Her question was answered by a nicker from the stall next door as a black and white face emerged. "Diablo!" Issie grinned at him. Diablo was Aunt Hester's favourite stunt horse, a piebald Quarter Horse that could do all sorts of tricks, including playing dead when a gun was fired – a trick that had almost scared Issie and her friends out of their wits the last time they were at Blackthorn Farm.

In the stall next to Diablo was the enormous draught horse Dolomite. The big bay with the white blaze stood at nearly sixteen-three hands, while, in the stall right next to him, was Titan, the dinky miniature pony who couldn't have been more than ten hands high!

"Dolly and Titan obviously aren't any use as riding-school ponies," Hester said. "You'd need a ladder to mount Dolly."

"What about Titan?" Stella asked. "Couldn't one of the little kids ride on him?"

Hester shook her head. "Titan is a true miniature, a Falabella. They're not really bred as riding ponies; they can only handle very light weights on their back – although he can tow a cart."

In the stall next to Titan was a dark brown pony who was around thirteen hands high. "This is Molly, one of my new ones," Hester said. "She's a Blackthorn Pony that I've been schooling up. Very well mannered – the perfect learner's pony."

"How many ponies will you need?" asked Issie.

"That depends on how many students enroll," Hester said. "The ad has only been up on the *PONY Magazine* website for a few days and we already have five keen pupils lined up."

"Do any of them actually know anything about riding?" Kate asked Hester.

"The twins, Tina and Trisha, have experience," said Hester. "They're ten years old and they've been having weekly lessons since they turned eight apparently. I was planning to put them on Paris and Nicole. They'll be perfect for more advanced riders. The youngest rider so far is Kitty – she's eight and mad keen on ponies according to her mum, although her brother George, who is ten, sounds like a handful. Both of them have had riding lessons, so they know the basics."

"Which ponies will you put Kitty and George on?" asked Issie.

"I'm not sure about George, but I was thinking that Kitty could ride Timmy, the sweet chestnut with the star on his forehead. He's a Blackthorn Pony too, no vices and thoroughly bombproof," Hester said. "The oldest girl is eleven. Her name is Kelly-Anne and she insists she's a bit of an expert – but she seems utterly green to me, if you know what I mean. I'm going to put her on Julian. He's a bit of a plodder, quite safe for an absolute beginner."

Issie and Stella exchanged nervous glances. Up until now the idea of running a riding school had seemed like fun. But now that they were here it all seemed kind of daunting. Next Monday they would have actual pupils arriving. And some of the riders weren't much younger than they were. What would they say when they saw that their instructors were just a bunch of kids?

"I thought you three could draw up a lesson plan and a timetable this afternoon, then we've got time to iron out the kinks during the week before the riders arrive," Hester continued.

"Lesson plan?" Stella squeaked. "Won't you be doing that? I mean, we won't actually be taking the lessons all by ourselves, will we?"

Hester shook her head. "I'm not expecting you to do everything by yourselves. But it's good to have a game plan so you can cope without me. Aidan and I have a lot of work to do just keeping the farm running so it's possible you'll be left alone in charge at least some of the time." Hester noticed the terrified looks on the three girls' faces. "Something wrong?"

"Ummm… no…" Issie managed.

"Good!" Hester said brightly. "Well, I think that's enough of a tour of the stables for today. You can meet the rest of the ponies later. Shall we get back up to the house and you can unpack your things? You've all got your usual rooms. I hope that's OK?"

Issie's bedroom was the first room off the landing at the top of the grand wooden staircase. She threw her bags down on the enormous four-poster bed and then threw herself down next to them. The huge room was papered with antique horsey wallpaper and hanging above the fireplace was an enormous oil painting of Avignon, Aunt Hester's great grey Warmblood stallion. In the portrait Avignon was running free, his beautiful silver mane flowing in the wind. Issie lay on the bed and gazed up at the painting, taking in the beauty of the horse, the arch of his neck, the flare of his nostrils, the deep, dark eyes staring back at her.

"All settled in?" Aidan's voice startled her. He was standing in the doorway holding a duffel bag. "I'm moving into the last room down the end of the hall."

Issie was confused. "Why aren't you in your cottage down by the stables?"

"It made sense to move out," Aidan said matter-of-factly. "We needed somewhere to put all the kids so we turned the cottage into a sort of dormitory. I'm staying here in the main house until they leave." He stepped into Issie's room and shut the door conspiratorially behind him. "Hey," he said in a low, stagey whisper, "we need to have a secret meeting."

"What about?"

"Dinner," he said. "I want to sort out a roster before the kids get here. We need to stop Hester spending too much time in the kitchen – for obvious reasons!"

Aidan was right. Issie's aunt might be able to run a riding school. But it was an entirely different matter to feed a riding school. Hester was, quite possibly, the world's worst cook. Her dinners usually ended up as blackened, inedible mounds in the oven. Her baking was so bad that even Butch, the resident farm pig, turned his nose up at it. Unfortunately Hester had already been in the kitchen that very morning. When the girls came downstairs after unpacking they found her waiting for them with a plate of scones for afternoon tea. They were like bricks with raisins in them.

Stella picked one up and took a bite. She instantly regretted it. "Ow, I fink oif broken a twooth!"

"There is no way she's cooking dinner," Issie muttered to Aidan as she choked down a mouthful of her scone.

"We'll sort out that roster," Aidan agreed.

Cooking and cleaning rosters, riding timetables, lesson plans. There was lots to be prepared before the new pupils arrived. "Can't we do it all later?" Stella grumbled as they sat down at the kitchen table with pens and sheets of paper. "I mean, it's only Tuesday. We have nearly a week to get all this done and it's a lovely sunny afternoon and we've been cooped up in the truck all day. I want to go riding."

"We didn't come here for a holiday!" Kate said. "We've got work to do. Don't you want to be organised when the riders arrive on Monday?"

Hester surprised everyone by agreeing with Stella. "We could work on the rosters and timetables tonight," she suggested, "and I've got a stable full of riding-school ponies who could all do with some exercise." She looked at her watch. "If we get down there now, there's enough time for a quick bit of schooling in the arena before dinner."

Nobody needed convincing. The girls dashed up to their rooms to get their jodhpurs on while Aidan and Hester went ahead to the stables to get the ponies ready.

"I saw the cutest little grey pony grazing next to the arena when we arrived. I wonder if I can try that one?" Stella said.

"I like the chestnut one with the star on his forehead and the three white socks," Kate said. "What's his name again?"

"His name is Timmy. And your ankles will drag on the ground if you ride him!" Issie giggled. "Hester will probably put you on one of the palominos."

Issie knew which horse she would be getting. Hester was bound to put her on Stardust, after they had bonded so well on the set of *The Palomino Princess*.

As they neared the stables it looked like Issie was right. When Aidan emerged from the stalls he had Stardust all saddled up and her reins in his right hand. It seemed like a lifetime since Issie had ridden the pretty palomino. She felt a shiver of anticipation as she strode towards the mare. "Hey, girl." Issie reached out a hand to stroke her glossy, treacle-coloured neck. She was about to take the reins from Aidan when she heard her Aunt Hester's voice behind her.

"Issie! There you are! Come with me. I've got your horse ready too."

Issie was confused. "But I thought I'd be riding Stardust, Aunty Hess?"

"Oh, I'm sorry, dear. I thought I told you," Hester said. "Aidan is on Stardust today. I was hoping you would take on a new mount that really needs the work."

"What?"

"The skewbald troublemaker," Hester said, gesturing to the last stall in the loose-box row. "I want you to ride Comet."

As if on cue at the mention of his name, Comet thrust his chestnut and white face over the Dutch door and let out a cheeky whinny. Issie looked suspiciously at the skewbald pony.

"He needs riding. He gets so frightfully bored standing in the loose box," Hester said. "It's his own fault of course. If he wasn't such a troublemaker, I'd let him back out to graze with the others… I mean, you can't leave him in the paddock because he jumps out and you can't leave him in the loose box because he tries to destroy it."

As if to confirm this, Comet began banging and scraping the bottom half of the Dutch door with his hoof. *Get me out of here!* he seemed to be saying.

"Naughty Comet! Stop that!" Issie said firmly. She grabbed the skewbald by the reins, unbolted the stall door and led him out into the yard.

Hester had already tacked him up for her and Issie noticed that Comet looked quite different in a saddle and bridle. He was one of those skewbalds with vigorous splashes of white all over his withers and rump. They trickled down his legs finishing up with four white socks – a bit like someone had spilt a can of white paint over him. Even his chestnut tail looked like it had been streaked with a paintbrush.

Once you put a saddle on, though, Comet's colouring was less obvious. The saddle blanket completely covered up the white marks on his withers and back. He almost looked like an ordinary chestnut with four white socks, except when you looked from the other side you could see a big splodge of white on his hindquarters that looked a bit like a map of India.

As Issie led Comet out into the yard and over to the mounting block the pony danced along beside her, lifting his legs up in a high-stepping trot. When he was sure that everyone was watching him he raised his head and gave a high-spirited nicker, calling out to the other ponies.

"Comet! Stop being such a show-off!" The skewbald skipped about on the spot as Issie tried to steady him long enough to put her foot in the stirrup.

Issie knew she needed to be firm with this pony. Comet was green and he had shocking bad manners. Ponies were supposed to walk quietly beside you, not skip about. But she didn't have the heart to be too tough on him. There was something about his grand attitude and silly antics that just made her want to giggle. Comet strutted about as if he was a superstar instead of just a little skewbald gelding in the paddock at Hester's house. Besides, Issie was beginning to realise that Comet didn't respond well to authority. He was a stroppy pony and if she wanted to bond with him, she was going to have to do things his way.

"Steady, Comet!" Issie gave up on using the mounting block as the pony kept dancing around her. As Comet circled she moved swiftly with him, slipping her foot into the stirrup and, before the pony even knew what was happening, she was bouncing up into the saddle and had landed lightly on his back. "Good boy!"

There is that moment when you sit on a horse for the very first time and you ask yourself, *How does it feel up here? Are we right for each other? Do we click?* You can never really know for sure straightaway. It takes a long time to get to know a horse. But in those first minutes in the saddle, as you ask them to walk, trot and canter for the first time, you get an inkling, almost like a sixth sense that tells you whether you really belong together.

Right now, Issie didn't realise it but she was unconsciously, instinctively, feeling this new horse out. She adjusted her position and felt the sturdiness of Comet's stocky frame, compact and solid underneath her. He was only fourteen-two, which meant that officially he qualified as a pony, not a hack, and yet Issie could sense that he had the attitude of a much larger horse.

As she gathered Comet up and asked him to step forward into a walk and then a trot, Issie felt almost instantly that he was exactly the sort of horse she liked – responsive and peppy. Issie only had to give him the lightest touch with her legs to get him moving.

"Take him on a lap or two around the arena to get used to his paces," Hester advised her. Issie nodded and asked Comet to trot. He did so immediately, his stride covering the ground in a floating trot with his hocks coming underneath him nicely. His canter too was bouncy and active. Issie felt a thrill of excitement tingle up her spine.

"He's got lovely paces, Aunty Hess!"

Hester smiled. "He's still green, but he has loads of potential. I think you'll get on famously."

As if to confirm this, Comet raised his head and let out another loud whinny, calling out to the other horses as if to say, "Look at me!" Issie laughed and gave Comet a slappy pat on his glossy neck.

"Well, Comet already thinks he's famous – I guess that's a good start."

Chapter 5

What is a riding instructor supposed to look like? Issie had fretted about it all morning as she got dressed. Today the riding-school kids would all be arriving and Issie, Stella and Kate had to look the part and impress their new pupils.

She thought about Tom Avery. He always cut such a commanding figure at the Chevalier Point Pony Club in his cream jodhpurs, tweed hacking jacket and a cheesecutter cap on top of his thick thatch of dark, curly hair. A riding crop was permanently in his hand – not to use on the horses, but to thwack against his long leather boots for emphasis when making a point. Issie had flirted with the idea of wearing a cheesecutter cap like Tom's when she was getting dressed, but decided that it looked a bit too much. She had decided to go with the riding crop, however, and she carried this in her right hand as she walked into the kitchen.

"Ohhh, I wish I'd thought of that," said Stella. Stella and Kate both had on their best instructor outfits too. Like Issie, they were wearing long boots and jods. Stella had on a pink Ralph Lauren polo shirt and Kate was wearing her short-sleeved shirt and her Chevalier Point Pony Club tie, which looked very smart.

"When are they due to arrive?" Kate asked, pacing back and forth, too nervous to eat her toast, which was going cold on the kitchen table.

"Any time now," said Issie. "Hester went off in the horse truck an hour ago to pick them up at the train station."

"Do we need to go down to the stables then?" asked Stella. "Hester said we should meet her there to welcome them."

"I guess so," Issie said, looking around nervously. "Hey, where's Aidan?"

"He's meeting us down there," Kate said. "He said he had to finish fixing something. I heard him hammering." It turned out that Aidan had been adding a new top railing to the paddock closest to the stables.

"I've made the fence half a metre higher all the way around," Aidan said with satisfaction as he threw his tool belt down in the corner of the stables.

"So you think it will hold him?" asked Issie.

Aidan nodded. "With that new rail the fence is almost one metre fifty. It would hold a deer. There's no way that little skewbald Houdini is escaping again."

"Poor Comet," Issie said. "He's been so fed up with being stabled all week. I bet he can't wait to get back outside."

Since their arrival at Blackthorn Farm, Issie had spent all her spare time riding Comet. Not that she had much spare time. Hester hadn't been kidding when she said there was a lot to get ready before the kids arrived. The ad on the *PONY Magazine* website had been successful. There were now eight riders signed up to arrive today at Blackthorn Farm Riding School.

"They should be here by now," Aidan said. "It only takes half an hour to drive back here from the train station…"

As he said this, there was a cacophony of barking as Hester's dogs, Nanook the Newfoundland, Strudel the golden retriever and Taxi the black and white sheepdog, all bounded out of the door of the stables to greet the horse truck that was pulling up in the driveway.

"That'll be them now," Aidan said.

"Well, shall we go and meet them then?" asked Issie, although she showed no signs of moving.

"Is my tie straight?" Kate asked nervously.

"I feel like I'm going to throw up," groaned Stella.

"There you are!" Hester said as the girls finally emerged through the wide sliding doors at the front of the stables. The young riders had all emerged from the truck with their bags and were standing beside Hester, staring back at the girls expectantly.

"Everyone, I'd like you to meet your instructors," Hester said. "This is Isadora, Stella and Kate. These girls are senior members of the Chevalier Point Pony Club. They are all B certificate riders with their own horses and loads of experience under their belts. They will be your tutors here at Blackthorn Farm Riding School and I want you to listen to them and do as they say at all times." The kids all nodded at this.

"You can leave your bags here for the moment," Hester said. "You'll be staying in the stable manager's cottage, but first I'm sure you want to meet the horses you'll be riding."

The riders all followed her through the stable doors and there were gasps of amazement from a couple of the younger ones as they saw just how vast and impressive the stables were once you got inside. Hester led them through to the centre of the stable block where a row of hay bales had been piled up to serve as seats.

"We've matched you up with your mounts based on your ages and riding abilities," Hester explained. "In the stalls here today are the horses that you'll be riding for the next three weeks."

Hester began with the two red-headed girls sitting on the hay bales at the end. The girls were so similar they were clearly identical twins. "This is Tina and her sister Trisha," Hester said. "They're from Wellington. How old are you, girls?"

"Ten," said Trisha.

"Tina and Trisha attend their local riding school each week. Is that right?" Tina and Trisha nodded vigorously. "You girls will be on Paris and Nicole," Hester told them. "Matching hair and matching horses!" Tina and Trisha looked pleased with this and instantly began discussing between themselves which one would have Paris and which one would get Nicole.

The next two girls were much younger, perhaps around eight. "Lucy and Sophie have only had a few riding lessons. They can do the basics like rising to trot,"

Hester explained to Issie, Stella and Kate. Then she turned to the two girls. "We've put you on Molly and Pippen. Lucy, you've got Pippen; he's the little grey in the stable here."

"He's beautiful!" Lucy said breathlessly. Sophie was just as impressed with Molly.

"These will be your ponies for the holidays. You'll be totally responsible for them and will feed, groom and care for them as well as riding them, OK?"

Lucy and Sophie were instantly up from the hay bales and glued to their ponies' sides. Sophie even produced a carrot that she had been carrying in her pocket for the whole trip to the farm in anticipation of this moment. She held out her palm to feed it to the eager Molly.

Hester moved on to a girl with white blonde hair and a boy standing next to her who had the same hair and was clearly her brother. "Kitty and George..." Hester continued, "who are both horse-mad according to their mum."

"I'm not horse-mad," George said. "Kitty is. Mum makes me have lessons and she made me come on this stupid holiday because she couldn't be bothered booking two school holiday programmes. I'd rather be riding a BMX."

Hester looked slightly taken aback at this. "Well, George, how about if you ride Diablo?" she said. "He's the perfect colour for a cowboy like you and he knows all the best tricks. He can count to ten with his hoof, you know." George looked quite impressed by this. Kitty, on the other hand, was standing there quietly, not daring to say a word. It was almost as if she couldn't believe her luck being here at all. Unlike her brother, she obviously adored horses. She looked so desperate to ride a horse, any horse, that you could tell it wouldn't matter which.

Kitty," Hester said, "I think we'll put you on Timmy." Hester opened the top door of a loose box to her right and there stood a chubby little chestnut pony with a star on his forehead and three white socks. He was quite clearly one of the Blackthorn Ponies, stocky with a shaggy mane and tail.

"I love chestnuts!" Kitty said. "They are my absolute favourite colour."

"Well, that's worked out perfectly then," said Hester.

She continued along the queue to the second boy who also looked about eight years old. He had a thick mop of dark brown hair and chubby cheeks. Hester looked at him suspiciously as if he might start on about BMX bikes too if she gave him the chance. "You'll be on Glennie,

Arthur." Hester gestured to the cattle pens just outside the back door where a dapple-grey Blackthorn Pony had his head over the fence and was watching them intently.

They had now reached the last child in the row, a sullen-looking girl with dark hair cut into a blunt-fringed bob. "And last but not least we have Kelly-Anne," Hester said. "Kelly-Anne will be on Julian."

Kelly-Anne looked at Julian as if he were something she'd had to scrape off the bottom of her riding boot. Julian, who was a rather ill-tempered little brown butterball of a pony, stared straight back at her with exactly the same expression.

"He looks useless!" Kelly-Anne said. "I don't want him. I want that one!" She pointed across the stable at Comet who was minding his own business for once and standing peacefully with his head over the loose-box door.

"Kelly-Anne, I'm sorry, but at this school you ride the horse you're given," Hester said quite patiently. "Comet is not a beginner's pony."

"I'm not a beginner. I'm a really good rider, so I want the best horse," Kelly-Anne piped up.

"Have you been riding long, dear?" Hester asked. "Do you go to pony club or do you have a local riding school?"

"No," Kelly-Anne said dismissively. "I don't like pony club, it's dumb. Besides, I can already ride, I don't need lessons. I have ridden loads and loads of times and I can do jumping and cantering and everything!"

"Well," Hester said, her patient tone slipping a little, "even the best riders have lessons. I'm sure you'll learn a lot from listening to Issie and Stella and Kate. When it comes to horses we can always learn more, can't we?"

Kelly-Anne didn't look at all convinced by this. "I knew this camp would be useless," she muttered as she stomped back to the horse truck to grab her bag.

Stella watched her go and then leant over and whispered to Issie and Kate, "There's always a Natasha Tucker in every group, isn't there?" The three girls exploded in a fit of giggles and had to rather unprofessionally hide in the tack room and pull themselves together while Hester led the young riders through the stables to Aidan's cottage to show them where they would be sleeping.

There was one room for the girls and the other bedroom was for George and Arthur. The girls had claimed that the sleeping arrangements were unfair as there were six of them in one room and only George and Arthur in the other. But then again, none of the girls actually wanted to move in and share George and Arthur's room. "Boy germs!" Lucy had shrieked, so that was the end of that complaint. That left the lumpy sofa in the living room. "For the dorm room monitor," Hester explained. "The girls are going to take turns staying out here at the cottage to keep an eye on you all."

This was news to Issie, Stella and Kate. It also didn't go down very well with the Blackthorn riders. "We don't need babysitting, you know," George said, clearly insulted by the idea.

That afternoon was pronounced "free time". Issie and Aidan gave the riders a tour of the farm, introducing them to Hester's performing animals. The younger riders stayed back to feed the goats, the rabbits and the chickens while the others went with Aidan to find racquets for the dilapidated old tennis court and fishing lines for catching eels in the duck pond by the cottage.

After dinner that night – big platters of spaghetti with tomato sauce and cheese cooked by Kate and Stella – it was time to relax before the first full day of riding tomorrow.

"You can watch TV until 9.30 then it's lights out," said Hester sternly. "We have early nights at the farm because we need to get up early too. You must all be back here dressed and ready for breakfast by 7 a.m."

There was a groan from George at this and Kelly-Anne looked sulky as usual, but the others seemed cheery enough as they stacked their plates and headed back down the hill for their first night in the cottage dormitory.

Issie was just about to get changed for bed herself when Aunt Hester knocked on the door of her room.

"Would you mind taking the first shift down at the dorm tonight, Issie?" she said. "I know the cottage is perfectly safe, but I think it's a good idea to have you there to make sure our guests are all right. Just for the first night at least. I know I'm a bit of a worry wart…"

"Sure, Aunty Hess." Issie grinned. "I'll look after them."

Issie stepped out on to the back verandah with her sleeping bag rolled up under her arm. She pulled on her boots and switched on her torch. It was funny how much darker the night was when you were in the countryside, she thought. No city lights, just the moonlight and the stars and the white beam of her torchlight as she walked across the lawn towards the cottage.

The lights were already out in the cottage. But as Issie

approached, she could see the flicker of a flame, possibly a candle, burning in the kitchen.

That's weird, she thought. Hester would never leave a candle on at night – it was too dangerous. What were those kids up to? As she came up to the front door of the cottage Issie was about to turn the handle, but something made her hesitate. Instead, she crept to the left of the door where a small, low window meant that she could see into the living room inside. It was hard for her eyes to adjust and Issie had to press her nose up against the glass to see in.

At first, she could hardly believe what she was seeing. Sitting there in the middle of the room, cross-legged in a circle around the candle flame, were the eight young riders. Their heads were shrouded in blankets so that they looked a bit like medieval monks. One by one, as if taking part in a mystical ceremony, they were picking up the candle and passing it to each other. Finally, the candle had travelled all the way around the circle until it came into the hands of George, who put it back down on the floor. George gave a wicked smile and looked at the two youngest children, Lucy and Sophie. The girls looked completely terrified. Issie couldn't hear what he was saying, but as George spoke Sophie looked like she might cry.

George looked at her with a devilish grin and then he blew out the candle! The cottage was now pitch-black! Issie couldn't stand it any longer. She had seen enough. She burst through the door and there were shrieks and screams from the startled kids inside as she switched on the light.

"What are you doing?" George squeaked.

"I came to check on you," Issie said, trembling. "And it's just as well!" She looked around the room at the frightened faces. "Now, who's going to tell me... what's going on?"

Chapter 6

Issie looked around the room at the faces of the terrified young riders. "Why are you all sitting here in the dark? What are you doing?"

They sat there mutely. No one was willing to answer. Issie looked at George, who had blown out the candle and was still holding on to it, looking the guiltiest of all of them.

"George?" Issie said. "Do you want to tell me what's going on here?"

"It was Arthur's idea!" George blurted out. "He started it!"

"Did not!" Arthur snapped back.

"Started what?" demanded Issie.

George hesitated. "We've been telling ghost stories,"

he said. "It was a competition to see who could tell the scariest one."

"Trisha is winning so far!" added Kitty. "She told that one about the hand with the hook, you know, in the forest, when they hear the tapping on the roof of the car? And then they find the hook stuck in the door?"

"That story was so lame!" Kelly-Anne groaned. "I never wanted to do stupid ghost stories in the first place. They're for babies."

"You're just in a sulk cos no one was scared of your story!" George shot back. Lucy and Sophie, the youngest ones in the group, were silent during all of this, huddled together in the corner under a blanket.

"Are you girls OK?" Issie asked. "Is this too scary for you?"

"No way!" Sophie grinned. "I love ghost stories!"

"We told the one about the bloody fingers!" beamed Lucy.

"Can you tell us one, Issie?" Tina asked.

"Go on!" Trisha begged.

"No," Issie said firmly. "It's lights out time. It's too late to be up telling ghost stories."

"But it's only ten o'clock; it's not even late!" Sophie said.

"Just one story and then we'll go to bed," added Tina. There was a murmur of agreement from the circle.

Issie sighed. "OK then. But after I tell you a story, everyone has to go to bed and straight to sleep, OK?"

Lucy and Sophie made a space in the circle between them and Issie nudged her way into it.

"Wait!" Arthur said, leaping up to grab the matches so that he could relight the candle. Then he switched off the light and the cottage was once again in darkness apart from a flickering flame.

Issie pulled a spare blanket up over her head like a hood, took the candle from Arthur and sat silently for a moment, the soft glow of the flame illuminating her face. "You won't have heard this ghost story before," she said in a low voice, "because what I'm about to tell you isn't a story at all. It is absolutely real. And it happened right here at Blackthorn Farm." She paused. "Are you sure you are brave enough to hear it?"

"Yes!" George and Arthur were both desperate for Issie to begin.

"Have you ever heard of the Grimalkin?" Issie asked. They all shook their heads. "The Grimalkin was a giant black cat that roamed the hills of Gisborne," Issie continued. "When I first heard the stories about him, they said he had escaped from the circus or the zoo and was living in the hills, wild and dangerous. Of course, no one really believed in him. They didn't think he was real. But I knew he was real because I saw him."

"Did you really?" Kitty said. "How big was he?"

"Big enough to eat a horse," said Issie. "The first time I saw him was just outside this cottage," she continued, "walking along the railings of the cattle pens. I could see him in the moonlight; he was jet black with this tail that was at least two metres long…"

"You're making this up to scare us!" Kelly-Anne objected.

Issie looked at her with a steely gaze. "I am not. You can ask Aunty Hess when you see her in the morning if you like."

"Shut up, Kelly-Anne!" George snapped. "The rest of us want to hear about the Grimalkin."

Issie had the sense to spare them the really gory details of that awful night when she and Aidan had found Meadow's body. The big black cat had killed the calf by slashing its throat with its powerful claws. Issie still had nightmares about poor Meadow, lying there with her rust and white coat soaked with blood. There was no need to give Sophie and Lucy nightmares too.

Huddled under their blankets, the Blackthorn Riders hung on Issie's every word. There was an audible groan of dismay when she finally finished her story and switched the lights back on.

"Was that all really true?" Tina asked. Issie nodded.

"Do you think there are still Grimalkins out there?" Lucy said, peering out at the blackness beyond the window.

"No, the Grimalkin is gone. I saw the ranger kill him. There's nothing out there now." Issie looked at the tired faces surrounding her in the candlelight. "OK, bedtime then," she said, shooing the riders out of the living room so that she could set up her bed on the sofa. "Let's go!"

"I told you we don't need a babysitter," George grumbled.

"What?"

"Yeah," Tina and Trisha agreed. "Please, Issie. We want to stay down here by ourselves. We don't need anyone to look after us."

Issie looked at the lumpy sofa. It was barely long enough for her to fit on and it looked horribly uncomfortable. She had to admit she would rather be in her enormous double bed back at the manor.

"OK," she said reluctantly. "But I need all of you to

get into bed before I go." There was a groan from George and Arthur, but no one argued with Issie this time. As she switched out the bedroom lights she heard Lucy's voice in the darkness.

"Issie?"

"Yes, Lucy?"

"You know how we asked you to tell us a ghost story."

"Uh-huh."

"Well, that wasn't really a ghost story at all, was it? I mean, the Grimalkin wasn't actually a ghost. He was real."

"I suppose so," Issie said.

"Do you know any real ghost stories?" Lucy asked. "With proper ghosts in them?"

"Yeah, I do," Issie said.

"Will you tell us them?" asked Lucy.

"Maybe. But not tonight, Lucy. Go to sleep."

As Issie walked through the kitchen towards the cottage door she switched on her torch and swept the room, making one last check of the house before stepping outside into the cool night air and locking the door behind her.

The torch beam picked out a circle of light on the damp grass in front of her feet as she walked back across the lawn towards the main house. It wasn't far to walk.

All she had to do was wind her way between the trees behind the cottage and then cross the vast, sloping back lawn to the main house. She could see the back verandah light shining ahead of her, acting as a beacon guiding her way.

As she walked Issie thought about Lucy and how she wanted a "proper ghost story". She remembered Lucy's question, "Do you know any real ghost stories?" *Yeah*, Issie thought, *I really do*. Should she have told Lucy and the others about Mystic? There had been times when Issie felt desperate to tell someone about him, like she was going to burst if she kept her pony a secret any longer. For a moment in that room tonight she had considered telling the kids her own true story. She wanted to tell them that ghosts could truly be real – that Mystic was dead, but he was still with her somehow. He had come back to her, not as a ghost, but as flesh and blood, like a real horse. He was her horse and he always would be.

Issie wanted to tell them. But something stopped her. She was suddenly filled with the enormous weight of the dark truth that she held within her. At that moment she realised that Mystic wasn't something you could tell kids as a bedtime story. The sacred bond she shared with the grey gelding was too special to be turned into a campfire tale. Mystic had been her best friend. Now he was like her guardian angel. He was her secret and she shared it with no one – that was the way it had to be.

Issie had been so deep in thought that she was halfway across the lawn before she noticed the noise. In fact, even when she did finally notice it, she wasn't really sure whether she had actually heard something. Was it her turn to imagine ghosts now? No! There it was again! The noise sounded a bit like the crunching of branches underfoot. It was as if something or someone were following her. Issie spun around, shining her torch beam in a circle. Then she stopped and trained the beam on the garden to her right, where she thought the noise was coming from.

Issie kept her torch pointed on the garden. There! In the shadows. She could have sworn she saw a branch move. She shone the torch on the spot, but whatever it was had gone. She tried to listen again, but all she could hear was her own heart beating. All those ghost stories were getting the better of her!

Then she heard the rustling sound again. Closer this time. It was coming from behind the trees just beside her. She could hear branches crackling as something moved through the undergrowth.

"Is there someone there?" She could feel her palms sweating. "This isn't funny!" Issie's pulse quickened. She thought about what Lucy had said back at the cottage, about there being another Grimalkin. Maybe she was right. How did Issie know there had only been one? Ohmygod, what if...

Out of the shadows now a dark shape came towards her across the lawn. As it loomed closer Issie shone the torch beam directly at the creature. Not a black cat as Issie had feared, but a chestnut and white skewbald pony.

"Comet?" Issie groaned. "Comet! How did you get out?" Issie already knew the answer. Sure enough, when she led the skewbald back to his paddock she found the gate was still shut tight. Comet, must have jumped.

"One metre fifty!" Issie whistled. "And in the dark too!" She turned to face Comet, who was looking extremely pleased with himself.

"Comet!" Issie said firmly. "You have to stop this. No more jumping out or Aunty Hess is bound to put you back in the loose boxes. And you wouldn't like that, would you?"

For a moment there, Issie fancied that Comet actually understood her. The skewbald pony looked at her with sorrowful, deep brown eyes, as if to say, *Sorry, it won't happen again.*

Issie couldn't help but giggle at his apologetic expression. "OK then," she said, opening the gate, "I'm giving you one last chance." As Issie released her grip on his halter the skewbald trotted off merrily across the paddock. Issie shook her head as she watched him go. Would he still be there by the morning? Hester would have a blue fit if he jumped out again. Maybe Issie should just give up and lock him up now in the loose boxes herself?

Issie trained her torchlight on the paddock, searching for Comet. And then she felt her pulse quicken as she caught something unexpected in the beam. There was another horse in the paddock with Comet! She had only caught a glimpse of him for just a moment, but she was sure of it! Searching frantically in the darkness, she waved the torch beam back and forth trying to find the horse again. There! He was standing next to Comet. She could see him quite clearly this time. She could even make out the grey dapples of his coat, the flash of silver mane. Her heart leapt as she realised who it was.

"Mystic?" Issie called out. "Is that you?" She held the torch with both hands to keep it steady, worried that if the light beam slipped away even for a moment then the grey horse would disappear and she wouldn't be able to find him again.

"Hey, boy?" Issie called out. She was close now, almost there… Issie kept expecting the horse to vanish, but he was there. He stood perfectly still in the torchlight and his black eyes shone back at her. He was waiting for her. She reached out a hand and touched the thick, coarse strands of Mystic's silver mane. "Hey, boy," she breathed softly. "It's good to see you."

Mystic nickered softly as Issie stepped closer to him and leant against his shoulder, wrapping her arms around the pony's neck, burying her face deep in the grey pony's mane as she hugged him tight.

Their embrace was interrupted by the sound of Comet moving behind her. From the moment Issie had met Comet she had sensed there was something special about the skewbald pony. Maybe Mystic sensed it too? Certainly, it was no coincidence that Mystic was here. It meant something.

"Are you here to keep an eye on him?" Issie murmured to Mystic. "Maybe you can convince him to stay in his paddock for the night for once?"

The grey gelding seemed to acknowledge his new task as Comet's babysitter. He gave a soft nicker at Issie's instructions, then wheeled about and trotted off into the darkness, fading out of her sight. Comet raised his head up as Mystic disappeared, then he trotted after him, following the grey horse across the paddock.

Issie grinned. If anyone could help control a wayward pony like Comet, it had to be Mystic. She stood there for a moment longer in the dark, flashing the beam of her torch where the horses had been. But they were too far away for her torch to penetrate now, lost in the pitch black at the far side of the field.

"G'night, Mystic," Issie murmured. "Keep him safe, OK?"

Issie walked back to the manor deep in thought. As much as she was thrilled to see Mystic again, her horse's appearance had left her worried. If Mystic was here then it meant trouble of some kind.

As she took off her boots and put her torch down on the table by the back door, she felt a chill run down her spine. She walked through the kitchen and was about to head upstairs to her room when something made her stop. There was a light on in the small alcove off the kitchen that Hester used as her office. Issie tiptoed in her socks across the parquet floor and peered through the door of the alcove. Her aunt was hunched over her desk, a mound of paperwork stacked in front of her. Hester took off her reading glasses to rub her eyes and as she did so she caught sight of Issie standing behind her. Startled, she dropped her glasses and then scrambled to pick them up again so she could see who was standing in the doorway.

"Issie! I thought you were sleeping at the cottage. You gave me quite a turn!" Hester looked tense.

"The kids threw me out. They're fine. I came back here to sleep," Issie explained. "What are you doing, Aunty Hess?"

Hester readjusted her spectacles. "A bit of book-keeping – the farm accounts, that sort of thing." Issie looked at the mound of bills on the writing desk in front of her aunt.

"Is it true, what Aidan said? You might have to sell the farm?"

Hester took her glasses back off and rubbed her eyes a second time. "Yes, well, Aidan's jumping the gun a bit. I'm not selling it just yet. We have enough money in the emergency coffers to see us through for another month. Perhaps two months if we scrimp."

"What will happen after that?"

"Mortgagee sale, I expect. I want to take the horses with me, but where would we go? I won't be able to take them all. Or the other animals – or Aidan for that matter."

"How much money do you need?"

"A windfall of around $25,000 is all it would take," Hester said. "I've been buying lottery tickets so that's bound to pay off soon I should imagine."

She looked at Issie with tired eyes. "I am doing everything I can, favourite niece. And I cannot tell you how much it means to me that you are here to help me." Hester smiled weakly. "Anyway, I'm sure we'll muddle through. So stop standing in the doorway looking at me with those sorrowful eyes. You look like one of my jersey cows with that expression!" She waved Issie out of the office. "Off you go to bed and stop worrying! You have a rowdy group of riders to teach in the morning."

Issie stood there for a moment longer but her aunt was firm. "I said goodnight, Isadora."

"G'night, Aunty Hess."

Upstairs in her room, Issie lay on her bed and stared at the painting of Avignon on her wall above the fireplace. Why was Mystic here? The grey horse wanted to help in some way, but how could he? Even Issie couldn't help. What Blackthorn Farm really needed was money – and she didn't have $25,000.

Chapter 7

At breakfast the next morning Hester dropped another bombshell.

"I've just had a call from old Bill Stokes who lives down by Preacher's Cove," she told the girls. "There's been an accident. There was a landslide in the cove and Bill has found six of my sheep trapped on a ledge with no way out. He said they're very distressed, must have been stuck there all night. I told him I'd drive down there with Aidan this morning and winch them up to safety with the horse truck."

"This morning?" Issie squeaked. "But, Aunty Hess, it's the first day of the riding school."

"I know it's leaving you in the lurch," Hester said, "but I've got no choice, Issie. Those poor animals are in a frightful state – it can't wait."

Hester saw the worried looks on the girls' faces. "You've got your lesson plan. I'm sure you'll be fine."

Issie wasn't so sure. "George, and Kelly-Anne will be the worst," she muttered as they walked down the driveway to the stables. "They're too busy picking fights with each other to listen to us. And Kelly-Anne thinks she knows everything."

"You have to treat them just like horses," Stella insisted. "Don't show any fear or they'll pick up on it."

"You're right," Kate said. "You just have to take control of that lesson, Stella, and show them you're in charge."

"Me?" Stella stared at Kate as if she was crazy. "Not me! I'm not teaching them. You are! You're the head instructor, Kate – you're the one with the most experience and everything. Those riders are bound to listen to you."

"You're kidding!" said Kate.

"Go on!" Stella grinned. "Issie and I will be there right behind you to back you up! Won't we, Issie?"

"Yep!" Issie grinned. They were right behind Kate too – hiding behind her and giggling as they made her go first through the stable doors to meet the riders.

"Right!" Kate said, reluctantly taking command and addressing the eight pupils sitting on the hay bales. The riders were dressed in their jods and boots ready to get started. "Before we even begin to think about getting on our ponies, what do we need to do first?" Eight faces stared blankly back at her.

"We have to catch them of course!" Kate smiled. "Follow me to the tack room." She led the eight riders into the tack room. Hung neatly on the walls on named pegs were rows of halters and bridles. "Now who can tell me which one is a halter and which one is a bridle?" Kate asked.

Trisha and Tina's hands shot up. "The one with a bit and reins is the bridle. The halter doesn't have a bit. You use the halter to catch them and tie them up while you're grooming and stuff," Trisha said.

"Very good!" said Kate. "Now can you all please pick up the halter of the horse that you'll be riding, grab a carrot each out of the feed bins and let's go catch our ponies." This proved to be easier said than done.

"We didn't have to catch our own ponies at our last riding school," Lucy said. "They had them all ready for us to ride when we arrived."

"I can't undo the strap!" Sophie groaned, struggling

to pull the stiff leather through the buckle.

Meanwhile, Stella was busy with George, who had managed to put a halter on Diablo, but had somehow got it upside down and couldn't figure out what he had done wrong.

"Is anyone else having problems?" Kate asked. She looked over at Kelly-Anne, who had managed to get her halter done up but had the lead rope wrapped tightly around her hand. "Always hold the lead rope at the shank and don't wrap it around your hand like that!" Kate called out to her. "What you're doing is dangerous. If Julian bolts on you and the rope tightens, you could end up getting dragged along by your pony or with a broken finger."

"I know what I'm doing!" Kelly-Anne snapped back. "Stop being so bossy." Still, she unwrapped the rope that was twirled around her hand and held it correctly the way Kate had shown her.

"Has everyone got their halters on?" Kate called out. "Right. Let's lead them back to the loose boxes."

Once they were inside, the riders were all shown how to tie a slip knot to tether the ponies and then Kate led them to the tack room.

"Your gear should be stacked next to the nameplate of your horse," Kate explained. "You've each got a bucket with your own grooming kit. You should have a hoof pick, a curry comb, a sweat scraper, a sponge, a dandy brush, body brush and a mane comb each. Can you all check your kits?" The riders all dug about in their buckets and tried to identify the various bits of their grooming kit.

"Your saddles and bridles always go in the same place in the tack room and your racks are name-tagged with your pony's name," Kate continued. "There will be a prize each week for the person who keeps their tack and kit the tidiest and cleanest…"

There was a groan from Kelly-Anne at the idea of cleaning gear. "Are we actually going to do any riding today? You want us to clean the ponies and stuff? It's like we're doing your work for you!"

"Grooming your horse is an important skill you need to learn," Kate said. "Can anyone tell me why we bother to groom before we ride?"

"To make our horses look pretty?" Lucy offered.

"Yes, but what else?" There was silence. "Grooming a horse isn't just about making them look nice," Kate said. "It also gives you a chance to check for injuries, to see if your horse has a saddle sore or if there's a stone stuck in a shoe. Even if you are in a screaming hurry, you should always give your horse a quick groom all over to check that it is OK."

"Now," Kate said, "when I call your name, can you come up please and grab your bucket of brushes and your tack. And remember to carry the saddles with your arms through the gullet the way we showed you."

Lucy and Sophie were both struggling to carry their own saddles, so Issie helped them to lug their gear back to the loose boxes.

"Will you help us put the saddles on too?" Sophie asked. "The thing is, when we ride at the riding school they always have our ponies ready for us."

"So you've never even groomed a horse before? Or put on a saddle and bridle?" Issie was stunned. "That's awful. Horses aren't just furry bicycles that you can park up at the end of the day, you know!" The girls giggled nervously at this.

"Come on," Issie smiled at them, "it won't take you long to learn. I'll give you a grooming lesson right now."

And so Issie showed Sophie and Lucy how to groom their ponies, starting at the head and working back towards the tail, using the body brush on the soft parts of the horse where the saddle went, and the dandy brush to scrub the mud off their ponies' hocks.

"I think I'm hurting him!" Sophie wailed as she snagged her mane comb in Pippen's thick grey mane.

"He's fine," Issie reassured her. "Ponies' manes really aren't very sensitive."

Lucy, meanwhile, was trying to pick out Molly's hooves, but kept getting nervous and shrieking every time Molly tried to help by obediently picking up her feet. It took forever for Sophie and Lucy to get Molly and Pippen groomed, and even longer to saddle up.

"Are you lot ready yet?" Stella stuck her head over the stall door. "It's almost lunchtime and we haven't even started riding!"

Eventually, all eight riders had their ponies tacked up, their helmets on and their stirrups at the right length, and they were riding around the arena.

"Keep two horse lengths between you and the horse in front of you," Kate called out as the riders walked around. "And trot on! Rising trot, everyone. Come on, Arthur, keep Glennie moving!"

"He won't go!" Kelly-Anne, who was bouncing about in the saddle like a sack of potatoes with wobbly hands, was having trouble getting Julian to trot.

"Just put your legs, try and keep your hands still and don't jag him in the mouth. He'll move forward," Kate instructed. But Kelly-Anne wasn't having any of it.

Kate, Issie and Stella were forced to watch in horror as Kelly-Anne lifted her legs up and away from her pony's sides and then brought them down again with a bang, giving Julian an almighty boot in the sides and digging her heels hard into his ribcage!

Julian, not used to being kicked in the tummy, got such a shock that he bolted forward into a frantic canter and Kelly-Anne, who hadn't been expecting him to move quite so suddenly, let out a squeal as she lost her balance. Julian, realising his rider was in trouble, came to a sudden stop and Kelly-Anne flew forward, out of the saddle and landed smack flat on her bottom in the middle of the arena in front of the entire ride, whereupon she immediately burst into floods of tears.

"Well, that's a brilliant start," Stella muttered to Issie under her breath as Kate rushed forward to help Kelly-Anne up, grabbing Julian's reins with one hand.

"Are you OK?" Kate asked as she picked Kelly-Anne up off the ground.

"I'm fine. He's a stupid horse. I was just making him go!" Kelly-Anne said defiantly.

"That's not how you make a horse go!" said Kate.

"Well, that's how I do it," Kelly-Anne sniffed.

"I can see that!" said Kate. She turned to Issie and Stella. "I think we'd better run through some basic rules before we even try the rest of them at a canter."

"Uh-huh," Issie nodded.

"I think I saw a whiteboard and a felt pen in the tack room," Stella said. "It might help if we write them down!"

When Stella returned a few moments later with the whiteboard, she had already written a title across the top: The Blackthorn Farm Riding School's Five Commandments

"Umm, Stella? Aren't there supposed to be ten commandments?" Kate asked.

"They'll never remember ten!" Stella said. "Five is enough to start with."

"OK," Issie said to the riders. "Can anyone tell me the first rule? What is the most important thing when you are riding?"

"Ummm, being nice to your pony?" Sophie said.

"Excellent!" Issie said. "What else?"

A hand shot up from one of the other riders. "Ummm, don't kick?" Tina said.

Pretty soon everyone had their hands up (except for Kelly-Anne, who was still in a sulk about being told off)

and in no time at all Stella had written up her list.

The Blackthorn Farm Riding School's Five Commandments

1. Always treat your pony with kindness. A good rider
    makes their pony happy.
2. Never kick your pony to make him go. A squeeze is
    enough.
3. Never yank on the reins to make him stop. A squeeze is
    enough too!
4. Do not flap your arms and legs. You are a rider,
    not a chicken.
5. A good rider is quiet in the saddle. Keep your heels down,
    your eyes up and your hands steady.

The lesson was short and simple that morning. The girls made their pupils clamber around in the saddle doing round-the-world, before swinging their legs to the front and the back to do heel clicks. Then they played the Mounting Game. Stella popped a series of yellow, red and blue feed bins on the ground. The riders had to dismount and pick up an object out of their grooming kits before remounting, trotting up to the bin and throwing the items in one by one. They had to dismount again to get the next piece until their grooming kits were empty and the bins were full. They finished the morning session by making all the riders show them the perfect position in the saddle.

"You need to think of a straight line from your ear to your elbow to your heel," Issie said as she adjusted Lucy's leg so that it was back against the girth. "You must maintain that vertical line at all times."

"Can anyone tell me what other straight line you must keep at all times?" Stella asked.

"Umm, is it the elbow to the bit?" asked Tina.

"That's right! Imagine a line straight from the horse's bit to your elbow that means your hands are in the right position."

"That's easy," Kelly-Anne snorted.

"Yes, but you haven't actually tried moving yet, have you?" said Stella. "It's easy to maintain the perfect position when you're just sitting there, but wait until you start trotting – or cantering!"

"Yeah, you had the perfect position until you fell off on your bum!" George grinned at Kelly-Anne.

"George!" Issie cautioned him. "Everyone falls off.

Horsey people have a saying: you have to fall off seven times before you are a real rider."

"Anyway," Kate looked at her watch, "I think we've all had enough for the morning. It's lunchtime. Let's get these ponies untacked."

It took almost as long for Lucy and Sophie to unsaddle the horses as it had taken for them to tack up. As Issie helped them, she drilled the girls on their general knowledge.

"We'll play Pony Questions," Issie told them. "Let's see who can be the first one to give me the right answer. Are you ready?" The girls nodded.

"What colour is a piebald?"

"Ohh!" Sophie's hand shot up. "Black and white!"

"Excellent! And what is another name for a piebald? The name the Americans use? We should really use it for Diablo because he's a Quarter Horse..."

"A paint?" Sophie guessed.

"That's right!" said Issie. "Next question then. Who can point to their horse's fetlock?" Lucy pointed to the bottom of her pony's leg.

"Very good, Lucy!"

The girls loved Pony Questions and were begging Issie for more as they walked back up the road from the stables. When Issie finally arrived in the kitchen she found Aidan valiantly defending the last piece of chicken pie for her.

"Are the sheep all OK?" asked Issie.

"They're fine," Aidan said. "We got them all up the bank again and then Hester dropped me back here so I could help with lunch. She's gone to help Bill Stokes fix the fence – the landslide took out a whole section along the Coast Road."

Aidan passed her the pie. "George and Arthur both wanted to eat your piece," he explained. "You'd have been forced to survive on one of Hester's leftover scones."

"Ughh!" Issie took the plate gratefully. "Thanks! I'm so starving. It's been a tough morning."

"Want to sit outside?" Aidan asked. They walked out to the back verandah and sat down on the steps that led to the garden with their lunch plates on their laps.

"So how are your students?" Aidan wanted to know.

"They can all ride," Issie said. "Well, I'm not so sure about Kelly-Anne, but the rest of them can. They don't know the first thing about ponies though. It's like they've had everything done for them."

"You'll sort them out," Aidan said. "In three weeks time they'll all be riding like experts."

"I don't know about that," Issie groaned. "They're probably desperate for the weekend to come so that they can go home and get away from us bossing them around!"

Aidan shifted about uncomfortably and looked down at his feet. "Yeah, I was thinking about that, about the weekend. I know you've got lots to do during the week with the riding school and everything, but I was thinking maybe this Saturday, when you're not working, we could pack a picnic and go for a ride. With the film work drying up I've had some spare time to build a cross-country course across the farm. It's pretty basic, but there are about ten jumps and some of them are quite good. We could ride the horses over a couple of them and then go for a swim at Lake Deepwater…"

"That sounds cool!" Issie said, "I'll tell Stella and Kate and…"

"No!" Aidan blurted out. "I meant just the two of us. You know, like on a date." Aidan looked at her and as his piercing blue eyes locked with her own Issie suddenly felt her heart hammering in her chest, pounding so loud that she barely heard the words that came next.

"Issie… do you want to go out with me?"

Chapter 8

Aidan's words hung in the air. He had asked her out!

"Aidan, I, umm…" Issie didn't know what to say.

"Never mind," Aidan said, looking uncomfortable. "I was just thinking that… look, it's OK. You don't have to…"

"No," Issie said. "I mean, no, I want to. I mean yes. My answer is yes. Yes, Aidan, I'd love to."

"Great!" Aidan looked relieved. "Great! I…"

"Hey, you two!" Stella was suddenly right there behind them with her lunch plate in her hands. "Is this a private conversation or can anyone join in?"

"Actually…" Issie began, but it was too late as Stella sat down, squeezing herself in between Issie and Aidan.

"Come on, make a bit of room!"

"Here, you can have my seat," Aidan said. "I'd better go anyway. I'll see you back at the stables in an hour, OK?" Aidan stood up to leave and Stella took his place.

"So?" Stella said to Issie as they watched him walk off. "How are things with Aidan then?"

Issie felt herself blushing hot pink. "He just asked me out."

"Ohmygod!"

"We're going to go on a picnic to the lake on Saturday."

"But it's only Tuesday. That's ages away!"

"I know!" Issie groaned. "I wish it was Saturday now. It's going to feel like forever."

"What did he say exactly?" Stella said. "I want to know all the details!"

"We're going riding to try out this new cross-country course and go swimming at the lake."

"Cool," Stella said. "I'll tell Kate. She loves cross-country. What time are we going?"

"Ummm…" Issie didn't know what to say. "It was just going to be me and Aidan."

Stella's smile faded. "Oh."

"But I can tell him!" Issie said. "If you and Kate want to come too, we could all go together…"

"No," Stella said. "That's OK. It's a date. You don't need us tagging along." She gave Issie a disappointed look. "You go with Aidan. We'll go together another time."

The girls hardly saw Aidan or Hester at all that week. Hot on the heels of the drama with the stranded sheep, Hester received a call from Ranger Cameron. He'd spotted a Blackthorn mare running wild with a young foal at foot, up on the back ridge behind the lake. Hester and Aidan set off to try to catch her, leaving the girls in charge of the school once more.

"You'll be fine. You girls know what you're doing," Hester tried to reassure Issie. "I'm on my mobile if you need me. Just keep working your way through the lesson plan we made up."

According to the lesson plan, Wednesday was games day. Issie, Stella and Kate organised a barrel race, flag race, bending poles and an egg and spoon competition. Tina and Trisha, who turned out to be complete and utter daredevils, won every single competition between them – except for the egg and spoon race, which Arthur won on Glennie. Everyone was suspicious that his egg had been stuck to the spoon with chewing gum, but Arthur insisted he hadn't cheated.

Thursday was spent on basic flatwork and pony care. Friday morning was flatwork too and all the riders were excited because they'd been told they'd finally be doing some jumping in the afternoon.

"Has anyone used cavaletti before?" Kate asked the riders as they gathered in the centre of the arena after lunch. The eight riders all shook their heads. "Cavaletti are great for developing your pony's gymnastics. Can anyone tell me what that means?" Kate asked.

George sniggered. "What like doing forward rolls and cartwheels and stuff?"

"No, I mean gymnastic jumping," Kate said. "We're going to do what showjumpers refer to as 'gridwork'." She walked to the middle of the arena where two rows of white painted cavaletti were lined up.

"Cavaletti are not big jumps," she explained. "Their purpose is to teach you how to stay balanced and get a rhythm going. Plus, they'll make your ponies learn to think and lift their feet. Can everyone get into two-point position like I showed you please?" said Kate. "And take your stirrups up to jumping length first. We're only going to be jumping very small cavaletti today so two holes should do it."

Kate, Issie and Stella worked their way down the row of riders, checking everyone's jumping position.

"In two-point position we stand up in our stirrups a little and balance on our knees and our bodies tilt forward," Kate explained. "Let's try to get our positions sorted in the arena without jumps first." She made the riders trot around the school. "Everyone sitting in their normal position, excellent… Now… two-point!" she shouted and the riders all tilted forward. "And back again!" Kate instructed.

"My legs are getting tired," Kelly-Anne whined.

"You haven't even started jumping yet!" said Kate. "You'll get used to it. Put all your weight into your heels, balance on your knees. Now we're going to try our two-point over the cavaletti. Tina, you go first." Tina trotted towards the white jumps.

"Look up!" Kate shouted. "Never, ever look down at the bottom of the jump. If you look down then your horse will stop. You must look where you want to go – up and over the fence."

"That was cool!" Tina was beaming from ear to ear as she finished.

"You're next, Kelly-Anne," Kate called. "Hurry up.

Kelly-Anne! You must look up!" As Julian approached the cavaletti Kelly-Anne ignored Kate's advice. Instead, her eyes went straight down to the ground where the first pole was. Julian was a well-schooled pony and there was no way he was going to jump a cavaletti if his rider was looking at the ground. He didn't know what else to do so he stopped dead in front of the poles.

Kelly-Anne let out a squeal, "Stupid pony! Get up!" And before anyone could stop her she had lifted her riding crop up high and brought it down hard on the brown pony's rump. "Jump, you pig!" she yelled. Julian didn't have a clue what was wrong. Why was this girl hitting him? He gave an indignant snort and leapt to one side as Kelly-Anne squealed and struck him again. This time she brought the stick down hard on his shoulder. Julian was panicking now; the whites of his eyes were showing as he backed away from the cavaletti.

"Kelly-Anne, stop it!" Issie rushed forward. "He doesn't know what you want him to do. You're just scaring him!"

"He's a stupid, stupid pony!" Kelly-Anne said. She was so furious, so lost in her anger that Issie could see that any drop of common sense she might have had was quickly disappearing, consumed by her fury.

"Give me the whip, Kelly-Anne," Issie said coolly.

Kelly-Anne didn't respond. She glared back at Issie, who reached out and grabbed the riding crop out of her hand. "I said, give me the whip!" she snapped. "And don't ever think about riding like that again – or I'll have you sent home from this school and you won't be back."

"I was just teaching him who's boss," Kelly-Anne insisted.

"You weren't teaching him anything except how to be afraid of a girl who doesn't know how to ride," Issie snapped back.

Kelly-Anne looked at Issie as if she was going to explode. Then she jumped down, threw Julian's reins at her and stormed off. "I don't want to ride him anyway," she fumed as she stomped towards the stables. "He's just a dumb learner's pony!"

"Shall I go after her and try to explain why what she did was wrong?" Stella asked as they watched Kelly-Anne flounce off.

"Leave her," Issie sighed. "Let's get on with the lesson. I'm going to tell Aunty Hess tonight. I won't put up with her treating Julian like that. It's got to stop now."

When Hester heard about Kelly-Anne's behaviour she agreed. "I've taken her aside and had a good talk to her," Hester told the girls as they set the table for dinner. "She's on a good behaviour bond. The riders are all going home first thing in the morning anyway, so that will give her the weekend to cool down. When she comes back to the school on Monday, I expect her to have a new attitude."

Apart from Kelly-Anne, who was now in a permanent sulk, everyone was in a cheery mood at dinner. Hester had defied the odds by turning out a decent meal for once, including a steak pie that was entirely edible.

"I have some news," she told the girls as they tucked gratefully into their unburnt dinner. "Tom Avery is coming to stay."

"What?" Issie just about choked on her pie in surprise.

"He called today and told me that he was planning to come down this weekend with Dan and Ben to prepare for the Horse of the Year. They were going to keep the horses at a stable near the showgrounds, but I suggested that they come here instead."

"Do we have enough room for them?" asked Issie.

"Of course. We've got loads of grazing and spare loose boxes. Tom says he and the boys were planning to camp in his horse truck, and now they won't have to. They can stay here at the house instead for the next fortnight. We have loads of room," said Hester. "Plus, Avery has offered to pay board and grazing costs for the ponies – and right now every bit helps."

"When do they get here?" asked Aidan, looking less than impressed at the idea of Dan turning up.

"Tomorrow lunchtime," Hester said. "So I'll need a bit of help first thing in the morning getting their rooms ready and preparing stalls for the two new ponies."

"But tomorrow is Saturday!" Issie blurted out. She was thrilled that her instructor and pony-club friends were coming to stay, but did it have to be tomorrow? She had been waiting all week for her date with Aidan and now there was no way she could leave the farm for the day.

"I'm sorry," Issie told Aidan when they took their dishes to the kitchen. "About the picnic, I mean."

"That's OK," said Aidan. "I figure we can still ride."

"What do you mean?"

"We've still got a couple of hours in the morning before they get here and there are no lessons going on in the arena," Aidan said. "What about if we saddle up Destiny and Stardust and do some showjumping training?"

"Really?" Issie felt her heart race. It had been ages since she did proper jumping.

"Sure, the cavaletti are already set up and I can build us a jumping course too," Aidan said. "That is… if you want to?"

"I do!" Issie said. Then she hesitated. "There's just one thing, Aidan. I don't want to ride Stardust. I want to ride Comet."

"Really?" Aidan was surprised. "Issie, Comet is pretty green. I've taken him over cross-country jumps when we've been out riding, and he's done a bit of gridwork over cavaletti, but Stardust has had far more proper schooling in the showjumping ring."

"I know," Issie said, "but he's a natural jumper, Aidan. I've seen him." She smiled. "He didn't need any training to learn how to jump out of his paddock, did he?"

Aidan grinned. "No… no, I guess he didn't."

Comet seemed to know that something exciting was happening the next morning when Issie arrived at the stables. The skewbald pony moved about anxiously in his stall as she entered.

"Easy, boy," Issie cooed softly under her breath as she slipped the bridle over his head and did up her own helmet straps, before slipping on her riding gloves. "Let's go."

In the arena Aidan and Destiny were already warming up. "I've set up a showjumping course," Aidan said, gesturing to a small circuit of jumps that he had built at the far end of the arena, "but I thought we should start with some cavaletti."

The two riders did exactly the same gridwork that the kids had been doing earlier that week, practising their positions and making the horses trot through the cavaletti. As she worked him over the cavaletti Issie couldn't help smiling at Comet. His confidence as he took the jumps was like nothing she had ever seen before. He was such a bold jumper – and such a show-off! Issie had to try not to giggle each time they finished and Comet gave a dramatic flick of his tail, a bit like a horsey version of a high-five, thrashing the air emphatically.

"You are funny, Comet!" Issie gave him a slappy pat on his glossy neck and turned to Aidan.

"He's going brilliantly, isn't he?" said Aidan. "They seem pretty well warmed up. Shall we try them over some proper jumps?"

The first fence in the course was parallel rails, the second was a hog's back, then you turned left to approach the double, which had just one stride between the fences and quite a decent spread on the last fence. The fifth and final fence was the biggest by far and was made up of blue and white painted rails with hay bales stacked underneath.

Issie and Aidan both dismounted to walk the course together. "The striding is pretty easy," Aidan said. "You have to turn quite sharply to take the hog's back after the parallel rails, and then there's one stride in between the first and second fence of the double."

Issie stood next to the hay bales. It was a big fence. The bales came all the way up past her waist almost to her chest.

"It's one metre twenty," Aidan said. "Destiny and I will be jumping this height at the Horse of the Year."

Issie nodded. She had jumped a fence the size of the hay bales loads of times before on Blaze, but never on Comet. She felt the butterflies in her tummy beginning to flutter. Cavaletti were all well and good, but what would the skewbald be like over such big jumps with a rider on his back?

"I'll go first, OK?" Aidan said.

Issie didn't know whether it made it better or worse that Destiny took the five fences so effortlessly. The black stallion positively flew over the double, barely bothering to even put in a stride, and took the hay bales at the end with ease for a clear round.

"Good lad!" Aidan gave Destiny a slappy pat on his broad black neck as he pulled the stallion up to a halt next to little Comet. "Do you want me to put the fences down for you before you go?" Aidan asked. The jumps were at the right height for a horse like Destiny who was sixteen-two, but for a little pony like Comet these were big fences.

As Issie eyed up the jumps, there was something about the way Comet danced and skipped beneath her that made her think he was almost trying to say, *I can do this! Let's go!*

"No. Leave them," Issie said. "I think we'll be OK."

When you watch horses showjumping on TV, they make it look so simple. Even the biggest fences seem to be no big deal. But when you are actually riding in the showjumping ring in real life, facing a massive fence made out of painted rails, it's quite a different story.

Issie had a brief moment as she turned Comet to begin her warm-up circle when she felt her nerve falter.

What if Comet didn't jump? If the pony suddenly stopped or swerved she might lose her balance and fall. She shook her head, as if trying to shake the bad thoughts out of her brain. She remembered what Avery had told her about staying positive and tried to imagine herself soaring cleanly over each fence.

"Steady, Comet," she said firmly. The skewbald was tense with anticipation. Issie tried to ride him into a steady canter as she approached the first fence. There was a moment, a couple of strides out from the jump, when it looked like Comet was going to refuse, but he simply put in an extra stride to get deeper into the fence and leapt it cleanly. He took the hog's back too with ease and put in a perfect stride between fence one and two of the double combination.

As they turned to face the hay bales Issie felt herself stiffen in the saddle and the butterflies returned. She looked down at Comet who was pulling like mad against her hands, filled with his own pure love of jumping, and she sat back in the saddle and let him go. Comet put in two huge canter strides, gathered himself up and absolutely flew over the hay bales, giving a high-spirited victory buck as he cantered away on the other side.

"Oh, well done, Comet!" Issie had a grin on her face

a mile wide as she pulled the skewbald to a stop and let go of the reins to give him a pat on both sides of his neck. "Good pony!" The sound of applause from the side of the arena made her look up.

"Excellent round!"

"Tom!" Issie was surprised to see her instructor standing there, clapping vigorously.

"That's quite the horse you've got there," Avery called out to her. "What's he called?"

"Comet," Issie said. "His name is Comet."

Avery ducked down, slipped between the rails of the fence and strode across the arena towards Issie and Comet. He ran his eyes over the horse, his face serious, clearly deep in thought. "Nice solid bone, strong hindquarters," Avery murmured as he assessed him, "and a scopey jump too. I haven't seen a pony jump like that in a very long time…" He looked up at Issie. "Well, it looks like I got here just in time."

"In time for what?"

"To start your training." Avery patted the skewbald's neck. "Issie, Comet is a superstar in the making. We'd better get cracking." He paused. "That is, if we're going to enter him in the Grand Prix at the Horse of the Year Show."

Chapter 9

Issie was stunned. Did Avery really think that Comet was good enough to jump at the Horse of the Year? Surely her instructor was joking?

"I'm completely serious," Avery insisted. "This pony is a natural athlete. I was watching him over those jumps and he's got a terrific bascule."

"What's a bascule?"

"A good jumper will stretch his neck out and tuck up his front feet over a fence so that he almost looks like a dolphin flying through the air," Avery explained. "That's called a bascule. It's absolutely crucial in a showjumper. Comet has it. With a little training to perfect his technique, that natural ability could be enough to earn him a clear round in the pony Grand Prix at the Horse of the Year."

Issie vaulted down off Comet's back and landed on the ground beside her pony. The cheeky skewbald was listening intently with his ears pricked forward, as if he knew that Issie and her instructor were talking about him.

"He can clear any fence on the farm," Issie said as she told Avery about Comet's habit of jumping out of paddocks. "He's totally fearless!"

"Well," said Avery, "let's see if we can harness his natural talents. We've got two weeks before the Horse of the Year qualifying rounds to get some solid schooling in. I think the best plan is for you and Comet to join in on my jumping lessons with the boys." Avery saw Issie's uncertain expression. "Is there a problem?"

"It's just that I'm supposed to be working, Tom. I won't have time…"

"Don't worry," Avery said. "You can fit it in. Hester needs the arena during the day for her riding school anyway so I've agreed with her to use it in the evenings. We'll switch on the floodlights and have jumping practice after dinner each night. That means you'll have time to teach the school during the day – although you'll be pretty exhausted by the end of the day, I should imagine."

Issie grinned. "That sounds brilliant!"

"Where's my training squad got to anyway?" Avery looked over at the stables. "I asked those boys to put their horses away in the loose boxes ages ago. What is taking them so long?"

As he said this Dan and Ben emerged from the stables with halters in their hands. When Dan saw Issie his face lit up. He gave her a wave and began to run across the arena towards her. Then he caught sight of Aidan, who was still working Destiny around the showjumping course, and his expression suddenly turned dark.

Aidan had caught sight of Dan too and didn't look pleased to see him either. He took Destiny over one last fence and then pulled the stallion up and trotted back over to join the group.

"Aidan!' Avery said. "Good to see you again! You've got Destiny going very nicely."

"Thanks, Tom," said Aidan.

"You know Dan and Ben, don't you?" asked Avery.

"Yeah." Aidan reached down from his horse to shake hands with Ben and then put his hand out to Dan. Dan hesitated for a moment and then reluctantly took his hand and shook it as the boys exchanged a gruff hello.

"I was just asking Issie if she wanted to take part in Horse of the Year training in the evenings now that we're here," Avery told Aidan. "Do you want to join us too? We'll give the horses a day to settle in and then our first training session will be on Monday."

"Absolutely," Aidan said. He stared directly at Dan. "If Issie is doing it then I'll definitely be there. I wouldn't miss it."

On Sunday night, when the Blackthorn Riders had returned from their weekend at home, everyone sat around the dinner table and discussed Avery's training sessions.

"What about us? Can Kate and I do it too?" asked Stella. "I mean," she added grumpily under her breath to Issie, "unless it's just you and Aidan, like a date." Issie felt the sting in Stella's comment, but Avery didn't notice the tension between the two girls.

"Absolutely," he agreed. "I'm sure Coco and Toby are both capable of jumping the heights we'll be doing at the training sessions if you girls both want to join in."

The younger riders seemed very excited by the idea of proper showjumping training.

"What about us?" Arthur asked. "Can we all come and watch?"

"I don't see why not – if that's OK with you, Hester?" Avery said.

"I think it's a great idea," Hester agreed. "We'll make sure we have an early dinner and then you can meet up at the arena. You'll learn a lot from watching other riders. I'm sure all of you will pick up some excellent technique tips."

Kelly-Anne looked doubtful about this. "I don't want to watch," she said. "I want to ride too." There was silence and then a giggle from some of the other kids.

"What?" Kelly-Anne glared at them. "I've done loads of showjumping and it's easy. I could totally compete at Horse of the Year if I had Comet instead of stupid old Julian!"

"No, you couldn't!" Arthur said.

"I could so!" Kelly-Anne snapped back.

"Gee, Kelly-Anne," George rolled his eyes. "You are such a fibber!"

"I am not!" Kelly-Anne's face was red with anger. "You don't know anything about horses anyway!" There were daggers in her eyes as she pushed her chair out from the kitchen table, stood up and stomped out of the room.

Kelly-Anne wasn't the only one who was in a dark mood at dinner. Stella was clearly in a huff with Issie. As for Aidan, he was barely speaking for some reason and kept glaring at Dan across the table.

"Did you notice that too? He's, like, so totally jealous!" Kate insisted when the girls were gathered in Issie's room later that evening.

"But why?" Issie said. "I've already told him that Dan isn't my boyfriend."

"Maybe," replied Kate, "but it's hard not to notice the way Dan keeps looking at you all the time. And did you see the evils Dan was giving Aidan? He's just as bad!"

"Well, I wish they'd both stop it," Issie sighed. "They can't carry on like this for the next three weeks."

It wasn't just the boys who had Issie worried though. How long could Stella carry on being in a bad mood? Ever since Issie had mentioned her date with Aidan, Stella had been acting really weird. Something was definitely bothering her. She had been really quiet lately. And Stella was never quiet!

Stella would talk to Issie if she needed to, like in the arena when they took the riding lessons. But she wasn't her normal perky, chatty self, and whenever Issie tried to talk to her about what was wrong, she just shrugged and walked away. Issie didn't know what to do. It had seemed like such a good plan for Issie to come here and help Hester. But was she really helping? Right now everything Issie did just seemed to make matters worse.

"Right!" Avery said, eyeing up the riders who were standing in front of him. "I hope you're ready for a workout tonight. We need to get these ponies and horses really fit over the next fortnight – and the best way to do that is lots and lots of circles and flatwork to supple them and get them listening, and then gridwork with the cavaletti so that they develop muscle and rhythm."

Ben looked crushed by the idea of flatwork and cavaletti for two weeks. "But aren't we going to do any big jumps?" he grumbled. "The horses will have to do big jumps in the competition, won't they? Isn't that what we should be practising then?"

Avery nodded. "Absolutely – we'll be doing a few big fences, but not too many. It's important not to overjump these horses. There's too much risk of an injury or making them sour on it. We're going to build up with some smaller courses before the qualifying rounds in a fortnight, and after that we'll start to put the jumps up a notch and tackle some big courses."

Ben didn't look convinced by this argument. You could see he was just itching to take Max around the course of painted rail fences that Avery had set up at the far end of the arena.

"Now, I see you all have your stirrups at jumping length already," Avery smiled. "Very good. But tonight you needn't have bothered."

"You mean we're not jumping at all now?" asked Ben, trying to keep the frustration out of his voice.

Avery shook his head. "No, Ben, you will be jumping – you're just not going to be using your stirrups. We're going to ride without them." He walked over to Ben and quickly slipped both the leathers and irons off his saddle so that Ben had his legs dangling with no stirrups.

"Can you all strip your leathers off the saddle please and hand them over to me?" Avery told the rest of the ride.

"Ohmygod! This feels weird," Stella said as she slipped her stirrups off the saddle and let her legs hang loose down at Coco's sides.

"How are we going to jump without any stirrups?" grumbled Ben.

"You don't need stirrups," Avery insisted. "In fact, relying on your stirrups can teach you bad habits. Learning to jump without them is good for you. It will teach you not to get too far out of the saddle as you go over the fences and you'll be forced to balance and use your knees effectively."

He turned to the riders. "Are we all ready? Let's start work then. Aidan? Can you lead the ride please. Get them working around the arena at a walk and then do a sitting trot in the corner of the arena and come through the cavaletti in your two-point position without stirrups."

There were a few shrieks from Stella and a bit of giggling and bouncing about as the riders got used to trotting without stirrups. But then things got serious as they did the cavaletti course for the first time and they could all see what Avery meant. Without stirrups they were relying on their own body to hold their position and stay in the saddle, and after a few drills back and forth through the cavaletti all of them had a much better seat.

"Excellent," said Avery. "Keep your eyes up, Stella! That's it! Good stuff!" He called all the riders back into the centre of the ring. "Now," he told them with a straight face, "knot your reins please."

Stella couldn't believe this. "You mean we're going to jump with no stirrups and no hands!"

Avery grinned. "Trust me, Stella. It's not as scary as it sounds."

As the horses came bouncing back through the cavaletti at a trot, all the riders managed to stay in the saddle despite having no stirrups and knotted reins. Issie had to hold Comet back as they approached the cavaletti. The skewbald could still get a little fizzy and overexcited when he was taking fences, but as he settled in with the rest of the ride he began to calm down and soon he was trotting the poles like a dream.

"How is he feeling?" Avery asked her as Issie pulled Comet up when they were all getting their stirrups back.

"Really good!" There was a huge smile on Issie's face. "He's a bit hard to hold sometimes though."

"He'll settle down," said Avery. "He's just fresh, that's all." He turned around to the other riders. "That'll do for tonight!" he called out to them. "Good lesson, everyone."

"I can't believe it!" Ben muttered. "When are we going to do some really decent-sized fences?"

It seemed Avery was in no hurry to use the showjumps that were set up at the other end of the arena. For the rest of the week he kept up the same routine, drilling his riders over the cavaletti so that, by the end of it, all of them were quite happy jumping without their stirrups or reins.

The following week, it looked like Ben was finally getting his wish. Avery began to set up a proper jumping course for them to ride. But if the riders had been expecting to jump huge fences, they were disappointed. Avery had built the course with the jumps set low, at a metre high. "We don't need big jumps," he reasoned. "This week is all about learning arena craft. You must be able to ride a showjumping course with technical skill and take the best possible line at a fence. Then, no matter what height you are jumping, your horse will always be in perfect balance."

Comet was a talented jumper, but he wasn't the easiest horse to control. He was inclined to get a little hot and excited when he jumped. "You need to use your seat to control him," Avery told Issie as she took him around the course. "Sit back in the saddle if you want him to slow down. Don't fight him with the reins or he'll just get stroppy with you. Work with him; focus on being a partnership."

Issie worked hard, concentrating on what Avery told her to do, and by the end of the second week she felt like her bond with Comet had strengthened even more.

On Saturday, after the riding school had gone home for the weekend, Avery's riders gathered in the living room of the manor for a squad training meeting.

"The qualifying competition is being held tomorrow," Avery said. "We'll be trucking the horses into the local Gisborne pony-club grounds at 6 a.m. so everyone needs to set their alarm clocks for 5.30 a.m." There was a groan from the riders.

"Meanwhile," Avery continued, "I thought we'd better get the paperwork sorted." He picked up a stack of papers and handed them to Aidan. "You all need to fill in one of these. Can you pass them around please, Aidan?"

"What is it?" Issie asked.

"Your entry form for the Horse of the Year," said Avery.

Issie looked at the entry forms in front of her. Her eyes scanned the long list of competitions and categories.

"I'm thinking of entering Destiny in the Horse of the Year novice category," Aidan said.

Dan, who was also riding hacks now and could no longer enter the pony ring, glared at Aidan. "That's the event that I'm entering on Madonna."

"Then I guess I'll be riding against you," said Aidan gruffly.

"Suits me," Dan bristled.

"What's this one here?" Stella tried to pronounce the word, "The pussy-ance?"

"It's pronounced pwee-sonce," Avery said. "The word 'puissance' is French – it means powerful. It's a high jumping competition basically. The riders jump a brick wall, which gets higher and higher with each round. There are five rounds and it's a knockout competition. If you don't get over the wall, you're out. The idea is to keep jumping until everyone is eliminated. Whoever gets over the highest wall in the last round will be the winner."

"How big can the wall get?" Ben asked.

"The highest a horse has ever jumped in a Puissance competition is two and a half metres."

"Ohmygod!" Stella was amazed. "That's huge!"

Avery stood up and stretched out his arm as far as it would go above his head. "It's about another half a metre taller than my hand," he said.

"I think I saw a Puissance on telly once," Stella said. "The wall was so big you couldn't see the horse at all – all you could see was his ears sticking over the top before he jumped it!"

"How can they jump if they can't even see over it?" Ben boggled.

"The Puissance is all about courage," said Avery. "Once the fence gets to that kind of height, your horse must be truly brave and have faith in his rider because he won't be able to see what's on the other side."

Issie looked back at the entry form and finally found the event she was planning to enter. "This can't be right!" she said. "It says here that the pony Grand Prix has prize money of $15,000! Is that a misprint?"

Avery shook his head. "No. There are over half a million dollars in prizes at this year's Horse of the Year. This is the richest show in the hemisphere. There'll be riders from all around the world competing."

Issie felt her tummy churning with nerves. "Maybe we should enter something else?"

Avery shook his head. "If you qualify, I definitely think it's worth a shot to take on the pony Grand Prix. The jumps are big, but Comet has the ability to do it."

Issie felt her heart racing. "Really? Tom, do you think so?" She looked back at the entry form: $15,000 in prize money! If she won she'd make enough money to help Aunt Hester save Blackthorn Farm!

For a moment, Issie felt so elated at the thought that

she could barely breathe. And then her eyes went to the entry details at the bottom of the form and she felt as if someone had punched her hard in the stomach and knocked the wind clean out of her. There at the bottom of the form was a list of fees. The numbers were quite clearly printed in large black type. Entry fee: $500 per rider, per event.

Five hundred? That was crazy! She didn't have five hundred dollars and she had no way of getting that much money. Her plan was over before she even had a chance – probably her last chance to help her aunt save Blackthorn Farm.

Chapter 10

How was Issie going to come up with $500? "There's no point in worrying about that yet," Kate pointed out to her. "We've got to make it through the qualifying rounds before they'll even let us enter Horse of the Year."

The event on Sunday was the last of the district jump-offs. With the finals happening the following weekend, this was the one and only chance for Avery's riders to qualify. The riders were all feeling the pressure as Avery pulled the truck up at the Gisborne Pony Club grounds that morning.

"Only the top ten riders in every event will gain enough points to make it through to the Horse of the Year," Avery told the girls, who were riding in the front with him. "If you don't make it through today's competition then you're out. End of story."

"So there's no pressure then?" Stella said sarcastically. She was busily studying the schedule for the day's events, although Issie suspected that she was mostly reading the schedule as a way of avoiding talking to her. Her long silences during the trip to the club grounds had made it pretty clear that she was still barely speaking to Issie.

"You're lucky!" Kate told Issie when they got out of the truck and began unloading the horses. "It was much worse being in the back with the boys. Dan and Aidan just keep getting at each other all the time! Honestly," she shook her head, "I don't understand boys!"

Things only got worse once the riders saddled up. The running order for the competition was divided into hacks – that's horses fourteen-three hands high and over – and ponies, which are fourteen-two and under. Dan and Aidan were both riding hacks, and that meant that they were riding first.

Both boys were taking the contest really seriously. Their rivalry had been obvious all week at training, but it finally came to a head when they were warming up in the practice arena. There was one jump, a blue and white crossed rail, set up for the riders to practise over before it was their turn in the ring.

The competition was getting hot and Dan was due to ride next. He'd been waiting for his turn and circling Madonna in the practice arena. At the last minute he decided to try one last practice jump and lined up the chestnut mare to take the crossed rails. He didn't seem to notice that Aidan was already riding towards the same jump from the other direction.

"Hey! Get out of my way!" Aidan shouted as he saw Dan riding straight at him. Dan had to put in a last-minute change of direction, yanking at Madonna's head to swerve to get out of Aidan's path.

"Hey, watch it!" he shouted angrily back at Aidan.

"What?" Aidan said. "You're kidding? That was totally your fault! You knew I was going to take the jump. You should have stayed out of my way."

"Well, maybe I'm sick of staying out of your way," Dan shot back at him. He pulled Madonna up to a halt. "I've got to ride now. We'll finish this later," he said coolly.

"Count on it," Aidan replied.

Issie, who was back at the horse truck getting Comet ready, had no idea about any of this. She didn't see the fight at the practice jump and she didn't see Dan and Aidan ride their event. In fact, she would never have found out about what happened next if it hadn't been for Comet's saddle blanket. She had been saddling the skewbald up when she realised she had left her usual blanket behind at the farm.

"Don't worry," Avery had said. "I've got a couple of spare numnahs that should be perfect. They're in the crawlspace above the kitchen."

Horse trucks always have a crawlspace in them – a platform that is built at the top above the living area. Often, when riders go away on long trips in their trucks to compete, they will sleep on a mattress in the crawlspace. Avery had been planning to sleep there himself on this trip, but since they'd had a change of plans and he was now staying at the manor, he'd shoved all sorts of things into the empty space – including spare saddle blankets.

Issie had climbed up the ladder to the crawlspace and was lying on her belly, feeling around in the half-light for the saddle blankets, when she heard the stomp of footsteps in the living space underneath her. She could hear two voices quite clearly and she recognised them immediately. It was Dan and Aidan, and if they sounded mad with each other before, now they were furious.

"You could have lost me the competition today with that stunt over the practice fence," Dan fumed.

"Me?" Aidan was flabbergasted. "Dude! You cut me off. And you did it on purpose!"

Dan snorted. "That's ridiculous. Why would I do that?"

"You know why," Aidan said. "Because Issie chose me and you can't stand it."

Dan glowered at him. "You're dreaming, man. I don't know where you get the idea from that you're her boyfriend, but you're wrong."

"Why don't you just back off and leave me and Issie alone?" Aidan said, his face dark and brooding under his black fringe.

"I was about to say the same thing," said Dan. Then he looked Aidan square in the eyes. "Listen, it's time to settle this, right? So how about we do it in the arena?"

"What do you mean?"

"The Horse of the Year," Dan said. "We've both qualified to ride in it, right? So what about if we make a little bet?"

"What sort of bet?"

"I should have thought that was obvious," Dan replied.

Aidan looked at him. "You mean bet on who gets Issie?"

"Uh-huh," Dan said. "Whoever wins the competition gets to be her boyfriend."

Aidan looked at him. "So if I win, you'll back off and leave me and her alone?"

"Yeah," Dan said. "If you win. Which you won't."

Aidan bit his lip, then he shook his head. "This is stupid. Issie will never agree to it anyway."

"Then we won't tell her," said Dan. "This is just between you and me." He put out his hand. "Or are you too scared to take me on?"

Aidan looked Dan in the eye. And then he took his hand and shook it hard. "You've got a bet."

Upstairs, in the crawlspace of the truck, Issie felt herself trembling. She was shaking partly out of fear – she would have hated to have been discovered right now – but mostly out of pure anger. How dare those boys bargain with her as if she were a Bella Sara card to be traded? They were totally crazy! She held her breath and lay perfectly still in the crawlspace for another minute or so and then slowly stuck her head out to make sure they were gone. There was no one there.

As she backed out down the ladder her heart was still

beating like mad. She couldn't believe what she had just heard! At moments like these, Issie realised, there was only one person in the world that she could talk to about stuff like this. She needed her best friend right now. Unfortunately, Stella wasn't speaking to her.

Issie looked at her watch. She was due at the arena to compete in ten minutes. That didn't leave her much time. But she knew she had no choice. Stella was her best friend. How could things have got so messed up? She needed to talk to her desperately and straighten things out. Issie couldn't possibly concentrate on the competition and riding her horse until she had made things right with her best friend.

Luckily for Issie, Stella wasn't too hard to find. Her red curly hair was easy to spot across the fields. Issie could see her by the main arena, leaning over the railings by herself and watching the last of the hacks compete in the open classes.

As Issie approached Stella she thought of everything she wanted to say. She wanted to say that she never meant to make Stella feel left out. She wanted to let Stella know that she was her best friend in the world and that she would never let a boy come between them. She wanted to tell Stella that they were best friends forever and it was a silly fight and she missed her. But, in fact, when she arrived at Stella's side with tears shining in her eyes, all she said was, "I'm sorry!" and that was enough. Before Issie knew it, Stella had said she was sorry too and the two friends were hugging and giggling and saying, "Let's pretend it never happened, OK?" And Issie was telling Stella the whole story of the contest between Dan and Aidan and they were pulling faces over how crazy boys were and then laughing so hard they were gasping for air.

"Ohmygod!" Stella said. "This is like the best thing ever! They've made a bet and the winner gets to be your boyfriend? What planet are they on?"

Issie shook her head. "It's like they're medieval knights in a jousting match and I'm the fair maiden."

"Well, fair maiden." Stella did a little bow and a curtsey. "Who dost thou think will win your hand?"

"I don't know," Issie said.

"Well, it doesn't matter who wins, does it?" Stella said. "They don't get to decide who gets you. You should be the one who gets to choose."

"Stella, that's just the problem," Issie looked serious. "I guess I've been trying for ages. You know, to choose between Aidan and Dan..."

"And?"

Issie sighed. "I don't know. I can't decide."

"Well, if you want to know who I'd choose…" Stella was about to offer her opinion when Issie froze and looked at the arena.

"The open hack event has finished!" she said. She checked her watch. "Ohmygod! The pony Grand Prix qualifier is next and I haven't even got Comet saddled up!"

"Come on," Stella said, breaking into a run beside Issie. "Let's get back to the truck. I can saddle Comet while you get changed. It's OK, we'll make it in time."

"Isadora! Where have you been? You're due at the practice arena now!" Avery was far from pleased as Stella and Issie came running towards the horse truck.

"Sorry, Tom," Issie said. "I lost track of the time."

"It was my fault really," Stella added. "Issie came to find me and I made her late."

Avery looked at them both and shook his head. "I have no idea what the pair of you have been up to, but lucky for you I've already saddled Comet up." He tossed Issie her helmet. "Put this on and grab your boots. Let's go."

As Avery gave her a leg-up on to Comet's back, he offered Issie some last-minute advice. "This is a qualifying competition. There's no clock to beat; all you have to worry about is jumping cleanly. Get a clear round and you'll be guaranteed a place in the Horse of the Year."

Avery tightened Issie's girth by a hole and checked her stirrup length. "Now, you've walked the course twice already this morning. Do you know which route you're taking?" Issie nodded.

"OK, then give him a brisk trot around to warm him up, and pop him over the practice rails a couple of times before you go into the arena." He gave Comet's gear a final check, "You're all set. Any questions?"

Issie shook her head. Any questions she had about whether she was ready for this, about whether Comet was truly ready, would be answered in just a moment when they rode into the ring.

As Issie warmed her horse up around the practice ring, she took the same approach with Comet that she had done right from the start. The skewbald was so headstrong that he liked to do things his own way. *Well, fine*, Issie thought, *let him run the show. Let Comet set his own pace and find his own stride between the fences. Interfere with him as little as possible and never, ever fight him. Just stay one step ahead of him, anticipate, be ready to react.*

As Comet danced about in front of the practice jump, it was as if he expected Issie to take a firm hold on his reins and pull him back. But she didn't. Instead, she gave the pony his head and stayed perfectly calm. She focused her energy on keeping him steady and straight, letting the pony relax as he approached the jump, as if the cross-rails weren't even there and she didn't care. Once Comet had taken the practice jump and understood that Issie wasn't going to try and control him or yank on his mouth, he calmed down too. Now Issie gathered Comet up, holding him just a little with the reins so that he rounded his neck and brought his hocks under him. She looked over at Avery, who was standing on the sideline with Stella. Avery nodded back to her as if to say, "That's it, you've got him ready to go."

Issie nodded back and, at the sound of her name being called, she entered the arena. There weren't many people here at the qualifying rounds today, but even a very small audience was good enough for Comet. As he came through the flags and took the first jump he gave a dramatic tail flick. Over the first fence he kicked his hind legs out with a baroque flourish, putting much more air between him and the jump than he actually needed to. Then he approached the second fence and took that with the same outlandish jumping style.

"He jumps like a circus pony," Stella giggled.

"Yes," agreed Avery, "but look how cleanly he always takes a fence. The way he kicks his hind feet up like that so that they never so much as scrape a rail. I've spent years training my showjumpers to take fences so cleanly. Comet does it naturally."

Out in the arena, Issie felt her adrenalin surge as Comet cleared fence after fence with ease. Issie tried to stay calm, to keep a firm but light hold on the reins, controlling her pony simply by sitting up in the saddle if she wanted him to slow down, letting Comet control the pace. As they rounded the corner to set up the final combination in the course, a double with a bounce stride in the middle of it, Issie felt that Comet was cantering a little too fast, and for the first time on the course, she checked him with a sharp signal on the reins. She knew it was risky. Comet might overreact, fight her pressure and go even faster. But the skewbald didn't argue with her at all. He slowed his stride just as she had requested, and then took off perfectly over the first fence, bouncing in and popping back out over the second with that trademark flourish of his hind legs. Issie felt a thrill tingle through her. Not because they had just got a clear round and made it through to the Horse of the Year Show. Something much more important had just happened in the arena; Issie and Comet had experienced that breakthrough moment. When she asked Comet to slow down and he took her cues without a fight, both horse and rider knew that they were truly working together. It was a partnership. And if they could maintain that partnership, they would be unbeatable.

Chapter 11

Issie pressed her ear up against the receiver and listened to the ring tone. She could hear the phone ringing once, twice, three times… Please, please pick up! She was just about to hang up again when finally the receiver clicked and there was a familiar voice at the other end of the line.

"Hello? This is Amanda Brown speaking."

"Mum?" Issie croaked. "It's me."

"Issie?" Her mother sounded concerned. "It's nearly eleven o'clock at night. Are you OK?"

"I'm fine, Mum. Are Blaze and Storm OK?"

"They're fine, Issie. I checked them this afternoon. Is that why you called?"

"No…"

"Issie, is there something wrong?"

"I'm fine, it's just… ummm… Mum? Can I borrow $500?"

There was silence on the other end of the phone for a moment and then Mrs Brown's gentle voice. "OK, Issie, why don't you start at the beginning and tell me just what's going on."

Half an hour later Issie had told her mother everything. She told her all about the farm being in trouble and Comet, and how she'd been training him to win the pony Grand Prix and had already made it through the qualifying rounds.

"…And the prize money is $15,000! It's almost enough to save the farm!" Issie said. There was silence at the other end of the phone. "So… umm what do you think?"

"I think that $500 is a lot of money," Mrs Brown replied matter-of-factly.

"I know it is, Mum, but I really think Comet can do this," said Issie. "I'll pay you back. I have some savings from when I did *The Palomino Princess* and I was going to use that money to buy Blaze a new winter rug, but you can have that and…"

"All right," Mrs Brown said quietly.

"What?" Issie was stunned.

"I said all right. Yes, I'll lend you the $500." There was silence on the phone line. "Issie? Are you still there?"

"Uh-huh. I just can't believe you said yes."

"Neither can I," Mrs Brown said. "Now I'm going to give you my credit card number to put on the entry form and if I were you I'd shut up and write it down before I change my mind about the whole thing."

After she hung up the phone, Issie went upstairs to her bedroom. She propped up the envelope containing her entry on the mantelpiece underneath the portrait of Avignon. Then she lay down on her four-poster bed and stared up at the ceiling. She was in a state of shock. Was she really going to do this? She was entered in the biggest competition of her whole life on a horse that was green as grass and she had just asked her mum to give her $500 to do it!

It wasn't that Issie was having second thoughts, or an attack of nerves. No. What she was feeling now was pure adrenalin and excitement at the thought of taking Comet into the show ring and proving to everyone what an amazing horse he really was. She knew the heart and the courage that Comet had; there was no doubt in her mind that he could do it. It was up to Issie now. If she could ride her best, if she did everything right and didn't make any mistakes then they could totally ace this.

With only a week to go until the competition, she needed to get really serious about training. The Horse of the Year was next Sunday and this week was going to be the most testing time of her life.

"Issie! Issie! George keeps poking his tongue out at me! Make him stop!"

Issie sighed. She had been expecting this week to be gruelling, but she hadn't figured on this! Not only did she have a heavy training schedule, but she still had her riding-school duties to contend with as well. That included keeping George in line when he tried to tease his sister.

"I wasn't doing anything!" George objected when Issie told him to stop pestering Kitty.

"George, please circle Glennie through the arena so that you are at the rear of the ride," Issie instructed. "If you two can't behave when you're riding next to each other then it's better if you stay at the back. Kitty? Can you get Timmy trotting a bit more rhythmically please?

He's moving like a slug at the moment. Put your leg on and get him striding out. One-two, one-two! Excellent! Much better!"

For the past week, Issie, Stella and Kate had been leading a double life, training the young riders during the day, grooming and cleaning the stables and feeding the kids their dinner before saddling up their own horses and riding their evening training sessions with Avery.

"I feel ready to drop," Stella complained as the girls lay on Issie's bed that evening. "Those kids are a total nightmare. George is out of control and Kelly-Anne has such a bad attitude."

"Well," Issie said, forcing herself to stand up again, "forget about them for now. It's time to get down to the stables and get ready for team training."

Stella groaned and didn't move. "I don't know why I'm even bothering with training. I'm not even riding in the stupid Horse of the Year." Coco and Stella had managed two very good rounds at the qualifying competition – unfortunately, neither of them were good enough.

"I only got twelve faults," Stella whined. "Can you believe that wasn't enough to qualify?"

"How do you think I feel?" Kate said. Toby, Kate's

rangy bay Thoroughbred, was a well-schooled jumper, but when they got to the showgrounds on the day he had trotted up lame. Avery thought it was probably just a stone bruise. There was a farrier working at the showgrounds who had come straightaway and replaced the shoe, but Kate hadn't been convinced that Toby was one hundred per cent so she decided not to compete.

"He doesn't seem to be lame now though, that's the main thing," Kate said, trying hard to be cheerful about it. "Hopefully he's totally sound again and we can do the training for the rest of the week."

As Avery had promised, the fences had got bigger this week. The riders had been doing substantial showjumping courses, working on getting their striding correct between jumps and learning how to hold their horses back between fences.

The showjumping course had grown too. Avery had packed his horse truck with his own equipment from Winterflood Farm. One of the new jumps that he had built was a wall constructed out of red painted "bricks" that were made from lightweight wood. Avery had even added the finishing touches by putting a tall conifer plant at either corner of the wall.

On Thursday night Avery lined up the riders in front

of the brick wall and they watched as he added in an extra row of bricks to make it higher.

"Now, I know none of you are actually entered in the Puissance this weekend," Avery said, "but we're going to practise it anyway. It's a good way to find out what your horse's limits are, just how high they can really jump."

"So how does it work?" asked Stella. "We just take turns jumping the wall until someone has a refusal or knocks down a brick and then they're out?"

"That's pretty much it," Avery said. "There are actually two fences in the Puissance. You have to jump a basic painted rail fence before you turn to take the wall. The painted rail will stay at the same height for the whole of the competition. Only the wall gets bigger each time. And actually, you are allowed a refusal. You'll only be eliminated if your horse refuses three times, or if you knock a brick or choose to withdraw because the jump gets too high."

Avery looked back at the wall. "I've set it at a metre ten to begin with. There's a maximum of five rounds in a Puissance, so tonight we'll be raising the height by ten centimetres each time. We should finish at a metre fifty – if anyone makes it that far. OK," he said, "who wants to go first?"

"I will!" Aidan and Dan both answered at once. The boys glared at each other.

"Aidan, you can go first," Avery decided before they could start squabbling. "The rest of you, start warming your horses up."

The first round, unsurprisingly, saw all six riders go clear. "Too easy!" Ben called out as he cantered back to Avery after clearing the wall without any trouble on Max. He was eating his words a few minutes later when Max knocked a brick out in the second round.

In round three, Kate withdrew on Toby, who seemed to be having a problem again with the same leg that had gone lame the other day. "He's probably fine and I'm just being a fusspot," Kate said to Avery, "but I don't want to jump him too high if he is a bit sore."

That left Stella, Issie, Aidan and Dan still in the competition. The wall had been raised to a metre forty for the fourth round. On the sidelines the Blackthorn Riders were all cheering and shouting.

"Boys against girls! Boys win!" called a voice from the arena railing. Issie turned around to see Arthur's cheeky face staring up at her.

"Don't count on it, Arthur!" she shouted back.

There was whooping from the girls on the sidelines as

Stella turned to face the wall at one metre forty – and then cries of dismay as Coco refused and Stella flew forward on to the mare's neck and had to struggle to stay on. She turned her pony away from the wall and trotted her back over to Avery. "I think that's Coco's limit," she said. "That's way the highest we've ever jumped in our whole lives!"

Avery nodded. "I agree. Good decision to stop her there, Stella – and a great jumping effort."

The boys on the sidelines had their second disappointment when Dan attempted the metre forty wall and Madonna dropped her feet and knocked out a brick.

"Bad luck," said Issie as he rode off. Then she pushed Comet into a canter and began to prepare to take the wall for the fourth time. Comet popped easily over the painted rails – and even more easily over the metre forty wall, giving his usual heel flick and clearing the top of the fence with room to spare!

The girls on the sideline went wild – except for Kelly-Anne, who was creeping Issie out by sitting on the railing all by herself and staring at Comet with greedy eyes.

Issie was the only one to make the height of a metre forty so far. That just left Aidan to try his luck. "Get ready for a jump-off," he grinned at Issie as he breezed past her at a canter to face the warm-up fence.

But there wasn't going to be a jump-off at all. Destiny did exactly the same thing that Madonna had done, dropping his hind legs just enough to dislodge a brick and dashing his chances to the ground.

"Issie wins on round four!" Avery announced.

There was much bragging from the girls on the sideline and Kitty was pulling faces at George. "Girls rule!"

Avery walked over to Issie with a broad grin on his face. "That was very nicely taken at a metre forty," he said.

Issie beamed. "Comet took it easily."

"He's got an amazing jump in him," Avery said, "and a very clean pair of hind feet." Then he added cryptically, "It'd be interesting to see just how high he could go."

The next day, the girls decided that since the kids had enjoyed watching the Puissance so much, they would have one of their own for the riding-school pupils.

"Cool!" George yelled. "A chance for the boys to win their glory back!"

Stella rolled her eyes, and Kitty looked nervous.

"We're not going over the big wall like last night, are we?"

"We're going to use the wall," Stella said, "but we'll make it much lower. We're going to start it at twenty centimetres."

The riders were all lining up ready to go when Kelly-Anne rode forward on Julian with a face as sour as month-old milk. "I don't think it's fair," she said, fixing Issie with a determined look. "Julian is a useless jumper so there's no way I'll win."

"Kelly-Anne," Issie said through gritted teeth, "we've been through this a million times. Julian is actually quite a good showjumper and he's perfectly capable of doing jumps like this."

Kelly-Anne sneered. "I was watching you last night. You think you're a really good rider, but you're not. It's just because you have a good horse. That's why you won't let me ride Comet, isn't it? I bet I could ride him just as well as you can! Go and saddle him up for me! I want to ride Comet!"

For weeks now Kelly-Anne had been the riding school's resident pain in the neck. She was rude to the other riders, mean to the horses and grumpy to her instructors, but this was the worst, most miserable outburst yet. Issie didn't know what to say. But luckily, as it turned out, she didn't need to say anything because Aunty Hess was standing behind the riders and had heard everything.

"That's it, Kelly-Anne!" Hester barked. "You've had plenty of warnings. That's the final straw. You should never speak to a riding instructor like that."

Kelly-Anne stuck her bottom lip out. "But I wasn't doing anything. I was just saying…"

"I heard everything you said, Kelly-Anne." Hester's voice was firm but calm. "You can take Julian back to the stables please. Stella will come and help you unsaddle him. I'm not willing to put up with this behaviour in my school any longer. I'm calling your mother, and you can pack your bags. You're going home."

Kelly-Anne was too stunned for once to bite back. She looked like she was trying very hard not to cry as she turned Julian around and headed back to the stables. The rest of the riders sat there on their ponies watching her leave.

"Serves her right!" George muttered.

"George!" Issie told him off. She had never thought she would feel sorry for a girl like Kelly-Anne, but at that moment, as she watched her riding back to the stables alone, she felt sympathy for Kelly-Anne for the first time.

Kelly-Anne didn't turn up for dinner that night.

"She's probably embarrassed," Hester said. "Let's leave her alone. I've spoken to her mother, and she wasn't at all surprised. Apparently she's been having some trouble at home. Her parents are going through a rather nasty divorce – which I didn't realise. Anyway, they sent her away to pony camp to keep her out of the firing line, so her mother wasn't exactly pleased to hear she needed to come and pick her up. She's coming to get her tomorrow after breakfast."

The punishment of being sent home was doubly cruel, Issie now realised. If Kelly-Anne's mum came to get her on Saturday, she wouldn't be able to come with the other riders to the Horse of the Year Show on the Sunday as they'd planned.

"It's her own fault," Stella said when Issie pointed this out. Still, Issie couldn't help but feel bad about being responsible for getting Kelly-Anne sent home. She knew how awful she had felt when her parents split up. Maybe she had misjudged Kelly-Anne a little.

Issie was exhausted by the time she went to bed that night. She had big plans to read her manual of

160

showjumping rules to make sure she was ready for Sunday, but the boring rule book made her eyelids immediately feel heavy and she gave up and switched out the light.

It was just before dawn when she was woken up by a sound outside her bedroom. Issie sat bolt upright in bed. She could have sworn she had heard hoofbeats outside – and her first thought was that Comet had jumped the fence again. Then she realised that she had left him in his loose box last night. It couldn't be Comet. Maybe she was imagining it? She slid out of bed and felt the cool wood of the floorboards against her bare feet as she tiptoed over to the window.

The sunlight was beginning to creep across the horizon. Issie guessed that it must have been about 6 a.m. In the early morning gloom, she could make out shapes and shadows on the lawn down below her bedroom. As she was standing there, with her nose pressed against the glass, she realised that one of these shadows, right in the middle of the lawn, was moving.

Issie stayed perfectly still. Was the shadow really moving or was she imagining it? There was no doubt in her mind a few moments later when the light picked out the colours of the shadow-shape and she saw a flash of dapple-grey, the shimmer of silver mane. The shadow on the lawn below was her horse. It was Mystic!

Issie pulled on a pair of jeans, not bothering to change out of her pyjama top, and hurried down the stairs. At the back door she shoved on her riding boots before racing across the lawn to the place where she had seen Mystic.

The horse wasn't there any more, but as she looked around, Issie thought she caught a glimpse of him again, heading between the trees towards the stables. Issie could hardly breathe. It was like her heart was in her throat, choking all the air out of her as she ran across the back lawn. By the time she reached the stables, she was gasping for air and had to bend over for a moment with her hands on her knees to catch her breath. She stood up again and looked around, expecting to see Mystic, but the grey gelding wasn't there. Had he been there at all or had she just imagined it? No, Issie had been quite sure it was Mystic on the lawn, but why was he here now?

Panic gripped her as a thought occurred. The last time Mystic was here he had been watching over Comet. Was that why the grey gelding was here? She looked down the row of loose boxes to the stall at the far end. It was still bolted shut, just as she had left it when she put Comet in herself last night.

"Comet?" she yelled out as she began to run up the row to the stall. "It's OK, boy, I'm here." Issie fell against the door of the stall and struggled to work the top bolt free to swing it open. Inside the stall, Comet didn't respond. The awful silence from behind the door gave Issie a chill of fear. Her fingers fumbled desperately as she opened the stall.

"Comet?" she said softly. She was still hoping that the pony would appear and thrust his cute little skewbald face out to greet her. But the minute she opened the top door she could see that this wasn't going to happen. She braced herself and stuck her head over, expecting to see the worst. But she wasn't prepared for what she actually saw. Her pony wasn't in his stall at all. The loose box was totally empty. Comet was gone.

Chapter 12

Stay calm! Issie told herself. Comet couldn't just disappear. That was crazy. She must be confused. Maybe she put him back in a different stall last night? Or perhaps Hester or Aidan had changed their minds and put him out to graze instead? No! She knew where she had put him last night – the stall she was standing in right now. She hadn't moved him and neither had anyone else. He had simply disappeared.

Issie took a deep breath. Horses didn't just disappear. She had to calm down and think clearly to make sense of this.

Acting on a hunch, she ran out of Comet's stall, sprinting all the way down the stable corridor to the tack room. Her blood pounding and heart racing, she grabbed the tack-room key from its hiding place on a nail behind the hat on the wall and fumbled to work the padlock. The lock was fiddly and her hands were trembling. It finally came open and Issie barged straight through the door and into the dark room on the other side.

She switched on the tack-room light and began frantically scanning the racks of saddles and bridles. She soon found what she was looking for – or rather she didn't find it. Comet's saddle and bridle were both missing.

Well, that solved part of the mystery. Comet hadn't disappeared by himself. Someone had taken him. But who would do that? There was the shuffle of footsteps behind her and Issie turned to see Kitty in her pyjamas looking pale and scared beneath the stable lights.

"Ohmygod, Kitty!" Issie gasped. "Don't sneak up like that! You startled me! What are you doing here?"

"Kelly-Anne took him," Kitty said.

"What?"

"Kelly-Anne. She took Comet. She woke me up. I was asleep and I heard a noise and then I saw her dressed in her jodhpurs so I asked her where she was going. She said it was unfair, that she wanted to ride Comet but you would never let her. She wanted to ride him just once before her mum came to take her home. I told her she shouldn't do it, but she got really angry at me and made me promise not to tell anyone…"

Kitty looked like she was going to cry. "I'm really sorry, Issie. I should have tried to stop her. It's all my fault…"

Issie shook her head. "You did the right thing, telling me. And don't worry about Kelly-Anne. I'll find her and I'll get Comet back and everything will be OK, I promise." Kitty wiped her nose with the sleeve of her pyjamas.

"How long ago did she leave?" Issie asked her.

"Ages ago," Kitty said, sniffling. "She said she'd be back again by breakfast and no one would ever know she had taken him."

"OK, Kitty, I need you to do something else for me," Issie said. "Can you go and find Aunty Hess and tell her that Kelly-Anne has taken Comet and I've gone to follow her? Can you do that for me?"

Kitty nodded and then she turned and set off down the long corridor past the stalls and out the back of the stables, heading for the manor, leaving Issie standing alone in the tack room.

Issie's mind flashed back to that jumping lesson when Kelly-Anne had lost her temper with Julian. She still remembered Julian's wild eyes, the poor pony's terror and confusion as Kelly-Anne had whipped him again and again in front of the jump.

If she does anything like that to Comet, if she hurts my horse... Issie was almost shaking with anger. What did Kelly-Anne think she was doing? Comet was too fiery for her to handle. Kelly-Anne simply didn't listen and now she was going to get herself hurt – and Comet too!

Issie looked back at the racks of bridles and saddles. Kelly-Anne had a head start. She would need a fast horse if she wanted to catch up with her. Her first thought was Destiny. The black horse had a huge stride, plus he had grown up on the hills around the farm and he was sure-footed across country. But then she remembered that Aidan was planning to ride the stallion in the Horse of the Year. Taking Destiny on a ride like this the day before the event was crazy. The farm terrain was uneven and rough and there was every chance that Destiny might stand in a rabbit hole or throw a shoe. If he went lame then Aidan would be devastated and Issie would never forgive herself. No, she couldn't risk it.

Her next choice was Diablo. The piebald was fit and

almost as fast at a gallop as Destiny. She grabbed Diablo's saddle and bridle from the rack and ran down the corridor to his stall. The black and white Quarter Horse gave a nicker of surprise as she opened the door to his loose box and stepped inside.

"Hey, Diablo," Issie said. "We're in a hurry so no grooming today, OK, boy?"

She threw the saddle straight on to the piebald's back and did up the girth. Then she adjusted the stirrups to a short length. She was going to be riding fast and for the sake of speed she would need to stay up in two-point position in the saddle the whole time.

As she slipped on Diablo's bridle and did up the throat lash, Issie heard noises out in the corridor. "Kitty?" she called out. "Are you still here? I thought I told you to go up to the house?"

But when she led Diablo out of his stall there was no one there. Issie looked back down the row of stalls. They were all shut tight apart from Comet and Diablo's boxes. The place was empty. She turned again to lead Diablo out the back of the stables through the open doors towards the paddocks and that was when she saw him.

Standing in the doorway, framed by the dawn light,

was a grey pony. Issie could see the soft bloom of his dappled coat and the thick silvery mane shining, his coal black eyes staring intently at her.

"Mystic!" she called out. The grey gelding raised his head and nickered to her, and Issie waited, expecting her pony to come to her as he always did. But he didn't come closer; he shifted about restlessly, dancing this way and that, shaking his mane in agitation.

"Mystic?" Something was wrong. Issie dropped Diablo's reins and began to run towards him, but it was too late. Mystic had already turned on his hocks and set off at a canter, disappearing through the stable doors and out of sight.

"Mystic!" Issie began to run faster, her blood pounding, pulse racing. Why didn't her pony wait for her? When she reached the stable doors and ran outside she almost expected him to be gone, and was a little surprised to see him standing waiting for her next to the paddocks beyond the cottage. "Mystic!" she called out. The grey gelding didn't move. Issie didn't understand. Mystic had never been like this before. Why wouldn't he come to her? Then the thought occurred to her. *He wants me to follow him!*

Well, she realised, she wouldn't get far like this. She

needed Diablo. When Issie had dropped Diablo's reins to run off after Mystic, the Quarter Horse had remembered his stunt training and stayed rooted to the spot where Issie had left him at the far end of the stables.

Issie spun around to face him, put her fingers to her lips and blew a short, sharp whistle. Diablo reacted to this cue as if on pure instinct. Without hesitation, he broke into a canter, his hooves clattering on the concrete floor of the stables as he ran to Issie's side.

"Good boy, Diablo," Issie said, grabbing the reins and swinging herself swiftly on to the stunt horse's back. "Let's go."

Mystic was still standing by the paddocks waiting for them, but the moment he saw Issie and Diablo emerge from the stables he turned away and began to canter ahead of them, towards the back fence of the paddock and the rise of Blackthorn Hill. The countryside beyond the fenceline was hilly and the terrain was rough and covered with scrub. There was no path or clear ground to ride over. Issie would never have come this way herself. She would have ridden along the well-worn ridge track. But she quickly understood why Mystic was leading her this way. It may be more dangerous, but it would take half the time.

Issie clucked Diablo into a canter and they began

gaining on Mystic, who was heading straight for the back fence. Issie scanned the fenceline, looking for the gate. She didn't realise the flaw in Mystic's plan until it was too late. There was no gate. If they were going to get to the other side, they were going to have to jump their way out.

Issie looked at the fence. It was a post and rails, about one metre twenty. Comet would clear a fence like that easily. But could Mystic and Diablo? As the grey gelding approached the fence, Issie held her breath. She needn't have worried. Mystic took the fence with ease, his legs forming a graceful arc above the rails. He looked just like a dolphin diving, Issie realised. A perfect bascule!

She was getting close to the fence herself now and, considering she had never even seen the piebald jump a fence before, let alone ridden him over one herself, she decided she would just have to ride hard at it. As Diablo approached the back fence she heard him give a nervous snort, as if he had only just realised what she was asking him to do.

"You can do it, Diablo!" Issie said, putting all her faith into the horse, willing him to take the jump. Diablo sensed her confidence and, as he came into the fence he didn't hesitate; his stride stayed steady as he took off and flew over the rails, landing cleanly on the other side without breaking stride. "Good boy!" Issie gave him a firm pat on his black and white patchy neck, her eyes remaining on Mystic, who was now galloping on ahead of them, across the rough gorse and scrub towards the crest of Blackthorn Hill.

As they galloped on and up the hill Issie caught a glimpse of some cross-country jumps to her left and remembered what Aidan had said about building a course across the farm. As she rode over the crest of Blackthorn Hill and looked down on the valley she could see several cross-country obstacles scattered over the paddocks below. To her left now she could also see the winding red snake of dirt that was the ridge track. Her cross-country route must have saved her at least twenty minutes, maybe more. Had she caught up with Kelly-Anne and Comet? Maybe she had even overtaken them? She looked up and down the track. Where were they?

There was a whinny from Mystic, who was already barrelling back down the other side of Blackthorn Hill, ducking and swerving his way around blackthorns and gorse as he headed helter-skelter at a gallop towards the valley below. Issie's eyes followed the grey gelding, and then her heart leapt as she caught sight of another horse ahead of Mystic in the distance. It was Comet! The skewbald was about half a kilometre ahead. She could see him clearly next to one of Aidan's jumps.

"Come on, Diablo." Issie clucked the horse into a gallop, through the scrub and the long grass, following Mystic down the sheer face of the hill.

If you have ever galloped downhill, you will know that it's terrifying. It would have been hard enough for Issie galloping downhill on the ridge track, but here on the uneven ground of Blackthorn Hill, with Diablo dodging this way and that to avoid the prickly gorse and blackthorn bushes, it was a total nightmare. All Issie could do was hold on and stick to the path that Mystic had taken ahead of her, trusting in the grey gelding to show them the safest way to go. Issie bit her lip to hold back her fear. She wanted to tell the little grey pony to slow down, but as they drew nearer she became even more afraid of what lay ahead.

Kelly-Anne had obviously tried to take Comet over one of Aidan's cross-country jumps, a stacked logpile, and something must have gone wrong. Very wrong. Comet was standing stock-still and Kelly-Anne was no longer on his back. Issie could see her body lying sprawled and motionless on the ground next to the jump, with Comet standing over her. Comet raised his head a little when he caught sight of Diablo and Mystic, but other than that, the skewbald didn't move a muscle. He was standing next to the girl, still as a statue! But Comet never stood still. He was always dancing about. Something was definitely wrong!

As they came into closer range Issie could finally see why her pony wasn't moving. Instinctively, she pressed Diablo on to gallop even harder. She couldn't afford to slow down; she had to reach her horse before things got any worse. Comet wasn't standing next to the logpile, he was standing in the logpile. His front leg had somehow got wedged between two rails of the rustic fence. He was standing perfectly still because he had no choice. If he moved or tried to pull his leg free, the pony would rip the skin from his cannon bone or even break a leg as he tried to wrench his hoof out.

At the sight of Issie and Mystic, the skewbald gave a frantic whinny and began to try and free himself.

"Comet! No!" Issie called out. He had to stay still until she could reach him. She urged Diablo on faster now. She had to get to Comet.

Please, please don't move, she thought. *Stay still just a little bit longer, Comet. I'm coming…*

Chapter 13

As she pulled Diablo up next to the logpile, Issie wanted more than anything to rush to Comet's side, but first she needed to see if Kelly-Anne was OK. Issie vaulted off Diablo's back, running over to the girl, who lay motionless on the ground.

"Kelly-Anne?" Issie put her hand on her shoulder and shook her gently. She didn't move. She must have been knocked out cold from the fall. Quickly, Issie tried to remember what they had taught her in the first-aid sessions at pony club. *Don't move her, and check her breathing.* She looked at her chest and could see it rising and falling. Good. Kelly-Anne was definitely breathing.

"Kelly-Anne, can you hear me?" Issie tried again. This time there was a groan and the girl murmured, her eyelids fluttering. She was waking up.

"What happened?" Kelly-Anne said groggily.

"You've had an accident," said Issie. "Don't try to move yet. Just lie still. I'll be back in a moment."

Now she was certain that Kelly-Anne was OK she was finally able to get a closer look at Comet. The skewbald had been standing still all this time, waiting patiently for Issie to come to him.

"Hey, Comet," Issie said. "It's going to be OK, boy."

At first glance, though, Issie wasn't sure things were going to be OK at all. Comet was shivering with shock. His flanks were damp with sweat and he was covered in mud. But what really worried Issie was Comet's leg. The pony's near foreleg was completely wedged through the shattered wood rails of the logpile fence. By the look of the angle, he had brought the leg down on top of the jump and his hoof had rammed straight through the wood. The weathered timber had splintered under the sheer force of the pony's hoof so that Comet was now stuck knee-deep in the logpile. Luckily, Comet had had the common sense to recognise his predicament and had stood still, waiting for his rider to free him. Only Kelly-Anne was in no fit state to help him at all.

How long had Comet been standing there like this? Issie wondered. And what would have happened if she hadn't arrived in time? Even now that Issie was here to help him, the skewbald was still in a perilous position. He was terrified. Issie could see the whites of his eyes and knew the pony was exhausted with stress and fear. How long would it be before he lost his cool and went into a frenzy, trying to free himself at any cost? Issie felt the panic rising in her too; she knew she had to act fast.

"Easy, boy," she cooed as she moved slowly towards Comet. She had to be careful. A sudden movement might spook him and if he pulled back he would wrench his leg horribly against the pointy barbs of broken wood.

"Easy, Comet," she said. "It's OK, boy," she whispered as she stroked the skewbald's neck. "Steady, boy, that's a good Comet, steady…" Her hands ran along his neck and down his near foreleg, the one that was wedged tight into the logpile. "Easy, Comet," Issie soothed him, stroking his neck and looking at the leg. "Stay still. I'll get you out, I promise. There's a good boy…"

"He's not a good boy, he's a stupid, mean pony!" It was Kelly-Anne. She was on her knees and looking dazed and wobbly as she struggled to clamber back up on to her feet.

"Kelly-Anne!" Issie said. "Don't get up. You've had a bad fall and you were knocked out. Sit down for a minute and catch your breath." For once, Kelly-Anne seemed to listen. She collapsed back against the logpile.

"No!" Issie said. "Not on the rails! You'll crush his leg if you sit there! Get off!"

Kelly-Anne staggered back up and looked at Comet. "It's his own fault," she said. "He wouldn't jump it. I was trying to jump the logpile and he wouldn't go over and then he stopped in front of it so I whacked him and he still wouldn't go over so I hit him again and then he did this stupid sort of bunny hop and I guess he must have landed on top of the fence and that was when I fell off…"

Issie felt her blood boil. She knew it! It was exactly the same back at the riding school when Kelly-Anne had terrified poor Julian.

"I don't want to hear any more!" Issie snapped. "It's always the horse's fault, isn't it? Well, I've got news for you, Kelly-Anne. It's your fault. You're a nightmare. You shouldn't even be allowed to ride. You don't know anything about horses and, even worse, you don't seem to care about them either!"

All the blood drained from Kelly-Anne's face as Issie said this. The girl stood there for a moment, too scared to speak. "I'm, I'm sorry…" she started.

"Don't be sorry," Issie said. "Be useful." She looked around frantically. "Take off your jacket!' she barked at Kelly-Anne.

"What do you mean?" asked Kelly-Anne.

"Just what I said. Take it off and pass it here."

"What are you going to do with it?" Kelly-Anne asked nervously as she handed the jacket to Issie.

"I'm going to wrap it around Comet's leg like a bandage so he doesn't hurt himself when we pull him out." Issie took off her own jacket too. Then, speaking softly to Comet the whole time, she bent down and wedged her hand through the logs and began to wrap the jackets around his knee and cannon bone. As Issie worked Kelly-Anne watched over her shoulder.

"What now?" Kelly-Anne said. "Do we just make him pull his leg out?"

"No way! We can't move him yet!" Issie said. "The poles are still wedged too close around his leg. We need to open them up a bit so he has enough room to get his hoof out."

Issie looked at the logpile. It had been built solidly like a true cross-country fence. It wasn't going to be easy to pull the logs apart. But the timber logs next to the pony's leg were already broken, so all she really needed was something to push between and lever them apart. Then if she could wedge the logs open another few centimetres, she would be able to get Comet's leg out.

"Give me your riding helmet," ordered Issie. Kelly-Anne didn't hesitate this time. She unbuckled her chin strap and passed Issie the helmet. It was dented in badly on the left side from the fall.

"It probably saved your life," Issie said, showing Kelly-Anne the dent. Then she looked around on the ground. "We need a big stick," she said. "Go and search over there and see if you can find something we can use as a lever to push the logs back while we shove the helmet in the gap. While Issie stood with Comet, reassuring him as she double-checked his bandages, Kelly-Anne searched the ground around the jump.

"How about this?" She lifted up a tree branch. The branch was about two metres long and as thick as her forearm. "Will this do?" Issie took the branch from Kelly-Anne and tried to bend it. The branch didn't yield at all. The wood was green and firm – perfect.

"That should be strong enough," Issie said. "Now," she instructed Kelly-Anne as she shoved the branch at a right angle in between the broken logs, "when I tell you, I want you to lean back on that branch and push down on it as hard as you can. That should prise the logs around Comet's leg apart for a moment. I'm going to shove your riding helmet in between the logs, which will hopefully hold them apart long enough for us to get Comet out."

Issie looked at Kelly-Anne. "Do you understand what you have to do? Are you ready?" The girl nodded.

"OK... now!"

As Kelly-Anne heaved against the branch the logs pulled apart and Issie managed to ram the riding helmet in right next to Comet's trapped leg.

"Keep holding it until I can get the helmet all the way in!" Issie shouted.

"I'm trying!" Kelly-Anne snapped.

As Issie forced the helmet in further, Kelly-Anne's strength faltered and she let go of the stick. There was a horrific cracking noise and Issie was gripped with panic. It sounded like the logs had snapped back and crushed the bones of her horse's leg!

She was relieved to realise it was actually the sound of the hard fibreglass shell of the riding helmet cracking under the pressure. Thankfully the cracked helmet held firm in the gap and the logs remained bowed apart, hopefully just enough for Issie to get Comet's leg out.

The sound of the helmet cracking had startled Comet too and the skewbald pony was now moving about restlessly. "Easy, boy," Issie murmured. "Easy, Comet. I'm going to get you out in just a minute. Steady now…"

There was now room to get both her hands right down into the hole and wrap them tight around Comet's fetlock. Issie lifted the fetlock gently and eased the leg out.

She felt her heart stop when she saw a dark trickle of blood soaking through the jacket that was wrapped around the cannon bone. She told herself to ignore the blood now covering her hands and to focus on getting her horse out. Issie kept lifting the leg, slowly, gently, talking to the quivering skewbald all the time, reassuring him with her voice. It seemed to take forever, but finally she managed to ease Comet's hoof all the way out from between the logs.

"Is he OK?" Kelly-Anne asked.

"I don't know yet," Issie said anxiously as she lowered Comet's hoof back down to the ground. She hastily unwrapped the makeshift bandages to check his leg. There was a lot of blood but the cut on his cannon bone wasn't deep. "I'll have to walk him and see."

As Comet took his first steps forward he seemed reluctant to put any weight at all on the injured leg, holding it up in the air.

"He's lame!" said Kelly-Anne.

"Wait a minute," Issie replied. "He's been stuck in that fence. It's only natural that he's going to favour that leg until he's sure it's OK…"

Sure enough, in a few strides Comet was putting his weight on all four legs again and was walking normally.

When Issie trotted him up to check if he was lame or not, miraculously it looked like the leg was totally sound. The cut on his cannon bone would probably need antibiotic cream, but it seemed to be superficial and other than that the leg was fine. Comet was going to be OK.

"He should be OK to walk home," Issie said with relief.

"Which one of us is going to ride him?" asked Kelly-Anne.

Issie looked at her with astonishment. "The weight of a rider on his back is the last thing Comet needs right now. Neither of us is riding him. You can ride Diablo. I'm going to walk back."

Issie looked up at the sun that was now rising over Lake Deepwater. "It should take us about an hour and a half. We'll take it slow to rest Comet's leg, but we'll still make it home before lunchtime in time for your mum to pick you up."

Kelly-Anne looked even more upset. "Please, Issie." She had tears in her eyes. "I don't want to go home."

"Why not?" said Issie darkly. "You don't seem to like it here much – I would have thought you'd be glad to leave."

Kelly-Anne shook her head. "That's why I ran away on Comet. I thought if Mum came and I wasn't there she'd just give up again and go home. She's going to be so mad at me. Everyone at home is angry all the time. It must be my fault because I know I make people angry. I don't try to, but I do."

Issie looked at Kelly-Anne, who was trying to hide the fact that she was now crying by making a curtain of hair out of her brown bob.

"Kelly-Anne?" Issie said gently. "I think maybe you're the one that's angry. About your parents, I mean. You've been taking it out on the horses since you got here, and on us. But it's not our fault your parents are getting a divorce. And it's not your fault either. These things just happen." Kelly-Anne nodded, but she kept her face hidden under the veil of hair.

"Your mum isn't angry at you. She was really worried about you when Hester said you'd been in trouble," Issie continued. "She told Aunty Hess that things were tough for you at home. And if we'd known what was going on with the divorce and stuff, maybe we wouldn't have been so hard on you."

Kelly-Anne parted her hair away from her face and looked at Issie. "Do I have to go home?"

Issie reached her hand down and helped Kelly-Anne to stand up. "I don't know," she said. "Right now, I think we just need to worry about getting back to the farm before we even think about that."

Kelly-Anne dusted off her jodhpurs and Issie was about to leg her up on to Diablo's back when the girl hesitated. "You got here really quick. How did you do it?"

"What do you mean?"

"I mean, how did you reach us so fast? I was way ahead of you, I must have been. There's no way you could have caught me up."

"I went straight over instead of taking the ridge track," Issie said, pointing back at the steep slope of Blackthorn Hill. Kelly-Anne couldn't believe it.

"But how did you know I was here?" she continued. "How did you know where to come?"

Issie didn't know what to say. She looked over Kelly-Anne's shoulder. There he was, cantering away over the hills in the distance. She smiled as she watched the grey pony, his mane and tail streaming out in the wind. He was almost out of sight now, rounding over the ridge that would take him out of view into the basin of Lake Deepwater. If it hadn't been for Mystic, they would never have made it here in time to save Comet. As for Kelly-Anne, she would never know how Issie had managed to find her that day.

"You were knocked out for a while," Issie told Kelly-Anne. "In fact, I wouldn't be surprised if you didn't have a bit of amnesia!" That seemed to shut Kelly-Anne up. Before the girl could ask any more questions, Issie changed the subject.

"You see that big hill up there to the right? Once we get over that we'll be back on the ridge track. It's all downhill after that. We'll be home in no time."

Issie gave Kelly-Anne a leg-up on to Diablo. Then she picked up Comet's reins and checked the skewbald's leg one more time before they began to head for home.

They had just reached the top of the hill when Issie heard the sound of hoofbeats coming from the other direction and a few moments later Hester and Aidan appeared, cantering around the bend on Stardust and Paris.

"Thank God! Are you both OK?" Hester called out. "Kitty told me everything. Why are you walking? What happened to Comet?" Issie told them the story while Kelly-Anne stood there looking suitably ashamed. The utter stupidity of her actions, taking off with Comet like that, had finally begun to dawn on her.

"Is he lame?" Hester asked.

Issie shook her head. "I don't think so. But I didn't want to ride him back just in case. He took a bad knock when his leg went through the logpile."

Hester looked at Kelly-Anne. "How does your head feel? I'll call ahead now and get the doctor to meet us at the house. He should come and check you for concussion."

"I'm fine, honest," Kelly-Anne said. "I'm really sorry. I know I've caused lots of trouble..."

"Aunty Hess," Issie said, "she really wants to stay. Do you think you could call her mum back and tell her that Kelly-Anne's been given a second chance?"

Kelly-Anne gave Issie a grateful look and then turned to Hester. "Please? I'll make up for everything and I'll do whatever Issie and Stella and Kate tell me to do."

Hester looked doubtful. "We'll talk about this back at the house. Kelly-Anne, are you all right to ride Diablo the whole way?" Kelly-Anne nodded.

"Issie, you can double home with Aidan on Paris and lead Comet," Hester added. "It'll be faster than walking."

Hearing this, Aidan rode forward on Paris. He looked down at Issie but he didn't get off to help her up. Instead, he just took his feet out of his stirrups and lowered a hand for her to grasp. "Slip your foot into my stirrup and I'll swing you up behind me," he said. Issie looked up at Aidan. She didn't return his smile and she didn't take his hand. "Come on, Issie, what are you waiting for?"

Issie wanted to tell him that she was still mad at him over the whole crazy bet he'd made with Dan. She wanted to tell him she knew everything and she thought the boys were both stupid. If Aidan thought that she was going to be his girlfriend because of some silly bet, he was so wrong.

"Issie?" Aidan's smile faltered. "Take my hand."

Issie paused for a moment. Now wasn't the time to talk about it. She had to get Comet home. She put her foot in the stirrup and grasped Aidan's hand tightly. "One-ah-two-ah-three!" Aidan pulled her up, swinging her around so that she was sitting right behind him on Paris's back like a pillion passenger on a motorbike.

Issie kept hold of Comet's reins with her left hand. "Put your arm around me," Aidan instructed her. Issie did as he said, wrapping her arm around Aidan's waist. He was wearing his favourite old tartan shirt. It smelt good, like fresh soap. She let her head rest against his back for a moment and felt the soft flannel of the shirt against her cheek.

"Are you OK back there?" Aidan called over his shoulder.

"Uh-huh."

"Then let's go home."

Chapter 14

Issie knew the Horse of the Year was a huge event, but she wasn't prepared for just how huge. There were literally hundreds of horses and riders gathered here at the Gisborne showgrounds. As Avery eased the horse truck across the grass looking for a parking space, the girls gawped out of the windows at the show riders with their glamorous horses tied up to their fabulous, expensive horse trucks.

The horses all had their manes perfectly plaited and their tack polished, and all the riders wore their best sparkling white jods, black or navy hacking jackets and velvet helmets.

"Ohmygod!" Stella squealed. "I just saw Katie McVean! And… I think that blonde girl next to her is

Ellen Whitaker! She's from England – I've seen her jumping on TV! Did you see her Issie? Issie?"

Issie didn't say anything. The tingle of excitement that she had felt when they set out from Blackthorn Farm that morning had turned into a tight ball of nerves in her belly. There had been so much drama in the past twenty-four hours, with Comet going missing, that Issie had almost forgotten about entering the pony Grand Prix and the $15,000 first prize.

Yesterday, when they got back to the farm, Issie had wondered if Comet would be sound enough to ride today. Even though the skewbald wasn't favouring his injured leg at all, Issie was still worried. She made a fuss over the pony the moment they got back, cooling his leg using ice packs and dressing the scratch wound to keep any inflammation down. This morning, before they loaded the horses on the truck, Avery had made her trot Comet back and forth down the stable corridor on the hard concrete. Issie was relieved when Avery said he couldn't see any signs of lameness at all and Comet was pronounced fit to compete.

But now that they were actually here at the Horse of the Year, Issie was almost wishing she had an excuse not to ride. She felt totally and utterly sick. What had she been thinking? She was completely out of her league! There was no way she could ride in the Grand Prix.

"Nervous?" Avery looked at her.

"Uh-huh," Issie replied. What she wanted to say was, *Turn the truck around and let's go home – I've changed my mind!*

Avery looked at her as if he understood exactly what she was thinking. "It's pretty daunting, isn't it? When you turn up at a place like this and see the competition."

"Uh-huh."

"Every rider gets nerves, Issie. The great riders are the ones who can put those fears out of their mind and focus on riding and doing their best." Avery smiled. "I wouldn't have brought you here if I didn't think you and Comet were ready for this, would I?"

"No," Issie said uncertainly, "I guess not."

"You may not have a fancy horse truck or a million-dollar horse, Issie, but you've got a pony with talent and the biggest heart I've ever seen," said Avery.

"And besides, you are just as fancy as them. You've got your own groom!" Stella piped up. "That would be me!"

Issie laughed. "Well, in that case," she grinned, "let's do it!"

If Issie's nerves were now gone, well, Comet had

never had any in the first place. The skewbald pony emerged from the truck in the same mood as always – acting as if he owned the place, prancing out of the horse truck with his tail held high and his neck arched like a stallion on parade.

"Comet! Behave!" Issie said as she led him in circles next to the truck trying to calm the little skewbald down.

As Aidan eased Destiny down the ramp of the horse truck and tied him up to the other side he couldn't help laughing at the antics of the skewbald pony. "I don't think Comet has realised that Destiny is actually the stallion here – not him!"

Issie smiled. It was true. Destiny wore a red tag on his bridle today, the mark that a horse was a stallion and that other horses should be wary of getting too close. Stallions were supposed to be watched at all times at horse shows because they might be wild or vicious to other horses. In fact, you couldn't get a more well-mannered horse than Destiny. While Comet skipped and danced about the place, Destiny stood like a perfect gentleman as Aidan unwrapped his floating boots and began to plait up his mane.

Dan, meanwhile, was unloading Madonna from the horse truck and had led her past Issie, tying the chestnut mare up next to Ben's brown gelding Max. He walked around the truck to where Aidan was busy plaiting up the big black horse's forelock.

"Ummm, Aidan?" Aidan looked around and saw who it was.

"Yeah."

Dan put out a hand. "I just want to wish you luck, man." He seemed to mean it as he stuck his hand out.

Aidan too looked like he genuinely wanted to make friends as he grasped Dan's hand and shook it firmly. "Me too. I mean, good luck to you. May the best man win and everything…"

"Do you think they're serious?" Stella said, watching the boys as she stood next to Issie and Comet.

"Uh-huh. Totally," said Issie.

"That is so lame!" Stella giggled. "You have to tell them you know all about their stupid bet. Let them know they can't get away with it!"

"I was going to say something to Aidan yesterday," Issie groaned, "but it was just too embarrassing. It's all so stupid!"

"It's kind of funny though, isn't it?" Stella grinned at Issie. "So, come on. We're best friends, right? And you still haven't even told me – which one do you want to win?"

"That's the whole problem," Issie sighed. "I really don't know."

The Horse of the Year Show had already been underway for two days. Today was considered to be the big day for showjumping, though, with all of the big prize money competitions happening in the main arena.

Dan and Aidan had already reported to the competitors' trailer to get their numbers, which they now wore on their chests. The hacks were jumping first today. Issie would ride in the afternoon in the pony ring.

"They're on in twenty minutes," Stella said, looking at her watch.

"You go ahead to the grandstand and save me a seat," Issie told her. "I'd better go check in at the riders' tent first."

The schedule of the day's events had been posted up on the pinboard outside the competitors' trailer. Issie ran her eyes over the competitor list for the pony Grand Prix to see if she recognised any of the other riders. One of the names on the list leapt out at her. *Ohmygod*, Issie thought. *Just my luck!*

"Well, well, Isadora!" Issie turned around and saw the familiar sour face and stiff blonde plaits of her arch pony-club nemesis – Natasha Tucker!

"Hi, Natasha," Issie said. "I was just checking the competition lists. I see we're both entered in the pony Grand Prix."

Natasha looked at Issie suspiciously. "I didn't even know you were riding at Horse of the Year," she said. "The last time I checked you didn't even have a horse to ride!"

"That's my horse. The skewbald over there," Issie said, pointing to Avery's horse truck where Comet was skipping about and trying to steal hay out of Max's hay net.

"Really?" Natasha tried unsuccessfully to suppress a cruel giggle. "Ewww! A skewbald! They're so ugly! How can you stand to ride him?"

"I think he's beautiful," Issie said, defending Comet. "Anyway, I'm not concerned with how he looks. It's how he jumps that matters."

Natasha sneered. "Well, he doesn't look like Grand Prix material to me!"

"I guess we'll see," said Issie flatly.

"I'm riding the Grand Prix and the Puissance today,"

Natasha continued. "I'm on Fabby, of course. He'll do for this competition, but I'm hoping to pick up a new ride while I'm here as well. You know Ginty McLintoch, don't you? She trains all our horses and Mummy has asked her to keep an eye out for a new pony for me. Mummy says she's willing to spend mega-money on a really special pony that can take me to the Pony-club Champs this year."

"But what will you do with Fabby?" Issie was aghast at the way Natasha chopped and changed ponies as if they were nothing to her.

Natasha ignored this question and looked over Issie's shoulder, her eyes narrowing as she spied Dan mounting up on Madonna next to Avery's horse truck. "Is that Dan?" she asked. Then a slightly bitter tone crept into her voice. "Is he here with you?"

"Uh-huh," Issie said. "He's riding in the next event – novice hack over one metre twenty." Issie paused and then added, "Aidan is riding in it too."

"Ohhh," Natasha said, "I might go and sit in the stands for that. It sounds like it will be worth watching."

"Yes," Issie had to agree, "I guess it will be."

"What is she doing here?" Stella pulled a face as Issie arrived with Natasha in tow and sat down next to Stella and Ben in the grandstand.

"Don't ask!" Issie rolled her eyes.

Kate was in the grandstand too, trying desperately to wrangle the kids. "It's like herding cats!' she grumbled. "They all keep dashing off in different directions!"

"Bottoms on seats now, everyone! You are representing the Blackthorn Farm Riding School – show some manners!" At the sound of Avery's booming voice, Lucy, Sophie, Arthur, George, Tina, Trisha, Kitty and Kelly-Anne all immediately fell silent and sat as still as statues.

"Hi, Issie!' Kelly-Anne beamed up at her, waving furiously. Issie smiled back. She was glad she had managed to convince Aunty Hess to let Kelly-Anne stay on after all.

"I really think she's learnt her lesson this time," Issie had said, standing up for Kelly-Anne. And it seemed that she had. OK, she was still a bit of a know-it-all, but at least she was trying. At their last riding lesson on Saturday, Kelly-Anne hadn't uttered a word and had done everything Kate told her to do. Not only that, she'd helped out with the younger kids too, unsaddling Lucy's horse for her and helping Sophie to mix up Pippen's hard feed after the lesson was over.

"Why isn't Aunty Hess here?" Issie wondered as she looked around. She could have sworn she saw Kate give Stella a strange look at this question.

"Umm, Hess had to go and pick something up. She'll be back soon," Kate said.

There was a crackling noise over the tannoy and then the announcer's voice came through crisp and clear. "The next event in the main arena here today is the novice hack over one metre twenty. This event will be judged on the total points accumulated over two rounds. All riders will complete two rounds."

Issie looked down from the grandstand at the horses warming up below. She could see the boys working in their horses. Dan on Madonna and Aidan on Destiny. She felt a tight knot growing in her tummy.

"I'm going to get an ice cream," Stella said. "Do you want anything?"

"No, thanks," said Issie. "I'm really not hungry."

The knot in Issie's tummy got worse as the competition progressed. Dan and Aidan were the last two riders to go, and so far no one ahead of them had gone clear in the first round.

"It's a difficult course," Avery noted approvingly. "The fences aren't huge, but there are lots of tricky questions for the horses to answer." Avery pointed to the red and white triple that finished the course. "That's the bogey fence," he said. "Hardly anyone has made it clear through that triple."

Issie could barely bring herself to look as Dan rode into the ring on Madonna. The chestnut mare looked stunning, her coat glowing in the sunlight. Dan too looked handsome with his black showjumping jacket and crisp white jodhpurs. As he took the first fence, Madonna tucked her feet up beautifully and cleared it easily, and Issie felt her heart beginning to race. Would Dan go clear? It certainly looked like he might as he took the second, third and fourth fences with ease. As Madonna approached the double she did a funny stride and then had to pop in an extra stride at the middle of the fence, which meant that she bashed her hind legs on the rails.

The crowd held their breath, but the rail didn't fall. Dan was still clear. Over the next three fences too his luck held. Now all that was left was the triple. Madonna approached the triple with a perfect stride, ah-one she was over the first fence, ah-two and the second, ah… no! There was a collective sigh of disappointment from the crowd, who were hoping that this would be the first clear round of the day. Instead, Madonna managed to knock the very last rail with her front legs and down it came. Four faults!

"That still keeps him in the front running," Ben said, watching intently. "And there's only Aidan to come."

Aidan looked tense as he brought Destiny into the ring. Issie could see that Destiny was straining against the reins, making it hard for Aidan to hold him and get his striding right between fences.

As they came through the start flags Issie saw Aidan check the black horse firmly to let him know he meant business. Destiny arched his neck and his canter became bouncy and forward as he popped neatly over the first fence. The crowd clapped as Destiny took the second, third and fourth fences with ease and then romped over the double as if it wasn't even there. By the time Aidan came down the final line to face the triple, he hadn't knocked down a single rail. If he went clear through the triple then he would be the only rider to make it through the first round with no faults.

Issie held her breath as Aidan took the last turn into the triple a little too tightly, not leaving himself much time at all to settle Destiny into a steady stride before the first fence. Destiny seemed to manage it though. The black horse took the first fence… one, then two… he was clear so far. You could hear the silence as the crowd waited to see whether he would make it over the last fence – and then came the thunderous applause as the black horse cleared the final fence and raced through the finish flags. Destiny had gone clear! Aidan had done it.

The man on the tannoy crackled back into life again. "Aidan MacGuire on Blackthorn Destiny goes clear, putting him out in the lead as we enter the second round." He explained, "So with four riders sitting just behind Aidan MacGuire on four faults each, we still have a real battle on our hands!"

"Can Dan still win?" Stella whispered to Issie.

"Uh-huh," Issie said. "He's only got four faults. It's accumulated points and there's still one more round to come."

The jump-off course had been tightened down to eight fences and, as was the tradition in these events, the rider with the worst score from the last round rode first. That meant the leader from the last round, Aidan, would be riding last.

As the riders took their second round it became clear that, once again, the triple fence was the bogey. None of the riders seemed to manage a clear round. Then it was Dan's turn. Issie watched as he circled Madonna around in a warm-up lap.

"Go, Dan!" Ben shouted from the stands as Madonna came through the start flags and positively flew over the first fence. The kids were shouting out too, cheering every time Dan went clear over a fence. Issie, meanwhile, sat quietly watching. She wanted Dan to do well – of course she did. But did she want him to beat Aidan and win the bet?

As Dan lined up for the final triple she felt her heart catch in her throat. Madonna took the first fence beautifully, and the second and... as Dan cleared the third fence for a clear round Issie heard the crowd go crazy. Dan had done it! He had gone clear!

"Now this makes the competition interesting!" boomed the tannoy man. "Dan Halliday has gone clear in the second round. That means our last rider, Aidan MacGuire, has to go clear also with no time faults. If he collects a single rail, he will slip back in the rankings to equal Dan Halliday. If he takes two rails, he'll fall behind Dan to second place!"

The tension showed on Aidan's face as he brought Destiny back into the ring. Aidan nodded to the judges and heard the bell that signalled that he could start. He pushed Destiny into a canter and the black horse took the first fence with a clean take-off, clearing it neatly.

"Go, Aidan!" Kate, Stella and the kids were shouting their heads off now as Aidan took Destiny over fence after fence without a fault.

As Aidan turned to face the triple Issie felt her heart pounding. She had been so confused for so long about Dan and Aidan that she didn't know what to think. Now, as Aidan lined up to take the final jump, suddenly her heart made up her mind for her. She realised she had been jumping with Aidan over every single fence. Wishing him over the jumps. At that moment, she knew at last how she really felt.

"Go, Aidan!" she yelled so loudly that Stella and Natasha, who were sitting next to her, nearly jumped out of their skins.

Aidan looked at the triple ahead of him and managed to judge his stride perfectly at the first fence. Then trouble struck. Destiny miscued his take-off for the second fence and took down a rail. The error left him disunited as he approached the third fence and the top rail fell from that one too. There was a collective sigh from the crowd as the man on the tannoy crackled back to life.

"A very unlucky eight faults there for Aidan MacGuire, putting him back to second place. That makes our winner of the one metre twenty novice hack event… Mr Dan Halliday on Madonna! Second place is Aidan MacGuire on Blackthorn Destiny and third goes to Justin Jones on Tribesman. Would all the riders come into the arena for prize-giving please?"

"Issie?" Stella looked at her friend. "Are you OK?"

Issie shook her head. She wasn't OK at all. Dan had won. Aidan had lost. Issie had finally made up her mind and she knew what she wanted… she knew who she wanted. And now it was too late.

Chapter 15

Issie wasn't even looking at Dan and Madonna as they took their victory lap around the arena. Her eyes never left Aidan. From the grandstand she watched as he slid down off his horse. She saw him quietly whisper something to the black stallion as he stroked his muzzle, as if horse and rider were consoling each other over their loss.

Then she saw Aidan look away from Destiny and up at the grandstand, his eyes searching for Issie. At that moment he looked so heartbroken, so miserable, that Issie realised she couldn't stand it any longer. She had to talk to him! She stood up and began to move towards the exit.

"Hey! What's going on? Where are you going?" Stella said as Issie pushed past her. "Issie? What's happening?"

Issie stopped and turned to Stella. "It's all wrong. I wanted Aidan to win."

Stella looked confused. "But, Issie, if you wanted Aidan to win then why didn't you just choose him in the first place?"

"Because I didn't know I wanted him to win until just now!" Issie replied.

"What's going on?" Arthur piped up.

"Issie wanted Aidan to win!" said Kitty.

"But why?" Lucy asked.

"Issie, is Aidan your boyfriend?" asked Sophie.

"Yes. I mean no… I mean, he should be. Ummm… Stella, can you get them some more ice creams? I gotta go!" Issie hurdled the back of the bench seats and began to run along a vacant row of seating towards the grandstand door. The only person she wanted to talk to right now was Aidan. She had to tell him how she really felt about him.

She was almost back to Avery's horse truck, making her way there as fast as she could by darting in and out between the other trucks and floats, when she heard a voice beside her. "Hey, Issie!"

It was Dan. He was on Madonna and he had a huge smile on his face. Madonna looked pleased with herself too. She was dancing about, the gold tassels of her red winner's sash flapping against her chest as she moved.

"Did you see the jump-off?" Dan asked as he slid down off Madonna's back and landed on the ground next to her.

"Yeah, I did," Issie said. "Ummm… you jumped brilliantly. It was a really good round and you deserved to win."

Dan looked at her face and suddenly his smile disappeared. "So why do I get the feeling that you're not happy that I won then?" he said.

Issie looked at Dan. She couldn't speak – she was finding it hard enough just to breathe! *You have to do this*, she told herself. Dan didn't deserve to be messed around. Now that she knew how she felt about him and Aidan, she had to say something…

"I know about the bet."

"What?" Dan looked nervous.

"You and Aidan. I heard you. I was in the horse truck when you were talking and I heard you…"

Dan froze like a rabbit in the headlights. Issie knew about the bet! "I never really meant it!" he babbled. "It was just a silly thing to say. You didn't think I really expected you to be my girlfriend, did you?" Then he looked at her. "That is, unless you want to. Be my girlfriend, I mean."

Issie looked at Dan. "Dan, I… can't."

It felt awful that moment. The crushed look on Dan's face, the desperate hot flush of embarrassment as he tried to act cool, as if he didn't care that she had turned him down.

"I was just being silly. I didn't mean it…" he said again. He avoided meeting her eyes by busying himself with adjusting Madonna's martingale.

"I'm sorry," Issie said softly.

"Hey, I said I never meant it, all right?" Dan said, still refusing to look at her. "Don't worry about it, OK?" He put his foot back in the stirrup and sprang up on to Madonna's back. "I gotta go. I need to get to the judges' tent and collect my prize money: $10,000! Can you believe it?"

Issie shook her head. She wanted to say something, anything that would make things the way that they used to be between them, but she didn't know what to say. "Dan, I…"

"Anyway," Dan said coolly, turning Madonna so that he had his back to Issie, "I'll see you later."

Issie watched helplessly as he rode away. Dan trotted

off for a few strides and then something made him stop and pull Madonna up to a halt. He turned back to her. "Issie?"

"Uh-huh?"

"Good luck, OK? For the pony Grand Prix." He smiled at her. "I really hope you win."

Issie smiled back. "Thanks, Dan."

"Do it for the Chevalier Point Pony Club!" He gave her a wave, then he turned Madonna again and trotted away.

Issie stood there for a moment watching him ride off. It might take a while to get totally back to normal, but she knew now that things were going to be OK between her and Dan. It had been good to talk to him. But now all she really wanted was to find Aidan and…

"Isadora! There you are! I've been looking all over for you!" Aunt Hester was striding over the showgrounds towards her. She was wearing her best black jodhpurs and a pink shirt and carrying a large picnic basket.

"I've brought a surprise with me," Hester said. At first Issie thought her aunt was referring to the picnic basket, and she was so busy staring at it that she didn't notice the woman with long dark hair and a broad smile on her face who was walking just behind Hester.

"Hello, sweetie!"

"Mum?" Issie couldn't believe it!

"Mum! Ohmygod! What are you doing here?" she squealed as she ran to Mrs Brown and gave her the most enormous hug.

"What? Do you think I'd miss the chance to see my daughter ride in the pony Grand Prix?" Mrs Brown laughed.

"I just picked your mum up from the airport this morning," Hester explained.

Issie still didn't believe it. Her mum was here!

"I fed your horses their breakfast and then I got on the plane," Mrs Brown said breezily.

"Are they OK?" asked Issie.

"Blaze and Storm are fine," Mrs Brown said. "I asked Pip at the pony club to keep an eye on them until I get back."

"I'm so glad you came!" Issie grinned.

"Hess says you're riding just before lunch?"

"Uh-huh. I was just on my way back to the horse truck now. I suppose I should start getting him ready."

"Well, come on then!" said Mrs Brown. "I've heard so much about Comet. I think it's time I met this superstar pony of yours."

Issie was still desperate to talk to Aidan. She had been hoping that he would be back at the horse truck with Destiny when she got there, but they were nowhere in sight.

"I think he had another class to ride in," Stella said as she reached the truck to join them.

Issie wanted to go and find him, but with her mother here and the time ticking by until her competition started, she figured that her conversation with Aidan would have to wait. It was time to get ready to ride.

"All you have to worry about is getting yourself dressed," Stella told her. "I'm your groom, remember."

"Yeah, but…"

"Hey!" Stella said. "I've got it covered, OK? I can look after Comet. I've even got myself an assistant."

"An assistant?"

"Hi, Isadora!" Issie looked over Stella's shoulder and saw Kelly-Anne standing nervously to the side of the horse truck. "Stella said I could help her get Comet ready… if it's OK with you?"

Issie looked at her. "Do you know how to do gamgee bandages?"

Kelly-Anne shook her head. "No, I don't."

Issie smiled. "That's OK. This is a good chance for you to learn how to do them properly. Stella will teach you how to put them on."

"Here," Stella said, passing Kelly-Anne a roll of bandages and a wadge of stuff that looked a bit like cotton wool. "I'll do the first one and then you can copy me and do the next one, OK?"

Issie left them to it and went inside the horse truck to get changed. She pulled on her white jodhpurs and long black boots. She opened the closet and stared at her riding jacket. It wasn't actually hers – it was an old one of Hester's. It was a little bit big for her and a tad moth-eaten, but it didn't really matter. It would have to do.

Issie was just slipping off her T-shirt and putting on her shirt when there was a knock at the door of the horse truck and her mum stepped inside. She was holding a black box tied with a black and white grosgrain ribbon.

"Before you put that old jacket on, you might want to open this." Mrs Brown smiled as she passed the box to Issie. It was filled with lilac tissue paper, and beneath the tissue there was a brand-new navy blue riding jacket.

"Oh, Mum! It's gorgeous!" Issie couldn't believe it.

"When you phoned me the other night for the entry money, I realised that you didn't have a showing jacket to wear," Mrs Brown said. "So I called Hester and asked her what I should get you."

"Thank you!" beamed Issie.

"There's a tie in there with it," Mrs Brown pointed out. "A navy jacket and a red tie. The Chevalier Point colours. I thought they'd bring you luck."

Issie pulled the jacket out of its tissue paper. The navy fabric was so dark it almost looked black. The jacket had a velvet collar, also in navy blue, and a single vent up the back. It was a classic showjumper's jacket.

"I hope it fits," Mrs Brown said. "You're growing so fast these days I find it hard to tell what size you are!" Issie slipped on the navy jacket and did up the buttons. It was a perfect fit.

"Thanks, Mum!" she grinned. Then her face fell. "But I already owe you $500! And now this jacket…"

Mrs Brown smiled. "The jacket is a gift. And don't worry about the $500."

"But if I don't win this event then I won't be able to pay you back or help Aunty Hess with the farm…"

"Issie, you're only fourteen. That's far too young to

take the weight of the world on your shoulders," Mrs Brown said firmly. "You need to put all of that out of your mind. All I want is for you to go out there and do your best and have fun, OK? That's all anyone is asking of you."

"OK, Mum." Despite what her mother said, Issie was still feeling the butterflies beginning to churn in her tummy. There was $15,000 in prize money up for grabs in this event. If she won then she could give the money to Hester and maybe she wouldn't have to sell the farm and… Issie tried to put those thoughts out of her mind. Her mum was right. She had to focus on riding, not winning.

Mrs Brown looked at her watch. "It's nearly eleven," she said. "I'm going to go with Hester now and get a good seat in the stands. I'll see you afterwards."

As her mother opened the door of the truck Issie called after her. "Mum?"

"Yes?"

"I'll try to make you proud of me."

There were tears in Mrs Brown's eyes as she looked at Issie. "Oh, honey, I'm already proud of you. I always have been." She gave Issie one last hug. "Here, let me straighten your tie… perfect!"

She looked at Issie and smiled. "Now get out there and good luck!"

The grandstand was already crowded as Mrs Brown, Hester, Stella, Kate and the kids hurried to their seats.

"With $15,000 at stake this is one of the premier pony events in the Southern hemisphere," the announcer's voice crackled over the loudspeaker.

"$15,000? That's big money!" Stella gave a low whistle.

"Yeah, big jumps too! Look!" Kate pointed down at the arena. "They're huge."

In the warm-up arena down below, Issie was looking at the ring and thinking exactly the same thing. "Tom?" She looked nervously at Avery, who was holding on to Comet's reins as he gave her some last-minute advice.

"Take a deep breath and take your time," her instructor said. "Remember, the main thing is a clear round; speed doesn't matter in this event." Issie nodded.

"And watch the turn into that last double," Avery added. "Don't take it too tight on the corner! Remember what happened to that last rider – it's a big fence: you need three decent strides to take it."

Issie nodded and turned Comet towards the arena. She was the last rider to go, which put her in a lucky position. Earlier, she had watched Natasha come in and put in a nice round on Fabergé, with just one rail down for four faults. The fences were challenging, and there had been only one other rider who had done better than Natasha and gone clear. If Issie got a rail down, she'd have four faults too, just like Natasha. But if she went clear, she'd be ahead of Natasha and in the jump-off for first place.

The grandstands were packed and there was a round of applause from the crowd as Issie cantered into the ring. Issie nearly lost control as Comet bolted forward at the sound of their clapping, yanking the reins clean out of her hands. She managed to grab at the reins and had to pull hard to get Comet to a halt. As they stood in the arena she realised that the pony was actually trembling beneath her. "Easy, Comet," she soothed him. "What's wrong?"

She didn't have a chance to find out. There was a loud clang as the bell rang, signalling the start of the round. According to the rules, that meant Issie now had only one minute to get her horse through the flags and start her round or she would be disqualified. The clock was ticking. She had to ride now.

"Come on, Comet." Issie worked the skewbald in a canter circle to try to settle him then took a perfect line over the first fence. Comet seemed to relax again and took the fence nicely, tucking his feet up and clearing the rails, but as he landed on the other side the crowd let out a cheer and their cries made Comet surge forward again in a panic.

"Comet!" Issie tried to hold him, but the skewbald was too strong for her. He was rushing his fences and refusing to settle into a steady stride. Every time Issie lined him up for a jump Comet would hear the crowd cheering him on and lose his cool and charge the fence. She was lucky to make it over the first half of the course, but by the time they hit the big oxer in the middle of the course Issie knew they were in trouble. Comet rushed it so fast that his striding was all wrong, and he took off in a flying leap way, way earlier than he should have done. Issie squealed in shock as the pony jumped too soon. Instead of coming down on the other side of the fence, Comet brought his hind legs down on the back half of the jump, scattering poles everywhere.

The skewbald kept cantering on, but Issie was now

terrified. He was totally out of control. Issie's fears were instinctively picked up on by Comet. As he reached the next jump he panicked and screeched to a halt in front of the fence at the last minute, baulking to one side. Issie hadn't been expecting this. Comet had never refused a jump before! She was thrown forward on to the skewbald's neck and nearly fell off. She had to grapple her way back along his neck and into the saddle like a gymnast to avoid the twenty faults she would have got for a fall. But once she was back in the saddle she realised it didn't matter anyway. She already had four faults for a rail down and four for a refusal – plus her horse was shaking so much there was no way she was going to make it around the rest of the course.

Issie looked up at the judges' tent and slowly raised her riding crop up to her helmet in a salute.

"What's she doing?" Mrs Brown asked Kate. "Why is she saluting in the middle of the course like that?"

Kate looked down at Issie from the grandstand. She couldn't believe it. "She's retiring. That salute means that she's just quit. She's out!"

"That was an unfortunate round for pony Grand Prix newcomer Isadora Brown and Blackthorn Comet," the announcer said. "She has retired from the competition and is out of the running for the $15,000."

Issie was devastated as she left the arena. All that training, all those hopes of saving the farm – and now here they were, eliminated in the first round!

Comet had calmed down as soon as they left the arena and the noise of the crowd had died down, but Issie was still shaking from the experience. This had been it. Their big event. How could it have all gone so wrong?

As she walked Comet around to cool the pony down Avery rushed over towards her. Issie shook her head miserably as she saw her instructor approaching as if to say, *I know, it's my fault, I messed up*.

"Having a few problems in there?" asked Avery.

"I guess I panicked, Tom," Issie said. "Comet got spooked by the crowds and then I couldn't concentrate and it all kind of fell apart and…"

"It's not your fault, Issie," Avery said. "I'm kicking myself. I should have thought about it earlier. It's the noise of the crowd. Comet's not used to it. I should have thought of this before you went in there. But at least it's not too late to fix it."

He put his hand into his pocket and pulled out what looked like a crocheted doily, the sort that sits on your nan's bedside table. Issie noticed that there was something unusual about the doily – it appeared to have two pointy bits in the middle of it.

"It's an ear net," Avery explained as he began to fit the doily over Comet's ears. "It will muffle the sound and cut out the crowd noise."

"Will it really work?"

"It should do," Avery said. "Lots of professional riders use them to block out the crowd noise and help their horses to focus. I'm betting that Comet's problems in the ring just now were purely because he's not used to all that racket." Avery patted the skewbald on his white striped face." Anyway, there's only one way to find out."

Issie was confused. "But, Tom, it's too late. The pony Grand Prix is over. I've withdrawn."

Avery looked at her, "Well, yes and no."

"What do you mean?"

"I've entered you in another event." Issie couldn't believe it.

"What?"

"The pony Puissance," Avery said.

"But, Tom. Why? It must have cost you $500! You're

going to lose your money! You saw him in the ring just now! It was a disaster!"

Avery put his hand on Comet's neck and looked up at her. "Issie, the Puissance is a completely different event. It requires a pony with exceptional bravery, and a rider who can put all their trust in their horse." He looked at her. "Comet can do this. I know he can – that's why I paid your entry."

Comet lifted his head up as Avery said this, as if he knew that they were talking about him. Issie looked at his bold chestnut and white face. Avery was right – Comet had more courage than any pony she had ever met. If they quit now, she would never know what he was really capable of.

"OK, Tom," she nodded. "We'll do it."

Avery smiled at her. "Excellent. The competition begins in an hour. That gives us enough time for a quick lesson in showjumping Puissance-style."

Comet, who seemed to realise that something was going on, began to dance beneath her. "Steady, Comet," Issie soothed him. "You're getting a second chance in that ring, boy," she whispered. "We both are."

A sense of determination gripped Issie now as she turned to her instructor. "We're ready," she said. "Let's go."

Chapter 16

Issie felt her tummy tighten with nerves. The Puissance had begun, but there were several other riders to go before it was her turn in the ring. Issie kind of wished she was going first. It would have been easier in a way to get it over and done with. That way you didn't have a chance to get nervous. As Avery gave her some last-minute advice on jumping technique she tried to listen, but it was hard to concentrate. As she looked at the jumps in the arena her mind kept going back to her round in the Grand Prix. It had been a total disaster! And now she was going back into the ring to face the biggest jumps of her life? This was crazy!

"The key," Avery was telling her, "is to get your horse in quite deep to the fence to get a good bascule over the jump." He put down his riding crop about two metres out from the practice jump. "Imagine that this crop marks your take-off point," he said.

Issie looked at the practice jump which Avery had fixed at a metre forty. To Issie, even the practice jump looked utterly huge.

"I've never jumped that high before," she said.

"Yes, you have!" Avery said. "Remember the Puissance training that we did at home? Comet took one metre forty easily. We never got the chance to see how much higher he could go, but I think he can do even better than that. I think he can win this event."

"Uh-huh," Issie said, sounding unconvinced.

Avery looked her in the eyes. He could see now that something was wrong. "Are you nervous?"

"A little," Issie admitted.

Avery nodded. "It's perfectly normal to be nervous. But somehow you need to lose your fears before you enter that arena. Showjumping is all about keeping your cool."

"I know, Tom," said Issie. "It's just that when Comet got spooked in the arena in the Grand Prix and I nearly fell off, I guess I kind of lost my nerve a bit…"

"He was only panicking because of the noise, Issie," Avery said.

"I know, I know, and he has the ear net now and everything… but, Tom, those are big jumps in there!"

Avery looked at her. "Comet is a very smart horse. He knows exactly what you're feeling. If you panic then he'll panic too. If you relax then he'll relax. Do you understand?"

Relax! Issie looked across the arena at the crowded grandstand. "Yeah, right! How can I? This is the Horse of the Year pony Puissance!"

Avery looked at her intently. "Take a deep breath and listen to me," he said. "You had a rough ride in the Grand Prix, but you and I both know that Comet can do this. He's a superstar, Issie. You have to give him the chance to prove it."

Issie took a deep breath and slowly let it out again. In her heart, she knew Avery was right. Comet was a star. Hadn't Issie known that from the very first day they met? Avery saw it straightaway too. Even Mystic knew it. Wasn't that why Mystic had been watching over Comet ever since Issie arrived at Blackthorn Farm? Mystic had helped her to find the skewbald pony that day when Kelly-Anne had taken him. Mystic believed in Comet. Now, after all they had been through, maybe it was time for Issie to make a final leap of faith and truly believe in this horse too.

Issie took another deep breath and this time, as she exhaled, she willed herself to be brave, to trust absolutely in her horse. She felt the butterflies in her belly dissolve as she breathed all the nervous energy out and took another new breath in again.

"Are you ready?" Avery said.

"Yes, Tom," she smiled. "I'm ready – and so is Comet."

"We're up to competitor number twenty in the pony Puissance," the announcer called. "Isadora Brown on Blackthorn Comet."

As she rode through into the arena and looked at the first fence Issie felt a tingle up her spine. Not from nerves this time, but from excitement. She wanted to do this.

"Come on, Comet," she whispered to her pony. "You and I know you're the best jumper here – and now we're gonna prove it to them."

With his smart new ear net on, Comet was no longer bothered by the crowd noise. The pony was totally unfazed and every inch the showjumper as Issie worked him around in a bouncy canter and headed towards the first fence. Comet took the painted rails with ease, flicking up his heels as he went over and giving a grunt of satisfaction as he landed on the other side as if to say, *Piece of cake!*

"Steady, boy." Issie turned him and gathered him up again for the brick wall. Even though she knew it was just made of wooden blocks, it looked really solid and scary. She swallowed her nerves and felt a surge of power from beneath her as Comet pricked his ears forward at the fence and approached it in a rounded canter, with one stride... two... three strides and over! They had gone clear! The crowd clapped politely. It was only the first round. Most of the thirty young riders competing in this event would go clear in this round. But there were still four rounds to go after this – and with each round, the brick wall would grow.

"The field stewards are now raising the wall to one metre forty," the announcer told the crowd in the grandstand.

The second round was far more dramatic than the first. One metre forty was enough to knock out quite a few competitors. By the time the wall was raised again for round three, there were only eight riders left.

The loudspeaker crackled back to life. "The wall is

now being set at one metre fifty," the announcer called.

"One metre fifty? You might as well give up now! You'll never make it over that on your ugly skewbald!" Issie turned around to see Natasha Tucker pouting at her from the back of her grey pony Fabergé.

"Did you see me and Fabby in that last round?" Natasha said. "Fabby just flew over the fence. Puissance is his speciality." She looked darkly at Issie. "I really do expect to win this."

Issie couldn't believe it. Of all the people to be in a jump-off with, did she have to be riding against Stuck-up Tucker?

Natasha's smugness got even worse a few moments later when she rode the next round and Fabergé went clear over the one metre fifty wall. Issie watched Natasha ride out of the ring with an unbearably pleased-with-herself look. She wasn't the only one to go clear. Three other riders had already made it round and the pressure was really on.

Avery's last-minute advice for getting over the wall this time was short and to the point. "Don't think about it too hard," he said to Issie as she entered the ring. "Just jump it!"

Comet did exactly that. Issie came into the ring, popped neatly over the painted rails and then turned

Comet to face the wall. She counted his strides out loud under her breath to keep herself focused. "One, two, three!" As the skewbald took off this time Issie realised just how big the fence was. One metre fifty! That was as tall as she was! She had just jumped herself!

For the fourth round the fence went up to one metre sixty. Issie looked at the brick wall and tried not to get freaked out. She was pretty sure now that the wall was so tall Comet wouldn't even be able to see over it.

"We're down to the final two rounds," the announcer said. "With only five riders left, it remains to be seen who will make it over this wall and into the jump-off for the final round."

Issie looked at the four other riders. She couldn't believe she had made it so far. She was in the fourth round. If she could get over the fence this time then she would make the final jump-off.

She looked over at Natasha Tucker. Natasha was circling Fabergé outside the arena now under the watchful eye of a horse-faced woman with long flame-red hair and tan jodhpurs.

"Who's she?" Issie asked.

"You really don't know?" Avery was surprised. "Issie, that's Ginty McLintoch. She's trained some of the best showjumping riders. She has some of the best horses in her stable too." Avery pointed at Natasha's grey pony Fabergé. "The word is that Ginty charged the Tuckers top dollar for Fabergé. She's renowned for having a real eye for horse flesh. Ginty has customers who are willing to pay big bling for a talented pony…"

The loudspeaker crackled back into life. "We're in the fourth round of the pony Puissance here at the Horse of the Year with Natasha Tucker on Fabergé next into the arena."

Issie watched as Natasha rode into the ring. Natasha's eyes were set at the jumps with steely determination. Issie had noticed that she brandished a hot pink riding crop in the previous rounds. This time when Natasha was a couple of strides out from the wall she used the crop, bringing it down hard against Fabergé's flank and screaming, "Get up!"

Poor Fabergé looked thoroughly shocked at being hit for no reason and his canter became disunited, but he managed to take off cleanly somehow and still cleared the wall.

Avery shook his head. "That's a classic Ginty McLintoch rider for you," he sighed. "Ginty trains all her students to use their whips as soon as the fences get big."

"Actually, I don't think Natasha needs any encouragement when it comes to using her whip," said Issie. She watched Natasha ride back out of the arena with a huge grin on her face. And Natasha's grin got even wider a few minutes later when the next three riders all failed to make it over the wall.

"Only one rider has made it over the wall so far. Now it's time for our last competitor, Isadora Brown on Blackthorn Comet," the announcer said.

As Issie took Comet into the ring this time she tried to remember everything Avery had told her about bringing the pony in deep to the fence and not holding him back. As she popped Comet over the painted rails she felt the pony arc up beneath her and she knew for certain as she turned to face the wall that Comet was ready to do this.

Up in the grandstand above her, though, the others weren't so sure.

"Ohmygod!" Stella squealed. "That wall is totally huge!"

"I can't look!" Kate had her hands over her face and was peering through her fingers.

"Is it safe for her to jump a wall that size?" Mrs Brown asked Hester.

"You must be joking!" Hester said without thinking. Then she saw Mrs Brown's distraught face and added, "She'll be fine, Amanda. She'll get over it no trouble – you watch!"

"Come on, Issie!" Tina, Trisha, Lucy, Sophie, Kitty, Kelly-Anne, George and Arthur were screaming at the top of their lungs.

Down in the arena, Comet's ears swivelled as he heard the shouts of the crowd. But the ear net had muffled the noise and he didn't lose his cool. Neither did Issie as she lined the skewbald pony up to the wall, took a deep breath and rode him forward at a fast canter. Comet took four big strides and then leapt straight up in the air. It almost looked like the pony was climbing the wall rather than jumping it as he rose up and over. Then he did a neat flip with his hindquarters, flicking his fetlocks up in the air so that they too flew above the bricks.

"Is she over?" Kate asked, peeking through her fingers. "Did she do it?" Her question was answered by the roar of the crowd going wild. Issie was clear!

"We are down to just two competitors in the final round. Natasha Tucker on Fabergé and Isadora Brown on Blackthorn Comet," the announcer said. "The course stewards are now raising the wall. They've taken it up another ten centimetres this time. That means final height for our pony Puissance today will be one metre seventy!"

As the stewards added another row of bricks to raise the height of the wall, Issie tried to stay calm and keep Comet working at a trot around the warm-up area. A metre seventy! *It's OK*, she told herself, *that's just ten more centimetres, hardly anything at all. Comet can do it.*

"Issie!" A voice called out to her. She looked up and saw Natasha Tucker riding towards her on Fabby. There was something wrong though. Issie couldn't place it at first and then she realised what it was. Natasha was smiling at her.

"Issie!" Natasha said. "I just wanted to ask you something. It's just that, well, the ground is quite hard and I don't want to hurt Fabby's legs more than I have to and I was just wondering... well..."

"What?" said Issie.

"I was just wondering if you want to call it quits at round four," Natasha said. "We could tell the judges that we're both stopping now and then they'd call a draw and we'd both share the first and second prize money." Natasha gave Issie a smile. "What do you think? Do we have a deal?"

Issie looked at the wall. Maybe Natasha was right. An extra ten centimetres meant that the wall was totally huge now. Way bigger than anything she had ever jumped in her life. She looked back at Natasha, and then she remembered what Avery had said about horses being able to sense fear. At that moment, Issie could sense it too. She realised that Natasha was afraid. Afraid of the wall and afraid of losing to Issie. That was the difference between these two riders now. Sure, the wall was huge, but Issie still believed she could do it. She believed that Comet could jump it. And she wasn't afraid. She was ready.

"Thanks, Natasha, but I want to ride," she said. "I want to see how this one turns out."

Natasha's smile instantly transformed into a scowl. "Your loss," she said. "Just remember I gave you your chance to be a winner, OK?"

"Natasha Tucker on Fabergé into the ring please!" the announcer called.

"Good luck, Natasha," Issie said.

"What-ever!" Natasha snapped back as she turned Fabergé and rode into the arena. The steely determination was still there on Natasha's face, but this time as she took the first fence and turned to face the wall, Issie saw something else in there as well.

Fabergé sensed the change in his rider too. As they came in to take the wall this time, Issie could only just see the very tips of the grey pony's ears above the wall. She saw Fabergé approach and then get ready to take off and then, at the very last moment, Natasha lashed out with her whip. At the same time, though, she stiffened and hesitated and Fabergé felt the conflict of being struck by this girl who was afraid to go over the wall. Instinctively, the horse became afraid too. Instead of leaping, at the very last moment he planted his feet and slid to a stop. Natasha, who hadn't been expecting this, flew clean over his head and straight into the wall. There was a loud gasp from the crowd as the bricks and rider all tumbled down in a great heap, and then a sigh of relief when Natasha stood up and dusted herself off.

"And unfortunately for Natasha Tucker and Fabergé that fall means disqualification in the final round," the announcer said. "Our stewards are just taking a few moments to rebuild the wall and then we'll have our last competitor, Isadora Brown on Blackthorn Comet."

In the grandstand the crowd went completely silent as Issie entered the ring.

Comet seemed to know that every eye in the place was on him. The little skewbald had always known he was a star, and now that he had his moment to show them, he was loving it! Issie could feel the fizzing tension in his chestnut and white body. The little horse was almost trembling with excitement and eagerness as he took the painted rails with ease and came around the corner for the last time to confront the wall.

As Issie approached the wall this time she tried to clear her mind. *Don't think about how big it is,* she told herself, *and don't think about the danger. Just think about being on the other side.*

Professional showjumpers will tell you that once the fences start getting really big, jumping feels totally different. There is a moment when it doesn't feel like you are jumping at all; it feels like you are flying. It felt like that now as Comet took the wall. As the pony leapt up and up, Issie felt the world fall away behind her, and then she was in midair. As they crested the top of the wall it felt like they were in slow motion, floating there for a moment, before they came down the other side.

This time, all the ear nets in the world couldn't have muffled the noise of the crowd. The grandstand went wild with applause as the little skewbald landed on the other side. They were clear. They had won!

"Isadora Brown and Blackthorn Comet are the winners of the pony Puissance!" the announcer called. "A fantastic jump at one metre seventy and a well-deserved win for the prize of the Puissance Cup!"

"I get a cup?" Issie couldn't believe it. "Tom, did you hear that? I get a cup!"

"You get more than that," Avery beamed at her.

"What do you mean?"

"Issie, you just won $15,000!"

"What?" Issie couldn't believe it. She had assumed there would be some prize money for the Puissance, but she had never dreamt it would be that much! "Why didn't you tell me I was jumping for that much money?"

"Because it would have made you nervous," Avery said. "I figured you were coping with your nerves quite well. I didn't want to say anything that might throw you."

"Ohmygod!" Issie still couldn't believe it.

"Go on!" Avery grinned at her. "Get into the ring for prize-giving!"

Issie had to laugh as they took their victory lap of the arena with their trophy and the red sash tied around Comet's neck. This was Comet's moment and boy did the skewbald know it. He pranced about the ring with his neck arched and his head high as if to say, *I told you all that I could do it, didn't I?*

As they cantered out of the arena, the whole gang from Blackthorn Farm was on the sidelines to meet them.

"Mum!" Issie jumped down off her horse and gave her mother a huge hug. "We did it!"

"Wasn't he a superstar out there?" Mrs Brown said.

Issie hugged Comet tight around his neck. The pony wouldn't stay still though; he was still prancing about, making the most of all the attention.

"Comet, I can see you are going to be completely unbearable to live with from now on!" Issie giggled.

Hester sighed. "Isadora, he was already unbearable before. I can see that I'm going to have to build some paddocks with bigger fences when we get him home."

"That might not be necessary," said the woman striding towards her. Issie recognised the red hair and tan jodhpurs immediately. It was the same woman she had seen training Natasha Tucker. It was Ginty McLintoch.

"Hello, Hester," the red-headed woman said briskly.

"Hello, Ginty," Hester said. "I suppose you've come over to see our Puissance champion?"

"I've come to do more than that," Ginty said. "I've come to buy him."

"What makes you think he's for sale?"

Ginty looked Hester in the eye. "Don't play games, Hester. Everyone knows your farm is in trouble. I imagine that a cash injection from a horse sale is just what you need right now, and I'm here to offer it to you."

"He's not for sale, Ginty," Hester replied coolly.

"Oh, really?" Ginty raised an eyebrow and took out her chequebook. She smiled at Hester. "I've got a cheque here for $25,000 that says that he is."

Issie looked at her aunt. $25,000! That was more than enough money to save the farm and Hester and Issie both knew it. But her aunt wouldn't, she couldn't sell Comet. Could she?

Issie watched in horror as her aunt paused for a moment. Her face was expressionless as she looked at Issie. And then Hester reluctantly reached out a hand and took the cheque.

Chapter 17

Hester held the cheque in her hands and looked at it. Then she turned once more to the red-headed woman. "I'm sorry, Ginty. That's a lot of zeros you have written on here, but..."

Ginty looked Hester in the eye. "OK, Hester," she said. "If you want to play hardball. What do you want? Another $1,000? $2,000? All right, I'll make that a $28,000 cheque. I've got a client that this pony would be perfect for. She's looking for a new horse. And a horse just like this one could take her to the top." Ginty ran a hand down Comet's neck. "This pony will be perfect for Natasha."

Issie blinked. "You mean you're buying Comet for Natasha Tucker?"

Ginty looked taken aback. "You know Natasha?"

"We go to the same pony club," Issie said flatly.

"Well, she asked me to find her a new horse," Ginty said. "And I think I just have."

"Think again." Hester lifted up the cheque daintily between her fingers and ripped it carefully and cleanly in two.

"I'm sorry, Ginty, but I've been trying to tell you... Comet is not for sale. And even if he was for sale," she added, "you're talking to the wrong person. He doesn't belong to me."

Ginty stiffened. "Well, who is his owner then?"

"That would be my niece," Hester said, turning to Issie. "Comet's her pony, so Natasha will have the pleasure of seeing him at the next pony-club rally because Issie will be riding him there."

Issie was stunned. "Really? Aunty Hess, do you mean it? He's mine? To take back home with me and everything?"

"Absolutely!" Hester said. "That is, if you want him."

Issie didn't need any more convincing. "Of course I want him!" she said. She turned to Comet and threw her arms around his patchy chestnut and white neck.

"Well," Ginty sighed. "I think you're all mad, of

course. You won't get a price this good from anyone else in the business." She handed her card to Issie. "If you ever change your mind and want to sell him, these are my details. My offer still stands." Issie accepted the card and shoved it in her jodhpur pocket.

Ginty ran her eyes over Comet one last time. "That's quite the pony you have there," she said to Issie.

"I know," Issie replied. "He really is."

"Do you think we did the right thing?" Issie asked her aunt as they sat around the kitchen table back at Blackthorn Farm that evening. "I mean, should I have taken Ginty's money? It would have got you out of trouble – with the farm and everything, I mean."

Hester shrugged. "I suppose it would have been the logical thing to do," she said, "but then I was never really one for logic. Besides, I'm not sure that Comet would be worth all that money without you riding him. You and that skewbald were made for each other and I'm not about to split you up now. You've got a lot of adventures ahead of you yet. Maybe not at this farm – but I couldn't sell Comet to save this place. I just couldn't. Now,"

Hester looked around the table at Mrs Brown, Stella, Kate, Ben, Dan, Avery and Aidan, "shall I put the kettle on for tea then?"

Hester was just about to stand up when Issie shoved an envelope across the table to her. "Aunty Hess? I want you to have this."

Hester looked at the envelope in front of her on the table. She didn't pick it up.

"What is it?"

"$15,000," Issie said. "It's my winnings from the Puissance."

"Can I add something to that?" said a voice across the table. It was Aidan and he too thrust an envelope across the table at Hester. "It's $10,000. My winnings from the showjumping. I still came second in the novice hack – plus managed to ace a couple of other events on Destiny."

Aidan looked at Hester. "I want you to have the money. With my money and Issie's combined that makes $25,000. It's enough to save the farm for now. It will see us through until we get that next big film job."

Hester shook her head. "No. I won't let you kids do this. This is your money. I won't take your charity."

There was silence at the table – and then, finally, Mrs

Brown spoke. "I agree," she said. She turned to her sister, "You're right, Hess. I won't let Issie give you $15,000. That money could be her future. She could invest it and use it for university…"

"But, Mum! I want to do this…"

"Let me finish, Issie!" Mrs Brown said firmly. "I said I won't let you give it to your aunt, but I will let you invest it with her. That is, if Hester is willing to take you and Aidan on as her business partners." Mrs Brown smiled at her sister. "Hess, I know I always tease you about this place being a money pit, but since I got here I've been seeing things differently. It's beautiful here. I can see why you love it so much, and the riding school could be a real success in the future or maybe you could breed Blackthorn Ponies? If they all show as much promise as Comet then you could have a lucrative business on your hands selling up-and-coming showjumpers to people like Ginty McLintoch. Not to mention the film work, which I'm sure will pick up again."

Hester looked at her sister. "What exactly are you suggesting, Amanda?"

"I'm suggesting that you take Issie and Aidan on as your junior business partners."

Hester stared at the envelope on the table and then she picked it up and put it in her pocket. "Well," she said, extending a hand to an astonished Aidan and Issie, "I guess we should shake on that, don't you? I'm sure your mum can do some paperwork, Issie, and make it all official."

Aidan and Issie both took turns shaking her hand in stunned disbelief.

"Congratulations," Hester grinned at Issie. "You are now the proud owner of one skewbald gelding – and shareholder in an utterly barking mad horse farm!"

Leaving Blackthorn Farm was much harder this time. It wasn't just because it was Issie's farm too now. It was everything. The manor, the ponies, the kids…

"Even Kelly-Anne?" Stella had asked Issie teasingly.

"Well, maybe I won't miss Kelly-Anne," Issie said, "but even she hasn't been so bad lately."

In fact, since Stella had got Kelly-Anne to help out as groom at the Horse of the Year, there had been a real attitude change in her. On the last day of the riding school they had held a Blackthorn Farm Ribbon Day, and it was Kelly-Anne who had stayed up late the night before helping Issie, Stella and Kate to make homemade rosettes for all the riders.

There was a red rosette for first, blue for second and bright yellow for third place. Each rosette was made of ribbon with a round cardboard disc at the centre with *Blackthorn Farm Riding Club* written on it in scripty handwriting.

Issie, Stella and Kate were the judges for the Ribbon Day and they gave out prizes for loads of events. Kitty won most improved rider; Tina and Trisha won the prize on the palominos for the best dual jump. Sophie and Lucy had Molly and Pippen so shiny and well-plaited that they tied for first place in the best-groomed. George won the bending and Arthur won the flag race. Even Kelly-Anne joined in the competition in good spirits and won Best Rider over Hurdles, which she seemed to be completely thrilled about.

An official prize-giving was held on horseback at the end of the day and the rosettes were tied on to the ponies' bridles before all the riders did a victory lap together around the arena. Sophie was so thrilled with her yellow rosette that Issie noticed she was wearing it in her hair when she came to dinner that night.

Before they sat down to eat their dinner, the kids all raced off into the living room and returned with a cardboard box. "We've made prizes for all of you too," Sophie explained. From the box they produced a purple sash made out of crêpe paper for Kate that said Best Instructor. Stella got a homemade badge that said Most Fun Horsey Friend and Hester got one that said Favourite Holiday Organiser Ever.

"Well, they wouldn't give her one for her cooking, would they?" Stella whispered to Issie.

"We've got one for you too, Isadora," Kitty said. The kids gathered around the box and pulled out what looked like an old china teacup with a saucer underneath it. "It's a cup," Kitty said. "Well, I know it's only a teacup, but we thought it could be, like, a cup for winning the Puissance – and we've had it engraved and everything."

Issie looked at the teacup. It was cracked and it had a chip out of the saucer. "We found it in a pile of rubbish down by the stables," Kitty said. "It's not actually for you to drink out of or anything. It's to sit on your mantelpiece like a trophy."

"Thanks!" Issie smiled.

"Look at the engraving!" Lucy said.

Issie looked on the side of the teacup. The "engraving" was done in green felt tip. It said, *The Champion's Cup: awarded to Isadora Brown for Winning the Puissance and Saving Blackthorn Farm.*

Issie grinned. "Thanks, everyone – it's the best prize I've ever had."

The cup was placed alongside the other prizes in the centre of the table and Mrs Brown served up pizza and chips on to everyone's plates.

"I don't believe that this is our last dinner together before you all go home," Hester said. "It will be so quiet here when you are all gone. It's been so loud and full of life for the past few weeks. There's never been a quiet moment."

Actually, Issie thought, a quiet moment was exactly what she needed. A nice quiet moment when she could finally talk to Aidan about what had happened after Dan won the showjumping that day. She hadn't been able to talk to him when they were at the Horse of the Year. And then she was in Avery's truck sitting with her mum for the ride home. Since they'd been back at Blackthorn Farm it was just as Aunty Hess had said – there was never a quiet moment. It had been impossible to get some time alone with Aidan. Issie had finally resigned herself to the fact that she would never get a chance to tell Aidan how she felt. *Maybe that's a good thing*, she thought. If Aidan was really meant to be her boyfriend then wouldn't he have said something by now?

On their very last morning at the farm, Issie set her alarm clock for 5 a.m. It had become her ritual now, that every time she left this place she woke up before dawn and spent some time alone, feeding the animals breakfast, saying her own quiet goodbyes to all the horses before the rest of the world woke up and joined her.

When her alarm clock woke her up it was still pitch black outside, but by the time she was dressed and had pulled her farm boots on, the dawn light was already filtering through the trees on the horizon.

Down at the stables, Issie unbolted the stall doors one by one and watched as the horses all stuck their heads out to see who was there. Diablo stuck his head out first, and then Paris and Stardust.

"It's me," Issie whispered, moving down one side of the barn, feeding each of them in turn. "I've got carrots." At the mention of the word "carrot" there was a nicker from the first stall and Comet stuck his head over.

"Hey, boy," Issie grinned at him. "I'm taking you home today. You're coming to live with me. I can't wait for you to meet Blaze and Storm."

"So you're choosing him then?" Issie turned around to see Aidan standing behind her.

"Aidan!"

"I thought this was a competition between me and Dan," Aidan grinned at her, "but I can see now that the only one who's ever going to really win you over is Comet."

"No!" Issie felt her tummy somersaulting with nerves. "Aidan, that's what I've been trying to tell you, about the bet, the one you made with Dan…"

"It's OK," Aidan said, stepping closer to her. "I already know. I spoke to Dan and he told me what you said to him."

Issie was shocked. "You talked to Dan? When?"

"At the Horse of the Year," Aidan said. "I went to shake his hand and say congratulations on winning our bet and all that. He told me that the bet was off. He seemed to think that you wanted me to win…"

"I did… I mean, I do…" Issie was trembling as Aidan moved closer to her. Before she could say anything more he had put his arms around her and…

"Issie! There you are!" Avery's voice boomed through the stable.

Aidan jumped back at the sound of his voice, letting go of Issie. He tried to act casual. "I was, ummm, I was just feeding Comet a carrot…"

Avery raised an eyebrow at him. "Come on, you two!" he said briskly. "Breakfast is ready and Hester asked me to come and get you. We don't have much time. I want to be packed and out of here by 9 a.m. It's a long drive back to Chevalier Point with five horses in the truck."

Issie and Aidan both hesitated, hoping that Avery would walk on ahead and leave them alone again for a moment, but the instructor stood at the door waiting to escort them back to the manor.

"Well? Come on? What are you waiting for?"

The rest of the morning was much the same. "It's a big farm," Issie grumbled to Stella and Kate. "You'd think there'd be enough room for me to be alone with my boyfriend for five minutes."

"Boyfriend?" Stella's ears pricked up. "Issie, is Aidan really, finally, your boyfriend?"

Issie shrugged. "I don't know. I guess so."

"I thought he was your business partner," Kate grinned.

"That too," Issie grinned back.

It was a departure on a grand scale that day. Aidan was driving Hester's horse truck with all the kids in it to take them back to their homes now the camp was over. And Avery, Mrs Brown and the Chevalier Point gang were going home together in Avery's truck at the same time.

"That's the last of it," Issie said as she threw a sleeping bag into the storage box in the back of the horse truck. "You can bring the horses on now."

As Dan and Aidan walked Madonna and Max up the truck ramp, Issie, Stella and Kate went to get Toby, Coco and Comet.

Issie looked around the stables longingly one last time. She had almost kissed Aidan here this morning. She had been hoping that she might see him here again and get the chance to say goodbye, but it looked like there was no hope.

"Come on, Comet," she said as she led the skewbald out of his stall. "It's time for us to go home."

The horses were loaded, and so were the kids. Aunt Hester had handed everyone bundles of inedible jam scones to see them through the long drive through the Gisborne gorge, and they were all ready to go home.

"Right," Avery said. "Are we all onboard and ready?"

Issie jumped up into the cab next to Avery and did up her seatbelt. "Uh-huh. Everyone is in their seats. We're ready to…" There was a loud tapping on the driver's window. It was Aidan.

Avery wound his window down. "What is it?" he said. "We need to get going; we've got the horses onboard."

Aidan took a deep breath. "I know that, sir. It's just that I need to talk to Issie for a moment. It's something I wanted to say to her earlier, but we got interrupted and, well, I really need to talk to her."

Avery looked annoyed by this, but he turned to Issie. "Aidan's got something he wants to talk about, apparently. You've got one minute."

Issie leapt down out of the cab and Aidan grabbed her by the hand and dragged her back across the lawn so that they were standing a few metres away from the trucks underneath the falling petals of the cherry trees.

"Listen, Issie, about before," he said. "I never finished saying what I wanted to say and, well, I wanted to let you know that… I hope you'll be…" He stopped talking and looked up. Peering out of the two horse trucks were a dozen faces, all pressed up against the glass, watching them.

"Oh, great!" Aidan groaned. "Just what I needed. An audience!" He looked back at Issie. "I'm not going to talk about this any more," he said. "You know what I mean and you know what I'm trying to say. Now this is it. I don't care any more. I'm going to kiss you, OK?"

"But, Aidan!" Issie objected. "I can't. They're all watching us!"

Aidan smiled and pulled her closer. "Close your eyes then," he told her.

And she did.

storm and the silver Bridle

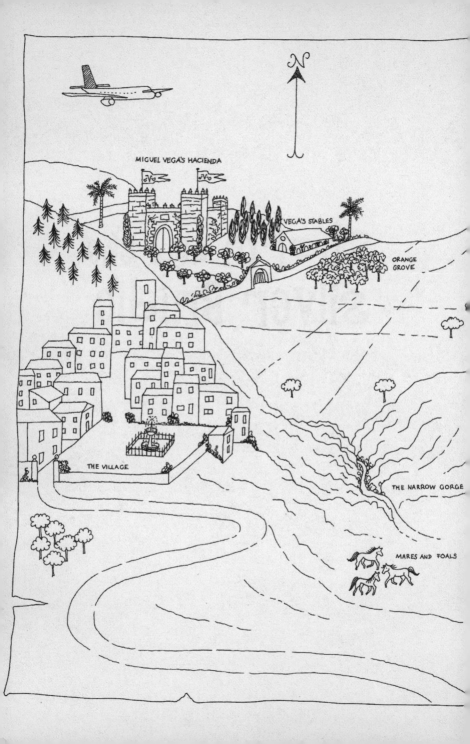

MIGUEL VEGA'S HACIENDA

VEGA'S STABLES

ORANGE GROVE

THE VILLAGE

THE NARROW GORGE

MARES AND FOALS

N

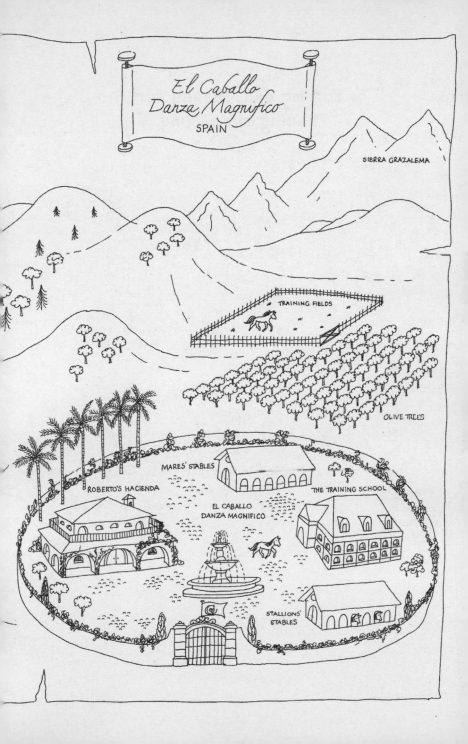

For my dad, thanks for
buying me a pony

Chapter 1

Anyone who knows anything about horses will tell you that there is no such thing as a white horse. A horse is never called 'white'. They are always referred to as grey.

Roberto Nunez shook his head and smiled at this. How silly these rules were!

He knew that horses could not be white. Yet how else could he describe the mares that were galloping towards him? These mares were as pure white as the snow that topped the distant mountains of the Sierra de Grazalema. They were as white as the stone walls that ran around the stables here at El Caballo Danza Magnifico.

Roberto Nunez's purebred Lipizzaner mares were as white as any animal in nature could possibly be. Their colour appeared all the more startling because it was in stark contrast with the coal-black foals that ran alongside them at their feet.

Although Lipizzaner horses are famous for being white, their foals are always born pitch-black. Gradually, as the foals grow up, their colour will change. As they mature, the Lipizzaners' dark coat will begin to prick here and there with tiny white hairs so that by the time the foals have grown into yearlings they have become steel-grey. At the age of three Lipizzaners are almost grown-up, and their coats have become even lighter, with dapples beginning to show through the dark steel on their hindquarters. In this way, their coats will keep fading until finally, at around the age of twelve, their dapples will have washed away and the Lipizzaner will be utterly and completely snow-white just like their mothers and fathers before them.

This was the way with the Lipizzaner. Roberto Nunez knew the breed well. At his *hacienda*, his grand estate here in southern Spain, he bred Andalusians and Lipizzaners, along with the highly strung, elegant, chestnut Anglo-Arabs that made up his internationally renowned troupe of performing horses known as El Caballo Danza Magnifico.

The mares that were galloping towards him now, driven carefully by his men, were part of his breeding herd. They had been grazing for the day out on the dry, rocky hillsides that surrounded his horse stud. Nunez liked to let the mares and their young foals roam free as much as possible. It toughened them up. It gave them spirit. But always he kept a close eye on his horses. Now, as night fell, he was bringing them home.

There were about two dozen mares in this herd, all ghostly pale, with the bloom of their grey dapples fading on their rumps. Their manes and tails were hogged off – cropped short, in the style that the Spanish always kept their breeding herds. It was funny, Nunez thought, how his mares were the ones who had their hair cropped short while the stallions, the male horses of the herd, were allowed to keep their long and silky manes.

Even without their manes, these mares were great beauties. To anyone else, they would have appeared almost identical, and yet Nunez could tell them apart at a glance. He simply looked at their faces and knew them instantly, in the same way that you and I might know a friend's face if we saw her in a crowded street.

For instance, one mare might have a Roman nose, a noble trait often seen in the Lipizzaner, while another mare would possess the dished face of the Arabian bloodlines that had also influenced this mighty breed. Some mares had the typical Lipizzaner characteristic of perfect almond-shaped eyes. Others were blessed with a smattering of the dainty freckles known as 'flea-bites' flecked on their cheeks.

These were Roberto Nunez's very best mares and they had been bred with the very best of El Caballo Danza Magnifico's stallions.

Roberto Nunez smiled now as he caught sight of one of his favourite mares, Margarita, with her pretty coal-dark eyes and her features so delicate she looked as if she might have been carved out of marble. At Margarita's feet was a jet-black foal. The foal was all legs, gangly and awkward, and only a few weeks old. And yet already Roberto Nunez could see the signs of greatness in him that came from being sired by one of the finest stallions in Spain.

"You see him, Marius?" Nunez said to the stallion beneath him. The great grey horse shifted about restlessly at the sound of his master's voice, and Nunez reached down and gave him a firm pat on his arched, glossy neck. "That is your son," he said proudly.

The progeny of Marius held the key to the future of El Caballo Danza Magnifico. Roberto Nunez knew it. And this foal was not the only one. He had discovered that there was another son of his mighty stallion, born far away from Spain – in New Zealand, of all places!

His head instructor, Francoise D'arth, had received a letter from a girl called Isadora Brown. The letter said that a foal had been born to her mare Blaze and that Marius was the father! Nunez could not believe it when he heard the news. But one look at the photos of the colt that the girl enclosed removed any doubts. He was clearly the progeny of Marius, as strong and handsome as his famous sire. And with the beautiful Anglo-Arab mare Blaze as his dam, the colt would be intelligent too.

The colt's name was Nightstorm – although in her letter the girl referred to him by his nickname. She called him Storm.

The thunder of hooves shook Roberto Nunez back to reality as the mares and foals rushed past just in front of him, heading in through the wrought-iron gates that led into the vast courtyard of El Caballo stables. As the herd ran past, Nunez searched again for Margarita and her foal and then laughed out loud as he caught a glimpse of the black colt in full flight, giving a high-spirited buck as he raced through the gates.

"You see, Marius?" Nunez murmured to the stallion. "Your son. He is coming home…"

Meanwhile, on the other side of the world, Issie Brown was having serious second thoughts about taking Storm away from Winterflood Farm.

"I don't know about this, Tom," she said, gazing uncertainly at her colt standing in his stall. "Are you sure he's ready?"

"Absolutely," Tom Avery said. "The journey will be no big deal. This is an important stage in his training."

"It's just that he's still so little." Issie's voice was quivering. "He's only just been weaned two weeks ago and he's never been away from the farm before—"

"Issie, he'll be fine," Avery said firmly.

"But Tom—"

"Honestly, Isadora!" Avery couldn't keep the exasperation out of his voice. "With the fuss you're making you'd swear we were taking Storm halfway around the world instead of ten minutes down the road. For Pete's sake! We're only driving to the pony club grounds! It's hardly a long trip, is it? Trust me, he's ready!"

Issie sighed. "You're right, Tom. I'm being silly."

She had to face the fact that Storm wasn't her baby any more. The colt was so grown-up he was already as tall as his dam, Blaze. He shared his mother's delicate Anglo-Arabian features too, although his big-boned, powerful physique and presence owed more to his sire, Marius.

Storm was six months old now. Had it really been that long since the stormy night when the foal was born? Issie remembered it so clearly, fighting the rain to get Blaze inside, sheltering in the stable as the lightning flashes lit up the pitch-black sky. The thunderstorm that had marked the colt's sudden arrival into the world had given him his name – Nightstorm. Issie had delivered him all by herself, and from the moment she saw the wee foal lying damp and newborn on the straw of the stable floor she had fallen in love with him.

The only living creature that loved Storm as much as Issie did was the foal's mother, Blaze. They were so alike, Blaze and her son. Even though Storm was a bay and his mother was a chestnut, the colt's broad white blaze that ran down his velvety nose made him look just like his mum. He was beautiful like her too, with those enormous eyes full of wonder, fringed with eyelashes that were so long they didn't even look real.

With his fluffy dark mane and doe eyes, Storm was as cute as a baby kitten. If Issie had been left to her own devices, she would have spoilt him rotten with cuddles and treats. But Avery knew better than to let her do that. Her pony-club instructor had made it clear right from the start that horses weren't pets to be mollycoddled and fussed over.

"That foal is going to grow into a big, strong horse one day, bigger and stronger than you are," he told her firmly. "So don't even think about teaching it some tricks that you might think are cute right now, but will turn dangerous later on when that colt gets older. You are training a horse to respect you right from the start."

Issie was beyond grateful when Avery offered to keep Storm at Winterflood Farm and help her with his training. Together they began to 'imprint' the foal, teaching Storm to wear a halter, to lead and to stand politely while they brushed him and picked up his hooves.

Still, there were some things that Issie simply couldn't bring herself to do. When the colt was five months old and Avery decided that he was ready for weaning, Issie knew she couldn't bear to watch Storm and Blaze be separated.

"Can you do it, Tom?" she said, with tears welling in her eyes. "I don't think I'll be able to stand it. It's better if I just stay home."

Avery understood. "It's a normal process for all mares and foals to be split up, but they'll be upset for a day or so," he said. "I think it would be best to keep Storm here at Winterflood Farm in familiar surroundings.

He'll feel more secure if he's in his usual field. I'll take Blaze down to the River Paddock."

And so on the day of the weaning Issie sat at home hugging her knees miserably and watching bad movies on TV, while Avery separated the mare and her foal for the first time.

Blaze had been frantic when she was taken away from her son. She had whinnied and whinnied and paced up and down the fenceline, with a heartbreaking expression on her face as she searched in vain for her baby. But eventually she calmed down and began to graze and make friends again with her old paddock mates Toby and Coco.

As for Storm, the little colt had bellowed for his mother solidly all day and into the night. Then, just before Avery went to bed, he heard the trip-trap of the colt's hooves on the gravel driveway. Storm had decided that no one was keeping him away from his mum any longer and had jumped out of his paddock!

Issie couldn't believe it when Avery called to tell her. "Well, on the positive side, at least we know now that he has the makings of a good showjumper," Avery said. Luckily the driveway gate had been shut and Avery had caught the colt before he got too far. "Don't worry," he told Issie, "I've put him back in the magnolia paddock this time where the fences are a metre higher. I doubt he'll get out again."

With his attempted jailbreak foiled, Storm seemed to resign himself to his fate and began to make friends with Avery's two horses, Starlight and Vinnie, who grazed in the paddock next to his. By the time Issie arrived at Winterflood Farm the next day she found her colt quite content with his new life without his mum, nickering happily over the fence to her.

"It's all part of growing up," Avery told her. "He's becoming a horse." Issie knew her instructor was right, but still, she worried about her colt.

Now Avery said Storm was ready for the next step – his first outing. For the past two weeks Issie had been practising with the colt in Avery's horse float. At first she had simply got Avery to park the float around the back of the house in Storm's paddock. She had dropped the ramp and let the colt sniff his way around it, putting one tentative hoof and then another onboard. Then, she had clipped a lead rope to his halter and led the colt all the way on and off the horse float, talking softly to him whenever he spooked or snorted, reassuring him that it was OK and nothing would hurt him.

By the end of the second week, Storm was so comfortable around the horse float that he would walk on all by himself and stand like a perfect gentleman as Issie fussed with his halter, tied up his hay net and then lifted the ramp and locked the colt safely inside. Once he was closed in she would leave him standing there for a few moments, just to let him see how it felt before she lowered the ramp and let him out again.

Today the routine would be just the same as the past couple of weeks, Issie told herself. Except today, instead of going nowhere and staying in the paddock, the horse float was attached to the towbar of Avery's Range Rover.

"Easy, Storm," Issie cooed to the colt. "We're just going to go for a little ride."

Storm lifted his legs in an exaggerated high step, wary of the leg bandages that Issie had put on him today to protect him for the journey. The colt raised his feet deliberately and precisely as he walked up the float ramp. Then he was inside and Issie was bolting the doors behind him before climbing into the Range Rover next to Avery.

"Is he ready?" Avery asked.

Issie took a deep breath and nodded. "Uh-huh. Let's go."

As the Range Rover rolled slowly down the driveway,

Issie twisted round in her seat and stared out of the back window at the float.

"Is he OK?" Avery asked her.

"He's fine, Tom." Issie turned to her instructor. "I guess I shouldn't have worried so much, but it's his first ride in the horse float, you know?"

Avery smiled at her. "The pony club is the perfect distance – just a few kilometres. That's a good first trip for him. It will get him used to travelling and being around other horses. It's all about breaking him in gradually to new experiences. We start him off by taking him to pony-club rally. Let him understand that it's not a big deal, just tether him to the float for an hour or so, let him look around, then bring him home again. By the time he goes out to compete at his first gymkhana or one-day event he'll be quite relaxed because he knows the drill."

Issie nodded. Then she turned back to stare out of the rear window again, keeping her eyes locked on the horse float to make sure Storm was still OK.

If she hadn't been so busy staring straight at the horse float she might have noticed the car that was trailing behind them to the pony-club grounds. It was a black sedan with tinted windows, and it had been following them ever since it pulled out from behind the trees next to Winterflood Farm.

The black car kept its distance, travelling slowly behind them all the way to the pony club. When Avery pulled up to open the gates of the Chevalier Point club grounds, the sedan pulled over and parked out of sight behind the hedge across the road. A tinted window was lowered and a pair of binoculars appeared. Through the binoculars, dark eyes were watching Issie and her colt. They watched as Storm came down the ramp of the float, the binoculars trained directly on the colt as he looked about excitedly, letting out a shrill whinny, calling to the other horses. They saw the way Issie held the colt's head firmly and talked to him all the time, and the way the colt responded to her voice, calming down as she handled him.

Then, satisfied that they had seen enough, the tinted window was rolled shut again and the black car silently drove off.

If only Issie had seen the car, she might have realised that there was something suspicious going on. But as the black sedan swept out of sight, she had no idea of the danger they were in. She did not know what was to come – for her, and for Nightstorm.

Chapter 2

Issie might not have noticed the black sedan, but it was hard to miss the sour-faced spectacle that greeted her as they pulled into the club grounds.

Natasha Tucker had spent pretty much the whole season at pony club trying to make Issie's life a misery. As Avery steered the truck through the gates and Issie caught sight of the girl with the stiff blonde plaits glowering malevolently at her it was clear that today was going to be no different.

Issie knew precisely why Stuck-up Tucker had her in her sights. Ever since the Horse of the Year Show, when Issie and her skewbald pony Comet had beaten Natasha, the girls had openly been at war. Natasha was still furious that Issie's aunt Hester had refused to sell Comet to her.

Natasha's trainer, Ginty McLintoch, had offered Hester a huge amount of money – $28,000! But Hester had turned her down and given the skewbald showjumper to Issie instead.

Natasha didn't take no for an answer. She always got what she wanted and, despite the fact that she kept telling Issie that skewbalds were ugly, she had decided she wanted Comet. Ginty McLintoch had approached Issie twice since then on Natasha's behalf and offered to buy the skewbald gelding. But each time Issie said no – which just infuriated Natasha even more.

Issie would never have given up Comet. She had really bonded with the skewbald since she brought him home to the pony club at the beginning of summer. Now summer was over – and so was pony club. The weather was turning rainy and miserable and the club grounds were already getting boggy. Today would be the last rally for a while. For the next month or so, during the very worst of the weather, the club would be closed and most of the Chevalier Point riders, including Issie, had decided to spell their horses over this time, leaving them unridden until conditions improved.

Issie had been torn when she realised that bringing Storm along today meant she would miss her chance to ride Comet at the final rally of the season. She had even thought she might be able to ride Blaze to pony club today for the first time in ages. After all, Storm had been weaned so the mare was able to be ridden again. But Avery had convinced her to leave Blaze and Comet at home. It was more important, he said, to use this opportunity to give Storm his first experience of the grown-up horsey world. This was a vital part of the colt's training, letting him get used to new sights and sounds, and other horses. Not that there was any point in trying to explain that to Natasha.

"So why are you bringing your foal to pony club? What's the point of that?" huffed Natasha as she strode over from her fancy blue and silver horse truck where she had been standing to watch Issie unload Storm. "Trying to show off, I suppose. You always have to be the centre of attention, don't you?"

"I am not showing off!" Issie was taken aback. "Coming here is part of Nightstorm's training. Avery says—"

"Avery says, Avery says…" Natasha sing-songed back. She cast a glance over her shoulder to make sure Avery was still inside the horse truck and couldn't hear her before she went on, "You know, some of us don't care what Avery has to say. He's just a pony-club instructor. If he was any good then he'd have his own private stables, wouldn't he?"

"Like Ginty McLintoch, I suppose?" Issie said archly. She was fed up with Natasha banging on about her fabulous, expensive lessons with Ginty, and complaining about Avery's 'dated methods'.

"Ginty McLintoch says she'd never teach at a pony club," Natasha said. "She says she's too professional to lower her standards—"

"Natasha!" There was a call from the blue and silver horse truck and Mrs Tucker appeared on the ramp, looking flustered. "Natasha! What's going on? Are you going to unload your horse or do I have to do everything?"

Natasha groaned out loud at her mother's command, but she did as she was asked and walked back over to her truck, following Mrs Tucker back inside. A few moments later she emerged again leading a horse. Issie had been expecting to see Natasha's elegant rose-grey, Fabergé. Instead, the horse that appeared was a striking chestnut, about sixteen hands high, with a glossy coat, perfectly pulled mane, flowing tail and two white hind socks.

"His name is Romeo and he's a purebred Selle Francaise – a French sport-horse!" Natasha said proudly as she led him past Issie and tied him up.

Issie was stunned. "What happened to Fabergé?"

"Fabby's gone," Natasha shrugged. "He was never talented enough for me. Ginty was supposed to find me a new horse at Horse of the Year, but really there was nothing there that measured up to my needs." Natasha said this last part with a nasty sneer and Issie knew this was a dig at Comet. "Anyway, that's when Mummy suggested that Ginty fly over to Australia and look for a new horse to bring back. That's where she found Romeo. She insists that Romeo is the perfect horse to take me to the national pony club champs, and—"

"Got a new horse then?" Stella interrupted as she rode up to join them. "Is that because Fabergé kept bucking you off?"

Natasha gave Stella a filthy look. "That wasn't my fault! Fabergé is too highly strung. Ginty says that's why we weren't clicking."

"Natasha, I don't know how you can expect to 'click' with a horse if you just keep getting new ones every time something goes wrong!" Stella shot back.

"It's called upgrading," Natasha sniffed. She cast her eyes over Coco. "You know, you should really think about upgrading too, Stella. You're so huge your legs are almost dragging on the ground on that pony. What's the matter? Can't your parents afford to buy you a new one?"

Stella seemed genuinely hurt by this and Natasha, pleased with the success of her put-down, decided that was the end of the conversation. "I'm glad this is the last rally of the year," she added icily as she turned to lead Romeo away to the washing bays. "That means I won't have to put up with you two again for the next few months."

"God, she is such a cow!" Stella said, pulling a face behind Natasha's back as she watched her walk away. Then she vaulted out of the saddle to stand beside her horse. "Never mind what Stuck-up Tucker says, Coco, I still love you!" Stella threw her arms around Coco's neck, giving the mare a snuggle. Coco, who didn't particularly like snuggles, put her ears back a bit.

"You are getting a bit big for her though, aren't you?" Issie said gently.

It was true. The girls were fourteen now and Stella had really grown this year. Coco was only thirteen-two hands high and Stella looked enormous on her. Her legs were so long they almost wrapped right around the mare's tubby brown belly.

"I know…" Stella said. She cast a sneaky sideways glance at Coco, as if she was checking to see if the pony was listening, and then whispered dramatically to Issie with her hand over her face. "I don't really want to talk about this in front of Coco, but I've been looking in the 'ponies for sale' pages in *PONY* magazine. Mum and Dad said that I can sell Coco and get a new pony in time for summer and they're taking me to look at this fourteen-two roan next week…"

"Stella," Issie whispered back, "you do know that you don't have to whisper, don't you? Coco can't understand English."

"Coco understands every word I say, don't you, Coco?" Stella giggled, stroking her mare's forelock.

While the girls were talking, Storm had been standing obediently tied up beside them, his head held high, watching everything that was going on around him with bright, wide eyes. Mostly though, he was looking intently at Coco. He gave a high-pitched whinny and stretched to the end of his lead rope, craning his neck to get closer to her.

"Hey, Storm!" Stella said. "Do you want to say hello to Coco?"

Issie nodded. "That's why we're here. Tom says it will be good for Storm to socialise with other horses."

At first, Storm stepped back nervously when Stella led Coco over. After a few moments, though, his curiosity got the better of him and he came closer, stretching his neck out so that he and Coco were touching noses. Coco responded with a stroppy squeal and put her ears flat back, trying to nip at the colt. Nightstorm skittered back to get out of her way.

"Coco! Be nice! He's just a baby," Stella scolded. She stood Coco still and waited for Nightstorm to try again. This time the mare reluctantly seemed to accept the colt's presence. They nickered to each other softly, as if they were making horsey conversation, and within a few minutes they were standing quite happily together.

"Where's Kate?" Issie wondered.

"She's waiting for the farrier," Stella said. "Toby threw a shoe."

"We have to get her to introduce Toby to Nightstorm too," Issie said. "Maybe the three of them will be best friends – just like us."

Issie, Stella and Kate had been inseparable from the moment they met. Issie's mum always said that the girls were so alike they must be sisters. This was kind of a joke, because the three of them didn't actually look anything like each other. Issie had olive skin and long, dark straight hair just like her mum. Stella was a redhead with curls and freckles and Kate was tall and lanky with short-bobbed blonde hair and pale blue eyes. "Never mind looks. On the inside, where it matters, you three girls are cut from the same cloth," Mrs Brown would say, smiling and shaking her head. "Utterly horse-mad!"

Issie looked at her watch. Quarter to nine. The rally was about to start and she was absolutely dying of thirst. She had just enough coins in her pocket to use the drinks machine in the clubroom.

"Stella," she said, "can you do me a favour? Can you watch Storm for a couple of minutes? I want to get a drink."

"I want one too. I'll come with you," Stella said.

Issie shook her head. "Tom said I shouldn't leave Storm alone by himself."

Stella looked at Storm, who was happily nibbling at his hay net. "He's not alone. He's with Coco," she said. "He'll be fine. We'll only be a minute."

"I know, but…" Issie wasn't sure about this, but she didn't want to be a drama queen. After all, they were only going to the clubroom.

"OK, OK!" she caved. "But we have to be quick, all right?"

The two girls raced across the paddock to the clubroom and bounded up the steps. Issie dug into her pockets and hastily fed the change into the drinks machine. She listened for the clunk-clunk, and then stuck her hand into the hole to retrieve her can of Coke.

"Ohhh, I might get some crisps too!" Stella said. "I love crisps for breakfast." She grinned at Issie as she put her money in the vending machine.

"Come on. We better get back," Issie said nervously. She was beginning to regret leaving Storm. Avery had been quite firm when he told her not to leave the colt tied up by himself. If anything happened she wouldn't forgive herself.

Issie stepped out of the clubroom and looked back towards the horse float where Storm was tethered. "Ohmygod!" she said.

"What's wrong?" Stella said. But Issie didn't answer her. She had already leapt off the clubroom steps and was sprinting back across the paddock.

Issie could feel her heart pounding in her chest as she ran towards the horse float. Storm was standing where she had left him – but there was a dark figure next to the colt, with one hand grasping Storm's halter.

"Hey!" Issie yelled as she ran across the paddock. "Hey!"

At the sound of Issie's voice, the dark figure turned round. It was a woman. She was dressed in crisp white jodhpurs, long black boots and a black shirt. Her face was hidden behind dark glasses and the dramatic sweep of her long dark hair, but that didn't matter. Issie had recognised her even before she caught a glimpse of her features.

"You came!" Issie's face broke into a broad grin as she ran towards the woman. "I hadn't heard anything for so long, I had almost given up!"

The woman, who had been gently stroking the colt's muzzle, whispered something to the young horse and let go of the halter. She stepped forward to greet Issie, giving her two brisk kisses, one on each cheek, just as the French always do, before wrapping her in her arms in the most enormous hug.

"Isadora!" the woman cried. "*Bonjour!* It is so good to see you once again!"

Issie couldn't believe it. It was Francoise D'arth. The famed French horsewoman, head rider of El Caballo Danza Magnifico, here at Chevalier Point!

The last time Francoise had arrived in Chevalier Point with her troupe of dancing Lipizzaners and Anglo-Arabians she had turned Issie's world upside down.

Francoise had recognised Blaze – only she said her name wasn't Blaze at all, it was Salome and she belonged to El Caballo Danza Magnifico. The mare had been stolen and now they wanted her back. Issie hadn't wanted to believe her, but Francoise had proof. The Frenchwoman was amazed that she had found the mare again. Issie had no choice but to agree to return her. She was totally devastated when Francoise took Blaze away. Then, just when Issie thought she'd lost her beloved mare forever, Blaze was unexpectedly returned to her once more. Francoise claimed that "a mysterious benefactor" had paid handsomely for the mare, with instructions that Blaze be given back to Issie.

Issie had never discovered who this "benefactor" was, or why they had bought her horse back. Whoever it was, she owed them a great debt and she knew it. Blaze was hers for always now. And despite all that had happened, Issie still considered Francoise to be her friend. After all, Francoise didn't own El Caballo Danza Magnifico – she just worked for them. Francoise loved horses as much as Issie did – she was the one who had trained Blaze and she truly understood just how special the bond was between Issie and her pony.

When Issie had found out that Blaze was pregnant and Marius was the father she had written immediately to Francoise D'arth to tell her the exciting news. Francoise hadn't replied, but Issie figured that was because she was away on tour with El Caballo Danza Magnifico. After Storm was born, Issie had written to Francoise again, sending photos this time – and still no reply. And now, suddenly out of the blue, here she was!

Francoise turned her gaze to the bay colt. "He is beautiful, Isadora. Everything you said about him in your letters was true." She ran her hand down Storm's legs, feeling the strength of his bone and muscle. She could not hide the fact that she was impressed by this colt. "He is even more beautiful than in your photos. This horse is destined for greatness."

"I'm glad you like him," said a rather stern voice. Issie turned round to see Tom Avery standing behind her. "Well, this is a surprise!" Avery said with a tone that indicated it was not an entirely pleasant one. "What are you doing here, Francoise?"

"Tom!" Francoise smiled warmly. "It is good to see you again. It has been too long." She stepped forward and greeted him with a kiss on both cheeks. Avery's face betrayed little emotion as he waited for Francoise to continue.

"When I got Isadora's letter telling me that Blaze was in foal to Marius I was so happy," Francoise said. "Then I received the next letter, saying that a foal had been born, and well, of course I was very intrigued. I had to come and meet this colt."

"Really?" Avery cocked an eyebrow at her. Issie noticed

that he still wasn't smiling. "Is that all, Francoise? It's a long way to come just to say hello. I have a feeling that there is something you aren't telling us."

Francoise's cheery smile faded and was replaced by a rather more serious expression.

"*Oui*. Yes. You are right, Tom. There is more to tell you – and much that we need to talk about."

"I thought there might be," Avery said. "El Caballo Danza Magnifico wouldn't send you all the way here just to check on this colt."

Francoise nodded. "You are right." She looked at the colt standing in front of her. "I was told to come here and see for myself whether this young horse was indeed the son of Marius." Francoise paused. "I was told that if Nightstorm had the same great conformation and temperament as his sire then I was to pay as much as you asked and bring him home to Spain."

"Francoise, I don't understand." Issie looked shocked. "You mean you want to buy Nightstorm?"

"*Oui*, Isadora," Francoise nodded. "El Caballo Danza Magnifico have told me that I must – and at any price!"

"But he's my horse! You can't—" Issie began, but Francoise interrupted her.

"Please, Isadora, be calm and listen," she implored.

"The people I work for are very wealthy. They are offering you a great deal of money. This colt, your Nightstorm, is the progeny of their best stallion Marius, and you know that your mare Blaze was once their most favoured of all. You can see how valuable a colt like this might be to the stable..."

"I don't care!" Issie said. She could feel the panic rising in her. She looked pleadingly at her instructor. "Tom? She has no right to take him away from me, does she?"

Avery's frown had deepened, but he said nothing. Issie felt as if her throat had closed over and she couldn't breathe. She was choking as she tried to force the words out.

"Tom!" Her voice was trembling now as she spoke. "Tell her! Storm is mine. They can't do this to me, not again!"

Issie had every reason to be nervous and she knew it. *After all*, she thought to herself, *the last time Francoise D'arth came to Chevalier Point I almost lost Blaze*. Now the Frenchwoman was back and Issie felt her world spiralling out of control once more. Would she lose Storm too?

Chapter 3

Tom Avery wasn't the sort of riding instructor who liked to raise his voice. He never shouted at his pupils; instead he spoke to them with measured, calm authority. It was this very same tone that he used now as he addressed Francoise D'arth.

"Isadora is right, Francoise," Avery said. "The colt is not for sale. I'm sorry you wasted your time on this trip, but I'm afraid you're going to have to go back to El Caballo and explain that Nightstorm can't be bought – at any price."

Francoise nodded solemnly. "If that is your decision I will accept it. But you do not understand everything yet – there is so much more I need to tell you both. We must talk further. May I come and see you again at the farm tomorrow?"

"There's no point in trying to change our minds," Avery said, "but you are our friend, Francoise, and you're welcome any time at Winterflood Farm."

Francoise smiled at this. "Thank you. I shall come over in the morning then, yes? At about nine?"

She glanced again at Nightstorm. The colt had begun to sense that something was going on. His nostrils were flared and he was pawing at the ground anxiously. As Issie reached for his halter to calm him, Nightstorm pulled back and let out a shrill whinny, his head held high and proud.

"Easy, Storm," Issie soothed, stroking his muzzle as the colt trembled with excitement beneath her hands.

"He is restless," Francoise said softly. "It is time for him to go home, yes?" She looked pointedly at Avery as she said this.

He nodded in agreement. "Yes, Francoise. You're right. Maybe it is."

That afternoon back at Winterflood Farm, Issie spent longer than usual grooming and feeding Storm. When she turned him out in his paddock she realised she didn't want to let the colt go. She gave him a long, snuggly hug, scratching him on the rump the way he liked, and stroking his velvet muzzle for ages before she finally slipped the halter off his head and set him loose.

"You're worried about him, aren't you?" Avery said when Issie finally came back to the stables.

"Yes," Issie said. "Aren't you?"

"I know it must be hard," Avery said gently, "after what happened the last time Francoise was here, and everything you went through with Blaze... But Issie, this isn't the same thing at all. Francoise has no claim over this colt. It doesn't matter what she says, Storm's your horse and nothing will change that." Avery reached over and ruffled her hair. "Now go home," he smiled. "I'll see you in the morning."

Mrs Brown took one look at Issie's face when she came through the front door and knew instantly that something was very wrong.

"I get the feeling it didn't go well at the pony club?" Mrs Brown asked.

Issie shook her head. "No, Mum, it went fine... but Francoise was there. She's in town. She's come to see Nightstorm."

Mrs Brown was surprised at this. "Francoise's in town? But I thought you hadn't even heard from her? What does she want?"

"She wants Nightstorm," Issie said. "She's offered to buy him. She's coming to the farm tomorrow morning to meet with me and Tom. We told her that Nightstorm wasn't for sale, but she said she had things to tell us…"

"What do you mean?"

"I don't know," Issie said, "but whatever it is, it can't be good."

Mrs Brown dropped the pile of laundry she had been sorting. "What on earth is Francoise playing at? First of all she doesn't even answer your letters and then she just turns up and demands that you sell her your horse? What time is she coming tomorrow? I can't wait to tell her myself that Storm isn't for sale and give her a piece of my mind!"

Issie shook her head. "It's OK, Mum. I can handle it. It isn't like that…" Issie couldn't believe she was defending Francoise, but in spite of everything she was still convinced that the Frenchwoman was her friend. "Tom has already told her Storm isn't for sale, we're just going to talk about stuff."

"Are you sure?" Mrs Brown arched a sceptical eyebrow.

"You don't need me to come too? You can always call me on my mobile if you like and I can—"

"Mum, really. I'll be OK," Issie managed a smile. "Tom will be there to back me up."

Mrs Brown didn't look convinced, but she let the matter drop and didn't bring it up again that evening.

Issie went to bed that night feeling utterly drained after everything that had happened. Once she was actually in bed, though, she couldn't sleep. She kept thinking about Francoise's strange comment. What did she mean when she said that she had so much more to tell them? Why was Nightstorm so important to El Caballo Danza Magnifico?

Despite her worries, she eventually dozed off, but she'd only been asleep a little while when her subconscious took over and the nightmare began. In her sleep, she tossed and turned, and vivid images flashed through her head as she relived that fateful day at the pony club. The day that Mystic died.

Mystic had been Issie's very first horse. With his swayed back and a dapple-grey coat that had faded with age, he was hardly the best-looking horse in the paddock at Chevalier Point. That didn't matter to Issie, though. She adored Mystic and thought he was the most beautiful horse ever. To her, Mystic would always be the horse that she had loved first, the one who had changed everything.

In her nightmare, Issie was back at the pony club, and it was the day of the accident. It was all happening again, in heart-wrenching slow motion. She saw Goldrush, Toby and Coco break loose, then panic and bolt for the pony-club gates. And then, before she could think it through, she was following on Mystic, galloping after them, trying to head them off before they reached the deadly main highway.

As they struck the road she heard the clean chime of Mystic's horseshoes on the tarmac. The ponies were ahead of them – at any moment they might be hit by a speeding car! She rode Mystic forward, circling the three horses and driving them back up the gravel driveway to the club grounds, getting them clear of the traffic and out of harm's way. Then suddenly Toby, Goldrush and Coco were gone and it was just Issie and Mystic all alone on the road. Issie could hear the low rumble of the truck, smell the diesel and hear the squeal of tyres as the massive vehicle tried to brake. Mystic turned to face the truck, like a stallion squaring up to his opponent, ready to fight. As he did so, he threw Issie back and out of the saddle. Issie felt herself falling. She knew what would happen next because she had been there before. She would be thrown clear of the truck, but Mystic, poor, brave Mystic, would face it head on. And he would die!

"Mystic, no! NO!" Issie screamed. She was still falling, but the ground seemed a long way away. Falling, falling and then – she woke up. Issie sat bolt upright in bed, her heart racing and her sheets soaked with sweat. She found herself gasping, trying to catch her breath, trying to fight back the tears, then giving up and crying again just like she had done that day when she'd woken up in the hospital bed and her mother told her that her pony was dead.

Issie's mum and everyone had tried to help her get over it, but how do you ever recover from losing your best friend? And so she'd sworn she would never ride again. The idea of loving another horse had just seemed impossible.

Then Tom Avery had turned up with Blaze. He told Issie about how the International League for the Protection of Horses had found the mare half-starved and maltreated. Issie knew then that she had no choice but to take the mare on. She poured her heart into helping Blaze and, as the mare got better, Issie's spirit recovered too.

Still, Issie never let go of her love for Mystic. And it turned out that the grey pony never let go of her either.

Issie had always known that her pony was special – but Mystic was much more special than anyone could have realised. He was like a guardian angel for Issie – and for Blaze. After the accident at the pony club, the grey gelding came back to Issie. He returned whenever she really needed him. Not as a ghost, but a real horse.

Mystic had a sixth sense for danger. He had saved Issie's life so many times now she had lost count.

She had dreamt about Mystic before. Her dreams were often a portent of what was to come. As she sat there in bed, Issie became aware of just what the dream meant. There was big danger afoot – she could feel it. A dream like that? It meant Mystic must be here.

Issie jumped out of her bed and raced to press her face up against the window. She peered out into the inky night, trying to see down to the garden below her room. It was raining outside, and large rivulets of water snaked down the pane of glass, blurring her view. There! Something was moving down on the lawn. It was hard to make the shape out clearly in the dark, but it was something big – Issie could see the shadow moving back and forth. Was it Mystic?

Pulling on a sweatshirt over her pyjamas, Issie raced down the stairs and out of the back door into the garden.

The rain was getting heavier now and the grass was squelchy and sodden under her feet.

"Mystic!" she hissed under her breath as she peered into the darkness. "Mystic!" It was so frustrating having to be quiet, but she didn't want to wake her mum.

Issie stood still for a moment, listening carefully. At first, all she could hear was her own heart beating. She began to doubt herself. Perhaps she had simply been having a nightmare. Maybe it didn't mean anything after all? She held her breath now and listened again.

There! She heard it. A soft nicker, the sound of a horse, coming from the far end of the garden. "Mystic!" Issie called again, her voice strained with emotion. This time she heard the whinny quite clearly, and then came the muffled sound of hoofbeats trotting towards her across the well-mown lawn. Out of the darkness, a dapple-grey horse stepped forward to meet her.

"Mystic!"

The bad dream had left Issie so shaken-up that the sight of her pony actually standing right there in front of her made her instantly burst into tears once more. She wiped her cheeks roughly with her sweatshirt sleeve. She had to pull herself together.

"Hey boy," she murmured. She put out her hand to

touch her beloved pony and for a brief moment she wondered if Mystic would disappear again, nothing more than a misty shadow in the rain. Then she felt her fingers close around the coarse, ropey strands of Mystic's long, silver mane, and her hands touched the soft warmth of his dappled coat.

"Hey, Mystic, did you miss me?" Issie smiled. She was so desperately pleased to see her pony, yet his presence sent a chill through her heart. Issie realised immediately that if Mystic was here, then something was wrong. Very wrong.

The grey gelding seemed tense and anxious. He turned away from the house and began to trot back down the lawn towards the far end of the garden. Issie had seen him do this before and she knew exactly what he wanted her to do. Pulling on her boots, she followed him in the darkness, heading for the gate at the end that led to the street. Issie swung the gate open, taking hold of the pony by his mane so that he stood parallel to it. Then she climbed the wooden gate to the third rung and, without a second thought about what she was doing, leapt on to the grey pony's back.

Issie took a moment to get her balance, then tapped the pony lightly with her heels. He responded instantly, moving off at a brisk trot. As soon as they reached the grass verge of the road, Issie urged Mystic on from a trot into a loping canter. She had no saddle and the canter was less bouncy and easier to ride bareback. Issie had no reins either, but it didn't matter. She could have guided Mystic with her legs, but she knew better than to try and steer the pony. After all, Mystic had come to her with a warning and that meant he knew exactly where he was going. All Issie needed to do was wrap her hands into his long mane and hang on.

She gripped his mane tightly and bent down low over his neck as the rain began to fall harder. She realised she had been stupid to race out in weather like this, without changing into her jodhpurs and raincoat. Already she was chilled to the bone as the wind whipped her icy skin and the rain soaked her pyjamas. It was too late to worry about that now, though. Beneath her, Mystic's canter was almost hypnotic, rhythmic and steady, as his hooves pounded a tempo on the grass verge. There was no turning back.

Issie still had no idea where they were going. It wasn't until they had been riding for almost ten minutes when she saw tall rows of poplar trees rising up in front of them and realised they had reached the banks of the river. As Mystic turned along the esplanade she guessed they were heading towards Winterflood Farm. She felt a

chill up her spine. *Nightstorm was at Winterflood Farm.*
This couldn't be a coincidence – the arrival of Francoise
D'arth and now Mystic? No. It was clear that all of this
had something to do with the bay colt.

Beneath her, Mystic's strides lengthened as he reached
the wide grass strip that ran along the banks of the river.
They had ridden this path once before in the dark and
Issie had trusted Mystic then to get her there, just as she
did now. Instead of trying to slow the grey pony down, she
leant down low over Mystic's neck and let him gallop. If
Nightstorm really was in danger then they had to move
fast. There wasn't a moment to lose.

Minutes later, the clatter of Mystic's hooves on the
gravel driveway announced their arrival at Winterflood
Farm. As Mystic slowed to a trot, Issie vaulted off his back
and hit the ground running. She sprinted around the side
of Avery's house, taking the short cut past the tack room
and out the back of the house. She had put Nightstorm in
the magnolia paddock when they came back from pony
club. Her eyes flitted across the paddock now. She couldn't
see the colt anywhere.

"Storm?" Issie's voice was trembling as she called out
to the colt. "Storm?"

She fought her rising panic, took a deep breath, pursed

her lips and blew. Once, and then a second time. Storm always came when she whistled.

Issie strained her eyes in the darkness, looking for the colt. She couldn't see a thing. She tried shouting out his name again.

This time, the lights in the house went on and a few moments later Tom Avery emerged from the back door.

"Issie? I thought I heard you…" Avery was half asleep on the back porch of the cottage, tying his dressing gown and rubbing his eyes. "What on earth are you doing? It's the middle of the night!"

"Tom?" Issie said. "Where's Nightstorm? He's not in his paddock."

Avery shook his head.

"The weather report was for thunderstorms so I moved him inside. He's in the stables…"

Before Avery had finished speaking Issie was already moving, running hard towards the stables. Avery shouted something else after her, but she couldn't make out what he said. All she could hear was the rush of her own heartbeat, pounding in her ears.

When she reached the stables, she realised that Avery must have gone back inside to switch on the mains for the stable lights because they suddenly flickered to life above her head. There were three loose boxes in Avery's stables. The two at the far end were open and empty, but the one closest to the entrance was bolted shut. This was the stall that Avery usually kept Storm in, and Issie raced towards it now. With trembling fingers, she tried to open the door and was driven into a frenzy of frustration when she found that her hands were so numb from the cold it was impossible to work the bolt loose.

"Here!" A voice said. "It gets stuck sometimes. Better let me do it." Avery was standing behind her. He was dressed in his boots and an oilskin, which he must have stopped to pull on before following her, and Issie suddenly realised how mad she must look in comparison, standing here in her soaking-wet pyjamas and sweatshirt in the middle of the night. She stood aside and let Avery step forward to work the bolt loose and swing the stall door open.

When Avery opened the door Issie felt stunned disbelief. She had been expecting to find her colt injured or sick, but instead she was staring at an empty stall.

"I don't understand!" Avery said. "I locked him in myself!"

Maybe I'm still asleep, Issie thought, *maybe this isn't real. It's all part of the dream.* She wished it were true, but the prickle of the goosebumps on her freezing skin told her otherwise. She was wide awake and she understood now why Mystic had come to her tonight. She had dreamt that she was losing her horse, the most precious thing in the world. Now, in a sickening rush, she realised the nightmare was real. Once again, she had lost the thing that was most precious to her. She was too late. Nightstorm was gone.

Chapter 4

A quick investigation of the stables by Avery confirmed their suspicions that the colt had been stolen.

"Whoever it was must have broken into the tack shed as well," he said as he rejoined Issie. "They've used boltcutters to get in, but they didn't take anything – except Nightstorm's halter."

Avery looked at Issie, who was shaking like a leaf in her dripping-wet pyjamas. "You must be freezing!" he said. "We'd better get inside. We're not helping Nightstorm standing out here. We have to figure out what to do next."

Issie didn't move. When she finally spoke her words came out in a stutter because she was shivering, her lips blue and trembling from the cold. "We… we… need to find Francoise."

Issie and Avery were both thinking the same thing. Nightstorm's disappearance had to be connected to the sudden arrival of Francoise D'arth. The question was, how exactly was the mysterious Frenchwoman involved?

While Issie dried herself off and changed into one of Avery's sweatshirts and a pair of tracksuit bottoms, Avery phoned the number that Francoise had given them the day before when they'd met at the pony club.

Issie could hear him speaking briefly on the phone. She finished getting dressed, rolling up the sleeves of the sweatshirt so that her hands were poking out of the ends, and came into the kitchen to find Avery putting the kettle on.

"I'm making us some coffee to warm you up," he said. "You were like a block of ice out there in your pyjamas. How did you end up here in the middle of the night, anyway?"

"I… ummm… I had a bad dream," Issie said. "I guess I was half asleep when I left home, and I didn't think of getting changed and… anyway, what did Francoise say? Did you speak to her?"

"You could say that."

"What do you mean?"

"It was a pretty quick conversation. I told her what had happened and she said to wait for her to arrive before we did anything," Avery said. "She's on her way here now."

"Shouldn't we call the police too?" Issie said.

Avery shook his head. "She made me promise to wait until she arrived."

They didn't have long to wait. Francoise must have driven to Winterflood Farm like a demon, because by the time Avery was pouring the coffee they could hear her car pulling up in the driveway outside. Francoise swept into the living room. There were none of the usual cheek kisses or *bonjours* – she was tense as a cat that was about to pounce. Her face was dark with fury.

"When did this happen?" she demanded. "How long has the colt been missing?"

"Hey!" Avery said. "I think we're the ones who should be asking the questions here, Francoise. From the way you're acting now it's obvious you knew that the colt was in danger. Who's taken him? Is it someone from El Caballo Danza Magnifico? Is that why you're here?"

Francoise seemed deeply offended by this accusation. "Of course not! How could you even think that El Caballo would do something like that?"

"Well," Avery said, "it's a bit of a coincidence, don't you think? You turn up here one day offering to buy the colt and now he's gone? I think you need to tell us, Francoise. What's going on?"

Francoise shook her head. "We don't have time for explanations," she insisted. "For every moment that we speak they are getting further away with the colt."

"All right," Avery said. "If we don't have much time, then you'd better explain fast, Francoise. Tell me everything and then I'm calling the police."

"No! No police!" Francoise instructed. "I know these men and they are ruthless. If they think the police are involved they will kill Nightstorm. I will call my contacts and see what can be done, but I suspect it is probably too late. By now they will already have him on the plane."

"Plane?" Issie felt as if all the air had suddenly been sucked out of the room. She couldn't breathe, she couldn't think. What was going on here? What was Francoise talking about? "Francoise? What's happened to Nightstorm? Where is my horse?"

The Frenchwoman looked at Issie. "Isadora. I can understand how this looks, but believe me, El Caballo Danza Magnifico did not take your Nightstorm. But you are right, I do have something to do with this. When

I told you yesterday that I had been sent by El Caballo Danza Magnifico I was telling the truth. They sent me here to buy Nightstorm and bring him back to Spain. However, I did not tell you that I was also sent here to protect the colt."

"Protect him? Protect him from who?" Issie was confused.

"When I told my riders at El Caballo Danza Magnifico that Blaze was having Marius's foal, they were so excited," Francoise said. "In fact, soon the news of Nightstorm's birth was the talk of the local village." She shook her head ruefully. "Harmless gossip – or so I thought at the time. I didn't see the danger in it. I was stupid. I should have known that once certain men found out, they would do anything to get their hands on a colt born with such a bloodline."

"Do you mean one of the staff at El Caballo has taken him?" Issie asked.

"No, no!" Francoise seemed frustrated that no one grasped what she was saying. "Not from our farm. It is our rivals who have taken the colt! El Caballo Danza Magnifico is not the only great stud farm in Andalusia. There are others that also breed horses. These horsemen know only too well how valuable the progeny of a stallion as great as Marius can be. Especially now, with the race so near, and so much to lose…"

"Race? What are you talking about?" Avery shook his head in bewilderment. "Listen, Francoise, I know you say time is running out, but if these men already have Nightstorm on a plane to Europe then there's no way we can catch them now. Let's all take a deep breath. I think you'd better tell us everything, and start at the beginning this time."

Francoise looked as if she was about to argue with Avery, but then let out a heavy sigh, as if admitting defeat. "You are right. It is too late anyway to stop them. We might as well speak about this now." She shook her head sorrowfully. "I intended to tell you everything when I came here this morning, but not under these circumstances. This development is most unfortunate."

"You could put it that way," Avery said darkly. Then he softened. "I was making coffee just now. Would you like some?"

"*Oui*, yes please." Francoise managed a weak smile as she pulled out a chair and sat down at the kitchen table. Issie sat beside her while Avery poured them all a cup of coffee, and Francoise began her story.

"In Andalusia, where El Caballo Danza Magnifico has its stables, there are many famous horse estates, or *haciendas* as we know them in Spain. Each hacienda, of course, believes that they breed the best horses in the world." Francoise took a sip of her coffee and continued. "Over the centuries there have been many arguments over whose stable had the very best horses of all. And then one day, many decades ago, the haciendas joined together and decided to find out once and for all."

"And so they held a race?" Issie said.

"*Oui*, exactly," Francoise continued, "but not just any race, Isadora. This race was held in the middle of the village square, near the Sierra de Grazalema mountains. Twelve stables were invited to enter a horse in the race. One horse and one rider from each of the twelve, representing the most prominent and prestigious stud farms in Andalusia. The winning stable would be proven to have the best horses in all of Spain." Francoise paused. "There was much at stake in this race. To win meant great honour. To lose, to fail in this race meant great misfortune for your stable. You see, the winner would be allowed to handpick five of the very best horses from each of the other eleven haciendas. Imagine that! If you lost the race you would lose your greatest treasure – the best five horses in your herd!"

Francoise saw the look on Issie's face as she realised what this meant.

"You see how important this race is," she continued. "The winning hacienda would strengthen their bloodlines with the best horses from each of their rivals' stables."

Avery interrupted, "I've heard of this race, Francoise. They call it the race for the Silver Bridle. But I thought it was just a legend, something the *vaqueros*, the Spanish cowboys, took part in a long time ago."

Francoise shook her head. "The race is not dead. It has continued throughout the generations – it happens every ten years. Even now, in modern times, the race is as important as it ever was. Each stable wants desperately to win."

"And now the race is here again?" Issie asked.

"*Oui*," Francoise said. "Yes, Isadora. It is here again. El Caballo Danza Magnifico have selected the best horse in our stables, the stallion Marius, to run for us. If he wins, then we may take our pick of all the best bloodlines from the best stables in Andalusia. If he loses, then we lose our best horses too, just like the rest."

"I still don't understand," Issie said. "What does this have to do with Nightstorm? He's only a colt. He's far too young to race."

"You are right, of course," Francoise said. "He is too young to run. But he is the son of Marius – his bloodlines are beyond value. If we do lose the race then the winning stable will choose our best five horses to take. I do not doubt that they will choose Marius. We have only one other foal by him and he will get chosen also. And then where will that leave us? That is why I was sent here. At least if we had your colt then we would have a son of Marius and the bloodline could continue." Francoise looked worried. "Unfortunately, I was not the only one who realised this. Another rival hacienda had the same idea. Only they did not come here to buy your colt. They came to steal him."

"What will they do with him?" Issie asked.

"They will take him back to Spain, where they will hide him at their stud farm until the race is over," Francoise said. "You are right, Tom – I hate to admit it, but there is no point in trying to stop them now. These men will have been watching, planning and anticipating us, and will already have him on a plane. They have much money and great resources. They know the value of the son of Marius and they will stop at nothing to get him."

"But they can't just steal my horse and get away with it!" Issie couldn't believe what she was hearing. "Even if they get Nightstorm back to Spain, the police there must be able to arrest them!"

Avery agreed. "We should call Interpol. The international police. They must be able to act, force these men to give Nightstorm back."

Francoise shook her head. "And how will you prove to them that he is your colt? He has no brand, no microchipping, no papers. It seems unlikely, does it not, that a young girl in New Zealand would own one of the best Spanish colts with the finest bloodlines in Andalusia? No. Without proof that the colt is yours, the police will never believe you."

"Then what do you suggest?" Avery asked.

"I suggest that you leave it to me," Francoise said. "El Caballo Danza Magnifico will get Nightstorm back. We too have great resources – and we also have much to lose."

Much to lose? Issie couldn't believe it. Surely no one had more to lose than she did? Storm was her colt. She thought about how he must be feeling right now, all alone in a horse box, being loaded on to a plane, wondering where Issie was, feeling scared.

Issie was scared too, but at that moment she realised she had to put her fears aside. She had to be brave. Storm needed her.

"I want to come!" The words came as a shock to her even as she blurted them out.

"What?" Francoise was confused.

"Take me with you to Spain. If this rival stable, whoever they are, has my colt, then I'm coming with you to get him back."

"Impossible," Francoise stated firmly. "It is too dangerous. It is best that you leave this to us."

"Storm is the one who's in danger! He's never even been away from home without me before. He must be terrified!" Issie was shaking, not with the cold this time, but with anger. "I can't stay here and do nothing while they have him. I have to try and get him back. Please, Francoise."

Francoise turned to Avery for support. "Tell her that she is being ridiculous, Tom."

"I wish I could, Francoise," Avery replied, "but I'm afraid I'm on Issie's side. We can't be expected to wait here, not knowing what has happened to Nightstorm. If we come with you, surely there is a chance that we can negotiate directly with these men. We can make them see sense. I certainly think it's better than sitting here and doing nothing."

"We?" Francoise looked at him. "So now you are coming too?"

"It looks that way, doesn't it?"

Francoise sighed and shook her head. "You are both

impossible, I think. But you are also right. I would do the same if I were you. I will book the air tickets. El Caballo Danza Magnifico will pay your fares. There is a plane leaving tomorrow night. We should be on it. Pack your bags, and organise your passports. I will call you with details later and meet you at the airport."

And with that, Francoise disappeared out the door. There was the sound of her car squealing on the gravel driveway outside and she was gone.

"Well," Avery said, looking at Issie. "Looks like we're off to Spain then." His face dropped suddenly and Issie could tell from his expression that he had just remembered something. "Don't you have school tomorrow?"

Issie did have school tomorrow. In fact she had another whole week of school to go before the winter-term break. However, this was the least of her problems. She might have been able to convince Francoise to let her come to Spain, but convincing her mum to let her go halfway around the world to track down the horse thieves who had taken her colt? That would be flat-out impossible.

"Let me speak to your mother," Avery suggested. "I'm sure if I explain she'll listen to me."

"You must be kidding!"

It turned out that Avery was being a little optimistic when he said that Mrs Brown would listen to him. They had woken her at 6 a.m. and tried to put her in a good mood before they popped the question by making her breakfast. But it soon became clear that it would take more than bacon and eggs to bring her round.

"You expect me to let Isadora go to Spain with you to hunt down horse thieves?" Mrs Brown shook her head in disbelief. "Tom! This is crazy and you know it!"

"Mrs B," Avery began, "it's perfectly safe. We'll go over there and prove the colt is ours, talk to the authorities if necessary…" He locked eyes with Issie's mum. "Amanda, you must trust me. You know I would never put Isadora in any danger. But this is the best chance we have of getting the colt back."

"Why don't you just call the authorities and let them handle it?" Mrs Brown said.

"Call who exactly? Interpol aren't going to chase around Andalusia to get a girl's horse back for her!" Avery said. "Believe me, Amanda, if I thought there was any other way…"

Mrs Brown shook her head. "Then maybe we have no choice, Tom. Maybe we'll just have to let Nightstorm go."

Issie felt the blood freeze in her veins. "Mum? You can't mean that!"

"Issie, I can't let you go over there by yourself!"

"But I won't be going by myself!" Issie said. "Tom will be there, and Francoise too! They'll look after me. And I'll call you every day."

"This is madness, Issie. Apart from anything else you'll be missing school."

"Last week of term is just a muck-about week, Mum – everyone knows that. I've finished all my work." Issie looked at her mother with pleading eyes. "I'm fourteen years old. I'm old enough to do this."

"You're still my baby," Mrs Brown objected.

"And Storm is my baby," Issie countered, "and he's out there right now on his own and he's probably terrified. He needs me." She paused. "Mum, I can't leave him with those men. I can't just pretend that Nightstorm doesn't exist and go on with life. He belongs here, with me and with Blaze. I have to get him back. And you have to let me go."

Mrs Brown looked at her daughter's face, the strong determined set of her jaw, and the fierce wilfulness that burned in her. They were so alike, mother and daughter – both with their long, dark hair, willowy limbs and olive skin. But there were differences between them too – Issie was so headstrong, and so independent, just like her Aunty Hester. Mrs Brown was always amazed by the ferocity of the passion that her daughter possessed. Her love for her horses was beyond anything she had ever seen before. At that moment Mrs Brown realised that if she prevented Issie from doing this, she would be destroying that passion, crushing the spirit out of her daughter. No matter how painful, how terrifying it was, she had to make a choice.

"Issie," she said softly. "I hope I'm not going to regret this…"

"Mum! Please—" Issie began to argue, but her mother raised a hand.

"Don't," she said, shaking her head. "Don't fight me, Isadora. Just listen… because I'm telling you that I'm going to let you go."

Chapter 5

The man behind the glass wall gave Issie a stern look as she approached him, dragging her suitcase. "Documents!" he snapped as she fumbled in her pockets and pulled out her airline ticket and her papers. His expression softened when he opened her passport.

"You are from New Zealand?" He raised an eyebrow. "It is a long way to come to Madrid – halfway around the world!" His strict face broke into a kindly smile.

It had been a long way. Twenty-four hours in the plane without a proper stop. Over that time Issie had watched five movies and eaten three dinners – the plane never seemed to serve lunch or breakfast, it was nothing but never-ending dinnertime.

Issie's inner body clock felt completely mixed up by the

time they landed in Madrid. It was midday in Spain, which meant that right now, back home in New Zealand, it was midnight. Even weirder, she suddenly found herself baking hot. It was summer! Issie couldn't believe it. Yesterday she had been freezing in the cold and rain of winter, and now here she was on the other side of the world and it was a glorious, sunny day.

Francoise had warned Issie to pack for the summer heat with T-shirts and shorts, but she had still boarded the plane in her winter clothes. As she emerged from the air-conditioned airport on to the street outside she began to swelter instantly in her sweatshirt and jeans. The long flight had left her feeling sticky and exhausted. Her brain was swimming, and she was finding it hard to think straight.

"You've got jetlag," Avery told her. "Did you sleep at all on the plane?"

Issie had tried to sleep, but every time she closed her eyes all she could think about was Storm. Where was the colt now? Was he already here in Spain? Did horses get jetlag too? Did Storm feel just like she did? She wished she could be there with him, to let him know it was going to be OK, that she was coming for him and that she was going to bring him home again.

"We'd better get moving," Francoise said as they wheeled their suitcases through customs. "The next train from Madrid to Seville leaves in less than an hour."

The train station in Madrid turned out to be a giant tropical glasshouse. In the centre of it, enormous palm trees sprouted out of the ground, their thick, green leaves creating a jungle canopy. It wasn't like any train station Issie had ever seen. And the train wasn't like anything she had ever seen either. It was shaped like a space rocket.

"It goes like a rocket too!" Francoise laughed when Issie told her this. "Three hundred kilometres an hour. We'll be in Seville in a couple of hours from now and from there we drive on to El Caballo Danza Magnifico."

Tiredness finally overwhelmed Issie as they settled into their seats and she curled up, using her bag as a pillow, to be rocked asleep by the steady rhythm of the train.

It felt like she had only just drifted off when she was being woken up again, Avery's hand on her shoulder shaking her gently. "Issie, we're here."

Groggy from her nap, Issie followed Francoise out to the street.

"Alfie is supposed to be meeting us with the car," Francoise said as she scanned the parking lot. Her face broke into a broad smile as she spied a beaten-up old

Land Rover heading towards them. "There he is!"

The Land Rover pulled up and the boy behind the wheel gave a cheery wave before opening the door and leaping out to join them on the pavement. "Alfie!" Francoise gave the boy a kiss on both cheeks. "These are my friends, Isadora and Tom."

She turned to introduce the boy to them. "This is Alfonso. He is head of the stables at El Caballo Danza Magnifico." Issie's first thought when she'd seen Alfonso pull up in the Land Rover was that he looked a little bit like Aidan. He was about Aidan's age, with the same mop of dark hair. Now that he was standing right in front of her, Issie realised that Alfonso didn't really look like Aidan at all. He was much more tanned, and he had dark brown eyes that smiled readily whenever he did. His features were different from Aidan's too. Aidan's face was delicate and fine-boned, while this boy had the broad, rugged looks of a Spanish film star.

If he was good-looking though, Issie didn't really notice. It was sad but true that she was pretty much too lovesick over Aidan to look at any other boy. This wouldn't have been so sad if it weren't for the fact that she hadn't even seen him since he'd kissed her goodbye that day on the cherry tree lawn at Blackthorn Farm. It was so unfair, Issie thought, to finally, officially have a boyfriend, and never get to actually be near him. She longed to gaze once more into those pale blue eyes that Aidan kept half hidden under that long, dark fringe…

"Issie?" She was shaken out of her Aidan daydream by the sound of Avery's voice intruding sharply into her thoughts.

"Issie!" The voice prodded a second time. "Wake up! I said to give your bag to Alfonso so he can load it into the car."

"Sorry." Issie shook herself back to reality and reached out to hand Alfonso her bag. "I guess I'm a bit jetlagged."

Alfonso gave Issie a broad grin and took her bag.

"That's OK," he said. "How was your trip? Was the food on the plane actually, like, food, or was it totally gross?"

"You speak English!" Issie exclaimed with relief. She didn't know any Spanish and had been terribly worried that she wouldn't be able to understand a word that anyone said.

"Yeah," Alfonso said casually, "I picked it up from touring with El Caballo – we're overseas a lot with the horses so most of us know lots of languages. We can all speak English really well." He picked up Issie's bag and threw it in the back of the Land Rover and opened the passenger door for her. "Come on, *vamos*!" he said.

Issie looked at him blankly and didn't move.

"*Vamos* – that means 'let's go'!" Francoise laughed as she offered Issie the front seat next to Alfonso. Francoise and Avery climbed into the back seat, Alfonso put his foot down on the accelerator and the Land Rover roared into life, heading down the cobbled streets, making its way through the busy city towards the outskirts of town.

Within an hour they had left Seville and the Land Rover began to climb through the forest-clad hills of Andalusia. As Alfonso turned off the main road, pale dust flew up from beneath the car tyres and they began to make their way along remote dirt tracks through the rugged farmland that led to El Caballo Danza Magnifico. The Land Rover bumped and skipped along the potholed road, dust flying in through the open windows. Issie clung on to her seatbelt to stop herself being thrown about as the car bounced around.

Issie looked over at Alfonso, who was focused on the road. "You know, you don't look old enough to be driving this car, and you certainly don't look old enough to be the head of the stables."

Alfonso raised an eyebrow. "You're not happy with my driving?"

"No, I didn't mean that!" Issie stammered. "I'm sorry, that came out sounding really rude! I just meant—"

Alfonso grinned. "It's OK. I'm just joking. You're right. I'm only eighteen. Most of the riders at El Caballo are much older than me. But I've been in the saddle since the day I was born. It is in my blood."

Francoise leaned forward from the back seat to explain. "Alfie is the son of Roberto Nunez, the owner of El Caballo Danza Magnifico. Roberto is one of Spain's greatest horsemen. He once rode for the Spanish eventing team at the Olympics. As a rider in this country his career remains unrivalled."

"But your dad doesn't ride any more?" Issie said.

"Yeah, he still rides," Alfonso shrugged. "He's the one responsible for training all of our best stallions for the performing school. But he doesn't like to tour. He prefers the quiet life here in Spain with the herd."

"Will Roberto be there when we arrive?" Avery asked.

Alfonso nodded. "He went out this morning to bring in some of the mares, but he should be there to meet us when we get to the hacienda. It's not much further now. We'll be there soon. We're already on land that belongs to El Caballo. These olive trees that you see around you were planted by us. We grow oranges and olives here in the dry hills and the horses graze down in the valley, where the pasture is better."

"How long have you lived here?" Issie asked.

"All my life," Alfonso replied. "El Caballo has been my family's home for two centuries."

Francoise spoke up again from the back seat. "This place is steeped in tradition. When I left France and the Cadre Noir de Saumur to come and work here, I did not realise how long it would take to be accepted." Francoise laughed. "For the first five years they would call me 'the new girl'. It was a joke, of course, but it took them a long time to grow tired of it. Then, finally, one day, they said 'she is one of us now'. I have been here for ten years, and sometimes I still feel like I am the new girl…"

As Francoise was talking the Land Rover had been bumping and bouncing its way along the dirt road through the olive-clad hills. Now, as they came over the crest of the range, Issie looked down into the valley below. The sight that greeted her was one of the most beautiful she had seen in her entire life. The sunburnt fields were dotted with snow-white horses, mares with their coal-black foals at foot. To see these horses running free as a herd was like bringing a fairy story to life.

"Ohmygod! They are so beautiful!" Issie breathed.

Francoise nodded. "They are the very best mares. Roberto has a true eye for horses and it is his mastery that has made El Caballo Danza Magnifico stables the most respected in all of Spain. We have almost fifty horses here – stallions, mares and foals. Roberto loves his Spanish-bred Lipizzaners and also the Andalusians and his prized Anglo-Arabs – the bloodline of your mare Blaze."

The beauty of the horses was almost eclipsed by the sight of El Caballo itself. The grand, classical Spanish buildings of the hacienda were arranged around a cobbled courtyard with palm trees and fountains, and surrounding the estate was a high wall made of whitewashed stone. The entrance was marked by enormous black wrought-iron gates, which Alfonso drove through while Francoise pointed out the four main buildings of the hacienda.

"I will give you the full tour later," she said, "but in the meantime, let me quickly explain." She pointed to the building straight ahead of them. It was a rich golden mustard colour, the same colour, Issie noted, as the dirt under their car tyres. "That is the mares' stable block," Francoise said. Issie peered at the Spanish arches and could make out rows of loose boxes inside, set into archways of mosaic tiles.

Francoise gestured to the building next to it, which was larger still, with whitewashed walls this time, edged in the same mustard-ochre hue. "Our indoor arena is bigger than an Olympic arena," Francoise said. "We need as much space as possible to train the horses in the *haute école* movements and routines for our shows."

On the other side of this arena was yet another stable block with Spanish archways at the front. "The stallions' stables," Francoise explained. "We like to keep their quarters at a distance from the mares, of course."

Alfonso drove around the fountain, doing a lap of the courtyard, and then pulled the car up outside the front door of the most beautiful of all the buildings. It was a two-storey, stately Spanish villa, also with a grand archway surrounding the front door. To one side of the entrance, vines of brilliant orange and hot-pink bougainvillea grew against the white walls, their blooms splashing the villa with brilliant colour. Wrought-iron window boxes on the top floor were filled with candy-pink geraniums, spilling out and tumbling over the ledges. Seville orange trees groomed and shaped into tall topiary, stood on either side of the front steps that led to the door.

"This is the main house. You will be staying here with us for the duration of your visit," Francoise said.

Issie stepped out of the car and gazed around her in

disbelief. She smiled at Avery. "Can you believe this place?" she asked.

"I've heard a lot about it, but I've never—" Avery began, but he was interrupted by the rumble of horses galloping towards them.

Francoise looked up at the wrought-iron gates of the compound. "That will be Roberto now. He is bringing in the Anglo-Arabian mares from the far fields in the upper pasture where they have been grazing for the past weeks."

The rumble grew louder, and then suddenly Issie saw the first of the Anglo-Arabs appear through El Caballo's entranceway. For a moment her heart leapt – the mare cantering towards her across the cobbled courtyard looked just like Blaze! She was a deep liver chestnut, with a flaxen blonde mane and tail. Behind the mare ran half a dozen others just like her, some of them with matching colts and fillies at their feet. Issie's smile grew wide as she gazed at the beauty of these mares. They seemed to know exactly where they were going, trotting obediently through the main gates and across the courtyard to the stable block, each of them choosing a different archway to duck and weave through as they headed towards their loose boxes.

"They are like homing pigeons!" Francoise grinned.

Issie heard the crack of a stock whip at the gates and

saw that there were three men on horseback following the golden chestnut mares. Two of these men were on bay Andalusian horses, beautiful animals with long flowing black manes and elegant arched necks. The third man rode the most beautiful horse, an enormous dapple-grey stallion with a high-stepping trot and the most graceful physique of them all. Issie knew the stallion on sight – it was Marius! Nightstorm's sire.

The man riding Marius gave orders in Spanish to the other two riders, who followed in on their horses after the mares. Then he wheeled the great, grey stallion about on his hocks and cantered gracefully over to the steps of the villa where Francoise, Alfonso, Issie and Avery stood.

He leapt down out of the saddle and smiled at Issie. He was a handsome man, with the dark, swarthy skin of a Spaniard, kind eyes and thick waves of black hair. Tall and lean, he wore cream jodhpurs and long black boots. On the pocket of his white shirt a red C had been embroidered with the shape of a red heart set inside it. It was the same symbol, Issie realised, that she had seen branded on the haunches of the horses as they raced in to their stalls. The same symbol too, was printed in blood-red on the golden flag that flew at the gates of the compound. Of course! The C with the heart in the middle was the brand of El Caballo Danza Magnifico, Issie realised. And this man standing in front of them now had to be the owner of El Caballo Danza Magnifico, Roberto Nunez.

Roberto's smile faded and he looked serious as he locked eyes with Tom Avery. The Spaniard walked past Issie, Alfonso and Francoise and strode directly towards Avery, his face an unreadable mask. He came closer and closer until the two men were almost nose to nose, and then suddenly his face broke into a broad grin.

"Thomas! It has been so long! Too long!" His broad hands grabbed Avery by the shoulders and gave him a shake before he enclosed Avery in a swift bear hug.

The others stood there in stunned amazement as Avery, normally so cool and aloof, hugged him back. "Hello Roberto," Avery said warmly. "It's good to see you again."

"You two know each other?" Issie couldn't believe it.

"Know each other?" Roberto laughed. "Did this old devil not tell you?" He grinned and put an arm around Avery. "This man," he said, "this man, he is my brother!"

Chapter 6

Issie was stunned. Avery was Roberto's brother?

Roberto grinned. "Thomas and I haven't seen each other for twenty years. We met at the World Equestrian Games at Stockholm, Sweden. I was a brash young man, riding for the honour of Spain. Thomas was riding there too – he was the favourite to win against me in the three-day eventing." Roberto turned to Avery. "It was on the cross-country course there that this man gave up the chance for a medal in order to save my life. This is why I say that he is a brother to me. I trust him completely and I shall never forget the debt that I owe him."

Avery shook his head. "You don't owe me anything, Roberto. Anyway, that debt has been repaid many times since with your kindness."

"Wait a minute!" Alfonso was amazed. "You're *the* Tom Avery? Wow! Dad has talked about you for years. I never realised when he sent me to pick up someone called Tom from the train that it would be you. Dad has told me the most amazing stories about you."

"Stories? What kind of stories?" Issie was in shock. To her, Tom Avery was just her pony-club instructor. Sure, he was great with horses and everything, but the idea of him being some kind of legendary figure in this Spanish household was going to take some getting used to. "Why have you never told me before now that you were friends with the man who owned El Caballo Danza Magnifico?"

Avery gave her a wry grin. "I still have a few secrets left, Isadora."

"Issie is not the only one here who is surprised," Francoise said tartly. "Roberto did not mention this to me either."

"Oh, I did not want to bore you with stories of my glory days, Francoise," Roberto smiled. He looked at Issie. "But this is very rude of me! We should not be standing here on the doorstep. Where are my manners? Young lady, you must be tired after your long journey. Come inside! Francoise will show you to your room so that you can freshen up after your long trip." Roberto Nunez gestured towards the front door of the villa. "The guest rooms are ready and waiting. I will give you a chance to settle in. I have work to do myself this afternoon – we can all meet again to talk later at dinner."

Issie stepped inside the front door of the villa and found it to be even grander than she expected. The polished wood floors were strewn with elaborate Moorish rugs, the walls were painted in bright, earthy shades of ochre and tangerine and covered with antique tapestries and paintings of horses.

"Follow me," Francoise instructed, leading Issie past the living room, filled with vases of fresh roses, then the grand dining room and finally the library, its walls lined with books, before they reached the staircase which led to the guest rooms upstairs.

"I hope you will be comfortable here," Francoise said, opening the door. The room was beautiful. The walls were rustic plaster, washed in deepest pink, and the bed was covered with rainbow-striped blankets. Enormous mirrors trimmed with silver frames sparkled and glittered in the sunlight that streamed through the wide glass doors leading out to a private balcony.

"Do you like it?" Francoise crossed the room and drew back the rainbow-striped curtains to reveal a view of the cobbled courtyard below.

"It's amazing!" Issie said. "Everything is amazing. It's so beautiful here!"

"It is, isn't it?" Francoise said, gazing out over the hacienda. "When we travel away on tour with the horses we are gone for such a long time, and then to come home to this – it always makes my heart leap when we return here."

She pointed towards the stable blocks. "You see over there where we keep the mares? Salome – I mean Blaze – was born right there in those stables, in one of the foaling stalls."

Issie stared out of the window and felt a shiver up her spine. She knew Blaze was an El Caballo mare, but it had never occurred to her before now that this farm had once been Blaze's home. Her beautiful chestnut mare was actually born and schooled here, just as the rest of El Caballo's horses were.

"I remember I had only just started working for El Caballo back then," Francoise said dreamily. "It was foaling season and the mares due to have their babies were brought in each night, and I would sleep in the stables, to keep a close eye on them. Blaze's dam, Bahiyaa, was the most beautiful of all the mares in our stables so we were all waiting with great excitement to see what her foal would be like. We were not disappointed

– when Blaze was born we knew immediately that she was special. Oh, she was the most beautiful foal! I wish you could have seen her then! To witness the arrival of a new life, to see a new foal being born, it is so magical."

Issie's smile melted away as Francoise spoke. She too knew what it was like to be the one to deliver a newborn foal. When Blaze had foaled, it was Issie alone who had been there to help Nightstorm enter the world. In the excitement of her arrival here at El Caballo Danza Magnifico she had briefly forgotten the reason they were here in the first place. Her baby, her Storm, was somewhere here in Andalusia.

"You must want to rest now," Francoise was saying. "You have come such a long way. Perhaps you would like to take a siesta? We eat late here in Andalusia – dinner will be served at 10 p.m."

"No, Francoise," Issie said. "I know I should be tired, but I'm not."

Francoise smiled. "I understand. I am not either. I tell you what, why don't you have a shower and change into your jodhpurs? Meet me downstairs in ten minutes and I will take you on a tour of El Caballo and we can talk some more."

Ten minutes later, Issie came downstairs to find Francoise also freshly changed with her long black hair slicked back into a wet ponytail. She was wearing the traditional *vaquero* clothing of the Spanish cowboy – turned-up trousers with brown leather boots, a short cropped jacket known as a *chaquetilla*, and a wide-brimmed stockman's hat. Francoise handed Issie a hat too. "Put this on," she instructed. "The sun is hot here and you'll need it."

Francoise led the way back across the cobbled courtyard. At first Issie thought she was heading to the stables where the mares were, but then they kept walking past the mares' quarters, and Francoise took her past the fountain and through the archway that led to the stallions' loose boxes.

Issie had caught a glimpse of the mares' stables as they went past. They were in the old Spanish style, very traditional, stone stalls as dark and cool as catacombs. She had been expecting the stallions' quarters to be the same, but in fact they were quite different. On the outside they were classically Spanish too, but inside the loose boxes were all stainless steel and pale wood, sleek and ultra-modern.

"Roberto loves the history of El Caballo, but he is not always a traditionalist," Francoise explained as they walked down the row of stalls. "He rebuilt the stallions' quarters to match the best stables he visited when he was competing on the three-day event circuit in Europe."

Francoise reached one hand to the top half of the Dutch door on the first stall, slid the bolt and swung it open. There was a soft nicker from the stall and Marius appeared, craning his neck over the door to greet them.

"You know Marius, of course," Francoise said, reaching her hand up to stroke the nose of the grey stallion. Issie looked at Marius. Even though this horse was a fully grown stallion and Storm was still a colt, Issie could already see striking similarities between father and son. If she had ever had any doubts that Marius was Storm's sire, taking one look at the stallion made her absolutely certain that they shared the same blood. It was evident in the classical topline, the strong neck, shoulders and haunches. Marius was big for a Lipizzaner, almost sixteen-three hands high. Would Storm grow as big as his mighty sire? Would he look like this when he grew up?

Issie felt a shiver run through her. If she didn't find out who had stolen Storm, she might not have the chance to see him grow up at all.

Francoise grabbed a bridle off the hook behind her. "We only have Spanish saddles here, I hope that is OK?

They are quite different from the English ones, so I will show you how to tack up…"

Issie was confused. "We're going riding? I thought we were just taking a tour of El Caballo."

"We are!" Francoise responded brightly. "Did you think I was just showing you around the stables? I meant a tour of the land itself. And for that…" she said as she walked over to the next loose box, "… you will need a horse."

Francoise stood in front of the loose box and made a clucking sound with her tongue. "Come on, Angel," she said, softly coaxing. "It's OK, boy, it's me. I've brought someone to meet you." At the sound of Francoise's voice, the horse at the back of the stall gave a nicker and stepped forward into the light, thrusting his magnificent head out over the Dutch door.

He was a stallion, almost as big as Marius, and so handsome! Issie stared up at him. His face had the elegance of a classical Andalusian, with wide-set, soulful eyes and a dark, sooty muzzle. Unlike Marius, who still had grey dapples, this stallion's coat was absolutely white, as pure as parchment. His mane tumbled over his neck and shoulders, lustrous and pearly, like the foaming white crest of a wave.

The great beauty of this horse made it all the more

upsetting for Issie when she saw the scars. On the bridge of the stallion's nose, just where the noseband would normally sit, was a series of jagged gashes that had healed to form ugly scar tissue. The scars must have been caused by deep cuts into the stallion's flesh. The wounds were so profound they had left these heartbreaking marks as a legacy, destroying the stallion's otherwise perfect beauty.

Issie reached out a hand and touched the stallion's muzzle. He gave a soft nicker as she gently stroked his noble face, her hand running over the bumps and lumps, as if she were reading them like Braille beneath her fingers.

"How did he get these?" Issie asked Francoise.

"They were part of his training," Francoise said quietly. Issie was shocked.

"No, no," Francoise shook her head. "Not here. Please understand, Isadora, we did not do this to Angel. It was a rival stable. The hacienda of Miguel Vega. Vega is a great horseman – but a cruel one too. In Spain, there is a special noseband called a *serreta*. The *serreta* has sharp metal teeth that dig into the bridge of the horse's nose until he submits. It is very cruel. Throughout Spain, the *serreta* is considered an instrument of torture and is now banned. However, some horsemen, including Vega, continue to use them, even though it causes the horses unbelievable pain."

Issie ran her hand over Angel's scars once more. "So the *serreta* did this to Angel?"

"Miguel Vega did it to him," Francoise said angrily. "Angel once belonged to him. Vega put the *serreta* on him when he was less than a year old – to break his spirit."

"But if he's Vega's horse, then what is he doing here?" Issie asked.

"The race for the Silver Bridle," Francoise explained. "The winning stable gets to take five horses of their choosing from each of their rivals." Francoise reached out a hand to stroke Angel's silver mane. "When we won against Vega's stable ten years ago, I had just joined El Caballo. I was given the chance to choose a horse myself – and I chose Angel."

"I can see why," Issie said softly. "He's very beautiful."

"*Oui*," Francoise agreed. "But that is not why I chose him. I picked him because of his speed. Angel's bloodlines date back to some of the greatest racehorses in the history of Spain. His sire has won many, many races. And I knew Angel could be fast too. I thought that one day, when he was fully grown, he would be able to defend El Caballo Danza Magnifico against Vega's stables. He would race for us and bring home the Silver Bridle."

"So will he be racing this time," Issie asked, "against the other stables?"

Francoise shook her head. "I do not think so. Roberto wants Alfonso to ride for us in the race. A jockey needs to be light and quick and Alfie is the best in our stables."

"Well, why doesn't Alfonso ride Angel?" Issie was confused.

"Because Angel will not allow it," Francoise said. "Ever since Vega put the *serreta* on him Angel has been afraid of men. He trembles at their touch. He will not allow a male jockey on his back. He has thrown all of our best riders – including Alfie. Of course," Francoise added cheekily, "I'm sure you'll be fine."

"What!" Issie couldn't believe it. "You're joking, right? You don't really expect me to ride him? He'll throw me too!"

"You are not a man, are you?" Francoise smiled. "Angel has never thrown me. He will not throw you. It is only men that he fears, and rightly so, for it was a man – a brutal and cruel man – who did this to him."

"Poor Angel." Issie looked at the stallion's gentle face, those soulful black eyes. "Anyone who could hurt a horse like this must be a monster."

Francoise suddenly went very quiet and didn't respond.

"The brushes are in the stall," she said, changing the subject. "You can groom him while I fetch the saddles."

Grooming Angel proved to be quite different from brushing Blaze or Comet. For starters, the grey stallion was much taller than her horses at home. Issie tried tiptoeing at first and then had to give up and turn the grooming bucket upside down to stand on it so she could reach his mane. It usually took Issie no time at all to whip a comb through Blaze's mane, which was kept pulled short and neat, but Angel's mane was quite different. It was long and silky, like fairy-tale princess hair.

"Aren't you beautiful?" Issie said under her breath as she ran her body brush along the crest of Angel's magnificent neck. Then she caught sight of those scars once more and a shiver ran up her spine.

"Here you go!" Francoise's voice startled her back to reality. She passed Angel's bridle over to her and Issie was shocked when she saw that there were long black leather tassels hanging down the front of the brow band.

Francoise smiled. "Don't worry, it is not a *serreta*. That's just a *mosqueto*, a fly switch – all the horses here wear them."

Issie put on the bridle and then Francoise showed her how to put on the Spanish *vaquero* saddle. It was heavy, and twice the size of Issie's normal saddle, with a sheepskin pad on the top of it.

"It's like sitting in an armchair!" Issie giggled when Francoise legged her up.

Francoise led the two horses out into the courtyard and then mounted Marius. She smiled at Issie. "Have you ridden a stallion before?" she asked.

Issie nodded. "My Aunt Hester has a black warmblood called Destiny."

"Spanish stallions are quite different, you will see," Francoise said. "Angel has a temperament that matches his name. He is a sweetheart. I ride him all the time and he is very fit. Although," she added, "he may be a little fresh. I have not ridden him for two weeks."

Angel was indeed fresh. The stallion fought against Issie's grasp as they rode out into the courtyard, cantering on the spot with eagerness as she held him back.

"Follow me!" Francoise called over her shoulder as she pressed Marius on into a canter and set off across the courtyard towards the wrought-iron gates at the entrance of the hacienda. Issie followed, but she was still holding Angel back to a trot, afraid of the speed the stallion had in him.

Angel was sixteen-two, the same height as Destiny,

but he was much more muscular, with a broad neck and powerful haunches typical of his Spanish breed. Issie could feel the incredible strength this horse possessed, and it scared her. What would happen if she let the stallion get his head? She gripped the reins tight in her fists as they cantered out of the gates, holding Angel back as they trailed behind Marius.

"Are you OK?" Francoise looked back over her shoulder as she cantered on.

"Uh-huh," Issie nodded. She was still holding Angel back tightly.

"Let him have his head a little," Francoise said. "You can trust him."

Issie realised at that moment how she must look up there on Angel's back, her mouth held rigid with fear, hands stiff with nervous tension. She took a deep breath and did as Francoise said, relaxing her shoulders, softening her hands and releasing the reins a little. She was amazed when Angel didn't suddenly bolt off. He relaxed too and fell into a steady stride alongside Marius.

"Good boy!" Issie gave him a slappy pat. She sat up in the saddle and looked around her, beginning to enjoy the ride, taking in the beauty of the El Caballo estate. It was beyond gorgeous here, the fields full of mares and their foals, grazing or sheltering from the heat under the low-hanging boughs of the olive trees.

They cantered on, heading towards the rocky foothills at the rear of the estate, and as the ground underfoot began to get rocky Francoise pulled Marius up to a trot. "The footing is rough from here on," she said. Then she pointed at the hills ahead where bare, grey boulders marked the entrance to a narrow gorge. "We go through here," she said. "Follow me. It gets very narrow at certain points, only wide enough for us to ride in single file, but do not worry, the horses know this path well. It leads to the higher pasture, El Caballo land where the mares and stallions graze when grass is scarce during the dry months."

Francoise clucked Marius on and Issie followed behind. The sheepskin saddle was so comfy she tried riding a sitting trot instead of rising up and down and found it to be quite easy. Angel's trot was floaty, which helped a lot. She was already getting a feel for the stallion's paces, and she was sure that the horse was beginning to understand her aids too, listening to her cues. She could see Angel's ears swivelling back and forth, a sign that he was paying attention to her, as they negotiated their way through the gorge.

Not that Angel had any choice but to keep moving straight ahead. The gorge was narrow, with sheer rockface rising high on either side. Nothing grew here in the pale chalky soil except for a few tufts of tussock sticking out of the cliffs. Issie looked up and saw the gap between the cliffs above her and a thin river of blue sky floating over her head. Then she lowered her eyes to the front once more, her gaze set on Francoise's back as they rode on.

"It is not much further to the other side," Francoise called over her shoulder, anticipating Issie's question. And then, a few moments later, the narrow path became wider again and they were clear of the gorge and out the other side once more with flat, dry pasture stretching out in front of them.

Francoise pulled Marius to a halt. "This is the high pasture, the last of El Caballo grazing lands," she explained to Issie. She pointed ahead of her. "Do you see that orange grove and the brick wall with the turrets beyond the trees?"

Issie nodded.

"That is Miguel Vega's hacienda," Francoise said. "The orange trees mark the point where our land stops and his property begins." Francoise's eyes narrowed against the sun as she stared ahead. "It is only natural, I suppose, that the two best horse studs in Spain should be right beside each other like this," she said. "Vega's family has been here for centuries, just like Roberto's. Their ancestors knew that this lush, fertile land was the best place to raise horses. And it was only natural too, I suppose, that the families would become such great rivals."

Issie reached a hand down to stroke Angel's neck and, as she did so, she caught a glimpse of the stallion's profile and the ugly scars that marred his beautiful face. "I hope I never meet Miguel Vega," Issie said. "If he could do this to Angel then he must be horrible."

Francoise looked tense. "Isadora, I am very much afraid that you may have to meet him." She took a deep breath before the words came stumbling out. "Because we think it is Miguel Vega who has taken Nightstorm."

Chapter 7

Issie would have ridden to Vega's straight away to confront him and demand that he return the colt if Francoise hadn't grabbed at Angel's reins and held her back, calming her down until she saw sense.

"It is useless to go in there angry and without any plan," she said bluntly. "If you really want to get Storm back then we must be smart about it. Miguel Vega went to great lengths to steal your colt – do you really think he will simply hand him back again?"

Even in her fury, Issie had the sense to listen to Francoise. "I should never have brought you here like this," Francoise said. "I am sorry. I know it is hard, but please be patient, now is not the time. You will only endanger your colt if you rush off to face Vega now."

And so Issie cast one last, longing look at Vega's hacienda, and then turned Angel around under Francoise's watchful eye and followed Marius back into the gorge towards El Caballo Danza Magnifico.

She knew Francoise was right. Yet at that moment, turning her back on her colt had been unbearable. To be so near, and still unable to help him, was beyond painful. Francoise reassured her that it wouldn't be long to wait.

"We will get our chance tomorrow – at the *feria*. It is a huge festival, held every ten years to celebrate the race for the Silver Bridle. Vega is bound to be there. Roberto will tell you all about it when we meet for dinner tonight."

Dinner that evening was held in the main dining room and was a grand affair to celebrate the arrival of the guests. Issie hadn't been sure if she would like Spanish food, but everything tasted wonderful – there was deep fried calamari, fresh tomato bread and rich, hearty paella.

Alfonso had clearly been expecting to spend the meal talking to Avery about the good old days and his father's adventures, but Avery fobbed him off.

"I don't know what tall stories your father has told you

about me," Avery grinned, "but that was a long time ago. These days I lead a very quiet life."

"It doesn't sound very exciting," Alfonso said. "Who would give up international eventing to be head instructor at a pony club?"

"Alfie!" Roberto told him off.

"No," Avery said, "I know what he means. When I gave up riding, I had offers of all kinds of jobs, which I suppose you would call glamorous, but I wanted to do something that really helped young riders." He cast a glance at Issie. "Besides, a lot more action happens in Chevalier Point than you might think."

It was Roberto who brought the conversation around to Miguel Vega. As he told everyone at the table about what a monster Vega was and his fears that it was Vega who had taken the colt, Issie and Francoise exchanged looks. Issie wanted to blurt out the news about their ride today to Vega's hacienda, but it was clear from the swift kick that Francoise delivered under the table that it would be best not to mention it. Instead, she remained quiet as Roberto explained about tomorrow's *feria*.

"The parade is a great tradition, a chance for the haciendas to celebrate and show off their best horses before the race the following weekend," he explained.

"I would be honoured if you would both ride alongside us as guests of El Caballo Danza Magnifico."

"So all of the twelve haciendas will be there?" Avery asked. "Including Vega's?"

"*Oui*," Francoise answered him. "Especially Vega's. He would not miss this chance to boast – he expects to win this year. He will be there, riding his best stallion, the black giant Victorioso, the horse that he will ride in the race."

"Vega doesn't have a jockey from his stables who can ride for him?" Avery asked.

"Pah!" Roberto snorted. "Vega is too vain. The tubby old fool believes he is the best horse rider – the only one at his stables who is good enough to ride in the Silver Bridle."

"The rival haciendas assemble in the village square," Francoise continued. "The parade starts at the entrance to the square and follows along the same route where the race will take place."

"I don't understand." Issie was confused. "How can the race take place in the middle of a village square?"

"Isadora," Francoise said, "the Silver Bridle is no ordinary horse race. It is not run on a race track the way your thoroughbreds race in New Zealand. The race is meant to test not only the speed of the horse, but also the courage of the rider, and for this reason the race is run through the very streets of the village, the same way that our ancestors rode it two hundred years ago when the tradition began."

"On the street?" Issie couldn't believe it. She imagined horses running through the narrow dusty alleyways of the Spanish villages she had driven through on her way to El Caballo Danza Magnifico. "That would be suicide!" Issie shook her head.

"It is very dangerous," Francoise agreed. "The village square itself is quite wide, but not wide enough for twelve horses, as you can imagine. There is much shoving and pushing from the riders, and from the crowds who line the streets and cheer for each hacienda."

"How far do the horses run?" Avery asked.

"Three times around the square. Almost two kilometres – the same length as a normal horse race," Francoise said. "But not all of them will make it to the finish line. The course is dangerous and the jockeys are ruthless. They will fight tooth and nail to get a clear space as they gallop and there are always dirty tactics. Every time this race has been run, a horse has fallen. Many have been injured or even died in the course of this race."

"Why don't you just tell them you won't take part in the race? Can't you just say no?"

Alfonso shook his head. "You do not understand how deep this tradition is with us, Isadora. To win the Silver Bridle demands the utmost skill, the greatest courage. It is a test of true manliness. To refuse to race would be the mark of a coward."

"So you'll risk your best horse?" Issie was horrified. "You'll risk Marius, just to prove that you are a man?"

"Do not misunderstand my son," Roberto said. "We do not take this lightly. Yes, there are risks, for Marius, and for Alfonso also. But it is the way of our people, our tradition and our culture. I cannot turn my back on it, and neither can Alfonso. No matter what happens, El Caballo Danza Magnifico will take part in this race, just as we have done now for nearly two centuries."

"Don't you see, Issie?" Francoise looked at her pleadingly. "This is a good thing. If Alfie and Marius win the race, if El Caballo takes the Silver Bridle, then we get to choose five horses from every stable."

"So?" Issie said.

Francoise reached and grasped Issie's hand in her own. "So if we win, we can choose Nightstorm as one of the five. We can get the colt back."

Issie had never expected Roberto Nunez's hacienda to have email access. The traditional Andalusian stone villa was over two centuries old. The very last thing Issie had expected to stumble across was a hi-tech media room.

Issie had found the room by mistake before dinner that evening. She had walked in, thinking it must be the bathroom, and had been confronted by computer screens and electronic gadgets. Francoise had laughed at Issie's amazement when she spoke about it at dinner that night. "El Caballo Danza Magnifico performs around the world. We're a big international business, so naturally we are very well-equipped here."

After dinner, Francoise lent Issie one of the laptop computers from the office. "It is wireless, so you can access the internet and your emails from anywhere in the house, including your room," she explained.

The first person Issie emailed of course was Stella. It was an enormous long email all about everything that had happened so far. Issie told Stella about the shock of discovering that Avery and Roberto were old friends. She described in detail how beautiful and exotic the surroundings were at the hacienda. She wrote about riding Angel for the first time and Francoise's suspicions that Vega was the one responsible for taking Storm.

Stella emailed back immediately and her email was just one line.

Ohmygod! she wrote, **Alfonso sounds really dishy. Is he handsome? I bet he is! He probably looks just like one of the Jonas Brothers!**

Issie groaned when she read it. Typical boy-mad Stella!

Alfonso is really nice, Issie wrote back, **and yes, I suppose he is handsome. But in case you'd forgotten, Stella, I already have a boyfriend — his name is Aidan!**

Issie hadn't forgotten about Aidan. She thought about him all the time, even if she hadn't seen him for months since she left Blackthorn Farm. Aidan had sent her a few emails since then. He had written to say that the film job, the one that had previously fallen through, was now back on and they were back in the movie business. He and Aunt Hester had loads of well-paid work and the farm was now financially secure.

She was about to start on an email to Aidan when there was a knock at the door and Avery came in.

"Francoise told me you were doing some emailing," Avery said. "I just wanted to remind you to write one to your mum. I promised her that you would let her know once you'd arrived safely."

"OK," Issie replied. She stifled a yawn. What was the time, anyway? She looked at the clock over her bed. "Wow. It's nearly midnight." She was surprised.

"They stay up late in Spain," Avery said. "We'll have to get used to their timetable. They eat dinner at ten, they go to sleep at midnight and they have siestas in the afternoons. The whole place stops for a nap at three o'clock."

"Even the grown-ups?" Issie was amazed by this. "How long do they sleep for?"

"A couple of hours," Avery said. "They do it because it's too hot in the afternoons to do any work. It's the tradition here."

"Yeah, there are lots of weird traditions here," Issie said darkly.

Avery looked at her. "You mean the Silver Bridle?"

Issie nodded. "Tom, I just don't get it. Storm is my colt. Why do we have to wait to run some stupid race to win him back? Why don't we just go to Vega's stables and force him to give Storm to us?"

"I think we have to trust Roberto on this one," Avery said to her. "He knows the culture here and if he says the race is our best chance to get Nightstorm back from Vega, we have to go along with him."

Issie wasn't sure about this, but she was too tired to argue. "I'm gonna email Mum and then go to bed," she told Avery.

"Good idea," her instructor said. "Get some sleep. It's a big day tomorrow."

Chapter 8

Preparations for the *feria* took the entire morning. Saddles were polished until they glistened and every rider in El Caballo stables put on their best *vaquero* costume. It was the horses, though, who got the most attention. Their coats were groomed until they shone and their manes were plaited, not in the traditional English way seen at gymkhanas, but with thick double-rows of French plaits that ran in two braids down each side of the horse's neck from one end of the mane to the other. Their tails too, were dressed, the top halves plaited into a long French braid and then the switch of the tail elaborately knotted up at the end.

Issie was riding Angel again for the parade and had saddled him herself that morning with a rainbow saddle cloth for the occasion. The stable grooms had helped her get ready too, showing her the Spanish way of tying brilliantly coloured red, orange and violet bobbles into the stallion's mane.

By eleven o'clock all the riders were mounted and ready to go. Except for Francoise.

"What is taking her so long?" Avery checked his watch.

"Here she is!" Issie said.

Francoise emerged into the cobbled courtyard, not in her usual uniform of *vaquero* trousers and jacket, but in a hot-pink flamenco dress covered with large black polka dots. The dress hugged tight to Francoise's body all the way down past her hips and then turned into a riot of frills and flounces around her legs. She wore her hair tied back severely in a bun, with a gigantic red rose securing it in place.

"It is traditional." Francoise shrugged when Issie and Avery both stared at her wide-eyed as she walked over to join them, taking the reins of her mare. "Although I cannot say I am happy about having to ride side-saddle in this dress," she added grumpily. "One cannot control a horse properly riding side-saddle."

Francoise had chosen one of El Caballo's chestnut Anglo-Arab mares to ride to the *feria* today. Issie was riding alongside her, Roberto was riding Marius, and Avery had been given one of Roberto's best stallions, a bay Lusitano called Sorcerer. Six other *vaquero*s, including Alfonso, were also riding with them today, each of them on one of El Caballo's grey Lipizzaner stallions.

As the riders headed out through the gates of the hacienda they instantly fell into groups. Avery and Roberto rode ahead together laughing and chatting, at ease with each other as only old friends can be. Alfonso rode out at the front of them alone, holding the El Caballo flag. Behind all of them rode the El Caballo horsemen, and then Issie and Francoise, bringing up the rear. Apart from Francoise, who was riding a mare, Issie noticed that all of the other riders had something in common.

"Why does no one ride geldings here?" Issie asked Francoise as they trotted out of the El Caballo gates, heading up the dusty hillside road that would lead them the short distance to the village.

"In Spain it is only stallions," Francoise explained. "The Spanish stallion is not as wild and uncontrollable as other breeds. Indeed he is so well-mannered that even small children of three or four years old can be seen riding a stallion."

Francoise looked over at Issie's horse. "Angel is such

a typical Andalusian stallion," she said. "I remember when we first brought him to El Caballo as a young colt. He had been so badly mistreated by Vega and he was terrified of men, but even then he would always let me near him, and his nature was so gentle, so sweet. He is nearly eleven now, but he has not changed. Whenever I am home at El Caballo, I ride him each day and I marvel at how willing he is. He will do anything for you. You will see."

Issie knew what Francoise meant. When she had ridden Destiny there was always the sense of a power struggle between her and the black stallion. He was wilful, with a mind of his own. Angel wasn't like that at all – he was sensitive and willing to please. It made Issie even sadder about the scars on Angel's nose. Why would Vega use a barbed metal noseband on such a sweet-natured horse as this? It didn't make sense.

The village was on the hill rising up above El Caballo Danza Magnifico. It was a pretty sight with its whitewashed terraced houses with terracotta roofs all built right next door to each other. The houses all clustered around the central square, which was where Issie and the other riders were heading. They trotted their horses up the winding cobbled streets and gathered at the entrance to the square, where the other riders were organising themselves into their haciendas, preparing to parade under their racing colours around the fountain at the centre of the square.

Issie realised now that the red, orange and violet bobbles tied in Angel's mane were not purely for decoration – they denoted the colour of El Caballo Danza Magnifico's hacienda. As each of the twelve haciendas assembled by the entrance to the square their flag bearer rode to the front so that the other riders representing his stables could line up behind him. Each flag bearer held aloft the colourful banner that bore their hacienda insignia. El Caballo's flag was golden and in the middle was a red letter C with the red heart stamped inside it. Carrying the flag, Alfonso rode to the front of the El Caballo riders, smiling at Issie as he cantered past her.

"Look!" Francoise said to Issie. "It is so high up here, you can see all the way back to El Caballo. The hacienda looks beautiful, doesn't it?"

Issie looked across the square. Francoise was right, you could see the house and stables quite clearly from here. At the gates she could make out an El Caballo flag, the same as the one that Alfonso was carrying, fluttering in the wind on the flagpole.

There was a mood of anticipation now, as the flag bearers shouted out to their riders as last-minute preparations began. Issie wanted to get excited too, to get into the spirit of the *feria*, but she couldn't. She was still so desperately worried about Nightstorm. She hadn't really been concentrating when the flag bearers explained what to do, and she couldn't speak Spanish anyway. She suddenly felt overwhelmed and bewildered.

"It's OK. Stick with me," Francoise told her. She pulled her Anglo-Arab up to ride alongside Issie. "All we must do is ride once around the square so that everyone can admire our horses." And then she added under her breath, "Of course, this admiration comes at a price. Most of the haciendas are here trying to decide which horses they will claim from their rival stables if they are lucky enough to win the race."

Which horse would Issie choose if she won? The truth was, as she looked around at the stallions, mares, fillies and colts being paraded in the *feria*, Issie would have chosen all of them. Each horse seemed more beautiful than the next. And then, one particular horse caught her eye. He was a gigantic jet-black stallion, enormous, almost seventeen hands high, and solid with it. Unlike the other stallions in the parade, who all seemed to share the placid

Spanish nature, this black stallion had fire in his belly. He skipped and danced beneath his master as they rode back and forth. While the other riders in the parade marched obediently behind the flag bearer, the man on the black stallion paid no attention and rode ahead, circling his flag bearer and horses like a shark. Issie looked at the flag, which was bright yellow and black with a capital V surrounded by curlicues on either side   .

"Which hacienda is that?" Issie asked, pointing it out to Francoise.

Francoise didn't have the chance to answer Issie's question before a string of young horses came into view behind the yellow and black flag. The young horses were riderless, a string of colts and fillies, all wearing neck collars that joined together with leashes so that the line of horses formed a cobra.

Leading the cobra was a man on a grey stallion with a stock whip. He kept the young horses in line behind the man who carried the yellow and black flag. There were four colts in the cobra. The first three colts were almost identical, all of them steel-grey, with the classical physique of the Spanish Andalusian. But the fourth colt was quite different. He was a bay, with a broad white blaze and an elegant dished face with pretty

363

wide-set eyes. Issie saw him and her heart leapt.

"Storm!" she called out across the square.

Before anyone could stop her, she had turned Angel and was barging her way back through the crowded parade, going against the tide, pushing past the other horses and riders. She could no longer see Storm, he was lost in the crowd now, but she kept her eyes on the yellow and black flag that marked the spot where her colt must be.

"Storm!!"

There was no way the colt could possibly hear Issie's cries over the noise of the parade. Was she even getting closer to him? It was hard enough to hold her ground against the crowds who were pushing past her, going in the opposite direction. She kept losing sight of the yellow and black flag. Where was Storm?

Panic-stricken, she pulled Angel to a halt, took a deep breath and gave two short, sharp whistles – the same signal she used to call Storm in the paddock at home.

The bay colt heard her call and he returned it with a heartfelt whinny, letting her know that he was there.

"Storm!" Issie kicked Angel on again, heading in the direction of the colt's cry, forcing her way on through the crowd. Behind her, Alfonso had been the first one to realise what was going on. He had turned too and was trying to follow her through the parade, but his flag was making it hard to manoeuvre. Francoise was right behind him, making apologies to people as they barged through the crowd, pushing past the other riders as she tried to catch up.

There was a brief moment when the procession suddenly swelled around her and Issie lost Storm once more in a blur of horses and colourful flags – and then she urged Angel on and suddenly they were through and on the other side of the parade. The crowds had cleared and Issie was sitting there on Angel, staring directly at the man who held the cobra of colts.

"Hey!" Issie shouted at the man. "Where did you get him from? That's my colt!"

The man, who clearly didn't speak English, looked at her blankly as she pointed at Storm.

"You have my horse," Issie repeated slowly, "and I want him back."

The man shrugged at her and then turned away and shouted something in Spanish that Issie didn't understand. A moment later, the ranks of riders wearing the yellow and black colours of the hacienda opened up to let through the man on the gigantic black stallion, the one that Issie had first noticed in the crowd.

Now that she was closer Issie could see that although the horse was large, the man was not. He was short, and far too fat for the traditional *vaquero* costume that he was wearing. His gut bulged over the black satin cummerbund of his trousers. Underneath his black oiled hair, beads of sweat kept forming on his forehead and he dabbed at these with a white handkerchief. His eyes were beady and small, his face dominated by a very thick, bushy moustache.

"Hey *chica*! Little girl! What's going on?" the man on the stallion mocked her. "Do you not understand Spanish or do you think you are being funny? You're blocking our way. The parade has begun. Get a move on!"

Issie didn't move. "You have my colt," she said. "That bay colt there – he's mine and I want him back."

"You cannot make a claim on the property of Miguel Vega!" the man said dismissively.

"Miguel Vega is nothing but a thief," Issie said, shaking with fury, "and I'm not making a claim. I'm telling you. That colt does not belong to Vega – his name is Nightstorm and he is mine."

As Issie said this, Alfonso finally reached her side. "Are you OK?" He looked at Issie. She shook her head. "Alfonso, that's him. That's my colt. He's got Storm."

Alfonso turned to face the man on the black stallion.

"You've got a nerve stealing that colt and then bringing him here, Miguel."

Miguel? Issie suddenly clicked. Of course! This man in front of them was none other than Vega himself!

Francoise had joined them now. She had a steely look in her eyes as she rode past Issie and Alfonso, taking up position in front of them to confront the grinning man with the moustache.

"Miguel. You've gone too far this time. You know that the colt belongs to this girl and she has nothing to do with our feud, or the race. Why don't we settle this now? Do the right thing and give him back."

Vega gave a smirk at this. "You're mistaken, Francoise. The colt is one of ours. Look at the brand!"

Issie looked down at Nightstorm and as the colt danced about, fighting against his handlers, she caught a glimpse of his hindquarters. Freshly burned into his left haunch was the ~V~ brand of the Vega stables.

Vega sneered at Francoise. "You see? You insult Miguel Vega! I do not need to steal your feeble horses! I will win the five best horses in your stable anyway when Victorioso and I cross the line ahead of you for the Silver Bridle!"

All this time, as they had been standing there facing Vega, Issie had been struggling to control Angel. The stallion had been pacing and fretting beneath her, fighting her hands, desperate to get away from the man with the moustache. It hadn't occurred to Issie until now that Angel would have a lingering memory of Vega's cruelty, and that the stallion would be so terrified of his former master. She was struggling to keep him still so that she could confront Vega. "Steady, boy," Issie breathed, trying to hold the stallion as he danced beneath her.

"Ah!" Vega said. "I see you are riding Angel. He still bears the marks of my *serreta*." He laughed and reached out a hand to touch the stallion's scarred face. Angel instantly pulled back and Issie struggled once more to hang on to the reins and control him.

Vega laughed again and looked at Storm. "We shall soon see how this little one likes the *serreta*. He is almost old enough, I think, to begin his training."

"You leave him alone!" Issie shouted. Before she could stop to think about it she had kicked Angel on and was aiming her horse straight at Vega, her hand raised, ready to strike at the man with her closed fist.

"Hah!" Vega reached out his own hand and caught Issie's arm in midair, grasping her wrist tightly. "We have a young wildcat here! You need to control your child, Francoise! I might need to use the *serreta* on her as well."

"Let go of her!" Francoise egged her horse on, riding forward to reach out her hand and free Issie from Vega's grasp. As she did so, though, Vega's enormous black stallion reared up. Vega had no choice but to let go of Issie's wrist as the horse rose up underneath him. But Francoise was still riding forward to help her and as the big, black stallion came back down to the ground his front hoof caught a glancing blow on Francoise's shoulder.

Francoise let out a scream of pain and toppled forward from her side-saddle to land hard on the ground. Then her chestnut mare reared up in fright and suddenly there were horses loose everywhere and riders yelling and shouting in panic, jostling and shoving each other to try and get clear.

"Francoise!" Issie was trying to find the Frenchwoman, but she was out of sight on the ground, in danger of being trampled in the blur of hooves.

Alfonso fought the crowds too, struggling to reach Francoise, but it was Avery who appeared out of nowhere and managed to reach her in time. Realising the danger to anyone who was dismounted among the rabble of panicked horses, he stayed on his horse and reached down low to grab Francoise by the arm. Yanking her roughly to her feet, he grabbed her tight and threw her across the saddle in front of him. Francoise was clearly in pain, and had to use all her strength to cling on desperately as Avery rode to get them clear of the crowds.

"I've got her." Avery lifted Francoise to safety. "Issie! Follow us!" But Issie was already heading in the opposite direction, fighting her way back into the crowd to look for Storm. Vega's riders had all disappeared in the fracas and the colt was nowhere to be seen. She rode into the crowd, being barged and shoved by other horses and riders as she tried to force her way through to the last place she had seen Vega and her colt.

"Come on!" She felt a hand on her shoulder. It was Alfonso. "It's no use, Issie," Alfonso insisted. "Vega is arrogant, but he's not stupid. He knows better than to hang around after that. You won't find him now. He's already gone and he's taken Storm with him."

Issie ignored Alfonso. She kept looking, her eyes searching out the bay colt, hoping to catch a glimpse of Storm in the crowd of horses and riders.

"You'll get hurt if you stay in the way here," Alfonso said. "Come on, please. Follow me."

Alfonso led Issie and Angel out of the crowd, past the crush of horses and riders to a clear space where a row of park benches lined the far side of the town square.

There they found Avery, bent over Francoise who was lying very still on one of the benches, her breathing harsh and laboured.

"Is she OK?" Issie said, as she slid off Angel and ran to join them.

"It's my arm," Francoise said, gritting her teeth through the pain. "I think it's broken." She tried to sit up. "Did you get Storm? Where is he?"

Issie shook her head. "I don't know. Vega had him, he must have—" She couldn't finish her sentence. She couldn't bring herself to admit that her colt had been right there and they had lost him again. They had missed their chance to save the colt. Storm was gone.

Chapter 9

Back at El Caballo that afternoon the mood was dark. Francoise's arm was indeed broken. Alfonso had driven her to the hospital in Seville where they had X-rayed her and put the arm in a plaster cast before releasing her home again. Now she lay on the floral brocade sofa in the living room, with Avery and Issie fussing over her, plumping her cushions and bringing her fresh orange juice and pills to dull the pain.

"This is all my fault," Issie said. "I'm so sorry, Francoise. I shouldn't have lost my temper when Vega said he was going to use the *serreta* on Storm…"

"It is OK, really." Francoise smiled. "I do not blame you – it was this stupid flamenco costume!" She smoothed down the ruffles of her dress with obvious irritation.

"I could not stay on when the horse reared, with that ridiculous side-saddle and all these silly frills! Next time I shall wear my *vaquero* trousers!"

"I agree. Flamenco dresses are not appropriate attire for fighting on horseback," Roberto Nunez said sarcastically, as he entered the room carrying a tray laden with tea and cakes. He put the tray down on the coffee table in front of them and shook his head in disbelief. "I turn my back for a moment and what happens? When I turn round again I see all four of you at the other end of the village square, caught up in a fight with Vega! What were you thinking? Did you think Vega would just give the colt back? Alfonso? Francoise? You both know him better than that!"

"But Dad," Alfonso objected. "You weren't there. You didn't see Vega, the way he spoke to Isadora. He was so arrogant—"

Roberto cut his son off with a harsh look. "His arrogance will lose him the Silver Bridle, but only if we keep our heads. I expect my son to beat him in the race, not in a street fight."

Alfonso looked as if he was going to argue back, but Roberto waved away his objections with a brisk hand. "Go down to the stables and check on the horses," he instructed. "Make sure that none of them were hurt."

Alfonso looked annoyed, but he didn't argue. He nodded to his father and left the room.

"Well, one good thing has come of this," Roberto sighed. "At least we know for certain now that Vega has the colt."

"Does that mean we can call the police?" Issie asked.

Roberto shook his head. "I wish that were the case, but we still have no proof that the colt is yours," he said. "Vega has branded it with the mark of his stables – if anything, the colt now appears to be even more his property than he was before."

"But Storm isn't his!" Issie looked pleadingly at Avery. "Tom, we have to do something. I can't leave Storm with Vega."

"Issie, Roberto is right," Avery said. "Vega currently holds all the cards. If we go to the police now they won't believe us. It's our word against his. We must wait until the time is right…"

"When?" Issie said. "When will that be? After Vega has used the *serreta* on him, the same way he did to Angel? That man is a monster – and he's got my colt!"

"Isadora," Roberto cautioned, "I know how much you love your colt, but your impetuousness today has already got us into trouble. Now I must ask you to wait. Let us decide what to do."

"I'm sorry…" Issie was taken aback. "I wasn't trying to cause trouble… I didn't mean for anyone to get hurt…"

"I know that," Roberto said gently. "But for your own safety, Isadora, please, let us handle this. I do not want to see anything happen to you."

Issie looked around the room at Francoise and Avery. They were both silent, which Issie took as a sign that they were in agreement with Roberto.

She felt hot tears pricking at her eyes. *Great,* she thought, *now it's all my fault, and to make it worse I'm going to start crying like a kid in front of everyone.* "You know," she said, trying to focus on the plate of cakes in front of her as the tears blurred her vision, "I'm not very hungry right now. I think I'm going to go to my room for a while."

Issie left the living room, shutting the door behind her. She stood outside, pausing for a moment. What was she going to do now? Roberto had made it clear that he thought fighting to get Storm back was futile, and Avery and Francoise seemed to agree with him. Still, did they really expect Issie to sit back and do nothing while Vega had her colt?

What else could she do, though? Issie was halfway around the world, without her friends or her family. If she was home then she could rely on Mystic turning up to help her. But here, in Spain? She was on her own. In fact, she had never felt more alone in her entire life.

Issie slumped back against the cool stone wall of the hallway just outside the living room door. She let herself slide down the wall until she was sitting on the floor with her arms wrapped around her knees. She couldn't just stay here at the hacienda and do nothing!

She reached a hand to her throat and felt for her necklace. It was a friendship necklace, the sort where the heart splits in two and you keep one half and give the other half to your best friend. Francoise had given her this necklace. Issie wore her half of the gold heart on a gold chain around her neck. The other half of the heart was attached to Blaze's halter. Issie never took the necklace off. She liked to reach up and touch it sometimes, to remind her that no matter where she was, her heart was always with her mare, back in Chevalier Point.

Issie shook her head. That was what Roberto didn't understand. Storm wasn't just any colt, he was Blaze's son. She loved him with the same passion that she loved Blaze. And now Storm needed her. She wasn't going to let him down.

Filled with determination, Issie was about to push

herself back up off the floor and head up the stairs to her room when she heard voices coming from the living room. It sounded like they were arguing. She could hear Francoise complaining, "Your honour is all very well and good, but Miguel plays dirty."

Then she heard Roberto snap back. "I don't want my hacienda seen brawling with a common horse thief like Vega." Then suddenly the door swung open and Francoise D'arth came stomping out. She strode straight past Issie, muttering something to herself in French. She was heading straight for the kitchen and didn't cast a backwards glance, so she didn't see the girl crouched on the other side of the door frame, even though she swept so close to her that Issie felt the flounces of her flamenco dress as she breezed past. Francoise had left the living-room door open behind her, and this meant that Issie could hear Roberto and Avery's conversation. They were speaking to each other very seriously.

"*Madre Mia*, my friend!" Roberto said. "No one will listen to me today!"

"They're just trying to help. You know that, Roberto," Avery said.

"I know, I know," Roberto sighed, "but they underestimate Vega. Thomas, the man is a fat fool, but he is still dangerous. I don't want them to get involved with him and get hurt. You can see that, can't you?"

"What about the race?" Avery countered. "Couldn't Alfie get hurt then?"

"That is different," Roberto said. "The race is our tradition. It is the right way to win your colt."

"Issie just wants her horse back," Avery said. "She doesn't care about tradition."

"You must watch her closely," Roberto warned him. "She must stay away from Vega."

"I think you've made that clear to her," Avery said, "but yes, of course I'll keep an eye on her. You mustn't be too tough on her though, Roberto. She's in love with that colt."

"She is impetuous and too spirited…"

"… just like we were at her age," Avery responded. Then his tone grew serious. "She's the most talented rider I've ever trained, Roberto. I think she could be great one day. She's got what it takes."

"*Si*," Roberto said, "yes, I can see that. You were right about her. Everything you said has proven to be true. And the colt, he too is just as I expected, a true son of Salome and Marius."

Avery said something else that Issie couldn't hear and then Roberto spoke once more.

"Does the girl know that you are her *bonifacio*?"

"No," Avery said. "Not yet. The time has never seemed right. And now that we are here, with the colt in this much danger…" He paused. "Roberto, what is your plan for getting Storm back?"

"There is no plan. We will simply run the race," Roberto said. "Marius is the best stallion in Spain and my son may be a headstrong boy, but he is our best rider. He will run the race and bring honour to El Caballo Danza Magnifico. That is how the colt will be returned to us."

Pressed back against the wall listening, Issie felt her breath catch in her throat. Avery was her *bonifacio*? What did that mean? And was that really Roberto's only plan to get Storm back? She wasn't going to sit back and wait for them to win the race. For all she knew, Vega could be putting the *serreta* on Storm right now! The race was not the answer. She knew now what she had to do. Vega was so arrogant, after the fiasco today the last thing he would ever expect would be for someone to fight back. Well, that arrogance would be his downfall. She was going to get her colt back the same way that he had been taken from her. She was going to steal him.

In her room, Issie quickly pulled on her jodhpurs and grabbed her *vaquero* hat before heading back down the stairs and out of the front door. The moment she was outside she was struck by just how hot the sun was. It was mid-afternoon, the time when the Andalusian sun reaches its peak and the *vaquero*s, weary from the heat, take a siesta. This afternoon nap would last for a couple of hours, until the sun sank lower and they could return once more to their work.

The heat and the siesta would work in her favour, Issie realised. There would be no need to talk her way round the men at Roberto's stables and convince them to let her take Angel out. The men were crashed out asleep on their cots in the bunkhouse. There would be no one at the stallions' stable block to stop her.

Angel was standing at the back of his stall in the shadows as always, but the stallion came forward without hesitation at the sound of Issie's voice.

"Hey, boy." Issie couldn't help feeling pleased that Angel was responding to her already. She reached out and ran her hand down the stallion's noble face, finding herself filled with pity all over again as she felt the ugly scar tissue that Vega had inflicted.

She thought of Storm now, in the hands of Vega. She

couldn't bear the thought of the *serreta* being used on him. Well, she thought, as she snatched the bridle off the hook in Angel's stall, she didn't need to worry about that for much longer. She would saddle up now and ride to Vega's hacienda. Vega's men would also be having their siesta when she arrived. She would be able to slip in and take her colt back in broad daylight, before anyone even realised she had been there. All she had to do was saddle up before anyone noticed her and—

"Going somewhere?"

A voice behind her made her jump. She spun round and saw a man standing there, wearing the traditional *vaquero* costume of El Caballo. In the darkness of the stable she thought at first that it was Roberto Nunez. Then the man stepped closer and she could see his face.

"Alfonso!" Issie said. "You scared me half to death! Don't sneak up on me like that."

"Taking Angel for a ride?" Alfonso said.

"Uh-huh…" Issie began to try and think of a fib she could tell him, something he would believe, but she could see by the look on Alfonso's face that he wouldn't be fooled.

"Let me guess," Alfonso said. "You're going after the colt. You're going to Vega's stables to bring him back, all by yourself?"

"No! Well, yes, but…" Issie tried to stay cool, but instead she found herself babbling. "Alfonso, I have to do it! He's got Storm. I need to get him back before Vega uses the *serreta* on him. I know you can't understand how much he means to me—"

"Hey! Hey!" Alfonso cut her off. "Calm down, you've got me all wrong. I'm not trying to stop you." He reached out and took the bridle off the hook outside Marius's stall and then turned to her and smiled. "I'm trying to tell you that I'm coming with you."

Chapter 10

Galloping together across the sunburnt fields of the El Caballo, the two great grey stallions, Marius and Angel, made an impressive sight. "Alfonso, you don't have to do this, you know," Issie shouted out. "Your dad will be furious when he finds out."

Alfonso was ahead of Issie, but now he pulled Marius up so that the two of them were riding together. "First of all, you must stop calling me Alfonso," he shouted back at her. "My friends all call me Alfie – OK?"

Issie nodded.

"And second," Alfie continued, "my dad is not as bad as you think. He's a pussycat once you get to know him. Right now it's all 'honour this' and 'tradition that'. He'd never agree to let us steal the colt – but you watch, when we bring Storm back home, he'll be totally on our side."

Issie had her doubts about this, but she wasn't going to argue. She hadn't argued with Alfie either when he'd insisted on coming with her. After all, as he pointed out, he knew his way into Vega's stables and she didn't. With him on her side, Issie stood a fighting chance of getting her colt back.

The two riders slowed down to a trot as they neared the gorge, and it was easier to talk as they rode side by side. "Your dad and Tom have known each other for a long time, huh?" Issie said.

"Yeah, twenty years. They met before I was even born," Alfie said. "Then Tom moved back to New Zealand, so I never really knew him. He and Dad used to write to each other. Dad would always be really happy when he got a letter from the other side of the world."

"It's kinda cool how close they are. They've been inseparable since we arrived," Issie said. "I guess they have a lot to catch up on."

Alfie nodded. "It's great to see my dad talking about old times again. He doesn't usually have anyone to talk to about that stuff. I think he gets lonely, you know? It's really isolated here and, I mean, he has me of course, and his *vaqueros*, but when Francoise and I are away with El Caballo

Danza Magnifico it must be very quiet at the hacienda."

"Where's your mum?" Issie asked. "Why doesn't she live with you?"

Alfie was quiet for a moment. "She died," he said, "when I was six."

"I'm sorry…" Issie felt dreadful. What a stupid thing to say! She hadn't realised.

"It's OK," Alfie said, "honest. It was a long time ago. I hardly remember her now. My dad brought me up by himself. And Francoise too, I suppose. Not like she's my stepmum or anything like that, but she joined El Caballo not long after that and she's always kept an eye on me, you know?"

Issie nodded. "My dad didn't die or anything, but he left when I was nine. I don't really see him. It's just me and Mum."

"You've got Tom," Alfie offered. "He seems to look out for you."

Issie felt a sting of guilt when Alfie said this. "Tom would be really upset if he knew what we were doing."

"In that case," Alfie said, kicking Marius on, "he had better not find out and we had better not get caught."

385

They had reached the gorge now and Alfie took the lead on Marius. "Follow me, I know the way," he called back over his shoulder. Issie stuck close behind him until they reached the end of the gorge and they pulled up side by side once more and halted their horses. This was the same spot Issie had halted with Francoise when she had first set eyes on Vega's hacienda. This time, though, they'd be riding across the wide plains that lay in front of them, and sneaking into Vega's own stables to take back her colt.

On the horizon, Vega's hacienda looked like an ancient Spanish prison. The walls that surrounded the estate were two metres high and made of crumbling bricks and plaster the colour of dried blood. The top of the wall had pointy turrets, like a Moorish castle, and over the top of the turrets Issie could make out the rooftops of Vega's hacienda.

"Vega's stables are at the back of the hacienda," Alfie said. He pointed at the orange grove to the right ahead of them. "We can tie the horses up there and then vault the wall into the garden. Once we find your colt, we'll have to take him back out of the main gates – it's the only way."

Issie nodded at this.

"Ready?" Alfie asked.

"Uh-huh," she replied.

"Then let's go!" And with that Alfie clucked his horse on and Issie followed, galloping across the green fields towards the hacienda.

As they got nearer to Vega's house, Issie could have sworn she felt Angel tense up underneath her, slowing his stride a little. She didn't urge him on. Instead, she spoke gently to the stallion, reassuring him with the softness of her voice. She had seen the way Angel had reacted when they met the mustachioed man that morning at the *feria* in the village square. Angel had been terrified of Vega and Issie sensed the same fear in her horse now. This hacienda, Vega's stables, had once been Angel's home – and it was not a home the stallion was keen to return to.

Is it any wonder? Issie thought. After all, the stallion still bore the marks of the *serreta* that Vega had forced on him, and the scars ran deep, beyond the marks on his face, all the way to the hidden recesses of Angel's mighty heart.

"It's OK," Issie reassured him, giving Angel a stroke along his proud, arched neck. "We're not staying there for long, I promise. We just need to find Storm and get straight out again."

They had reached the cover of the orange grove now, and the trees kept them hidden as they neared the high wall that ran around the hacienda. Alfie leapt down off

Marius's back and put a finger to his lips to signal that they needed to be quiet now. Then he led Marius towards an orange tree and tethered the horse by his reins. Issie did the same, whispering softly to Angel as she knotted the leather to the bough of the orange tree next to Marius.

"I'll be back soon," she told the stallion.

"Here!" Alfie hissed at her. "Give me a leg up on to the wall and then I'll pull you up."

Issie legged him up as if she was helping him on to a horse and then Alfie balanced on top of the wall, checking that the coast was clear before giving her his hand so she could climb up too. Issie perched there for a moment, hidden between the turrets, looking down at the gardens in the courtyard below. It was a grand Moorish garden filled with mosaic-tiled fountains, overgrown lantana and rows of tall palm trees. A maze created from neatly clipped conifers ran all the way from the house to the buildings at the rear of the hacienda, which Issie figured must be the stables.

"Follow me!" Alfie whispered. He jumped like a cat into the lantana bushes and Issie promptly followed him. The maze hedging kept them hidden from sight as they crept on, making their way towards the crumbling brick archways that led to the stables.

Issie had been right. It was siesta time and the whole

hacienda was cloaked in silence. There was no sound here except the gentle trickling of the garden fountains and the dry chirrup of the cicadas. She followed Alfie down the stairs and across the cobbles, through the archways that marked the entrance to the stable block.

Inside, the loose boxes ran in rows up either side of the long corridor. There must have been at least thirty loose boxes stretching ahead of them, and the doors to the boxes were solid wood, all shut tight and bolted. "He must be in one of these stalls," Alfie said. He began to unbolt the door to the first stall. "Let's start looking. I'll take the left side, you take the right."

"No," Issie said. "I know a faster way."

It was risky, whistling for her colt, but they didn't have time to search every stall. And so she pursed her lips together and blew.

Two short, sharp notes rang out in the stillness. Issie waited but no reply came. She took another breath, ready to try once more, but before she could whistle a second time, a shrill nicker returned her call.

"Storm!" she called out. There was another nicker and Issie focused, trying to follow the sound of the colt's cry. It was coming from the end of the stable block!

At the far end of the stables, Issie could see the light

flooding into the darkness through an archway that she decided must lead outside.

"He's down there!" She broke into a run and began heading towards the light with Alfie close behind her. Ahead of her, she could see that a wooden five-bar gate ran right across the width of the archway, blocking it off. Behind this gate was a small lawn enclosure, bordered by high stone walls. It was a sort of secret garden, with beds of mint and pomegranate trees and gnarled, ancient bougainvillea vines climbing the walls. It was also a prison as far as Issie was concerned because here, with his head craning over the wooden gate to meet her, was her colt. It was Storm!

As he saw the girl with the long dark hair running towards him the colt let out another nicker, more urgent this time, demanding her attention.

It's me, I'm right here! he seemed to be saying. He gave more soft little nickers of excitement, pacing back and forth behind the gate.

Issie, meanwhile, was running so hard she thought her heart would burst. She sprinted down the corridor to the gates, and when she finally reached the colt she was gasping to hold back her tears and to catch her breath.

"I know, I know," Issie said, choking with emotion as

she put her arms around the colt's neck and hugged him tight, "I missed you too. I was so worried! But don't worry, I'm here now and I'm going to…"

Their reunion was cut short. There was the sound of footsteps on the cobbles behind her. Issie turned round, expecting to see Alfie. What she didn't expect to see was that behind Alfie were three *vaqueros*, all running down the stable corridor heading towards them.

"We've got company!" Alfie said as he reached her side.

"Thanks for the warning," Issie said darkly. "Now how do we get Storm out of here?"

"No time for that now." Alfie shook his head. "We need to get out." He looked around frantically.

"There!" he said, pointing to the bougainvillea vine that was climbing up the wall of Storm's enclosure. "That's our way out. We can climb up that vine and out over the wall." He vaulted over the gate and ran past Storm. He gave the vines a tug. "They're strong enough to hold us, I think. Come on!" he said, already climbing up and getting a foothold on the top of the wall.

Issie hesitated. She didn't want to leave Storm's side so soon after finding him. But she had no choice. If these men caught her here, like this… Issie might have been brave, but she wasn't foolish. She had no desire to find out for herself what a man like Vega was capable of if he caught her trying to steal back her colt.

She followed Alfie over the gate and ran for the vines, shimmying up so that she could get a handhold on the top of the wall itself and pull herself over. She was relieved to see that the wall led back to the orange grove outside the estate where they had tethered the horses. Alfie was already mounted on Marius and waiting for her. She hit the ground running, sprinting towards Angel, who was fretting and pacing nervously, looking like he wanted to get away even more desperately than Issie did.

"Come on!" Alfie said impatiently. "They'll be getting their horses now, they'll come after us for sure."

Over the wall behind her, Issie could hear the shouts of the men. The *vaqueros* had disappeared and Issie guessed that they must have gone back to the stables to get their horses.

"C'mon, Angel," she said, struggling to unknot the leather reins from the orange tree. "We've gotta go."

Marius and Alfie had already galloped off and were almost clear of the orange grove, and Angel was keen to follow them. The stallion's keen ears could already hear the sound that Issie now heard. The thunder of hoofbeats in the air as the *vaqueros* mounted up and rode out of the hacienda gates, circling back through the orange grove, riding hard to hunt them down.

Issie mounted up and turned Angel round. Ahead of her, they had about thirty metres to ride through the orange grove before they hit the open pasture that would lead them back to the gorge and El Caballo. They needed to get clear of these *vaquero*s quickly if they were going to make it home to safety. She gathered up her reins and was about to kick Angel, but instead, she let out a scream. There was something holding her back!

She looked down in horror to see a face leering up at her. It was a *vaquero* and he had his fat hands wrapped tight around her ankle.

Issie screamed again and pulled hard, but the *vaquero* had grasped her boot with both hands and was hanging on tight. He yelled out to the other horsemen in Spanish to let them know that he had her, and then he looked up at Issie's terrified face.

"Let go of me!" she shrieked.

"What were you doing? Trying to take *Señor* Vega's colt, eh?" the man replied.

"He's not Vega's colt!" Issie said through gritted teeth. "He's mine!" Her anger gave her a new surge of energy and she wrenched her foot once more, pulling so hard that the boot came clean off in the man's meaty paws.

Issie took her chance, and before the *vaquero* could make another grab at her, Angel had lunged forward and broken into a gallop, leaving Vega's man standing there holding nothing more than an empty boot.

Issie slipped her sock foot back into the stirrup and rose up out of the saddle as Angel galloped on. They were almost clear of the orange trees and ahead of them was the grassy pasture that led to the entrance of the gorge that would take her back to El Caballo. Ahead of her, Alfie and Marius had almost a two-hundred-metre lead on them. The boy and the stallion weren't slowing down to wait for them either, they were galloping flat out.

Issie looked back over her shoulder. Sure enough, there were two more of Vega's *vaquero*s giving chase. Both of them were on powerful Lusitano stallions, and their horses were already in full gallop and gaining on Issie, their strides chewing up the distance between them.

"Angel!" Issie whispered, rising even higher in her stirrups so that she was resting on her knees with her body low over the grey stallion's neck. "Angel, come on, boy. We need to stay ahead of them. Let's go! *Vamos!*"

The grey horse was already galloping, but as Issie asked more of him, he seemed to sense the danger and respond to the urgency of her plea. His stride suddenly lengthened and his frame extended so that the ground was swallowed up by his gallop. Issie bent down even lower and wrapped her hands in the stallion's mane, gripping tightly in case the horse swerved and she lost her seat. She needn't have worried. Angel was running as straight as an arrow towards the gorge, following behind Marius and galloping as if his life depended on it. His neck was flecked with foam and his flanks were heaving as he kept lengthening his stride, his pace increasing all the time as he drew further and further away from the horsemen behind him and closer and closer to the horse in front of him.

Issie could see now why Francoise had said that she chose Angel because of his speed. Although the stallion had the powerful muscles of an Andalusian, his gallop was more like that of a thoroughbred. He ran with a lightness and a grace that belied his burly physique. He had stamina too, maintaining his speed as Marius began to tire and drop back.

Marius had been way ahead of Angel, but now the distance between the two stallions had closed up so that the two horses were only a length apart. Angel was gaining more and more with every stride. Issie bent down even lower over the stallion's withers and kept talking to him, urging him on. Then Angel pulled up alongside Marius so that the two stallions were neck and neck and Issie and Alfie were next to each other.

As the two horses galloped towards the gorge Angel was powering forward with every stride, getting ahead of Marius and opening up his lead on the other stallion. For a moment, as Angel surged past the dapple-grey, Issie looked over and saw Alfie frantically urging his horse on, trying to coax the speed out of Marius to keep up with Angel. But it was useless.

As they reached the gorge Angel was in the lead, ahead of Marius by nearly two lengths, and the stallion still had plenty of running in him.

Issie cast a glance back over her shoulder. Angel had outrun Vega's men too. They had given up and pulled their horses back to a trot. They were far in the distance, no longer a threat.

It was then that Issie realised what had just happened. They had come here to get her colt and they had failed, but in the process she had discovered something almost as important. Angel was faster than Marius. The two horses had just been pitted against each other in the race of their lives – and Angel had won.

Chapter 11

Even though they had left the *vaqueros* in their dust back at the entrance to the gorge, Issie still didn't stop checking over her shoulder until they reached the gates of El Caballo.

"Are you OK?" Alfie asked her as he slid down off Marius's back and threw the reins over the horse's neck to lead him back to the stables.

"Uh-huh," Issie said. She vaulted down from Angel's back and as she hit the ground she felt the cobblestones beneath her sock foot and realised she only had one boot on. She had come so close to being caught! During the chase everything had happened so fast she hadn't had time to be scared, but now it was over, she realised that she was shaking uncontrollably.

Going to Vega's hacienda had been a stupid, desperate thing to do, she could see that now. The others were right – this wasn't the way to get her colt back. She and Alfie had been lucky to get away – in fact she never would have escaped if it weren't for Angel. She had never ridden a horse capable of such speed. Angel hadn't just outrun Vega's horses – he had raced them into the ground. Not only that, he had beaten Marius. There had been at least two hundred metres separating the stallion from Marius and yet he had caught him up as if Marius was standing still.

Angel's neck was wet with foamy sweat and his flanks were heaving from the run, yet his nerves were still wired up from his gallop and he didn't seem at all tired. Francoise had clearly been working on his fitness during her rides around El Caballo. The stallion was race-fit, and the gallop from Vega's hadn't exhausted him. In fact, it only served to excite him. As Issie tried to cool him down and bring him back to a walk, Angel kept skipping and dancing, refusing to settle as Issie led him back towards the stables. She spoke to the stallion in a soft, low voice, her tone calming him, as she stroked his broad, glistening white crest.

"He's fast, huh?" Alfie said as he led Marius up to walk back to the stables alongside her.

"Yeah," Issie agreed. "Francoise said he'd been bred for speed. I guess she was right."

Alfie nodded. He didn't look particularly happy. Finally he spoke again.

"He's faster than Marius," he said darkly. "He beat us, back there. I was riding as fast as I could when we left Vega's and you were way behind me, but you caught us easily."

Issie knew what Alfie was thinking. She was about to say something, but before she had the chance there was a shout from the stable block and Francoise and Avery came running towards them.

When Francoise saw the state the horses were in she knew immediately what they had done.

"Tell me you didn't!" she said, aghast, as she snatched Marius's reins from Alfie. "Tell me you didn't go to Vega's!"

"We did," Issie said, "and we saw Storm."

"We nearly had him too," Alfie added, "but Vega's men woke up and they chased us. We only just got away."

The look of concern on Francoise's face turned to anger. "I cannot believe this!" She shook her head in disbelief. "How could you both defy us like this? Alfie, your father told you that it was too risky to face Vega!"

"We weren't going to face him," Issie said. "We were going to bring Storm back."

"Don't play clever, Isadora," Avery said. "You know that Francoise is right. Vega is a dangerous man. I can't believe you two would be so foolish."

Issie was about to answer back, but when she looked at her instructor's face she saw something there that stopped her. She had never seen Avery so angry – and she realised at that moment just how deeply worried he must have been when he'd found that both Issie and Angel were missing.

"I'm really sorry, Tom." Issie bit her bottom lip. "I know it was a dumb thing to do, but I just wanted to get Storm back so badly."

Francoise shook her head, furious. "It is a miracle that you both escaped. I do not want to think about what might have happened if they had caught you."

"They nearly did catch Issie, but she got away!" Alfie said.

Issie shot Alfie a look, wishing that he would shut up. She didn't want Tom to know just how close she had come to being caught by Vega's men.

"I was at least twenty lengths ahead of her on Marius, and she caught me up," Alfie continued. "Angel totally outran Marius, I've never seen a horse go that fast. We were galloping flat out and he came up behind us like a rocket."

"Alfie's right. You should have seen him run," Issie

said. "Those *vaqueros* were right behind him one moment and then I asked him to run harder and he did it. He stretched out and there was no way they were going to catch him. He caught up to Marius and he passed him before we'd hit the gorge. He's fast all right, Francoise, just like you said he was."

Issie looked at Francoise, her heart racing. "Francoise, how far do you think it is from Vega's hacienda to the gorge?"

Francoise's eyes narrowed. She had already guessed what Issie was thinking. "It is about two kilometres, maybe a little more," she said.

"What are you talking about?" Avery was confused. But the other two knew exactly what Issie was driving at.

"She means the race," Alfie said. "The Silver Bridle."

Issie nodded. "Angel totally outran Vega's horses today. And he was faster than Marius. What if he could do the same in the race?" Issie held her breath for a moment and then she blurted out the words. "I think we should race Angel in the Silver Bridle. I think he can win."

"Isadora," Francoise said, "El Caballo Danza Magnifico already has a champion. Marius will be racing for us in the Silver Bridle. It has been decided."

"But why?" Issie said. "Francoise, you said yourself that Angel has the bloodlines of great racehorses in him. If he's faster than Marius, then shouldn't we race him instead?"

Francoise shook her head. "Angel has not been in training as Marius has…"

"…and yet he still managed to beat Vega's horses by at least twenty lengths!" Issie insisted. "You said you'd been riding him, Francoise, galloping him over the hills. Well, it's worked. He's fit and he's ready to race. Besides, we have a whole week yet before the race. We could train him."

"*Oui*," Francoise conceded, "yes, potentially it could be done. What you say is true. Angel is strong and sound but…" she shook her head, "… this is madness. It is not possible for him to race. Alfie is our rider. He is the best in our stables, and you know he cannot ride Angel."

Avery was confused by this. "Why not?"

"Because Angel is scared of men," Alfie responded immediately. And at that moment Issie realised why Alfie looked so distraught when they had been walking the horses back to the stables. Alfie was supposed to ride El Caballo's champion in the Silver Bridle. But what if Angel were really faster than Marius?

"I can't ride Angel," Alfie continued. "Believe me, I've tried. He's thrown me every time I got on his back. Vega using the *serreta* terrified him. It made him afraid, not just of Vega but all men – including me."

"It is not uncommon, this fear of men," Francoise said. "I have known many horses to object to having male riders. But in Angel's case? It is much more than mere objection. His fear of men is absolute. Angel cannot be ridden by a man."

"Francoise?" Issie said. "Francoise, what if it wasn't a man? What if it wasn't Alfie riding him? What if it was a woman?"

"That is impossible," Francoise said. "In case you haven't noticed, my arm is broken – and the race is just a week away. And anyway—"

"I didn't mean you!" Issie said. "I meant me. I can ride him."

The Frenchwoman shook her head. "No, no! Let me finish. It is not possible for you or any woman to ride. In the history of the Silver Bridle, the riders for each hacienda have always, always been men. Women do not race."

Issie furrowed her brow. "So are you saying it's against the rules for a girl to ride?"

Alfie shook his head. "It's not the rules, exactly. It's tradition. But traditions are strong here. You know what my dad is like."

"But your dad would understand. If Angel is the fastest horse then he'd want Angel to run, wouldn't he? If it's not actually against the rules? I mean, *if* I could convince Roberto, if I could get him to let me ride Angel, then they wouldn't be able to stop me?"

"No," Francoise admitted. "They wouldn't be able to stop you."

"Then we should ask Roberto to let me ride," Issie said.

"Now hold on a minute," Avery said. "Issie, I think you need to get a grip. Roberto will never allow this. The Silver Bridle is not just any horse race, it's a duel on horseback, a contest where horses and men routinely risk their lives to win."

"Tom is right," Francoise agreed. "The men who ride this race are battle-hardened. Once they are in that village square and the bell rings to signal the start, they will fight like animals to win."

"If I could get a good start and ride Angel like I did today then it wouldn't matter," Issie insisted. "We'd be out in front the whole way and no one would even have the chance to touch us."

"This is crazy even to talk about this," Francoise sighed. "Even if we were all in agreement, what then? You would still have to convince Roberto." She paused. "This race is of the utmost importance to him. He has focused all his energy on training Marius for this day.

It will be impossible for him to change his mind now."

"It's true," Alfie said. "You've seen my father in action, Issie. He's not a man who is easily persuaded."

Issie knew this was true. She found the idea of facing up to Roberto scarier than any horse race. Since they had arrived at El Caballo, Roberto had been the perfect host, kind and generous. But there was also something that made Issie nervous around him. Roberto had kept a cool distance from her ever since she arrived. And his conversation in the living room with Avery made it clear that he thought she was… what was the word he used? Impetuous!

To Roberto, Issie was nothing more than a troublesome kid. Convincing him that she was capable of riding in the race was not going to be easy.

"Francoise?" Issie said hopefully. "Will you ask him? Will you tell Roberto that Angel should race?"

Francoise shook her head. "No, Isadora. It would do no good. Roberto thinks you are just a child. If you want him to let you ride, then it is up to you to convince him that you can take on the *vaquero*s and beat them at their own game."

"Francoise is right," Alfie agreed. "My father is a man of honour. You stand a better chance of winning his respect if you ask him yourself."

"If you want to race Angel, it is up to you," Francoise said. "Isadora, you alone are the one. You must talk to Roberto Nunez."

Chapter 12

The indoor training school at El Caballo Danza Magnifico was a spectacular space. With its vaulted ceilings and horse tapestries hanging at the entranceways, it had the feel of a grand cathedral – one with an Olympic-sized dressage arena in the middle of it.

This training arena was the very heart of El Caballo Danza Magnifico. All the schooling for the *haute école* horses took place here. The spectacular shows that the Spanish stallions performed around the world required years of training and it all happened right here.

At this very moment the famed El Caballo stallions were in the middle of a training session, rehearsing their latest routine for the upcoming world tour. As Issie entered the school in search of Roberto her eyes fell upon the stallions and the vision took her breath away.

In the arena, twelve perfect, white horses were marching in unison, lifting their legs up in a high, exaggerated Spanish Walk. One by one the stallions wheeled about, pirouetting, striking off at precisely the same time to dance a half-pass back across the sand.

It was a performance that any horse-lover in the world would have paid handsomely to see, and here was Issie, all alone, with a front row seat, watching the greatest performing horses in the business at work.

She gazed on, enraptured, as the elegant stallions, their manes cascading down their necks like white silk, tails flowing behind them like bridal trains, began to circle the arena, showing off their extended trot – their legs flicking out in front of them like ballerinas *en pointe*, graceful and poised…

"Stop! Stop!" There was a voice over the sound system. The riders, immediately aware that something was not right, pulled their horses up to a halt and turned their heads to look up at the man above them, sitting enclosed in a glass booth that looked down over the arena. Issie looked up there too and saw Roberto, sitting behind the microphone in the booth.

Roberto spoke again into the microphone and his voice

echoed out through the speakers in the arena. "Very good pirouettes," he said, "lovely collection! But then what happened when you were doing the extended trot? I expect these horses to look like they are floating above the sand, not just trotting along like it's a hack in the park! Remember when you ask for the trot to really drive them forward with your hips to get their legs active."

He muttered something in Spanish that Issie didn't understand and then spoke again clearly into the microphone. "We're going to take it from the very start again. This time, I want to see their hooves strike the ground exactly on the beat of the castanets. OK? Let's take it from the top!"

Roberto was about to say something else when he spotted Issie at the side of the arena. He gave her a wave. "Isadora, you are welcome to come up and join me in here," he spoke into the microphone. "Use the steps at the back of the arena – the hallway leads you up to the booth."

Issie did as he said, walking between the rows of tiered seating towards the far corner of the arena until she found the stairwell that led up to the glass viewing booth where Roberto was sitting.

Roberto greeted her warmly with a kiss on both cheeks. "You came to watch the horses train?"

Issie didn't know what to say. She was too nervous to bring up the real reason for her visit. "Why did you stop them just now?" she asked. "I was watching them do the extended trot and I thought they looked OK. What was wrong with it?"

Roberto shook his head. "It was no good. Not enough elevation, not enough... magic. El Caballo Danza Magnifico has the best horses in the world – watching them perform must be more than just *OK*." He stressed the word as if he found it distasteful. "They must be magnificent. It is easy to produce horses that can perform a reasonable pirouette or half-pass, but here we are always striving to reach the utmost levels of the *haute école*. It is that final polish that will make the crowd gasp with delight or cry with pure joy. This is what we must aim for."

Roberto beckoned for Issie to take a seat next to him. Then he slid down the yellow button on the control desk in front of him and the lights in the arena faded to black. He pressed another button on the console and the music began once more, the sound of the Spanish flamenco. As the castanets began to strike up, Roberto slid the lights back on, the signal for the horses to enter the ring to start the routine again. Issie watched as they came in single file down the centre line of the arena, peeling off one by one in each direction.

"I've seen this before," she said to Roberto, "in Chevalier Point, when El Caballo was on tour. I saw them perform this routine."

"We have changed it a little since then," Roberto said. "There is a whole new dance for the Anglo-Arab mares to perform also."

He took his eyes off the Lipizzaners in front of him now and turned to look at Isadora.

"Tell me," he said, "how is Salome? The mare that you call Blaze. Is she happy in your country? She must miss her old life, running with the herd under the heat of the Spanish sun. She is so far from home, it must be very strange for her."

Issie had never thought about it like that before. As far as she was concerned, Blaze was home. OK, so the mare had grown up here at El Caballo, but she was Issie's horse now, and she knew Blaze loved her life in Chevalier Point.

"She's great," Issie said. "I haven't ridden her since Storm was born, and it's winter at home, but when the weather gets better I'll be able to ride her again."

Roberto smiled. "She is not an easy mare to ride. Anglo-Arabs can be highly strung and Salome is no exception. It is impressive that you can handle her. Avery tells me that you are a very good rider."

Issie squirmed nervously. This seemed like a good time to ask Roberto the question that she had come here with. "Roberto, I wanted to talk to you… It's about the Silver Bridle."

"What about it?" Roberto stiffened in his seat. He could see that Issie had something important on her mind.

"I know that you think that Marius can win the race," Issie began, "but what if there was an even faster horse in your stable?"

Roberto shook his head. "Impossible. I am quite certain. Marius is my best stallion. Alfonso has raced him against every horse in my stable to prove it!"

"Not every horse," Issie said.

Roberto looked at her. "And which horse is it that you suggest? Who do you think is faster than Marius?"

"Angel," Issie said. "I think Angel should be your champion to race in the Silver Bridle."

Roberto shook his head. "Did Francoise not explain to you?" he asked. "Angel is afraid of men. All of the men in my stable have attempted to ride him. He will not have a man on his back – not even Alfonso, and he is my best rider."

"Angel's scared of men – but he's not scared of women," Issie said. "He's not scared of me. I can ride him, Roberto!"

"You?" Roberto looked hard at her. "How old are you? Fourteen? You are not a grown woman. You are not much more than a child."

"I'm old enough. I rode him today – he was faster than Marius. You can ask Francoise and Alfie – they'll back me up."

Roberto raised an eyebrow. "You raced against Marius?"

"I didn't mean to race him – it just kind of happened. Alfie and I were riding back across the high pasture and Angel totally beat him to the other side. Marius had a twenty-length lead on us and we overtook him."

Roberto's eyes narrowed. "The high pasture? You were near Vega's hacienda?"

Issie winced at this. She had been hoping Roberto wouldn't question how she came to be racing against Marius.

"Umm… yeah, Alfie was showing me around. You know, a full tour of the estate," she offered. It was a feeble excuse, but Roberto seemed to let it slide.

"Anyway, it makes no difference if Angel beat Marius racing on the high pasture," Roberto continued. "The Silver Bridle is not raced on open fields. This is no ordinary race, it is a street fight, a rough contest, ridden by men who will stop at nothing to win. It is no place for a girl."

"But Angel can win. I know he can!" Issie said. "Please, Roberto, let me prove it to you. Let Angel race Marius again. We can race on the streets of the square this time and that will prove to you that I can handle it. Then you'll have to let Angel take Marius's place in the race."

Roberto bristled at this. "Have to? I do not have to do anything, Isadora. I understand that this race means a lot to you also – your colt is at stake. Still, it is up to me to decide who races for El Caballo. It is not your choice to make."

Issie opened her mouth to speak, but Roberto raised a hand. "Wait!" he said. "I did not say no, did I? If Angel is as fast as you say he is, then I want to see it for myself. We shall have a match race as you suggest. Tomorrow we shall take both the horses to the village square and see whether you are right. If your horse can run as fast as he did in the fields, then he will be our champion for the Silver Bridle. But if he does not win, then you must accept it, and stand back and let Alfie and Marius take up the flag for El Caballo instead. Does that sound fair?"

Issie was overcome with excitement. "Thank you, Roberto. Thank you for giving me this chance!"

"You have much courage for one so young." Roberto

smiled at her. "You will need all of it to best my son in this match race."

"I won't let you down," Issie said. "You'll see. Angel will prove how fast he is tomorrow."

Roberto raised an eyebrow at this, then he said, "Tell me, Isadora, what will happen if we do win the Silver Bridle?"

"What do you mean?" Issie was confused.

"You will get your colt back," Roberto said. "And what then? What will you do with him? Take him home to your pony club at Chevalier Point?"

"Why?" Issie said. "Is there something wrong with that? He's my horse!" She could feel her pulse racing now. What did Roberto mean? Was he planning to try and take the colt off her?

"Do not panic," Roberto said gently. "You must know by now, the colt is yours and no one at El Caballo would dream of taking him away from you."

"Then why wouldn't I take him home with me?"

"Because he is already home," Roberto said. "Isadora, look around you here. You are standing in one of the greatest horse training institutions in the whole world. This is where Nightstorm is meant to be. Leave him here with us and we will train him for you. He can receive schooling here with the best riders in the world. He'll be taught *haute école* movements, far above anything that he might learn at pony club. We could fulfil the destiny of his bloodlines, make him a true El Caballo stallion."

"Why would you do that? What would be in it for you?"

"You know how important Nightstorm's bloodlines are to us," Roberto said. "When Nightstorm comes of age, we would use him as a sire across our best mares. His progeny, his colts and fillies, would be invaluable for El Caballo. Then, with Nightstorm's training completed, and with our fields full of his foals, we could return him to you."

Issie didn't know what to say.

"Do not answer me now," Roberto told her. "Please, take your time and think about it. Search your heart. For you must know that this farm is Nightstorm's true home. Just as it is still the home of his mother, Salome."

"Her name isn't Salome – it's Blaze," Issie said, "and her home is with me in Chevalier Point, just like Storm."

Roberto was quiet for a moment. When he finally spoke, his voice was soft and low. "I can see the great love that you have for your horses, Isadora," he said. "It burns like a fire in you," and then he added, "but love does not always mean keeping things close to your heart. Sometimes it can also mean letting them go."

He looked down at the arena where the stallions were now finishing their routine. The Lipizzaners were taking their bows, each horse lowering itself down on to one knee to bow its head, while the riders on their backs doffed their hats to the imaginary audience.

"They have finished. I must go down to the arena now to discuss their training. They have much that they need to improve on," Roberto told her. "I am sorry our conversation must end here. But we will talk again, I am sure. With the race coming, there is much to be decided."

"Yes," Issie agreed. "There really is."

At dinner that night, Issie was surprised when Roberto poured her a glass of *fino* sherry, just like the adults had, and then raised his glass.

"I would like to propose a toast," Roberto said. "We are lucky to have friends here with us from across the world, friends who love and value their horses as much as we do. Tomorrow my son Alfie and Isadora will have their match race to see which of them will ride for the Silver Bridle and the glory of El Caballo Danza Magnifico. I wish them both luck. *Viva El Caballo!*"

"*Viva El Caballo!*" everyone cried, raising their glasses.

Avery, though, did not raise his glass. It was clear he was not happy with Roberto's decision, but he said nothing.

Issie, who was sitting next to Alfie, took a sip of her sherry. It was dry and almost bitter. "It doesn't taste anything like the stuff that Granny has in her sideboard at home," she said to Alfie.

"That depends on who your grandma is," Alfie smiled. He began to eat his paella.

"Umm, Alfie?" Issie said. "I know that the Silver Bridle is, like, a really big thing for you. I just want to say that I'm not trying to take your place. If there was any way that you could ride Angel instead of me…"

Alfie smiled at her. "Yes, the race is a big deal for me. I have been training for it my whole life. Ever since I was a young boy I knew I wanted to ride in the Silver Bridle and bring honour to El Caballo."

"I'm really sorry—" Issie began, but he cut her off.

"My ego will be bruised if you beat me, Issie, but the most important thing is for El Caballo to win against Vega, so that we can get your colt back and our horses too. If you and Angel are faster than me and Marius, then I will accept that."

"Thank you." Issie smiled.

"Hey!" Alfie said. "Don't thank me yet – you still haven't won. Don't get me wrong, I plan to beat you tomorrow, Isadora. Once we are lined up on that race course we will no longer be friends, we will be adversaries. My dad has given me instructions to treat you like any other rival for the Silver Bridle. Kicking, pushing, even biting the other riders, nothing is outlawed in this race. You must be prepared for anything."

"You're kidding me, right?" Issie couldn't believe it.

"We will see tomorrow, won't we?" Alfie replied.

Avery, who had been listening to their conversation, didn't say anything, but after dinner as they were all heading for their rooms he pulled Issie aside.

"I heard what Alfie was saying to you at dinner," Avery said. "Issie, I cannot believe you're going through with this. I never thought for a moment that Roberto would agree to it, or I would have put my foot down earlier." Avery looked serious. "This match race could get rough. I think you need to reconsider."

Issie shook her head. "I can handle it, Tom. I'm not scared."

"That's the problem. You should be," Avery replied. "Issie, I don't want to risk you getting hurt—"

"Please, Tom," Issie said. "Don't try and talk me out

of it. I've been feeling so helpless ever since we got here and everyone keeps treating me like I'm just this little girl. Now I've managed to convince Roberto to let me race, and if you force me to back out again then he'll think I'm just a silly kid."

Avery shook his head. "I'm not happy about this. I wish you'd reconsider. At least promise me you'll play it safe?"

Issie smiled. "You've got my word on it."

The match race was planned for early the next morning. Issie had woken up with her tummy in a tight ball of nerves and so she decided to skip breakfast. She pulled on her jodhpurs and boots and headed down to the stables. When she arrived, she found Alfie, Roberto and Avery already there waiting for her.

"Francoise has saddled up Angel for you. She's just getting Marius ready now," Avery told Issie. "We'll all be riding together up to the village."

Alfie smiled at Issie as he adjusted his helmet. "Did you sleep well?" he asked. "Are you ready to race?"

Issie was about to reply when she was interrupted by shouts coming from the stables. The grooms in the stallions' quarters were yelling about something. Issie couldn't make out what they were saying. She could hear Francoise's voice over all the others' though, and she sounded really upset. She was speaking in Spanish so Issie didn't have a clue what she was on about, but Roberto clearly understood her. His face fell as he heard Francoise's cries and then he was running for the stables with Alfie right behind him.

Avery and Issie instinctively followed after them, running across the cobbled courtyard. They had almost reached the stallions' quarters when Francoise emerged in front of them. She was leading Marius and immediately Issie could see that something was very wrong with the grey stallion. Francoise was trying to make Marius walk forward, but the horse was refusing to move properly. As Issie and the others looked on in horror, Francoise coaxed him to take a few more tentative steps, and it became clear that Marius was favouring his near front leg. The stallion was placing his hoof gingerly on the ground, as if he were afraid to put his weight on it. He made one more noble effort and tried to hobble forward for another stride or so, then he gave up and lifted the leg up, holding it aloft pitifully in midair. Issie saw Francoise shaking her head, and the look of complete despair on Roberto's face as the reality of the disaster they were witnessing sank in.

There would be no match race today. Marius, the great hope for the Silver Bridle, the finest stallion of El Caballo Danza Magnifico, was lame.

Chapter 13

It was a tense wait back at El Caballo Danza Magnifico while the vet examined Marius. When he finally emerged from the stallion's loose box, shaking his head as he spoke to Roberto, they all knew the news wasn't good.

"It's a ripped tendon," the vet confirmed as they gathered around. "My guess is that it was caused by the stress of galloping on hard, uneven ground. Has this horse been ridden fast across country recently?"

Alfie and Issie both looked guiltily at each other, thinking about their escape from Vega's hacienda.

"How bad is it?" Alfie asked nervously. He was as white as a sheet as he asked the question they all wanted the answer to. "Will he still be able to race?"

The vet nodded solemnly. "He'll heal all right – but

not in time to race on Saturday. An injury like this needs time, the leg has to mend. It'll be at least a month before he can be ridden again."

"Thank you, Hector," Roberto said quietly. "I appreciate your help, coming here so quickly to examine him."

"I'm very sorry it couldn't be better news, Roberto," the vet said. "I know how much this horse means to El Caballo Danza Magnifico. If it is any consolation, you should know that the injury could have happened at any time. Perhaps it is better for it to have happened now than for the horse to break down halfway through the race."

Roberto didn't say anything. He walked on with the vet towards the wrought-iron gates of the hacienda and the vet continued to talk as he got into his car, telling Roberto about the medication he had prescribed for Marius, and advising him on strapping the leg until the tendons began to heal.

As he drove off, Roberto walked back across the cobbled courtyard to join the others who had been standing watching in silence.

"Dad," Alfie began, "it's all my fault. I should never have taken him out and galloped him this close to the race. It was—"

Roberto raised his hand to stop him. "Alfonso, you

heard the vet. There was a weakness in his tendon and this could have happened at any time. If he had not hurt his leg in this way, then perhaps he might have broken down in the Silver Bridle and been beaten."

Roberto turned to Issie. "Isadora, you shall get your wish. You wanted to ride Angel in the Silver Bridle? You will get to do exactly that."

"You mean—" Issie started to say.

"Without Marius, I have to race another horse," Roberto said. "Angel is the fastest stallion in my possession. And I have no choice in the matter but to put you on his back. So it is decided. You will line up at the starting rope as our champion on Saturday. The fate of El Caballo Danza Magnifico, and of your colt, is now in your hands."

Back at the villa, Issie still couldn't believe what had just happened.

"Roberto must hate me," she said to Avery.

"Why on earth would you think that?" he said.

"Because this is all my fault. I was the one who decided to go to Vega's to get Storm back. If Alfie hadn't come with me then Marius would never have got injured…"

"… or he might have broken down during the race itself and it could have been much worse," Avery finished her sentence. "Issie, you heard what the vet said. That stallion's tendon could have ripped at any time. I know that Roberto doesn't blame you."

"He'll blame me if I lose the race on Saturday, though, won't he?"

Avery looked worried. "Issie, this is too much pressure for Roberto or anyone to put on you, making you responsible for the future of El Caballo. Listen, Roberto is my friend. I'll talk to him, tell him that I will race instead. I can ride Sorcerer – he's fast enough."

"No, Tom!" Issie said. "Angel is the fastest horse and you know it."

"Issie," Avery said, "I'm your guardian here and I'm putting my foot down. I'm going to ride in your place."

"Tom, you can't. I have to do this. Sorcerer isn't ready. You'll lose and then Roberto will lose his five best horses to Vega. He's already got Storm and he's bound to choose Marius – maybe Angel too!"

"Maybe," Avery said, "but I'd rather lose the horses than risk your life."

"There are always risks! What about riding at Badminton?" Issie shot back. "I bet that was a risk when you did it the first time. And how about when you rode at the Olympics? Did you know the risks then, Tom? Riders make their own choices. Now I'm making mine. I know it's hard, but you have to let me grow up. Let me do this. Angel can win this race, but he can't do it without me – please, let me ride."

"There are other ways, Issie," Avery said. "I don't want you to get hurt. It's too dangerous. You heard what Alfie said about the other riders. They'll fight you and you're too small to fight them back."

"No, they won't." Issie shook her head. "They won't fight me. Not if I get away fast enough at the break. Tom, what if I could get Angel out in the lead right from the start and stay there the whole way? If we were out in front and Angel could hold the lead ahead of the other riders then they'd never get the chance to push me around."

Avery considered this for a moment. "It could work, I suppose," he said, "but you'd have to be lightning-quick at the break to make sure you got out in front straight away."

"I've already thought about that," Issie said. "Angel has the speed to do it, he just needs the training, so that he'd be certain to take off from the start line before all the other horses."

"So you're going to teach him to break?" Avery said.

"No," Issie replied hopefully, "you are." She looked at Avery. "Please, Tom, I can't do this without your help. I need you to be my trainer."

The next day was Tuesday – which meant that Avery and Issie had just four days to train Angel before they faced Vega in the village square.

Avery had told Issie to meet him at the stables bright and early on Tuesday morning, and when she got there she found her instructor in the tack room.

"I've been making some modifications to Angel's saddle," he said. The traditional *vaquero* stirrups, cast from black iron and clunky as a suit of armour, had been removed. Avery had replaced them with lightweight stainless-steel stirrups. "I found these in an old box stacked under the saddle blankets – they're just what you need," Avery said. "Those other stirrups are fine for *vaquero*s who ride with their legs hanging long, but for racing you need smaller stirrups so that you can balance up high in the saddle."

Avery took the saddle out into the courtyard, and Issie followed behind him.

"Umm, Tom?" she said. "Where are you going? Angel is in the other direction."

"I know," Avery said, "but in case you've forgotten, Angel is not very fond of men and I happen to be one. Once you get on his back it will be almost impossible for me to handle him. So if you want me to teach you how to ride a racehorse we're going to have to do it before you get on his back."

"How?" Issie didn't understand.

Avery took the saddle now and slung it over a hay bale in the corner of the courtyard.

"Climb up on that," he said.

"You want me to ride a hay bale?" Issie frowned.

"Why not? Are you worried it's going to buck you off?" Avery grinned. Then he explained. "The idea is to get your position right in the saddle before you mount up on Angel. Racehorse jockeys have a different centre of gravity. They ride with very short stirrups. Hop up on the saddle here and I'll show you."

"OK, but I feel pretty silly," Issie grumbled as she clambered up and threw herself into the saddle. She let her feet dangle down because the stirrups seemed to be adjusted so that the leathers were really short.

"Put your feet in the irons and tell me how they feel," Avery instructed her.

"I feel like a bird on a perch!" Issie giggled. "Look how high my knees are! It feels weird."

Avery eyed her up carefully, and shook his head. "They're the perfect length, you just need to get used to them – you're riding like a jockey now."

"Well, I don't know how they do it," Issie said.

Avery climbed up next to her on the hay bales, crouching down as if he were the jockey on his horse. "You need to tilt forward like me. It's a bit like two-point jumping position. You keep your weight over his wither and stay low. Your aim is to stay off his back and let him run. It will make you twice as fast around the track."

"I don't get it," Issie said. "My legs are up so high, how do I make him go?"

"Urge him on with your arms," Avery replied, "and give him little taps with your ankles and increase these as you want to go faster. It's easy, really."

Issie looked at him quizzically. "How do you know all this?"

"I rode trackwork for a few years," Avery said. "I had big plans to be a jockey."

"Why didn't you?"

"I grew two feet too tall!" Avery grinned.

"So you never raced?"

Avery shook his head. "Afraid not, but I rode the training sessions like a demon. I even had a nickname.

They used to call me 'The Spaceman' because I had a knack of finding the smallest space on the inside rail and slipping through it. I'd sit back and wait at the back of the field until we were right down to the wire and then I'd kick on and make my move. Always go for the inside rail, Issie, that's the fastest way. No matter how small the space may look, if you're a smart rider you can make it."

Avery paused. "Not that you'll be riding with tactics like that. You need to get out in front of the other riders right from the start. It'll surprise them when you take an early lead. They won't be expecting it. Once you're out in front, Angel must hold that lead. He's got the stamina to maintain the gallop the whole two kilometres, for three laps of the track. If you ride the race like I show you, they'll be left in your dust." Avery smiled. "Anyway, are you ready to get off the hay bales and start training a real horse?"

Issie felt the butterflies surging in her tummy. "I guess so."

"Then let's go saddle up."

With Avery riding by her side on Sorcerer, Issie headed out of the gates of El Caballo. She was practising her new jockey position, standing up in her short stirrups, keeping her weight centred over Angel's wither, but she nearly lost her balance when Avery turned Sorcerer to the left and headed up the dirt road in the opposite direction from the village.

Issie was confused. "Aren't we going to the village to train in the square?"

Avery shook his head. "I talked to Roberto about it last night. We both decided that training Angel in the village is too risky. It's full of gossips and Vega probably already knows that Marius is lame and Angel is racing in his place. We don't need Vega's spies watching us while we train and telling him what we're up to."

"So where are we going?" Issie asked.

"Follow me, you'll see," Avery said.

The two riders cantered up and around the winding roads that led to the peak of the olive hills behind El Caballo and a few minutes later they had reached the rise of a hill overlooking flat fields. The fields directly below them were planted with olives, but beyond the olive trees was a flat, barren plain, perfect for riding trackwork.

"This is where we'll train him," Avery said. "Do you see those trees over there? They mark the edge of the course. Then you take him all the way to the old stone building there, and then back to me. That's about two kilometres – the same distance as the Silver Bridle."

Avery pulled a stopwatch out of his pocket.

"What's that for?" Issie asked.

"Timing you," Avery said. "On a decent track, a fast racehorse can do two kilometres in a little under two minutes thirty. I want to get a sense of how fast Angel is."

Avery scratched a line in the dirt with his shoe right next to a tall olive tree.

"This is your start line. Now I don't want you to take him flat out, the first time around just breeze him, OK?"

Issie looked puzzled.

"It's a racing term," Avery said. "It means ride him at a medium pace. Let him gallop, but don't push him."

Issie did up the strap on her helmet.

"Take it easy this time. We'll see how he goes," Avery said and Issie lined the stallion up.

"On your marks, get set... go!"

Avery dropped his hand and Issie took the cue, letting go of her tight grip on the reins. Angel lunged forward, breaking like a racehorse. His burst of speed was so sudden that for a moment Issie was left behind the stallion's movement and had to snatch at his mane to hang on. She looked down and saw the ground rushing beneath her, felt a sick sensation and a rush of nervous energy. *Don't look down and don't think about it*, she told herself firmly. And then she pulled herself back up into position and shook off her fears, focused on looking at the track ahead of her.

She was in sync with the grey horse's gallop now, moving with him, staying low over his neck, crouching like a jockey. As they rounded the first corner her arms were beginning to ache, feeling the strain of holding the stallion back. Avery had told her not to push Angel too hard, but she wasn't pushing at all – she was using every bit of strength she had just to hold him!

Issie's fingers were cramping from holding the reins so tight, the leather cutting into her fingers. Now, as she came past the trees that marked halfway on the course, she loosened her grip a little and Angel instantly took the bit and lengthened his stride. He was still fighting her hands, asking for even more rein, wanting to go faster.

"You want to go, huh, boy?" Issie whispered to him. She loosened the reins off more this time. She wasn't going to fight him any more. "OK, Angel," she said, letting the reins go slack, "time to go!"

As the great, grey stallion began to really lengthen his stride and extend his neck, Issie felt the wind in her face, blowing dust into her eyes, blurring her vision. She tried to stay low so that the horse's mane protected her, and focused all her energy into hanging on as they headed down the final stretch.

As they crossed the line, Issie saw Avery out of the corner of her eye, clicking his stopwatch. He looked pleased. Angel, meanwhile, was thrilling at the chance to run, so much so that it took Issie another few hundred metres before she could pull the stallion back to a trot and turn him round to return to her instructor.

"Well?" she said to Tom. "How did we do?"

Avery showed Issie the numbers on the stopwatch. "He just did two kilometres in two minutes twenty. Never mind the Silver Bridle," he said, "we should be entering Angel at Ascot."

Over the next two days Avery and Issie trained Angel at the fields. Avery would get her to gallop the horse flat out for a lap or two and breeze the horse for a couple more laps of the barren fields, before trotting him for another twenty minutes or so to cool him down.

Every time Issie rode Angel around the track, she felt more and more in the groove with the grey stallion beneath her. When Avery had first shortened her stirrups so that she was riding high in the saddle she had felt a little unstable, out of balance. Now, it felt like the most natural thing in the world to be perched up there on top of this enormous horse, feeling the wind biting into her face as the stallion ran at a gallop towards the finish line.

On the Thursday, Francoise and Alfie accompanied them to the training grounds. Francoise wore a shotgun at her hip and Alfie carried a length of white rope slung over his shoulder.

"What's that for?" Issie asked.

"You want Angel to be fast at the break, don't you?" Francoise replied. "Well, this is how they start the horses for the Silver Bridle. There will be a length of white rope strung across the square. The horses will line up behind it and then when the starter's gun goes they will take off. That is what we will now practise."

And so Issie spent the morning lining Angel up again and again behind the white rope while Avery and Francoise held each end. Alfie stood nearby with the shotgun and fired it into the air every time Francoise and Avery dropped the rope. At exactly the same moment, Issie dug her heels into Angel's sides, urging the stallion forward.

"We want him to make the connection between the gun firing and the rope falling so that he leaps forward on cue," Avery explained. And so they kept going, starting the horse over and over again, firing the gun and dropping the rope, honing his instincts so that after a dozen or so times, Issie didn't even need to kick him on, the stallion instinctively surged forward the moment the rope fell. By the end of the day all four of them were convinced that when the race day came, Angel would be the fastest horse at the break. Now all he had to do was stay in front.

"How is the training progressing?" Roberto asked them at dinner that evening. "Do we have a champion in our stables?"

Avery pushed his fork into his paella. "I think so," he replied.

"Victorioso will be the horse to beat," Roberto continued. "The black stallion is a threat, especially with Vega on his back."

"Angel can take Victorioso," Avery said with certainty. "He's fast, Roberto. Faster than any Andalusian has the right to be. When the race starts he'll be out in front. Issie just has to keep him there."

"Do not forget, you must be careful on the corners," Alfie told Issie. "The village square isn't built like a real race track. The turns are much sharper than they look."

"He's right," Francoise agreed. "The square is white chalk underfoot and very slippery. It is not uncommon for horses to slide and crash, and the houses are built so close to the streets if the horses don't stay on course they risk slamming into the walls."

"OK," Issie said nervously. "I'll be careful on the corners."

Roberto shook his head. "It is just as dangerous on the straight. There, the riders will try and grab you, your clothes, your reins, anything they can get their hands on. They will try and unbalance you, try and pull you off your horse so that they can get past you."

"Isn't that illegal?" Issie asked.

"Nothing is illegal in this race," said Roberto. "On the day of the Silver Bridle the village square will become a battleground. Do you truly think you are ready for that?"

Issie put down her fork. Suddenly she didn't feel so hungry any more. The race was coming and nothing could stop it now. Was she ready? She had to be.

Chapter 14

The next morning, when Issie sat down to breakfast with Avery, he told her that the training session was cancelled for the day.

"He's already race-fit and you've learnt every trick I have to show you," Avery said. "Why don't you just saddle him up and go off for a ride, just the two of you? Don't gallop him, just take him for a bit of a hack. Relax, get your head together."

Issie was happy to be left to her own devices. Last night's discussion of tactics at the dinner table had left her a bundle of nerves. Going for a ride by herself was the perfect way to calm down and mentally prepare herself for tomorrow's race.

At the stables, the grey stallion gave a nicker as she

walked into his stall, greeting Issie as if she were an old friend. The training over the past few days had made Issie even more aware of how special Angel really was. She loved his softness, how he could be so strong and focused when he raced, and yet so gentle here in the stables. In the afternoons, while El Caballo *vaqueros* were having their siestas, Issie would often come by to visit Angel. She would sit down in the straw at the side of his stall and chat away to the stallion as if he were Stella or Kate, talking to him about everything she was thinking, about how much she missed Storm, and about her life back in Chevalier Point with Blaze and Comet.

Sitting there next to the majestic stallion she felt completely safe, despite the fact that with a single sweep of his mighty hooves he could have struck her a mortal blow. She wasn't afraid. Angel was the gentlest horse she had ever met, unlike any other stallion she had ever encountered. The horse, for his part, seemed glad of her company. He would cock one ear as he listened to her idle chatter and then, if he got bored with Issie's endless stories, he would lower his neck, nudging the girl with his muzzle, which was his signal that he wanted her to scratch him in the sweet spot just behind his ears.

"No training today, Angel," Issie told the grey stallion

as she saddled him up. "We've got the day off. We're going to take a ride, just you and me."

The sky was clear and blue, and the early-morning sun was already warm on her bare skin as Issie rode into the cobbled courtyard. Beneath her, Angel was keyed up and ready to gallop, and she had to steady him back with her legs and her hands.

"Not today, boy," she cooed to the horse. "Save it for tomorrow, today we're just going to take it easy."

They cantered out through the gates of El Caballo Danza Magnifico and Issie was about to turn left towards the olive-tree hills and the race track, but something made her change her mind. Instead, she turned right, back around the white walls of the hacienda, through the fields where the mares and their foals were grazing, heading towards the gorge.

"We're not going all the way to Vega's," she reassured Angel, "I just want to go to the end of the gorge."

Once they had entered the gorge Issie held Angel to a trot, careful not to let him injure himself on the rocky terrain. She looked at the chalky cliffs rising up on either side of her, the slit of blue sky above her head.

It had been less than a week ago that Vega's men had chased Issie and Angel from his hacienda to this gorge when she had tried to steal her colt back. So much had happened in that short time! Throughout it all, though, Issie had never forgotten why she had come here. She was here to get her colt back. Now, as she rode on through the gorge, she realised she was riding towards Vega's hacienda, drawn towards the colt once more. She knew she couldn't get close enough to see him without getting caught, but she wished she could, just for a moment. She wanted to let him know that she hadn't forgotten him, that she was doing her best to get him back.

"Just one more day, Storm," she said under her breath, "one more day and you'll be with me again, I promise."

She was lost in her own thoughts as she trotted Angel on, heading into the narrow part of the gorge, a skinny path cut between the rocks, and it took her a moment to realise that there was a shadow in front of them, and it was moving towards them at speed.

She could see that it was a rider on horseback, but the sunlight was behind whoever it was, and the light was so strong it blinded her. It wasn't until they were much closer that she could make out who it was. The horse was an enormous black stallion – and the rider was none other than Miguel Vega.

Seized with panic, Issie tried to turn Angel round, but they were in the narrowest part of the gorge and turning here was impossible. She was in a frenzy now, trying to rein-back to get away, when she heard Vega's voice calling out to her.

"Wait! Do not run, little girl. I want to talk to you."

And then she was face to face with Vega, the man grinning stupidly at her, his bushy moustache twitching with pleasure at her obvious discomfort.

"The young *señorita*!" Vega said. "You came looking for me? What a lovely surprise!"

Issie felt her heart racing. "I wasn't looking for you." She tried to keep the fear out of her voice but she knew that Vega would be able to see that she was shaking. "Let me leave – I want to go home."

"Ah," Vega said. "You are afraid of Miguel Vega? Do not be scared. I only want to talk! It is fortunate that we have met here today. Why not take advantage of this wonderful opportunity that now presents itself to both of us?" His voice was as oily as his slicked-back hair. "I hear that Marius is injured and that you are the one who will now be riding against my hacienda in the Silver Bridle."

Issie nodded.

Vega smiled. "Excellent! Then luck is truly on your side, because this meeting may be most beneficial to you."

"What do you mean?" Issie was getting nervous. She had her hands and legs poised, ready to manoeuvre Angel quickly back in a half-circle to gallop off if she needed to, if Vega got any closer. Angel was ready to run too. He hated being this close to Vega, and Issie could feel the stallion's muscles twitching with barely controlled desperation to get away from the bully who had inflicted the pain of the *serreta* upon him so long ago.

The mustachioed man laughed and the fat on his belly wobbled beneath his cummerbund. "Look at you! As tense as a cat! Do not fear. I have no plans to hurt you…" A malevolent grin played across his face. "Why would I? I do not need to. Not when I still have your colt."

Issie's eyes widened in horror. "What do you mean? Is that a threat? What have you done to him?"

"I have not done anything to him… yet," Vega said. "What happens to him next is up to you."

Vega rode the black stallion a few steps closer, and Issie fought to control Angel as the grey stallion became more desperate than ever to get away from the man he hated so deeply. "Hold your horse still and listen," Vega snapped, "because I am making you an offer that you have no choice but to accept. I do not want to take any chances with the contest tomorrow. If you agree to hold Angel back, and make sure that you lose the race, then I will be generous. I will give you back your colt and you will be free to take him home. You have my word."

"You want me to lose?" Issie said.

"Oh, I am sure I will beat you anyway," Vega said boastfully. "Miguel Vega is a great rider. My horse Victorioso is magnificent. A little girl like you, a *chica*, you will never beat us. But then I figure, why take chances? I want your word that you will lose. I look forward to seeing the face of Roberto Nunez when you come in last."

"So if I lose the race, you'll give me back my colt."

"*Si, si*, of course," Vega said dismissively, "but you must not try to pass me in the race. If you try to take the lead at any stage I will know that you have betrayed me. My men will be watching you too and they will know that this is the signal to return to my stables and fix the *serreta* bridle on to your beloved colt. If you cross the line first, your colt will suffer for it. You must bow to my demands. It is the only way to save your beloved Nightstorm."

"How do I know you'll really give him back to me?" Issie asked.

"You have Miguel Vega's word as a gentleman," Vega

445

said. As he said this, he rode a step closer towards her and suddenly reached out a hand to grasp at Angel's reins. The stallion was too quick for him, though, rearing back and pirouetting on his hocks. All the time they had been talking, Issie had been inching the stallion backwards slowly. They had now reached a small gap in the rocks that was wide enough to turn and she did so now.

"Run then!" Vega laughed after her as Angel broke into a gallop. "But do not forget my kind offer. If you do not take it you are nothing but a fool, and your precious Storm, your colt, will suffer."

Vega made no attempt to chase after them. As he had already told Issie, he didn't need to hurt her. Not when he could cause her so much more pain by hurting the thing she loved most – her colt.

Issie spoke to no one about her encounter with Vega when she got back to El Caballo. She knew what Avery and Roberto would both say if she told them. They would tell her that Vega was not a man to be trusted, that even if she lost the race on purpose as he asked, he would not honour the deal. Her best hope still, they would say, was to win the race and get Storm back.

Issie knew this was probably true. But Storm was her baby, and if she won the race now it would be as if she were the one putting the *serreta* on him herself. It would be her fault when Vega's men strapped the spiked metal noseband to the colt's face and scarred him forever.

It was easy for Issie to excuse herself from dinner that night. Everyone expected her to have nerves the night before the race. She had stayed upstairs in her room, fretting about the decision that she was about to make. She realised now that even if she threw the race Vega would not give Storm back, and yet she could no more abandon her colt than she could betray El Caballo Danza Magnifico. It was the hardest choice she had ever had to make.

It was almost midnight. Dinner had been eaten and Francoise, Avery and Roberto were still gathered in the library talking tactics when Issie turned up with her pillow and her duvet.

"I thought I'd sleep in the stables tonight," she explained. "I want to keep an eye on Angel."

Francoise nodded at this. "I understand. My cot bed that I use when the mares are foaling is folded away in the tack room. It is easy to set up, you can put it in Angel's stall. Why don't you go and make yourself comfortable out there and let me bring you some dinner? I got the chef to keep a platter for you in case you were hungry after all."

Issie shook her head. "I don't want anything to eat, thanks, Francoise. I'll be fine."

"Then we'll see you in the morning. We leave for the village at seven." Francoise smiled gently at her.

"OK, see you then," Issie said.

"Goodnight Issie. Try and get some sleep out there, OK?" Avery said.

"I will," Issie said.

She wasn't certain that she would get any sleep, though. After the meeting with Vega today she was now worried that his men might try to sneak into the stables and hurt Angel during the night. She would put nothing past Vega – no dirty tactics were beneath this man. She would be sleeping with one eye open, looking out for trouble.

Angel greeted her with a nicker as she arrived in his stall with her bedding and the cot bed from the tack shed tucked under her arm.

"It's OK, boy," she said gently to the grey stallion. "It's just me. I thought I'd come and share your stall for the night."

Angel was happy to have a room-mate. But he could

sense that something was wrong. Issie usually lavished attention on him, but tonight she just sat on the edge of her cot staring out into the night. She looked like she had the weight of the world on her shoulders.

Issie sat up on guard duty for a couple of hours. Then she began to think that maybe this was part of Vega's master plan. He had her worried sick when she should be sleeping! If she didn't get some sleep tonight then she would be too exhausted to race tomorrow anyway.

She took one last look out of the stable door. There was no one around. She lay down on the camp bed and discovered that it was surprisingly comfy. The night air was warm, but she still tucked the duvet around her. In the stall next to her Angel stirred, moving his hooves in the straw.

"G'night Angel," Issie said drowsily. She fell asleep almost straight away, and it wasn't long before the dream began.

It was one of the strangest dreams she'd ever had. She was reliving everything that had happened in the past few weeks: Storm, the race for the Silver Bridle. In her dream it all became clear to her. When she woke up, sitting bolt upright on the camp bed, her heart was racing. Her dream had been the answer! She had figured it out. She knew how to save Storm and she knew exactly what she needed to do. But that wasn't why she had woken up. She was awake because she'd heard a noise in the corridor at the entrance to the stable block. Someone was there!

Angel heard it too. He raised his noble head, his ears pricked forward towards the stable entrance. "Do you hear it too, boy?" Issie asked. There it was! The scraping sound of someone, or something, moving on the cobbled stones. She looked up and saw a shape in the courtyard archway at the entrance of the stables.

"Francoise? Is that you?" Issie called. Perhaps the Frenchwoman had brought her dinner after all? The shadow didn't answer her. It did, however, begin to move, coming closer out of the darkness outside, heading towards the light of the stable loose boxes. "Hello? Who is it?" Issie was trembling now. "Francoise?"

Beside her in the stall, Angel moved about anxiously. She could make out the shape of a shadow moving in the darkness, now coming finally into the light of the stables.

And then suddenly Issie could see quite clearly who it was. The shock was too much for her, and she instantly burst into a flood of tears as she realised that it wasn't Francoise or one of Vega's men. It wasn't a human at all. It was a horse. It was Mystic.

Chapter 15

Tears were streaming down Issie's face as she rushed forward and threw her arms around the grey pony. "Mystic!" She was so choked with emotion she was struggling to get the words out. "Ohmygod! You don't know how glad I am to see you."

Mystic seemed just as pleased to see Issie too. He nickered warmly to her, nuzzling her with his sooty grey muzzle. Issie giggled as he did this, and began to pull herself together. She took a deep breath and used her sleeve to wipe her eyes and dry away the last of her tears.

"Mystic," she said, "I don't know how you got here, but I am so happy you came. Things have been so messed up. I must have fallen asleep because I had this dream…"

She'd woken up suddenly when Mystic had arrived, but

the dream had remained with her, and it was still flashing through her mind now, like a memory of something that really happened, all the details so vivid and real.

"Mystic," she whispered intently to the grey stallion, "I had a dream. And you were in it. You were there and you helped me to save Storm. That's why you're here, isn't it?"

Did she and Mystic share the same dream? Somehow she knew that he understood her completely and he knew what they needed to do.

Issie gave the grey gelding one last stroke on his sleek, dappled neck. Then she let her hand fall and stood back from her pony. "You have to go now. Until tomorrow, when the race begins," she said. Then she added cryptically, "You know I can't help you. You have to do it alone. You have to go and get him. I'm relying on you, OK?"

Mystic seemed to understand. He turned away from her and trotted back the way he had come, towards the entrance of the stables. When he reached the archway he stopped for a moment, silhouetted in the half light, his dark eyes shining as he stared back at Issie.

Then suddenly he wheeled about on his hocks, his silver tail flowing out behind him as he turned and cantered off across the courtyard. And then he was gone. As quickly as he had arrived in the stables here at El Caballo he had disappeared once more. Issie stood for a moment longer, staring out into the darkness. Was she right about this? Issie felt certain that she was connected somehow with the grey pony, that both of them had shared the same vision, and that Mystic would act when the time was right tomorrow and play his part. He wouldn't fail her.

Issie stood a moment longer, staring at the dark night outside. Then she turned round and walked back to the stall where Angel was craning his neck over the chain. He had seen Mystic too and he was wondering what was going on. Issie put out a hand and stroked the grey stallion's forelock.

"Not much longer now," she said to the stallion. Soon enough it would be dawn and the race for the Silver Bridle would begin. Now that Mystic was here, though, everything had changed. For the first time, as she stood there, Issie felt a surge of excitement at the thought of riding Angel in the race. A few moments ago she'd been in despair, but now she had a plan.

"It's going to be OK, Angel," she said to the big grey stallion standing next to her. "Mystic is here. And we're going to win."

Alfie! Wake up!" It was before dawn back at the hacienda and Issie was in Alfie's room shaking his shoulder gently. "Alfie!" she hissed. The shaking was not so gentle now as she gave him a shove and Alfie sat bolt upright in bed.

"*Madre Mia*! What's going on? Issie? What are you doing in my room?"

"Alfie, shhh, I have to ask you something," Issie said. "Listen, I need your help. I know a way to get Storm back. Vega has asked me to throw the race—"

"Vega? Throw the race? Issie, you can't—" Alfie began.

"Shhh!" Issie said. "I have a plan, but I'm going to need your help. You have to trust me, OK? I can't explain everything, but you have to trust me. Now are you in?"

Alfie took a deep breath and looked hard at Issie as if he were trying to make up his mind. Finally he spoke. "Of course I'm in," he said. "Tell me what I have to do."

The pounding rhythm of the Spanish flamenco filled the air as Issie, Avery, Roberto and Francoise rode towards the village that morning. Everywhere Issie looked, red roses littered the ground, trampled on the cobblestones beneath the horses' hooves. There were brightly coloured banners hanging from the windows of all the buildings. The sound of Spanish castanets and the joyous shouts of the supporters filled the air as the fans lined the streets leading to the village, all waiting to cheer on the jockeys from their favourite hacienda.

Twelve haciendas would compete here today and each of them was determined to outdo the others. Their rivalry began with the grooming and presentation of their horses. The spectators from each hacienda were on horseback and all dressed up in their team colours. Most splendid of all, though, were the twelve racehorses from each of the competing stables. Their manes were plaited with ribbons and bobbles in the colours of their hacienda and streamers were braided into their tails. The jockeys too were dressed in colourful and theatrical costumes. Each of them wore racing silks in hacienda colours that matched their horse's braids.

"I feel silly in this outfit," Issie grumbled as she rolled up the sleeves of her jockey silks. The silks were striped in the red, orange and violet colours of El Caballo Danza Magnifico, with a letter C and a red heart in the centre on Issie's back. "This shirt is too big for me."

"They were Alfie's silks," Francoise said. "I didn't

have time to alter them." She looked around. "Where is Alfie? He said he was going to catch us up. He'll miss the race at this rate."

"Ummm," Issie said, "I wouldn't worry about him. He said to tell you that he had something to do back at the stables. He'll be here later."

Now they passed the fountain that marked the entrance to the village square and Issie could see the track that they would race on, the sides of the streets swarming with people, waiting to cheer on their own hacienda.

As she looked down the wide white chalk streets of the square Issie knew exactly what lay ahead of her. This wasn't a game, it was real. Today she would be risking her life to win, riding against men twice her size and twice her age.

"Are you nervous?" asked Avery.

Issie didn't know what to say. This morning when she'd been telling Alfie her plan, she hadn't been nervous in the least. She'd been so certain that her idea would work. But in the harsh light of day, she was still a young girl, mounting up to ride against eleven men in a dangerous horse race that pitted riders against each other in a rough and tumble contest with no rules.

"Just remember our game plan," Avery said. "You've got to be away fast at the break, get out in front so that the other riders can't get near you. If they can't touch you then you can't be shoved around. Just keep Angel ahead of the pack and stay in the lead. He's got the speed to hold them off and the stamina to last the distance. Be careful taking the corners and then, on the third lap, when you're coming around to the final stretch, you can loosen the reins and really let him go, urge him on over the finish line."

Issie looked at her instructor, wondering how to explain what she was about to tell him. "That's just the thing, Tom, about our race strategy. I want to—"

The loud parp of a horn interrupted her.

"This is it!" Roberto said. "Time for you to line up." He looked at Issie and smiled. "I know you will ride your best for El Caballo Danza Magnifico. And that is all I ask. I am proud that you are riding for our stables, Isadora – you take with you the hopes and dreams for our future. Good luck, my brave friend."

He put out his hand and Issie shook it. It felt quite odd, shaking Roberto's hand. She had puzzled all morning about whether she should try to explain her plan to Roberto. Now, at the last minute, she decided that Roberto needed to know what was really going on.

"Roberto, I have to tell you," Issie began, "Alfie and I have this plan. Vega, he told me that—"

"*Vaqueros!*" A voice over the loudspeaker interrupted her. The announcer was saying something in Spanish.

"The race is about to begin. It is time for you to take your position at the start line now," Roberto said. "We will have time to talk later…"

He gestured to Francoise, who dismounted and handed the reins of her horse to Roberto, and then took Angel by the reins and led Issie over to join the other horses behind the white rope.

"What is it?" Francoise asked. "What were you trying to tell Roberto about Vega? Is it something about the race?"

Issie shook her head. "It's nothing," she said. She realised there was no point in talking about it now. They wouldn't understand. How could they when they didn't know about Mystic? Besides, the race was about to be run. Issie's plan was about to unfold. They would all see soon enough.

All this time, despite the noise, the crowds and the flags, Angel had been his good-natured self, as calm as ever. The grey stallion had been perfectly behaved on the way here and his manners had been impeccable as Issie rode him around the village square. But now, as they came back to the fountain where they would line up to begin the race, Angel's mood suddenly changed. The horse had spied Miguel Vega in the crowd ahead of them, sitting astride Victorioso, his mighty black stallion. At the sight of Vega, Angel's stride stiffened and he began to skip nervously, crab-stepping sideways beneath Issie, reluctant to step forward towards the start line.

"Easy, Angel," Issie soothed him. "Steady, Angel," she said firmly. Angel was trembling at the very sight of Vega. Luckily, Issie didn't have to line up right next to him. Two other riders from rival stables were positioned in the line between her and Vega, but that didn't stop the mustachioed man from leaning over in full view of everyone and taunting her.

"Remember my kind offer, little girl! We have a deal!" Vega called to her. Francoise looked up at Issie, confusion and shock on her face. "What is he talking about, Isadora? A deal? You bargained with Vega?" Her voice was stricken with panic.

Issie ignored Vega's taunt and his grinning face and looked down at Francoise. "Don't worry, Francoise. I can't explain now, but—"

"Issie... has he threatened you?" Francoise asked. "Listen to me! Vega is not to be trusted. What did he say to you?"

"Francoise... I—" Issie wanted to explain, but before she had the chance to finish the sentence there was another loud honk of the horn, signalling that the grooms had to let go of the horses now, and leave the jockeys to line up alone behind the rope, ready to start the race.

Francoise gave Issie one last, long pleading look and let go of Angel's reins and walked away. Issie watched her go. She wished she could have told Francoise, but there just wasn't time. The race was about to begin.

Issie took a tighter grip on Angel's reins and stood up in the stirrups of her saddle, ready for the rope to drop and the break to come. Above the sounds of the flamenco and the clacking of the castanets she could hear a louder rhythm, the sound of her heart pounding in her chest. She was about to risk everything and she knew it, about to turn her back on everything that she had agreed to with Tom and ride a different race, the race of her life. She hoped she was ready for it.

Beneath her, she felt Angel tense every muscle in his body, the rope pulling taut across his chest as the horses all lined up next to each other ready to run.

"On your marks," the voice on the sidelines shouted, "get set... go!"

The pistol sounded and the rope dropped. As the horses broke, Issie remembered Tom's advice. Get out in front of the rest of the pack and stay at the front. Ride in the lead and that way no one can touch you or try to hurt you. It was good advice – under normal circumstances. But Issie wasn't riding under normal circumstances. When the rope fell away, instead of letting Angel surge forward at the break as he had been trained to do, she did completely the opposite, holding the stallion back.

Angel tried to lunge forward, fighting hard against her hands. The other horses had taken off and he wanted to join them. He wanted to run! Issie's arms ached from the strain of keeping him back, but she held him firm, allowing the other riders to get a whole length's head start on the grey stallion before she finally loosened her fingers a little, leaned forward in the saddle and let him go.

Up ahead of her, Miguel Vega turned round and flicked a quick nod of approval at her. He could see what she was doing, holding Angel back so that the other riders were now ahead of her. From the sidelines, Roberto and Avery could see it too.

"What on earth is wrong with her?" Avery shouted over the noise of the crowd. "It looked like she was holding Angel back at the break! She's supposed to get to the front! What is she doing?"

Issie was at the back of the field, mixed up with the other straggling riders at the rear, and now she was in danger of precisely the thing that Tom Avery had feared. As the riders jostled and fought for position, Issie felt a hard blow on her shoulder as a jockey to her left riding a big bay stallion shoved her viciously out of his way. Issie let out a shriek, and tried to keep her balance, swerving to avoid the other rider. Then she pulled back hard on Angel's reins, forcing the stallion to slow down and drop even further back behind the field. She was now right at the tail of the race, the very last horse, trailing the leaders by almost eight lengths as they came around the square and back towards the fountain that would mark the end of the first lap.

"What is she doing?" Avery said again as Issie rode past them. Instead of focusing on the track, Issie seemed to be paying no attention to the race! She was staring out distractedly over the buildings, looking out towards El Caballo Danza Magnifico.

"She has lost her nerve," Roberto said. "She is too afraid to ride past them!"

As he said this, he caught sight of Francoise, who was running back to join them, pushing her way through the crowds to reach them. When she finally reached them she was exhausted, panting for breath as she tried to speak. "It's Issie…" she said, "… I think something is terribly wrong! I think Vega has got to her and threatened Storm."

"What do you mean?" Avery said.

"Look at her!" Francoise replied. "Don't you see? He's using the colt to blackmail her. That is why she is riding like this."

Francoise took a deep breath and the words came tumbling out. "Tom, I think she's losing on purpose. I think Issie is going to throw the race!"

Chapter 16

As Issie grappled with the stallion, holding him back, she caught sight of Avery, Francoise and Roberto watching her with disbelief from the sidelines. It felt awful to do this to them. Issie only hoped that her plan would work and she would have the chance to explain once the race was done.

Francoise had been right, of course, when she said that Issie was losing the race on purpose. She was holding Angel back, staying at the very rear of the field, letting Vega stay in the lead. It was all part of Issie's plan. She had to make Vega believe that she was really going to throw the race.

Issie knew Vega was not to be trusted, but she had no doubt that he meant it when he threatened to put the *serreta* on Storm. She knew he wasn't bluffing when he told her that if she got out in front, he would signal one of his men to return to the stables and put the metal-barbed bridle on the colt. And so she was going to hold Angel back until the time was right to strike. She had to let Vega keep his lead, for Storm's sake.

Beneath her now, as they came around to the end of the first lap, Angel snorted his objections. He had been straining on the reins since the break, and Issie could feel the leather cutting deep into her fingers as she gripped with all her strength to keep the horse back. Up ahead of her she could see the other riders. Vega was at the front of the field on Victorioso. He was at least ten lengths ahead of her now and there were ten horses between them. Issie needed to act soon, to put her plan into play. But right now she had no choice but to hang back. Vega's men were watching her suspiciously. Vega had told them to keep an eye on her. When she made her move, so would they. Timing was everything and so she had no choice but to hang on to the reins, try to ignore the pain in her fingers and wait. As she came around the village square this time she had a clear view to El Caballo and she looked down at the gates, hoping to see the signal she was waiting for. Her heart sank – there was no signal.

"Come on, Mystic!" Issie muttered to herself. "I'm depending on you. Where are you?"

Mystic, meanwhile, was galloping as if his life depended on it, racing across the green fields where the mares grazed around the white walls of El Caballo Danza Magnifico. The grey gelding wasn't alone. He was matched stride for stride by the leggy, bay colt who ran beside him. It was Storm! His head was held high as he ran for all he was worth, determined to prove that he could keep pace with the grey horse, sticking to Mystic's side like glue as they ran together.

This was Issie's master plan. It had all come to her like a vision in her dream last night just before Mystic had appeared.

Mystic was the answer. Issie couldn't save Storm. But Mystic could. While Issie was at the village taking part in the race, Mystic could go to Vega's hacienda, help Storm to escape, and bring him home. Mystic would be the one to rescue the colt – on his own.

The race created the perfect opportunity. Vega's men were all at the village square and the stables were deserted. There was no one watching the colt, Nightstorm was alone and unguarded. When Mystic arrived at the hacienda there wasn't a soul waiting to stop him.

Storm had gone mad with excitement when he saw the grey pony. It had been a simple matter for Mystic to encourage the colt to follow him by jumping over the five-bar gate. Storm had taken the fence just as easily as the paddock gate that he was only too accustomed to jumping back home.

The two horses had clattered down the cobbled stables, and straight out of the front gates as Mystic led Storm through the orange grove and across the pastures, towards the gorge.

All they had to do now was make it through the gates of El Caballo Danza Magnifico. Issie needed to be sure they were safe. She planned to win this race, but not until she was certain that her colt was truly home and free from the clutches of Miguel Vega.

That was where Alfie came in. He was a crucial part of her plan. Alfie would look out for Storm and signal to Issie the moment that the colt had arrived at the stables by running the El Caballo flag up the flagpole. The flag was the signal. Issie would see it flying and know that she was free to give Angel his head and try to win the race.

That was the plan. So far, Issie had carried it out perfectly. She had stayed at the back of the field, making it look like she was completely willing to lose this race, waiting until she was certain that Mystic's mission had been successful and the colt was safe at home at El Caballo again.

It was a good plan, but time was tight. Would Mystic get the colt back in time? Would she see Alfie's signal? She needed to know that Mystic's mission had been a success and that she could go ahead and try to win back this race – before it was too late.

As the crowds cheered around the village square, Issie kept holding Angel back at the rear of the other riders. They had turned the corner now to begin the second lap, and as she rode back around the square past the fountain, she could see down over the tops of the village houses once more with a clear view to El Caballo Danza Magnifico nestled in the valley below.

"Come on, Mystic!" Issie muttered. "We're out of time."

And then she caught sight of a vision that made her heart leap. A golden flag with a red heart was being raised up the pole so that it fluttered in the breeze. It was the signal! They had done it! Storm was home.

The sight of the flag was all that Issie needed to spur

her on. She felt a sudden chill run through her. Vega and Victorioso were still out in front and they must have been at least eight lengths ahead of her. She hoped she hadn't blown it. Had she left it too late to make her move? Too late to win?

On the sidelines, Avery, Roberto and Francoise were thinking the same thing. "She has lost," Roberto said. "Francoise is right. I think she has thrown the race on purpose."

"Issie wouldn't do that!" Avery snapped.

"No?" Roberto said. "Then how do you explain the way she is riding?"

Francoise kept her eyes on the race. "Even if she tries to claw her way back now," the Frenchwoman said ominously, "I do not believe she can do it. There is too much distance between her and Vega. The race is halfway through. She cannot possibly gain the distance on him in time to win."

At the back of the field, though, Issie was about to try and do exactly that. As soon as she'd come up with her plan she'd known she would have to win this race from the back, and not from the start. She had never been expecting to lead the pack. Instead, she'd known she would have to hold Angel and wait until Storm was safe, until the right moment to strike. And she knew she could do it. She had faith in the enormous speed of the horse she was riding.

"OK, Angel." She leaned down low on the grey stallion's neck and finally released the reins that she had been gripping so tightly since the race began. "Time to go, boy."

Angel, who had been leaning on Issie's hands, desperate to free himself since the very start of the race, responded instantly. He surged forward, his stride lengthening, making up the distance between himself and the horses at the very back of the tight-knit pack within just a few lengths.

The horses ahead of her all slowed down as they reached the treacherous corner turn, and Issie did the same, slowing Angel back just enough to make it around without skidding. She didn't want to risk sliding her horse into the crowds and the café tables that lined the streets of the square. As soon as she was back on the straight, though, she sped up again, asking Angel gallop harder. By the time they came around to the last corner of the second lap, Angel had caught up to the other stragglers. There were four riders grouped together at the rear in front of Issie. They were riding together in a tight knot, blocking Issie's path so that she couldn't get through. Angel had to slow down, settling in behind the pack for a moment as Issie decided on her next move. The safest thing to do would be to ride wide on the track, to go to the outside of the horses and ride around them. But Issie wasn't interested in the safest route, she was interested in the fastest. She pulled hard on the stallion's right rein and guided him to the inside, towards the small gap near the metal rails. She was going to pass through the gap, squeezing inside of the horses who were running ahead of them. She didn't have the luxury of time. The inside track was fastest and they would simply have to fight their way to get through.

"What is she trying to do?" Francoise screamed from the sidelines now. "She is riding through the other riders, she will get herself killed."

"No, she won't!" Avery yelled over the noise of the crowd. "She's making her move now, she knows what she's doing!"

As Angel made a dive for the gap, Issie looked to her left and saw the jockey on the horse beside her give her a filthy look. He wasn't about to be overtaken by a girl!

He had ridden the Silver Bridle before and he knew there were no rules in this race. He lifted his stick, ready to strike out at her, but before he could swing his blow Issie had ducked out of the way, bending down even lower in the saddle to sweep past as she clucked Angel on, kicking the grey stallion lightly with her heels to ask for more speed. The other jockey was left open-mouthed in her wake.

"Did you see that?" Francoise squeaked. "She is too small and quick. They cannot lay a hand on her. She is beating them at their own game!"

Now the grey stallion put on a surge of speed, his powerful haunches beginning to come into play, working to propel him to even greater strides. He raced past the next two horses as if they weren't even there, ducking and weaving his way through the field as Issie guided him on fearlessly. They were halfway through the horses now, in sixth place, as they approached the line for the third lap.

As they crossed the line for the third and final lap, Issie saw they were coming up towards a treacherous corner again. Angel was in full gallop and going far too fast to make it safely around the bend. Issie had to ignore the pain in her fingers and pull back on the reins with all her strength, fighting to get the stallion back under control and slow him down. She lost a little ground, but she knew it was the right thing to do, they had to make it safely round the corner.

Then disaster struck right in front of her. A rider had kept his mount going at full gallop, taking a risk that he would still somehow make it round the corner. He hadn't. His horse skidded into the pavement, knocking chairs and tables aside, and the crowd began to scatter to get out of the way. There was screaming and shouting as the horse crashed through a hawker's stall, trying to regain its footing. The horse's hooves scrabbled across the cobbled pavements and the jockey was flung out of the saddle and crashed to the ground.

Before anyone could help him, a second horse skidded at the same corner, also going far too fast, and got tangled in the fray.

The crowd immediately gathered around the horses and riders, trying to help them back to their feet. The horses were both standing up, their flanks heaving, the whites of their eyes rolling back from the fright. They were unharmed, but the crash meant they were well and truly out of the race.

"Get off the track!" Issie yelled as she galloped straight for them. She was still in this race and the people who were trying to help were now blocking her path!

"Out of the way! *Vamos*!" she shouted. The crowds scattered off the street just in time as she turned the corner with expert precision and raced on past. With these two horses eliminated there were only another two riders left standing between her and Vega. She was bearing down on them fast, and had tightened the gap. Less than four lengths separated her from the leader now.

Stride by stride, Angel was gaining on the other horses. As they came around the last corner of the third lap, heading into the final stretch, Issie knew it was time. She began to ride Angel like a race jockey, just as Avery had shown her, urging the horse on with her hands, talking constantly to the great, grey stallion, asking him to give her more. Angel was listening to her – he stretched out even further, sweeping over the ground with huge strides. He passed the other two horses in front of him as if they were standing still. Now, as they came into the final stretch, there was only Vega between them and the finish line.

"She will never take him. Victorioso is too fast and Vega is too clever to be beaten in the home straight," Francoise said.

Avery shook his head. "Issie can take him," he said. "Just watch her."

Out on the track, Issie was riding for all she was worth. Her head was tucked down low over Angel's neck as she kept talking to the grey stallion, asking him for more, asking him to edge up, stride by stride, chipping away at the gigantic black horse's lead. She knew Angel had the speed in him to take Victorioso. More than that, she knew the grey stallion had the courage, the will, to beat Miguel Vega.

As Angel began to pull up alongside Victorioso, Issie saw surprise on Vega's face. He hadn't been expecting this. And he hadn't been expecting what happened next.

The two horses, Victorioso and Angel, were neck and neck. The two great stallions were racing stride for stride so that Issie and Vega were alongside each other. Vega saw his chance. If this girl was foolish enough to come near him, he was going to make her suffer for it. He lifted one meaty paw from Victorioso's reins, and reached out his arm towards Issie to strike her.

He didn't get the chance. He didn't realise this too was part of Issie's plan. She had been anticipating this moment. In fact, she had been counting on it. She held Angel so that he was racing right next to Victorioso and the grey stallion got a real good look at Vega riding next to him.

At the sight of his enemy, Angel gave a snort of indignation and surged forward in a fresh burst of unmatchable speed that took him ahead of the black stallion. In two lightning strides Angel was out in front of Victorioso, leaving Vega in the dust behind him impotently shaking his fist as Issie catapulted into the lead.

All around them the crowd erupted in wild cheers and shouts, and flowers flew through the air as Issie and Angel passed the fountain for the third and final time and crossed the finish line. They had won.

Chapter 17

Two days after the Silver Bridle had been won, Issie faced yet another test.

As she stood in front of a line of the most beautiful horses she had ever seen she really didn't know if she could do it. They were all so stunning! How could she possibly choose one?

"Hurry up, girl!" A voice from behind her snapped angrily. Issie turned round to see Miguel Vega, dabbing furiously with his hanky at his chubby face as the beads of sweat trickled from beneath his *vaquero* hat.

"Don't rush me!" Issie grinned back at him. She stepped forward and walked down the row of horses until she reached a grey colt. He was a three-year-old Andalusian, with strong conformation, a well-shaped neck and a perfectly dished nose.

Issie looked back at Roberto. "What do you think?"

Roberto nodded. "An excellent choice, Isadora. This young stallion is the son of Victorioso, and his dam is one of Vega's favourite mares. I have long admired this horse and would love to have him in my stables." He smiled. "However, it is your decision."

Issie smiled back at Roberto, and then she reached out a hand and stroked the grey stallion on his pretty dished nose.

"We'll take this one!" she said.

Vega reluctantly signalled his men to lead the stallion away with the others.

"He's hating every moment of this," Avery muttered to Issie with a grin.

"Good!" Issie giggled back.

Vega had been forced to stand there this morning and watch helplessly as Issie, Roberto, Alfie and Francoise each picked a horse from his magnificent herd to take away with them back to El Caballo Danza Magnifico.

Since Issie had won the race for the Silver Bridle, she, along with Roberto, Alfie, Avery and Francoise, had been working her way around the eleven rival haciendas. At every stud farm, they had chosen five of the best horses to take as their prize. Vega's was the last of the eleven haciendas, and now that it was his turn to endure the claiming of the spoils of the Silver Bridle he wasn't liking the process one bit.

"Come on!" he snapped. "You have one left to choose. Make it quick. I do not wish to stand here all day!"

Roberto turned to face Vega now and his smile faded.

"We will not be choosing a fifth horse from you, Miguel."

"What?"

"You heard me," Roberto said. "We have chosen four of your horses today. The fifth horse is the colt that we already have back at our stables."

Vega looked at him suspiciously. "I don't understand."

"Nightstorm is Isadora's colt and you know it. We know you stole him from her. He was never yours to own in the first place. But, as a sign of goodwill, we are willing to let him count for your stables as one of the five horses you owe us."

Vega smiled at this. It seemed like a good deal as far as he was concerned. He had been furious when he had arrived home after losing the race only to discover the colt was missing from the stables. Vega figured one of his men must have foolishly left the gate open, and had given him up for lost until he discovered the colt was back at El Caballo. Now, to be offered this deal was a stroke of good fortune.

"There is a condition, though," Roberto continued. "We are doing this for one reason, pure and simple. We do not want you to have any claim over Storm. The colt will always bear the brand of your stables, but he is not your colt and you know it. He belongs to Isadora. And I am warning you now, if you ever touch him again, if you ever try to steal him or hurt him in any way, as a man of honour I shall be forced to deal with you myself. Am I making myself clear?"

Vega's smile crumpled. "Miguel Vega agrees to your terms," he spat back. "You have your deal, Roberto. And you have my horses. Leave now and let this be the end of all our dealings!"

"With pleasure," Roberto grinned. He turned again to look at Miguel as they left the hacienda. "See you in another ten years, Miguel!"

There was much talk about the horses they had chosen on the way home. Issie was pleased with the young grey stallion that she was leading beside her. Roberto had picked Victorioso, of course, and the black stallion was certainly a great prize. Francoise had chosen a snow-white mare from the same bloodlines that Angel shared.

"She will be good bloodstock for the future Andalusian herd," she explained.

Alfie had chosen a bay Lusitano foal.

"I think you chose him because he looks just like Storm," Issie smiled.

"Storm is much more handsome," Alfie said. "I can see why he means so much to you."

"I want to thank you again for helping me to get him back," Issie said.

Alfie grinned. "I had the easy job! Running a flag up a pole. I'm just glad that it worked out OK." Then he added in a whisper to Issie, "And maybe one day you'll explain to me exactly what really happened that day. How did you do it, Issie? All I know is that your colt came galloping in through the gates following this little grey horse. As soon as I saw them I raised the flag as you asked, and then when I turned round again – it was like the grey horse had just disappeared. You want to tell me what's going on here?"

Issie smiled back at Alfie. "Maybe one day. Meanwhile, let's just say that I owe you one."

No one, except for Issie, of course, really understood how the colt had managed to make his way back all by himself to El Caballo Danza Magnifico during the race.

Issie had simply pronounced that Storm was super-clever and had obviously found his way to El Caballo stables.

"But it makes no sense," Francoise had puzzled. "Even if Vega did leave the gate open and he got loose, how could he possibly know the way here on his own? He has never been here before."

Issie had smiled as she stroked the colt's fluffy bay coat. "I guess it's instinct," she said. "Horses always know the way home."

But where was Nightstorm's true home? Issie had been thinking a lot about that lately, ever since her conversation with Roberto in the training arena that day when he had offered to keep the colt here for her and school him as an El Caballo stallion in the traditional ways of the *haute école*.

Issie knew where her home was. She missed Chevalier Point terribly. She had been away for over two weeks and, even though she knew she would return home to soggy paddocks and muddy, shaggy ponies all pepped up from too much early spring grass, she still longed to be home again now that the excitement was over. She missed Blaze and Comet. She missed her mum. She missed Stella and Kate. To say she even missed Natasha Tucker would have been pushing it, but she was so homesick right now that if Natasha had turned up in Spain at that moment she might even have given her a hug!

Well, she thought, it wasn't long now. They would be home soon. Avery was busy making plans for their travel arrangements. It would be more difficult this time as they needed to transport Storm, so they would be travelling a different route.

"We'll leave tomorrow at midday," Avery told her when they all met in the library that evening for tapas. Issie had grown to love the exotic food. She was nibbling on a shrimp and had loaded her plate with tomato bread, chorizo and slices of Iberian ham. There was Spanish sherry too – a celebration for the adults, although Issie much preferred the fresh orange juice anyway.

"It will be a real pity to see you leave," Roberto told Issie. "I owe you a great debt. I never thought you would win the Silver Bridle and I must apologise for my lack of faith. You are indeed the great rider that Thomas told me you would be, and you are always welcome here at El Caballo Danza Magnifico."

"Thank you, Roberto," Issie said. Then she braced herself and asked the question that had been at the back of her mind ever since she arrived. "If you really owe me a great debt then there's another favour I need to ask of you."

"Certainly," Roberto said. "What is it?"

"Please," Issie said, "I really want to know… who was it that bought Blaze from you and gave her to me?"

Roberto shook his head. "I am afraid I am not at liberty to say. I promised I would never reveal the identity of your benefactor. I owe you a debt, Isadora, but there is someone else who I am even more indebted to—"

"It's OK, Roberto," Avery interrupted him. "It's time to tell her. She deserves to know."

Roberto raised an eyebrow at this. Then he nodded. "So be it. You are her *bonifacio*. It is your decision."

"*Bonifacio*?" Issie was puzzled. It was that word again! The word that Roberto had used when he was talking to Avery that night in the living room. "What does that word mean?" Issie asked.

"It means 'benefactor'," Avery replied. "Issie, it was me. I'm the one who bought Blaze for you."

Issie couldn't believe it. "But Tom, why? How?"

Avery smiled at the astonished look on her face. "Roberto owed me a great favour. Remember, I had saved his life once before. And he had sworn that if he could ever do me a favour, anything I asked for would be mine. I never thought I'd take him up on it, but when I heard about where Blaze was really from, I knew

484

that he would be willing to part with the mare for a fraction of what she was really worth. I knew I could buy her back for you."

"But why did you do it? For me, I mean?" Issie's voice was trembling. She felt as if she was going to cry.

"I guess I blamed myself for what happened when Francoise turned up and you lost Blaze." Avery shook his head. "You had only just recovered from losing Mystic and I was the one who had given Blaze to you. I wanted to make everything better, you see. I thought having a new horse, one like Blaze who really needed you to nurse her back to health, would help you to move on. And I was right, you and Blaze were so perfect for each other. Then, when Francoise arrived to take the mare back, I knew it had broken your heart. It was all my fault. I should never have given you Blaze in the first place. I knew the mare might have been stolen – I just never guessed she was from the famous El Caballo Danza Magnifico."

Roberto interrupted to continue the story. "When Thomas called me, I could not believe it. My old friend, my brother, whom I owed my life to, was calling to collect at last on the great debt I owed him. It made me very happy to let him have Salome. I could never refuse him, of course. And I promised him that I would never tell you who had been your benefactor."

"But why the big secret?" Issie asked.

"I didn't want you to know I'd bought Blaze," Avery said. "I thought your mum would try to pay me back what I had paid for the mare and I didn't want that. I didn't want you to feel that you owed me, because you don't. I was happy to do it. You've got the makings of a great rider, Issie, and I couldn't stand to watch you lose your horse. I lost a horse myself once, and I never really recovered. So I bought Blaze for you. I honestly didn't think I would ever tell you. As time went on, it just seemed easier to keep it a secret. And then when Storm was stolen and Francoise turned up, and we came here, I suppose I realised that I was being unrealistic trying to continue to keep it hidden. You deserve to know," Avery paused. "But I think it's best, don't you, if we keep this between ourselves? I'll tell your mother, of course, when we get home, but I don't really want the whole pony club to know about this. I can do without the kids all queuing up to get their mystery gift ponies from me!"

Issie giggled. "No, I can see that it would be a problem." She looked at her instructor, her eyes shining with tears. "Tom, I am so grateful for what you did for me."

"Don't be," Avery said firmly. "It was something I had to do. For me as much as for you. I'm just glad I could help."

Issie still couldn't believe it. She had come all the way to Spain to get her colt back and she had ended up with so much more. She knew the truth now, the real story behind the mystery benefactor who had given Blaze to her. It seemed like fate that she was here. Her path was destined to connect with El Caballo Danza Magnifico. This place had been Blaze's home. Her special mare had grown up here. And now, Storm had brought Issie here too. It had to be more than a coincidence, didn't it? Issie put her hand up to touch the gold half-heart that hung around her neck. She knew at that moment that the Silver Bridle was not their only reason for coming here. She knew she had something else that she had to do.

As Roberto poured a second glass of sherry for each of them, Issie excused herself from the group. "I'm going down to the stables to check on the horses," she said.

The night air was warm against her skin as she walked across the cobbled courtyard in the dark to the stables. She entered the stallion stables and Angel poked his head out of the stall immediately to greet her with a friendly nicker.

The big grey horse had run so bravely for her in the

village square. He had been given a hero's welcome at the finish line – and he had relished it. As the wreath of red roses was strung around his neck in the ceremony afterwards, Angel had stood proud and noble, his head held high. He wore the scars of the *serreta* now as a badge of his courage, rather than a reminder of the cruelty that had once been inflicted on him. He was the champion of El Caballo. Their greatest horse. His race would be spoken of throughout the generations, would become part of the legend of the Silver Bridle in the time to come. Issie had always known he could do it, but as they'd crossed the finish line ahead of Vega even she'd had to admit she hadn't known the grey horse could run quite as fast as he did that day.

"You're a hero, Angel, you know that, don't you?" Issie whispered to the horse as she stroked his satin neck. "A real hero."

The stallion nickered to her and Issie pulled a carrot out of her pocket for him. "Even a hero likes a pony treat now and then," she giggled.

Further down the corridor, at the other end of the stallion loose boxes, Storm was also waiting for his carrot. He had his wee colt nose poking up over the Dutch door. He could hear Issie's voice down the corridor and he nickered anxiously, calling for the girl to come to see him. Then he bashed one of his front hooves impatiently against the door of his stall, insisting that she pay attention to him.

"Yeah, yeah, I know, I'm coming!" Issie called back to him, laughing at the colt's bolshy new attitude.

He had grown up so much even in the past few weeks. He was getting bigger now, he would be a yearling soon, and then what? Issie felt gripped with uncertainty. Sure, she knew a lot about horses, but did she really know how to train a young colt, how to school and prepare a horse with the amazing bloodlines and potential that Storm had? She remembered Roberto's offer. He had told her that he would school the colt, make him a true El Caballo stallion, in exchange for the colt's own progeny, his sons and daughters, when he grew up and became a stallion. Issie hadn't wanted to listen at the time. All she could think of was getting Storm back and taking him home with her, home to Winterflood Farm where Blaze and Comet were waiting.

But where was home? Could it be that the colt's home was here? At El Caballo Danza Magnifico? Here, he could run free each day in the green, sweet pastures of Andalusia with the mares and their colts. He could be schooled, as Blaze had been, in the classical style of the *haute école*. He could be given everything that she could not give him back in Chevalier Point.

Issie unbolted the door of Storm's stall and walked inside. The colt stood perfectly still as she ran a hand over his soft bay coat. He knew this girl, he trusted her touch. She would never hurt him, never betray him.

"You know," Issie said, feeling the tears already rolling down her cheeks as she realised what she had to do, "you know I love you, don't you, Storm? I came here to get you back. I love you more than anything. But I think this is what I have to do."

"Isadora?" There was a sound outside the stall now and Issie looked up and saw Francoise standing there. "Isadora?" Francoise saw the tears running down Issie's cheeks. "What is the matter, what's wrong?"

Issie couldn't speak at first. She felt as if she was ripping her own heart out doing this. She knew, though, that it was the right thing to do. She had to do it for Storm.

With trembling hands, she reached around the back of her neck and undid the clasp of the gold necklace.

The necklace fell into the palm of her hand and she gripped the chain with the broken heart tightly in her balled fist. She couldn't bring herself to let go. Then she took a deep breath, wiping the tears away with the back of her fist, and reached out her hand to Francoise.

"Here," she said, her voice shaking. She passed the necklace to Francoise.

The Frenchwoman recognised it immediately. "Isadora," she said, "this is the necklace that I gave to you. Half of a gold heart. The other half is attached to Blaze's halter."

Issie nodded. "I've never taken it off, Francoise. Since you gave it to me, I've always worn it as a symbol of my love. No matter where I am, half of my heart is always with Blaze."

She pressed the necklace firmly into Francoise's hand.

"When I leave, Francoise, will you do something for me? Will you take this half of the heart and put it on Storm's halter? I want him to know, I want him to know…" Issie had to stop speaking for a moment as the tears overwhelmed her, and then she continued. "I want Storm to know that half of my heart now will always be here at El Caballo with him."

"You are leaving him here? In Spain?" Francoise said.

Issie nodded. "I have to, Francoise. I don't want to, but I have to. I know that now. You'll look after him for me, won't you? And it won't be forever, will it?"

Francoise nodded. "I will look after him, of course.

He is in good hands here. It is a very great thing that you are doing, a brave thing also."

"Don't!" Issie said. "I don't want to think about it or I will change my mind."

And with that she threw her arms around the colt's neck and embraced him for what she knew would be the last time in a long while.

"I have to go now, Storm," she said slowly, reluctantly letting go of him. "Francoise will look after you now."

She put her hand on her chest where the necklace had once been. "I don't need the necklace. You'll be right here, in my heart with me always," she said, biting her lip now to stop the tears. "And I'll come back for you," she told him. "One day. I'll be back. That's a promise."

STACY GREGG

PONY  CLUB SECRETS

Book Seven

Fortune and the Golden Trophy

This season Issie and friends are competing for a new prize – the Tucker Trophy. And Issie has to train the doziest Blackthorn Pony she's ever seen into a winner. That is if she can keep him awake!

Meanwhile, someone is sabotaging relations between riders and the nearby golf course... Could pony club itself be under threat?

HarperCollins *Children's Books*

Sneak preview...

As Issie rode down the long, poplar-lined driveway that led from Winterflood Farm Blaze seemed to take fright at every leaf that wobbled in the wind. When they reached the end of the drive and a pheasant flew up from the undergrowth beside them, Blaze startled and leapt forward as if she were about to bolt, but Issie held her back and calmed her down. She didn't panic at the mare's display of nerves and she never lost patience with her. Instead, she stayed relaxed in the saddle, whispering secret words to her pony in a soft, low voice, bonding with Blaze once more.

By the time they reached the wide grass verge of the riverbank that would take them to the River Paddock, Blaze wasn't spooking at all. She was still fresh though, and kept jogging, keen to break into a trot. Issie gave in and let the mare trot on, but Blaze still strained at the reins and Issie realised that the mare wouldn't be happy until she was let loose to gallop.

She also knew what Avery would say, that Blaze wasn't ready and they should take it slow, that galloping was a no-no. But at that moment Issie didn't care. She was desperate to blow the events of the past weeks away and escape from her own thoughts, if only for a moment. She needed to gallop just as much as her chestnut mare did.

Issie stood up in the stirrups, adjusted her weight into her heels and then gently let the reins slide through her fingers, inching them out slowly enough to give Blaze her head without losing control. She felt the mare rise up beneath her into a loping canter and then suddenly they were galloping, the grass below Blaze's hooves dissolving into a green blur as they sped on.

Issie could feel her pulse racing, the wind whipping against her face, cold air stinging her cheeks. It felt good. After the heartache of the past few days, being back on Blaze made her spirits soar. She was consumed by the rhythm of the horse beneath her, surging forward, leaving everything else behind.

Blaze was in full gallop now, her strides lengthening. Issie stayed low over the mare's neck and kept a tight hold on the reins. They were nearly at the River Paddock and she would need to slow the mare down soon, but not just yet.

As they came into view of the paddocks Issie found that she actually had to work quite hard to bring Blaze down from a gallop. The mare was bristling with energy and high spirits and didn't want to stop. But Issie worked the bit in her mouth and slowly Blaze gave in to her rider and began to canter and then, reluctantly, to trot.

Issie posted up and down in the saddle in a brisk rising trot, her eyes scanning the paddocks ahead of her. She was looking for Comet, but she was also trying to see if she could spot the other horses too. Kate and Stella both grazed their horses here at the River Paddock. Toby, Kate's horse, was a rangy, bay Thoroughbred gelding, while Stella rode a cheeky, chocolate-coloured mare named Coco.

In the shade of the willow trees down near the river, Issie caught sight of Comet. He was grazing happily next to Toby, but there was no sign of Coco. Issie's eyes swept the paddock. She couldn't see her anywhere.

Coco was probably hidden out of sight. There were lots of trees and dips and hollows in the River Paddock where a horse might be concealed. The mare was bound to be here somewhere.

Then Issie caught a glimpse of something and suddenly she wasn't so calm about Coco any more. At the far end of the paddock, beyond the willow trees near the river, there was something huge lying down on the ground. At a distance, it looked to Issie like the shape of a horse – and it wasn't moving. Issie felt a sudden surge of panic. It had to be Coco!

To be continued…